Recital of
the Dog

ALSO BY DAVID RABE

DAVID RABE

Recital of the Dog

GROVE PRESS

NEW YORK

Published by Grove Press
A division of Grove Press, Inc.
841 Broadway
New York, NY 10003-4793

Published in Canada by General Publishing Company, Ltd.

Library of Congress Cataloging-in-Publication Data

Rabe, David.
    Recital of the dog / David Rabe.—1st ed.
        p.   cm.
    ISBN 0-8021-1488-1 (acid-free paper)
    I. Title.
    PS3568.A23R4   1993
    813'.54—dc20   92-17307
                                                CIP

Manufactured in the United States of America
Printed on acid-free paper
Designed by Eve Kirch

First Edition 1993

10   9   8   7   6   5   4   3   2   1

William Louis Rabe

1906–1989

ACKNOWLEDGMENTS

I want to acknowledge Andy Winner for his first reading of this manuscript, Pat Toomay for his tireless, thoughtful readings, George Nickelsburg and his wife Marilyn for their special reading. To Alan Lightman I credit what's scientifically accurate. Points pertaining to painting were checked by Ernie Garthwaite. Thanks to Deborah Schneider. Thanks to Walt Bode, Ed Sedarbaum. Sadgurunanth Maharaj ki Jaya Muktananda and Chidvilasananda. Love to Jill and Lily and Michael and Jason. And to Blueberry, who, long after I had begun the writing of this book, found some cows to chase.

As we know, it is not the conscious subject but the unconscious which does the projecting. Hence one meets with projections, one does not make them. The effect of projection is to isolate the subject from his environment, since instead of a real relation to it there is now only an illusory one. Projections change the world into the replica of one's own unknown face.

—C. G. Jung
Aion

Every angel is terrible.

—Rainer Maria Rilke
Duino Elegies

BOOK ONE

Dogs

Chapter One

Before I lost my ability to paint, I spent hours each day slamming and smudging colorful oils onto canvas in patterns that appealed to me. Shapes emerged more often than not and with them my breath came more easily. In my brain a sense of painful constriction diminished. Quite frequently, feeling this flow of air and relaxation, I know I smiled. But then I killed a brown-eyed, ragged mongrel dog, and even now I can feel his muscle tearing in my bones. He bounded into the air. My rifle sight slid along beneath his leap. With the cows rumbling somewhere off to my left, I fired. I thought, as I watched him recoil, smashed and yelping, that I might paint him. He was a study in fierce but failing optimism. If desire could have saved him, he would have run from that field.

Instead, he took a sequence of wretched poses. At least that's what memory has for me. I see him reeling with impact and inventing a series of physiological strategies intended, no doubt, to extricate him from the disaster that had befallen him. Strictly experimental, they were of no practical effect. The bullet had already struck. The wound was mortal. They are nevertheless fixed in my mind, a set of stunning contortions:

one forepaw bent, the other straight, left ear folded, eyes full of alarm, rear legs angled out in perfect alignment. Then I blink and there he is again, his mongrel's tail wrapped around his ass and curled under his belly like a furled flag. Next he floats with his torso bent at the middle, his eyes full of glassy incomprehension. On he goes, front paws over his ears, hind paws pointed skyward, his back to the earth, stomach to the heavens, eyes filled with an odd repose. When he hits, he tumbles down a slight incline where the sun has burned the dirt to dust. Then he lies there brown and still.

As I say, my first thought was that I would paint him, and I have tried, but over and over the brushes fall from my hands. I stand, looking down from the height of my head to the floor, where the brushes lie unmoving once they have escaped my fingers. At first I thought I had grown clumsy, or inattentive, and I was simply dropping them, and I persisted, stubbornly, but I met the same results each time. Suddenly I was frightened that I was experiencing the first symptoms of some terrible disease, a disorder in my nervous system. I made an appointment with the local doctor. It was not lost on me that my fingers dialed without the slightest difficulty. I could comb my hair, brush my teeth, hold a spoon, a knife, a cup, a glass. I could drive my car. The only things that I could not control were my brushes. I felt embarrassed and ashamed, and called to cancel the appointment. I vowed to forget about the dog and to go back to work immediately on the project that I had begun only days before the creature appeared in my life. This was a series of family portraits whose exact style was yet to be determined. What I had so far was a male figure, the shoulders caught in a pair of black slashes, the torso tilted so that it seemed about to slip out from under the faceless head. Streaks that could become hands were gesturing toward me, the pale oblongs of upturned palms seeking some missing item. Reaching toward the canvas, I felt a tingle, then a kind of jolt. My fingers opened, surrendering to a fuzzy numbness, and the brush floated out of my grasp. Undeniably, the effects of my problem had spread, crippling my ability to render any subject at all. It seemed my only hope was to let some time go by, and I tried to reassure myself that, if I could just hang on, this whole nightmarish episode would disappear.

But that was more than a week ago, and my hopes have only diminished with every passing hour. I feel adrift, my spirit caught in an aimless trance. In the last few days, hoping to distract myself, I've entered into a quixotic pastime. When we first moved to this place, leaving the city behind, I imagined that the care necessary for a few cows and half a dozen chickens would provide a respite from my somewhat cerebral labors. I imagined my family drinking fresh milk and eating fresh eggs. The chickens proved annoying, and after the second month I sold them. The cows, however, I have managed to keep, or was driven to keep—something in their big eyes ringing a reciprocal chord in me. Now, I'm spending more and more time in their company, the four Guernseys, who seem my comrades and are somehow complicit in my predicament, for they stood witness to the deed. They were present when I killed the dog.

I can't remember exactly how the practice started, though I think it had to do with an impulse to reexamine the ingredients of the event itself, the sunlit afternoon, the cows, the dog. The rifle I had already put away in the basement, and the dog, of course, was gone. I remember seeing the cows off in the distance, afloat on the wavering green. I was on my way to feed them, planning to do no more than fork hay into the muck in which they stood. Perhaps what attracted me to them was the way they seemed so unaffected by what they had seen. All I know is that, once I mingled with their browsing heft, I was reluctant to leave. Though there were only four of them, they offered the consolations of a herd. My mind surrendered to an ache of animal yearning that was assuaged only by my association with their shifting flanks and slobbering breath.

From the first moment I stepped among them, they comforted me, and so they comfort me now, milling around and pursuing their interests contentedly as if nothing in their lives is strange, not even my extended visits. Bemused, I stroll about among them. If not exactly happy, I do at least feel hopeful amid their mooing stink and bulk. I lean against a dowdy hip. I fork hay into their trough. I run water into their tank. When two of them flop down in the mud, I flop down beside them. Together, we lie beneath the shade of the trees, watching the shadows of the leaves ruffle the ground. Their brown eyes peer into mine with a benign absence of comprehension, the thick slop of their brains quite porous in regard to the ethical consequences of the deed that brought us to this moment.

When I see my wife approaching, I rise and walk to the fence to meet her. I know she's worried. I smile as best I can. Before she can even

begin to ask the questions that have brought her down to me, her eyes
narrowing with concern and curiosity, I start to talk excitedly about how
fascinating the cows have become to me. "Their color, their texture. The
way the light dances in their eyes. It highlights their noses. The wetness, the moisture. I'm beginning to see what could be a rich and
evocative subject in them," I say.

"The cows?"

"Yes, yes." I remind her of the way that certain of my celebrated
predecessors found inspiration in the desert flowers of New Mexico;
Mount Ste. Victoire; the water lilies of Giverny; the dancing girls of the
Moulin Rouge. The cows, I say, will be my subject. I know I'm lying, but
I feel entitled. I feel that my predicament has liberated me from most
normal constraints. I can almost hear the doubts buzzing in her brain.
But she seems to doubt everything about me recently. Her attitude
toward every word out of my mouth and everything I do is shadowed
with suspicion and a tinge of mockery. She seems to have decided that
my personal concerns are an expression of rudeness to her explicitly, my
obsessive work habits are an affront, my need for frugality a deliberate
attempt to burden her with an irrelevant financial insecurity.

"Good thing that dog decided to leave them alone," she says.

I look at her as if she's changed in some drastic way. "Yes."

"What happened to him?"

She seems weirdly cheery. I'm staring at her, searching for hidden
aims beneath the gleam of her easy manner.

"I don't know what happened to him," I say.

"I sort of miss him."

"What?"

"He was impressive, racing about, the cows all—"

"The cows didn't like it."

"Well, no. They're cows."

I stare at her again, this time determined to expose the malice behind
such an attitude, an indulged and unsavory breeding ground. I'm struggling for a way through the perfection of her smile when she nods
sincerely and says, "I hope it works out."

"What?"

"The cows."

"I think it will."

"I hope so."

She glides away, climbing toward the house, her thoughts drawing her head down between her rising shoulders. My relations with her are shifting. Her praise of the dog has swept away some failing linkage between us. Her mockery of the cows feels alienating. But she doesn't know what's happened, I think. She's just talking.

Still something hurt and violent slashes across my understanding of her. It's a physical sensation, like a movement of bones in my chest. She's a tiny figure, receding from me as she strides the path, something valuable retreating with her. I loved her once. I wanted to be with her more than anyone else, we loved each other, our little boy was born. Now we peer at one another out of irritation most of the time, a cynical bewilderment building up behind almost every exchange.

When she pauses at the front door and turns to look down on me, I try to see myself from her vantage point. There I am on the wrong side of the fence, mud splattered on my shirt and face, my pants rolled up to my knees, my arm looped around the huge soft throat of a cow whose big eyes glow nervously with our unfamiliar intimacy. To view my behavior from her perspective is disorienting. I feel as if I'm betraying myself somehow. I hasten out of the pasture and up to the house, where I take a quick shower. I shave and brush my teeth and change into clean clothes.

It's later that day, somewhere toward the middle of the afternoon, when I see the Old Man. Something about him strikes me as odd. I'm driving around, looking at the light as it changes with the shifting of the clouds, the passing hours. The west, the north, the east, the south. Each has its particular texture and value and evolution. I'm chasing a twinge of color down a two-lane not far from my home, the fields of corn racing by, when I pass him. He's tacking up a sheet of paper on the splintering walls of a barn.

Seconds later, I realize that the figure I have just shot by is not just any old man, but the old man who owns the dog I shot. I don't know him well; we've never spoken, though his farm is situated near mine. Once a huge and thriving family business, it now goes largely untended. He lives there alone and leases out large sections, I've been told. Why didn't I go to him? I wonder. Tell him what his dog was doing. Why didn't I go to him and talk? I don't know. It never occurred to me. I could talk to him now. I could stop and tell him what has happened. When I start to consider this passing thought as a genuine option, my tongue goes dry like feathers in my mouth. I speed away, happy when a turn in the road thick with trees sweeps him from my view.

But on the following days he intrudes into my life again and again, and always he is attaching a sheet of paper to some object or wall. Though I don't want to think about him, his constant reappearance makes it impossible to ignore him. In the morning, I see him deploying his sheets of paper on the buildings that form the main street of our town. Around noon, he's hammering away at a telephone pole miles to the west. Late that afternoon, I spy him crouched at one of the endless fence posts that line the roads of the countryside, nails in his mouth, a hammer in his hand, a sheet poised to be attached.

Of course I'm curious to know what he's doing, but it feels prudent to keep my distance. I'm in the rest room of Jake's Filling Station, having stopped to gas up, pee, and get a candy bar, and I'm feeling defiant, I'm feeling enraged. I'm washing my hands and vowing to isolate myself from the Old Man and his sheets of paper, whatever they are. I don't know what he's doing. The hell with him. I'll go home and stay there. Pushing the button of the hot-air blower on the wall, I start turning my hands.

It's dusk when I step outside. Coming toward me across the pavement is a sheet of paper, skittering along. I recognize it as a dislodged poster, and the way it's headed toward me feels spooky. When it sticks against the stanchion of a sign advertising the station's gas price, I stare at it. Then it pirouettes, moving once more in my direction. It's several yards off to my left and about to go fluttering past when I lunge and snatch it up, feeling annoyed.

At first glance I laugh. The contents of the paper are an insult; they're preposterous. The death of the dog, which the Old Man knows only as an absence, has caused him to attempt things for which he is embarrassingly unprepared. At the center there is a detailed sketch of the dog, utterly unsophisticated and childish and somehow offensive. How dare he try to draw the dog? The rest is commonplace: a list of the animal's habits, a description of his physical traits, the offer of a small reward. At the bottom a phone number is nearly gouged into the paper. The crude lines, the blotches of shade are all struggling to render some emotion I cannot name, but the effort annoys and irritates me at the same time that it makes me jittery. It's weird, but I'm feeling dizzy. A chill comes racing out of the fading daylight. I can feel gooseflesh puckering the skin all over my body but particularly on my thighs and shoulders, as I'm seized by an urge to rush home and paint. I want to paint this dog and the Old Man who is his master. I want to paint how I feel in this instant. I hasten to my car and race off as if the pavement on which I had stood had just exploded. I am inspired, my sense of mission sharp, for I am convinced that I will find in this subject a limitless depth. I've tried before, but this is different. My earlier attempts were doomed because I had no intention of including the Old Man. That's why the brushes jumped from my fingers. But now I will succeed, my talent and implements serving me. Sitting on his back porch, awaiting the return of a yelping speck of joyous dog, the Old Man has been savagely affected. I must communicate a vacuum at his center, a sense of funneling darkness. A kind of deprivation in bold strokes of oil. In my fingers, I taste the pleasures I will find in my production of his shape. He must seem a chunk of earth come alive, yet eroding. He must seem to be falling backward into himself, as if there's an open sore in his belly into which his spirit is being retracted and covered over in a swirl of scars.

But as I reach the door of my studio, it's as if the night turns into a walk-in freezer. My arms seem slabs unrelated to my body. My hand, moving to turn the knob, hangs in the air, flopping like a fish. It slaps at the door. What is this? What's going on? It's just a dog, I think. A goddamn dog. I can't even open the door.

At home, I hear the sounds of my wife and son watching cartoons on the living room TV. Before them the screen is a flashing boil of color, against which their silhouettes are sculptured busts on the chair and footstool. I skulk away, leaving behind me the twilight geniality of the living room they share. In the kitchen, I telephone an old friend in the city, hoping to catch him in his third-floor walk-up situated several blocks north of the apartment where we used to live. It's only a year since I forced us to depart, hoping to find inspiration and peace in a steady diet of rustic solitude. I used to regularly climb at sunset to the rooftop of our building. Around me spread brick and granite, the steeples and other elements of an insensate vista infecting me with a disaffection I felt I must get away from.

When my friend finally answers, his clipped "Hello" prompts a torrent of words from me as I try to explain what has happened. Soon I'm asking him to drive up. I need to talk. As I make this plea, I hear an emptiness in my voice, a tone I cannot identify as my own until I connect it with certain nightmares whose exact content escapes me. When my friend at last gets a chance to speak, it's clear he understands how upset I am. His manner has changed from something dismissive to a stance of loyalty and mission. He has a business dinner scheduled, he explains, but he will try to rearrange it and call me back as soon as he can. When the phone clangs at me an hour later, he is at a gas station on the turnpike, already well on his way.

We meet at a local restaurant, whose unfortunate origin as a hunting lodge is evident. The floors are a raw planking, shellacked and sealed. The stained knotty oaken tables are overlooked by the heads of eight-point bucks mounted on the knotty timber. Their sightless eyes are like bubbles underwater. I do my best to explain the way things happened, trying to be both efficient and clear. I feel I'm making a quick pass over the facts, a kind of sketch to be deepened and filled in.

"This is the worst sort of thing for you—it just throws you," he says.

"I know. I know."

"If only you hadn't done it."

"Well, sure." I'm dissatisfied with what I've said so far, and I'm searching for a better version. The trouble is I don't know exactly what it is I'm trying to describe. It's more an ache of feeling than any set of ideas, and though shame isn't everything I feel, it's certainly prevalent and difficult to talk about. To the extent that my mood is characterized by these unsettled qualities, it's highly distracting. I'm trying to transform into words this knot of sensation and emotion that feels essential, like a prerequisite to understanding anything. Gradually, I see that what I'm wrestling with is my sense of my life as something wrapped around something else, like tissue around an unknown object. The enclosing material feels thin and soft and expendable, while the thing it conceals emits an imperious aura.

"What did I say?" I ask him.

"What?"

"What did I just say?"

"I thought I was talking."

"Didn't I say that I thought—something about my thoughts? I mean, I feel like there's something true in it."

"In what?"

"The way I feel. Even though it's—it's— Wait a minute."

"Sure."

"What I mean is that if I follow it—if I can follow it, there's something true I can get to. At least as far as my work."

"The work is at a complete standstill," he says.

"Yes."

"That's awful." He's downcast, as if the loss is intensely his.

"It's impossible."

"Well, I mean, it can't last forever."

"I certainly hope not." I laugh a little in the wake of that remark.

"You should have told him what was going on."

"What?"

"You should have called the old man, the farmer, and told him what was going on with his dog."

"That never occurred to me," I say.

"Oh."

"It never occurred to me." I glance at the logs that form the walls above the huge blazing fireplace. The heads of the dead deer hover in shadowy bands woven through the rising light. I don't know precisely what I expected from my friend, but I don't think I'm going to get it. I'm as perplexed as he is by the admission I've just made, but something in his response makes me want to get up and walk from the room.

Still, by the end of our meal I'm feeling better, and when I suggest that my outlook has improved, he emphatically agrees. I'm trying to more or less cede the responsibility of critical analysis to him. The fact that we are both laughing at regular intervals is good enough for me. We're drinking sherry and telling jokes about the horrors of city life. It's a tactic meant to serve as an oblique consolation to me. We both know what's going on, and every ten or fifteen minutes I take my cue and reaffirm my happiness at having managed to transplant my family far from the mayhem of the city. But then I start to sink a little. After all, my life in the country has hardly proven peaceful. I gulp the sherry, and he waggles his finger at me in a carefree warning as I order two more drinks.

The following morning I'm cruising down a sun-cooked lane of dirt weaving its way west toward the river, when I come upon the Old Man.

He's nailing a poster to the trunk of a half-rotted elm tree. Passing in my battered Chevy, I'm struggling to summon a response of pure indifference but I end up feeling a little numb. A quarter mile down the road I turn around, the wheels throwing up dirt from the shoulder. At the sight of him ahead of me, a savage fury assails me. But by the time I cruise past him I'm laughing at the absurdity of his behavior, and I'm mocking him with my secret knowledge of the truth that no number of signs will ever summon his dog back. Dead dogs do not arise to run or bark or lick the hand of anyone. Reversing my course once more, I roar by him for the third time in a matter of minutes. He never once glances up at me. I leave him enveloped in a swirl of dust.

My land is somewhat closer to the river than his and I end up lingering at its shores and brooding on the way he looked as the road and I conspired to cloud his existence.

Later, I start wishing my wife and I were not quite so distant at such a sensitive, difficult time. The move from the city has been hard on her, and the pity that I feel as I think of her has a concealed, dangerous bulk like floating ice. I glimpse a kind of gleaming visitation in which we are many years younger and happily walking down the city streets, hand in hand. Then the image begins to blur, and I'm leaning nearer as if to hear our conversation and steal a clue to our affinity. But as I hover there, a veil of estrangement is materializing between us. Soon I am left wondering if this vanished fondness reflects anything actual or merely the distortions of my baffled yearning. We hardly ever occupy the same room anymore. She comes in, I go out, or vice versa. She is busy with her needs to fill the cupboard, buy groceries, scrub the kitchen, go to work. And then there are her moods, the lists she makes, the phone calls, the night school she is planning to attend. I shouldn't really blame her for any of these things, and yet her actions strike me as precursors of something else, something drastic. Her behavior makes me uneasy. Evidently there are dozens of nursery school and community functions to which she must take our five-year-old son, Tobias, for she is constantly driving off. Always she yells her destination out the half-open window of her car departing our driveway, her attention not actually directed at me, the words garbled by the window closing back up, the car disappearing behind the trees.

In the hills across the river, nothing moves but the retreating sunlight.

There are no dogs, no cows, no people. As a child, I always wanted a dog. My grandfather had a dog, and that was the only dog I knew well, when I lived with him and my grandmother. Then the dog died, and it wasn't long afterward that my grandfather died, too. Grandpa, I think, trying to remember him but seeing his dog, a big old loose-limbed creature with long red fur. My mother came back for the funeral and she smelled of candylike perfume, and was accompanied by a man who wasn't my father. I didn't know who the stranger was, other than his first name, which I've now forgotten, or where my father was. He could have been anywhere, maybe even dead, for all I knew. Certainly he's dead now— though he might not be. But he probably is, since I'm in my forties.

When I feel that someone is watching me, I stand up and look around and see the trees, the shifting branches and shrubs behind which someone or something could hide. Everything is disappearing in the dusk. Next thing I know I am overcome with thoughts about dogs; the way they leap gracefully to take a stick from the air with glee and passion; the way they yelp to be stroked, feeling no shame in their need to be touched. In the changing sunset on the water I see reflected how dogs of every breed are openhearted and vulnerable. I can't escape the beauty of their fur and dutiful eyes; the care and diligence with which they learn to lead the blind. I think of their bravery, their courage, their playfulness and joy, which they maintain well beyond their puppyhood. They are deeply affectionate, yet their anger, when aroused and justified—such as when their master is hurt or their master's children endangered, or their tail stepped on—their anger is exhibited boldly. They have saved babies from fires, they have captured criminals. They possess the instinctive grace and muscular spontaneity of the very best natural athletes. They embody loyalty, yet they do not surrender their dignity easily.

On I go, knowing all the while that these are thoughts that should be resisted. Yet they haul at me, dragging me beyond the safety of my own prohibitions, pulling me into a moody darkness beneath the reasonable surface of my own advice. The grave shadows of evening lengthen to cover me like the earth I thought I would spread on the corpse of the dog after I carried him through the deepening trees and shrubs of the forest, his blood staining my shoulders, his drool falling from his slack jaw to my left hand. On my thumb, his spit clung for an instant before sailing away to spot my shoe. Dropping him in a kind of grotto of boulders, I put several rocks on top of him and then fled, leaving him only partly covered.

Now the moonlit river is creamy as drool and its surface remains unstirred. There are no dogs swimming. From the spectral hillsides there comes no barking, and through the grass, over the clumps of stones, and down the pathways, no dogs run. The descending dusk is void of yowling. Although I know it is unreasonable to consider myself the sole cause of these deprivations, I feel complicit. I feel there is no loyalty left on earth, no honor nor simple bravery, no padded footfalls nor sounds of sniffing, no undaunted pride nor affection anywhere.

Chapter Two

I awaken and look at the room through a disrupted wistfulness. On the dresser, the alarm clock is jangling. I feel I have been thrust up from a richness I was only beginning to appreciate. My wife is having trouble with Tobias. I can hear them in the kitchen, their quarreling voices rising up to me through the carpeted floor. But she has something else on her mind, and it's more complicated than it might first appear. I sense it instantly, and for a while I lie there, trying to decipher it, stationed at some midway point between sleep and full-fledged consciousness. The sounds of their quarrel reverberate against my awareness, which trembles like the surface of a pond about to open with something rising from its depths. Though she's railing at Tobias, I feel her real concerns are with me. Her anger is too huge for such a little boy. I know all this almost the instant I hear them. Certainly, I know it before I'm fully awake.

When I stagger down the stairs, seeking coffee, their argument is escalating, his five-year-old's resources pitted against her. She wheels toward me. "Did you hear that?" she says.

"What?"

"Can't you help me with him? He does nothing I tell him. He needs some discipline, some serious manly discipline. He needs to be slapped. He needs to be punished."

For a moment I stare at her before turning to Tobias, who meets my gaze with a defiance he cannot sustain. His stance is crumbling. He bolts from the room.

"Oh, you're right," she says. "You're right, you're right. I don't know why I even said that. Thank you for not doing it. What's wrong with me? Can you get him for me?"

"What?" I say.

She's looking at her watch. "Can you get him for me, please? I have to take him over to James's, for a play date. I'll wait in the car."

When she returns an hour or so later from having dropped him off, I'm still in the kitchen. As I watch her reordering the various appliances she used for breakfast, scrubbing the skillet, shoving cereal boxes back onto shelves, I try to explain that I am having trouble working but am optimistic that things will soon change.

"Things didn't work out with the cows?"

"What?" I say, feeling instantly uneasy.

"The cows," she snaps as if she's cursing me.

"No." Suddenly I've remembered the ploy I'd forgotten for a second. "It didn't."

"Too bad."

"Well, yes."

"Perhaps you're simply in the wrong line of work," she says, her anger freezing her words into little pellets.

"No. I don't think so."

"You can't work in the city, so we move to the country. Now you can't work in the country."

"It'll pass."

"What's the point?"

"You're in a bitchy mood," I tell her.

"Why not?"

Later that afternoon I grow restless, wandering amid the cows, feeling she's watching me. I jump in my car and head off, and I'm startled by the rage I feel when I spy the Old Man. Hoping to distract myself by spending a few hours repairing a window sash, I'm on my way to the hardware store in town when he pops into view less than a mile outside the city limits. Of course, he's tacking up a poster on a telephone pole. I pull my Chevy onto the shoulder and dash toward him, certain that I am going to confront him. Doesn't he know the dog is dead? I'm incensed at what has been happening to my life. My certainty that he is somehow to blame burns in the air between us. The dog is dead, I want to shout at him. The dog was cruel and arrogant. I killed him and I'm sorry, but on the other hand I don't really care. I have to be able to paint. If I can't paint, I'm nothing. I have devoted my life to painting, to trying to learn to be technically sound yet free of all doctrine and fashion, no matter how established, no matter how adored. I want to be original, yet sound and organized, and I hate what is happening to me.

I'm about ten yards away from him when I suddenly veer off. It's as if I hit a wall and bounce with a numbing jolt. I end up in an adjacent field. I don't know what I'm doing. I'm taking big long steps. Seeing some butterflies ahead, I decide to pretend I'm chasing them. Just as I'm beginning this deception, the numbness fades enough for me to recognize that I was flung off my original course by the fact that, as I got close to the Old Man, I realized that I had watched him nail a handbill to this exact telephone pole days ago. Now I'm wondering, Why is he back here? What's going on? Has someone been removing them?

Directly in front of me are a pair of monarch butterflies, and I reach toward them, compelled by the logic of my masquerade to try and capture them. All I want to do is to trick the Old Man about my purpose in pulling my Chevy onto the shoulder so near his dilapidated vehicle, but the wings of the one I grab grind to rubbish in my fingers. The second butterfly leaps upward. I swat at it and miss. After a moment I elevate the tiny corpse in a gesture of explanation toward the old farmer, but he is gone. Above me, the second butterfly twitches and departs, a clot of light.

Hurrying to the telephone pole, I stand and study the drawing hanging there. It's not a replacement of the original poster, but a revision, and it's very different. The space of scribbled bone between the hound's ink-drawn eyes has been widened, the tone of the gaze altered to contain a more piteous expression. Unmistakably this is a lost dog, a worried dog, a sad dog asking for help. The nose has been narrowed, the nostrils expanded to convey desperation. The rest is the same, the information, the habits, the reward, the phone number. But the weirdest thing about the changes is that, while the image now bears a diminished resemblance to the actual dog, its purpose as a drawing is much clearer. While the first drawing had been straightforward, somewhat neutral, I understand much more clearly what this picture wants from me. This dog needs help. I must look for him. The trouble is, of course, I know where to find him. My sense of culpability returns and with it comes a chill. When the weather changes, I think, everything will improve. A wind has been brought to bear on me and I feel cold.

Turning toward my car, I want to smile. It's a good idea. Driving along, I keep trying, but it's difficult; it's hard work, and I'm sweating as I rise up in the seat, looking into the rearview mirror and attempting to evaluate whether or not I'm smiling, and if I am, is it convincing?

I ease into a parking place in front of the hardware store, which is situated between a newsstand and a clothing store whose window display is a trio of soberly dressed mannequins seated around an aluminum and Formica table. The brassy entrance to the hardware store has racks of gleaming saws and tool chests on either side, and I saunter between them, doing my best to duplicate the manner of a homeowner arriving to purchase a sander, a plane, a hammer, some rope.

Hardly have I shut the door, however, when I am face to face with the Old Man. He passes by, his shirttail touching me, and I nearly yelp. He's traveling the aisles in the company of another elderly man, whom I recognize as the owner of the store—the both of them in their sixties if not their seventies.

"I mean, he's not your ordinary kind of dog," the Old Man is saying. "Don't ever suck up to people like your ordinary dog will, like they got no notion of who they are. You know Barney."

I fall into their wake, my sensibility overtaken by a fevered interest, though I know I must maintain a manner that is breezy and blasé.

"Barney's got it real clear what he's up to," the Old Man says, "and he's got his duties down, like to get me the newspaper, or to run up to me and sorta shake all over when I come home, we ain't seen each other for a long time. Boy howdy does he like to have his ears twisted both at the same time. But if he comes up to you and he wants his ears twisted and if you ain't jumpin' to do it, he's gonna walk away. Saleena's his mother—you know Saleena, she's still livin' over at the Murphy place. What a bitch she is."

"Oh, yeh," says his companion, his voice rumbling through the wall of his stomach.

"You know her—great black curly bitch droppin' pups all the time like the one and only thing she knew for certain was the world needed more dogs. You know the bitch I mean."

"Oh, yeh."

"She's got spirit, that Saleena. For a mongrel, I mean."

"You're damn tootin'. A good buncha dogs."

"I remember the day I took Barney from her litter—there was these six of 'em and I was tempted by the runt—I got it in me to maybe take the runt, but then there was this little curly one, he got his nose stuck up into the corner of the box and he's suckin' on the wood like it's a teat. So, 'It's him,' I says, and I can feel Saleena lookin' me over till she decides I'm all right. That's the kinda dogs they are. Not your ordinary dogs suckin' up to every piece of shit on two legs that might pat 'em on the head or drop 'em a bone. Not the kinda dogs to run off or get confused or hit by a car."

"Nosiree bob."

"So I figure what hadda happen is he was out sniffin' after some rabbit or lookin' for a cow to chase and play with and he was comin' up onto this valley—round them big white rocks over at the mouth of Big Toe Valley—you know the ones I mean. He's probably sniffin' a rabbit, thinkin' he'll catch it, so he was sneakin', and you know, his mind's on what he's doin'. And there was these city folks campin' there and sightseein', and they saw him and, 'cause he was so beautiful, they lured him over with a hunk of raw red hamburger meat, and then they threw this blanket over him is what I figure, and they threw him in this black trunk they had in the back a the camper they was in, which was blue, and they probably hadda throw out all the clothes that was in their trunk, which one of 'em did, and then they locked it up and drove off as fast as they could, headin' across the state line, headin' back toward the city where they come from, the goddamn sonsabitches, to steal my dog."

"The sonsabitches."

"But he'll be gettin' loose. He ain't just gonna sit and take it."

"Oh, no."

"He's probably bustin' loose about right now. Gnawin' through the rope. Headin' home."

"You bet."

"I better get on home and look for him."

"He'll be hungry."

I have been cold before but it was never like this. The air was always gray, and the sun burned distantly as it does right now beyond these windows; but there is a gloom in this grayness and the quality of the sun is estranged in a way that no explanation of miles of vaporous space can ever accommodate. Rather it seems that the sun must have been banished to an alien system, where it lingers now, the pulsing heart of a remote galaxy to which I do not belong. Such is the effect of the Old Man's story upon me, as I stand beside a wall laden with brass doorknobs.

"What'sa matter, mister?" says the store owner.

Looking up at him, I realize that I'm bent over at the waist and breathing cautiously, as if to ease a cramp. I turn my head away and see a calendar set to the month of June. "Is that calendar right?"

"Whatta you mean? You look awful pale."

"I'm cold."

"Maybe you got a fever."

I go to the local schoolyard, hoping to join in a game. But no one is there. After several minutes of standing around dejected under the netless basketball hoops and wondering where everybody is, the names of those I expected to find awaiting me start to fill my mind. I have not played in a place like this for years. When was that? What was I thinking of, coming here? When I was a child, a boy, I went to the schoolyard to play. That was a long time ago. No children here will ever know me. Around me the concrete is empty except for pebbles, bottles, and a beer can that I kick, clawing a scary noise out of the pavement. Surrendering at last to my desire for companionship, I begin to clap my hands.

The sun has fallen off the edge of the horizon, leaving behind a wound whose infliction caused no cry. The schoolyard is dark, the building so steeped in shadow it seems a windowless block. I start to review the names of people I once knew, people who held me in affection, the people I wanted to see: Bobby, Billy, Tommy, Sam, Fritz.

In the artificiality of my car I speed along, the eerie green of the instrument panel flickering over the blur of my fingers wrapped on the dark of the steering wheel. The Old Man, as I saw him in the afternoon, keeps rising up before me. He wants to tell me a story, and it's the story that he told in the hardware store, and the implications of his words press against my mind like boulders broken loose and threatening to crush me or compel me off into some unwanted direction.

I shut out the headlights and turn off the engine as I roll down the slight incline of our driveway. Exiting the car, I feel again the effect of a bullet whining from a barrel: the smell of cordite, the rush of velocity stinging the air. Then blood sprays across everything I know.

Following the beam of a flashlight into the forest, I lift the rocks off Barney and find a focus of maggots black and busy in a hole in his belly. His stomach that fed him is now feeding them. He seems to have no plans. The Old Man will be disappointed. His story was interesting but inaccurate. These kidnappers are grim beyond Barney's cunning. The flashlight in my fist is spewing a cone of clinical light to reveal a festering mass no dog could escape. It is true that an expression reminiscent of the wish to flee lingers in his eyes, but his paws are incapacitated by the events in his ribs.

I turn off the light and am surrounded by the dark full of wavering tree limbs and scurrying feet. I try to hear the maggots' munching. But I hear other sounds instead, among them my own voice. I seem to be trying to express a muddled sentiment whose purpose is to question the fairness of my condemnation of the maggots, when the dog would not lie there abandoned to their appetites if it were not for me. "Yet I can condemn them if I want to," I say. And I stand there proclaiming my condemnation of the maggots until a feeling of foolishness fills me. I might as well condemn the air or rain. I might as well condemn the whole of life. I hear the feathery fluttering of owls, the cries of bats and squirrels dreaming of one another, and snakes, and mad hawks, all forms of havoc. And I do condemn it all, I think. I do. The shifting tree trunks creak like floorboards, moonlight falling throughout the woods like wind. Trying to turn the flashlight back on, I drop it. My fingers seem broken. Time has slipped from beneath me like a hangman's device and the maggots have moved on to me, and in their impersonal manner they are picking clean the bones of my shins and ankles, moving on their tiny treads toward my knees.

When I get home, I find a note from my wife. She's gone out to dinner with another mother she met through a playgroup Tobias belongs to. A baby-sitter is tending Tobias and his playmate at the other family's house. I am told not to wait up; they'll probably be home late.

For a while I watch television, the gleam of the colors nearly making me sick. When the news comes on, the mask of the world is a boil of good and evil, old enemies vanishing, new ones arising. At the heart of it all I sense a corruption, a poison, the streets of the city crumbling under the birth rate, crime rate, the drug rate, the suburbs sinking under the divorce rate, an unsavory influence insinuating itself into our brains and being perhaps disseminated over the garish electronic waves of light into which I'm staring. The weatherman is heavyset and balding, his demeanor jovial unless I look deeply into his eyes, where something sordid stirs. I flick the remote device, muting the sound, and then I hit the power button. The room goes black. For several minutes I sit in the dark, feeling like a man who has come upon some forbidden pleasure. When my eyes adjust sufficiently for me to find the phone, I pick it up and call my mother. Though it's late where I am in the East, she lives in the West, in a desert state, so I know I won't be waking her.

"Hello," I say. "It's me."

"Of course. I recognized your voice."

"Did I wake you?"

"No, no."

I can feel a familiar barrier easing in between us as she gathers and deploys her impenetrable sweetness.

"It's not too late there, is it?"

"No, no."

It's a reflex for her to pretend she doesn't resent the trouble I cause her. It's been going on for years, my need to travel and paint an affront, something in the simple fact of my existence a burden.

"It's awfully late where you are, isn't it?" she says.

"Yes."

"How's Tobias?"

"Good."

"And Emily?"

"Good."

"You sound pretty chipper yourself."

"I am."

"That's wonderful. You sound wonderful."

"Oh, yes."

"I can hear it in your voice."

"Things couldn't be better."

"Not having one of your moods, I hope."

"No, no."

"That's so nice to hear."

"I'm doing well."

"I'm so glad to hear that. I was listening to the sweetest big-band music, and I was reading the most exciting, the most romantic story, so heart warming, and as I looked at the cover, the painting on the cover—it was of this beautiful, but noble, yet gorgeous woman and this tall, this heroic man—I could not help but think, Why doesn't my son do paintings like this—things that uplift people, that make them want to look life directly in the eye."

"What was Grandpa like?" I say.

"Grandpa?"

"When I lived with them."

"He was a dear, dear man. You know that."

"And Grandma?"

"Why are you asking?"

"Did he—did Grandpa—was he upset when his dog died? Do you remember his dog?"

"Of course."

"He was upset, wasn't he?"

"Well, he loved that dog."

"And did he, did he somehow blame me for the dog dying?"

"What do you mean?"

"I can't remember."

"I don't understand what you're asking."

"What?"

"It's such a strange question."

"I feel like he did, but I can't remember."

"I can't remember either. You had nothing to do with his dog dying, did you? I wasn't there, remember? I was away."

"I wish I could remember more from then. I can't really, you know. Just feelings. Splotches. Dots, you know."

"I don't really."

"Impressions. Shadows."

"I mean, we're all like that, really. It's best, I think."

"It was a terrible time—do you remember the time I'm talking about? I was very upset about a lot of things, and I stepped on the nail, then I fell off the roof of the shed and hurt my leg. Grandpa and Grandma were fighting all the time."

"They didn't fight."

"No, no. He ran away. Grandpa did. He ran away and nobody knew where he was. I was wetting the bed."

"I don't remember that."

"I was peeing in the bed."

"I wasn't there then."

"It was almost every night. You were there some of the time."

"No, no, I would remember that."

"I remember you being there some of the time. Not much, but—"

"No, no, that's just what you *think*. I was away a lot of the time. Remember?"

"You were there some of the time when this was happening."

"I don't think so."

"I remember you sleeping in your bed and you and Grandma talking. Then I ran away."

"I heard about that. I wasn't there."

"I got lost in the woods."

"I heard about that."

"What happened? Something happened."

"Well, you seem to remember everything pretty darn well."

"I don't. No, no, that's just the superficial stuff, the obvious stuff. These things are fragments, they're fragments. They're incomplete. That's what I'm saying. They're like clues, these things, clues to what I should be remembering."

"You don't sound like you need much help remembering anything, if you ask me."

"No, there's something else. Is there anything you can tell me about my father?"

"What? For goodness' sake, now you want to talk about that. You're just jumping around."

"There must be something."

"But you're just jumping all over the place. I don't know what you're talking about. We were talking about Grandpa, right?"

"Yes."

"Let's talk about him."

"And his dog."

"He was such a sweet man. He was always smiling. You need to smile more."

"I'm just trying to figure certain things out. I'm up late, that's all."

"So you're tired. Have you been drinking a lot of coffee?"

"I was up thinking."

"Have you been drinking a lot of coffee? You don't want to drink too much coffee."

"I drink some, but not too much. It's not—"

"You should call more often."

"Is there nothing you can tell me, then?"

"About what? Haven't I told you things? You want too much, sometimes."

"About my father, I mean."

"Oh."

"Yes."

"Well, there's one thing."

"What?"

"You can count your lucky stars you never knew him."

It's a little past midnight and my wife and son still haven't returned home when I climb into bed and drop off to sleep. But it's like icy water from which I bolt awake. I lie there for a while listening to the night sounds. The wind is laced occasionally with the passing of a car or truck jostling down the road in front of our house. After a while I start imagining myself getting out of bed and leaving the house. I see myself descending the stairs and walking through the door. In my reverie, I drive to the old farmer's field, where I park on the shoulder of the road. I lean against an ancient harrow I have noticed lying in a pasture several hundred yards from his house, the sweeping blades reminding me of a piece of sculpture depicting the rib cage of a prehistoric giant who met his end thousands of years ago. Light spills through numerous windows, but it falters before it reaches me. I watch the farmer's ill-defined silhouette appearing in one window after another. Then several clouds coalesce at the edges of the moon, and the old gray house begins to darken one window at a time.

Next thing I know, I'm rising from my bed and dressing. The night feels wintry. I drive quickly, and after parking my car on the shoulder, I pace into the field. The harrow blades are like icicles when I close my fingers on them. Before me stands the Old Man's house, several windows flooded with light. When a pair of clouds actually shift above me, coalescing at the edges of the moon, I start to feel weird. Bulb by bulb, window by window, the house is going dark. Soon it's a shadowy mass hardly distinguishable from the starless horizon. The angular edges and beams and boards start to express something more complex and insinuating than simple architecture. I find I'm clutching the rusted metal of the harrow's blades. When a wind comes up to tear at my fingers and the clouds slide off the edges of the moon, I head toward my car moving quickly, feeling squeamish, like a child about to be caught in some forbidden act. I'm almost running, my eyes fixed on the ground to keep from tripping, my shoulders hunched as if to ward off a blow. Then I look up for no particular reason, and the air seems filled with a force. The feeling brings me to a halt. Confused, I stand there as the moment opens up to show me what appears to be the future, in which I'm at work in my studio. Emerging on the canvas before me is the Old Man's house just as I glimpsed it seconds ago. In the field is the harrow and, behind it, I see a tiny figure dressed like me gazing at the house. The Old Man's head is a pale stain in the gleaming glass of the window as he peers out.

I'm having a vision, I realize, and before the startling sweep of its assertions the real world has been brushed aside. It's disorienting, but these sudden fictions have more vitality and verisimilitude than anything literally around me. It could be a series, I see, glimpsing the riches available in this night. First I went to the woods, and now I'm here. The hardware store could be included. The Old Man's posters. My worry. My phone call to my mother. My sleepless hours like a passing vehicle dropping me out to stand beside the harrow. And then would come the denouement, a celebratory alternative to this barren trek in which I now find myself walking alone. In lines and thickly applied paint, I will bring him to me. I will declare my wish to have him see me and emerge to join me. I will use an incandescent gray, like ash after the final spark has gone out, to characterize the sky. I will create him charging toward me on brittle legs across textured brushstrokes. Hand in hand, then, I will depict the two of us among the strokes, scumbles, and single-color areas as we look to the sky to seek a revelation, a benediction.

I'm standing by my car. The ideas for these paintings have a knotty, straining explosiveness. I want to do them all. God, I pray. Let me paint them. I'm praying like a child in a church, his mother gone, his father dead, his grandparents railing at one another in a nearby room, nothing intervening but the paper-thin walls through which he hears everything.

When I reach the front door of my house, the lights are out, the silence like sheets of canvas pulled down over the roof and staked into the ground in this gigantic encapsulation of the place, sealing it up. I ease forward and find the door.

In his little bed, Tobias appears flushed. I touch him gently, and he purrs. My fingers glide back and forth across his brow. In my bedroom, my wife is snoring. I undress carefully and then I slink down beside her, edging onto my back, hoping to go unnoticed, my eyes narrow and staring. Every time I close them, they pop back open as if some threatening occurrence has begun in the corner. Next thing I know, I'm spirited away. Whether I'm awake or asleep seems irrelevant, as I'm delivered to a stretch of unfamiliar terrain where I fill with an inexplicable nostalgia, a highly emotional recognition. The paradoxical nature of this place and my reaction to it is further developed when I almost immediately encounter a group of old friends who stare at me, their stony eyes incapable of recognition. Still they follow me around, until we all end up in a kind of classroom. The many desks are on piles of rocks and I am compelled to respond to a sequence of somewhat hostile and passionately complex questions. Through the pattern of my answers, the group is drawn toward a vivid but incomplete grasp of who I am, and then someone way in the back raises his hand and when I acknowledge him, he asks me if I own a gun. I tell him, *I am well prepared for answers that do not come.*

I end up outside. It's morning and the cold is continuing with a wind that begins to settle things. It's November, I see, but not the November with which I am familiar. This is a terrible November that is December, January, February, March, a pure and absolute winter. Leaves are torn from branches, while my face grows cold and red; I cannot smile without pain. I am perched on the railing of our back porch, my flannel robe open, my legs sticking out, as I sip my coffee. The cup is blue, and from the black of the coffee, steam is rising in a dainty spiral. I am trying to smile, for I am becoming frightened that soon everyone will begin to misunderstand my basic nature and affable attitude. It occurs to me I might find a way of smiling without moving my face and I try, and for the briefest of instants I feel that I am glowing.

That's when I wake up and see that it is still night and I am in my bed. The dark above me is impenetrable, and I feel that it is a wall that consists of rocks or dirt. But as I raise my hand up into it, I find nothing other than the inky and receptive air into which my fingers and then my palm and wrist advance, hidden from view.

Chapter Three

When I go again the next night, and the night after that, to stand beside the harrow in the Old Man's field, my regret is sharp but I feel expected in that bleak terrain. When I think of not going I feel anxious; I feel as if I'm violating a vow.

Unable to deny the strangeness of my actions, I determine to manage them in the most inconspicuous and least embarrassing way I can find. I don't want to have to talk about what I'm doing to anyone. I don't want to have to try to explain myself. Certainly not to my wife. When I imagine any attempt at justification, the impulses against which I'm fighting and am trying to explain seem to gain in significance, as if my words empower them. My hope is to defuse them by indulging in them secretly, so that when their magnetism passes, I can simply return to my life as if the interlude they fashioned never existed. Consequently, I start staying up late each night, reading and then slipping from the house sometime between midnight and one A.M., depending on when my wife goes to sleep.

Stationed at the harrow, I endure my vigil until three or four A.M., hovering in that field like a fixed moon before the planet to which I am bound. Some imminent event will soon clarify my purpose, I believe, delivering insight to break the rope that has drawn me there and left me, standing alone, growing colder. After my third night, I feel as if I'm freezing, and I can no longer meet my duties in my normal clothing. The following day I drive to the Salvation Army, where I purchase a huge old military overcoat with epaulets and oversized buttons. It's exactly what I want, something anachronistic, impersonal, and discarded. It grants me a portion of serenity and confidence when I put it on, as if by wearing it I will be a costumed stranger liberated from my own tastes and tendencies, my inhibitions and appetites.

However, that night when I return home in the predawn hours, I feel more agitated than ever before. Even with the coat, I'm chilled. I cook oatmeal topped with cinnamon to warm my innards with its lumpy sweetness, and sit at the kitchen table, worrying and feeling alternately anxious and depressed, waiting for the sun to come up. That part of me capable of impartial reflection labels my behavior odd and pointless. Yet these judgments merely irritate me because I know they're empty, like the advice of scholars with no real authority to affect the events they spend their lives examining.

When my wife walks in, I'm dozing at the table; or else I'm so absorbed in my preoccupations, I feel as if I'm sleeping. I don't hear her coming down the stairs. She looks at me and then starts pacing about beyond the milk and cereal packages on the table, her hands in the pockets of her corduroy robe decorated with tiny Indians galloping on little blue ponies.

"I'm not awake yet," she says. "I can't talk. How long have you been up?"

"Awhile."

I don't know what she's thinking, but I can tell she's not as casual as she would like me to believe. My first assumption is that she knows what I've been doing. But I decide to try to adopt a cordial demeanor while I chew and suck the soggy remnants of my oatmeal. I glance out the window. She fries an egg and watches her coffee drip through the basket and filter to slowly fill the carafe. Several minutes later, when she sits down at the table and begins a series of oblique references to her own sleeplessness during the night, I know that my earlier misgivings were correct. She had to go to the bathroom at two in the morning, she says. Then she didn't feel well. "I had cramps," she reports, shaking her head. "I ended up sitting up reading for quite a while. I don't know what time it was I finally got to sleep."

"You must have wondered where I was," I say.

"It crossed my mind."

"I'm sorry if I disturbed you."

"No, no, you're there, you know, or you're not there. In a way it's all the same. If you know what I mean."

"I think I do," I say, smiling. But I'm a little hurt at the way she seems to be saying she doesn't care about what I do or where I am. "I was out walking."

"Mmmm."

"I went for a long walk."

"I guess you did. Looking for inspiration, were you?" she says.

That seems to me to be as good an explanation as any I'll come up with, so I try to make the best of it. "That's right."

"Any luck?"

"I don't know yet. I have to go to my studio and give it a try."

"Well, all of us here," she says, "we will all just hold our breath."

I'm rising and turning toward the door, as if I intend to march out to my studio and get started right that second, when she grabs the sleeve of my coat, her fingers examining a six-inch tear starting at the wrist. She stares intently for ten or fifteen seconds, then releases my arm and glances out the window. "What's that?" she says.

I'm studying the flaw in the fabric that she has pointed out. The edges are ragged, the gap crossed by a mesh of failing threads. I've no idea what caused it.

"As if you don't know," she says.

"What?" I say.

"I suppose you don't know what happened to that coat. What in God's name are you doing with that coat on anyway? It's an overcoat. Where'd you get that thing?"

I don't want to get into a fight with her, and I also know that trying to explain the coat will necessitate an exchange I would much prefer to avoid, so I just start talking about the tear in the sleeve. Intending only a word or two, I listen as they add up, one leading to another, and before I know it I'm in the middle of an elaborate tale about slipping and falling down while seeking a moonlit view of the woods sufficiently original to rekindle my desire to paint. I have no idea whether or not she believes me, for her expression remains dissatisfied, but the conversation ends. Still, something in the way she shakes her head and glares at me just before she turns away seems to underscore, categorically, the oddity of my own behavior.

"I hope you don't think you're going to get away with this," she says, and stands up.

I wonder if I might tell her the truth; I'm thinking about it. But before I can speak, I'm overtaken by a demand for caution. Hasn't she been interrogating me? Even if she isn't suspicious at the moment, she will be sooner or later. I can't hide what I'm doing forever. We live in the same house. It makes no sense to give her any more information than I have to at the moment. She'll catch on sooner or later and start to berate me about the Old Man. After all, she was questioning me under false pretenses about the jacket. I don't know what happened to it. How can I be sure she doesn't know already what I've been doing, that she isn't following me around already? Gathering evidence. Certainly she's angry at me all the time. I can feel the edges of my sense of self-control fraying under the pressures of a buried wildness bucking against its confines. I mumble something regarding my contradictory feelings, the resentment and regret I feel over the chasm between us, but whatever I say, it must not be clear, because she suddenly rolls her eyes and slams the refrigerator door.

"Oh, shut up!" she snarls.

I walk from the room.

"Where are you going?" she yells.

Moving down a hallway, I see the door to the bathroom and the door to the closet and another door to the storeroom. A few more steps and I arrive at the base of the stairs to the second floor, which I have no alternative but to climb if I am to keep on moving away.

"Where are you going?" I hear her call from behind me.

"Sleep," I say. "Sleep."

"It's not night."

"I know."

"Promise me you'll do the shopping sometime this afternoon."

"All right."

"Promise. I have to take Tobias to see about getting into kindergarten next year."

"All right."

"I'll leave the list on the fridge."

The remoteness with which I experience her attempt to influence me is frightful and interesting and useful all at once. Her impact is a blur. "All right," I say again, intrigued by this grayish, insulating element that seems to be rising up around me like a full-sized sleeping bag being slowly zippered closed. "I'll take care of it," I call back to her, trying to reach through whatever it is enveloping me.

I stand at the bedroom window and watch her drive off. The bed looks inviting, but I head back downstairs and drive to the supermarket instead. For a while I wander the aisles, sickened by the gleam of the overhead lights and the clash of the colors and shapes crammed into the shelves. I don't quite know what I'm doing in these corridors of cans and produce, but I walk on. Guided by her list, I manage to fill the cart.

At the checkout counter, I am uncomfortable with the young man who loads my purchases into paper sacks. His efforts to aid me impress me as a kind of servitude that I feel debases him in ways he has refused to consider. When he transfers the bulging bags into my cart, I feel ashamed, and I keep my eyes averted.

Back in the kitchen, scrambling eggs, I watch the light maneuver in patterns on the cabinet above the stove. Something in the alterations of the colors conjures up a spell of optimism that turns me in the direction of the window. I feel myself drawn toward my studio, remembering the pleasant hours I once spent there. It wasn't that long ago. I went back and forth each day, imagining myself like one of those burly peasants in van Gogh's sketches, making my way through the trees. As rendered by his hand, those men and women were natural and uncomplicated, their qualities derived from the dirt upon which they trod and out of which their knobby bodies seemed to have sprung. To be natural in an equally spontaneous way was my goal. To find an approach, a technique responsive to the instincts of vision; to prepare and then let the work appear.

College in a remote, verdant corner of Pennsylvania had lasted two years, during which I mostly stared in dismay at a professor who, no matter what the period under discussion, declared that representational form and line were outmoded and should be discarded forever. Lines and paint were to be seen as nothing but themselves, he lectured. He met my periodic groans of opposition with a glare. Finally, from the recesses of the assembly hall, I roared: "As if they could ever be anything else!" It was a statement of a bitter fact as far as I was concerned. I fled his presence, leaving the classroom through a side door. My one bag wasn't hard to pack. I worked for the next eight years as a parking lot attendant and met my wife while parking her car. We married quickly and moved to the city, where at the end of the fourth year our son was born. We continued to live in the city, where she had lived previously and where she had many friends and a series of jobs, none of which appealed to her much. I continued parking cars and worked sometimes loading moving vans until, about four years after Tobias was born, I placed a number of pieces in a gallery and sold three, one for an astounding price. Not long after that my wife drank a bottle of wine one night and sat me down to talk. I felt certain she was going to confess the affair I believed her involved in. I even thought I knew who her lover was. Instead, she started talking about fears of growing old and complaints about the people who lived in the apartment above us. Since she was in her thirties and the elderly people above us were little more than a whisper above our heads, these concerns seemed to speak to me of a more generalized dissatisfaction. I made of her complaints an opportunity to introduce the option I had been entertaining for my own reasons. I wanted out of the city, and it seemed as if the time was right. Having sold some work, I felt a rising sense of opportunity and with it a rising sense of pressure and a need to find a way to work well more consistently. I tried to make the countryside sound like a solution to both of our complaints. When she expressed enthusiasm for my proposal, I found myself wondering whether or not her litany of grievances had been intended as a coded confession of her adultery. Whatever the case, I felt more certain than ever that I was right. Though I had no evidence, I had my intuition, my persistent, expanding instinct, which in its ethereal, magical way left me filled with helpless certainty regarding her betrayal at the same time that it compelled me to constantly and aggressively call my convictions into doubt. Because, if I were honest, I had to admit that they had no basis.

Upon our arrival in the woods, I was eager and serious. I felt reprieved from some onrushing censure whose crushing aims had seemed inescapable. In the first days, the fact that I owned a small but defined portion of this amazing vista seemed inconceivable. The rolling terrain struck me as a nearly supernatural visitation. The earth was gouged open with rocky escarpments and laced with creek beds and clusters of trees whose green was moist and thick, like gigantic beds of moss. The circle of the horizon exuded a sense of opportunity to which I responded. In this landscape was a mood, a kind of thrumming potentiality, by which I felt awaited, to which I felt destined. I would take no part-time jobs for the first year at least, and my wife didn't have to either, unless she chose to, which she did, working several afternoons and evenings each week as a dental receptionist. I constructed my studio carefully, a cabin with several removable panels in the walls and ceiling. I wanted to make available the variety of the light's developments, hoping that my abilities might be encouraged to operate sympathetically. My ideals were essential to me and, as if to rekindle them with each new day, I bore a candle through the predawn haze. I believed that the rising of the sun concealed a sacred event, a mythical education regarding color.

But now the path seems to offer access only to a wilderness, its edges overgrown in weeds and fledgling plants due to my recent neglect. I glance back and see that sometime during my ruminations I left the house and started toward my studio, as if I might actually go to work. Walking along, I keep looking back and forth between the house behind me and the studio ahead, whose white exterior is a fragment barely visible through the intervening trees. When a fallen tree limb brushes me, I stumble; the dead branches cling to my leg. It's a minor inconvenience, but I feel opposed. I feel defeated. The dreamy and distracted enthusiasm that hauled me out of my kitchen moments ago is disappearing in waves of mockery. I know I'm going to fail. I ache, whirling to retreat. Then I reverse myself. I fight my inclinations toward surrender with other inclinations that are equally my own.

In the end, an embittered stubbornness prevails, taking me by the throat and dragging me up the path and through the door and to my easel. But I cannot hold the brushes. Over and over they fall. I pick them up and they slip to the floor. My back begins to ache from bending. The creak of the floorboards precedes the creak of my knees. The canvas is blank except for an occasional splatter as the tumbling brushes scrape by. I end up on my knees, reaching up toward the canvas, my face splotched with color from the passing, airborne brushes. What is this? I think, as a drowning man might ask the water through which he sinks. I can feel my peril around me, I can nearly see it.

Grabbing up my palette, I hurl it against the wall. I yearn for a kind of liberation. The fresh paint smears the wood, while the old dried paint shatters into pebbles, and a corner of the palette breaks off. Gathering up the debris, I put it into the metal waste can beside the table. Quickly, I seize the brushes from the floor and race to dump them into the waste can, which I pick up, before hastening throughout the room, my mind methodical, my body a frenzy. I throw away every half-used tube of oil that I have preserved, along with those I have bought and stored unopened in anticipation of the prolific period I had hoped to find in the countryside. Every brush I discover is jettisoned. Even the huge tins of turpentine and linseed oil are flung away. Soon the waste can is full, and I start transferring its contents into the wrinkled green of a huge garbage bag, and opening several others, I stuff into them every canvas tainted by my stymied efforts in these miserable days. As if my inability to work is an infection that I have brought into this room, I feel the whole cabin is contaminated. I want to sterilize the room, cauterizing it against every reminder of my failures. Ghosts are in the brushes. No amount of soaking and squeezing could press the guilt from them. The paint thickening on the tabletop and on the remnants of the palette duplicates the gaudy juices that spill from wounds.

Now I'm dragging trash bags toward the door, and as I walk across the midday light projected through the window onto the floor, I feel some buried ember in me spark, and I start to believe that, because of this atavistic enterprise into which I have thrown myself, my skills might actually revive.

In the yard, I see a bird chattering on a limb. I ignite a wad of tissue that I then toss into one of the bags. After a moment the plastic flares. The turpentine, with an elongated and scorched growl, erupts into a scythe that rocks the nearby pine trees, raining needles to the ground. The branches recoil in a heave and rush of oxygen. I'm hoping for the best as I watch the towering flames plunge back to the piled plastic bags, which contort like a suffering flower, the final sacrifice in my attempted exorcism.

I have to drive thirty miles in order to replace what I have destroyed. My destination is a little college, where I park in a concrete lot whose periphery holds a series of half-court basketball courts, the foul lines painted onto the pavement below the chain net and metal backboards. Seized by a wistful memory that freezes me but will not clarify itself, I have to force myself across the gray of the pavement, like a frozen pond.

The buildings of this campus are all redbrick, the dorms, the class-rooms in a cozy sprawl amid cornfields. A bell rings, vibrating through the walls, and then the students themselves pour out. I hasten into their yammering ranks, boys and girls with bright clothes and shiny skin, happy hats and colorful clothes, hair of every length. My existence barely registers in the blaze of vitality filling their eyes. What little response they give me is a form of condescension masked by an artificial politeness. The result feels like mockery but I'm much too preoccupied to do more than note it.

Ahead waits the bookstore, an annex to one of the redbrick dorms. It's fronted by large plate-glass windows filled with school paraphernalia. Pushing through the wobbly revolving door, I head directly to the art supplies department, which is situated in the back in a tiny alcove squeezed between *photography* and a display of pennants and T-shirts. These stabs of green are adorned with the wild-eyed rocket ship that is the school logo. From various bins and racks I collect some basic oils. Some reds, yellows, greens, some blues. Raw umber, burnt umber, burnt sienna, cadmium red. They topple into my basket, where they are quickly joined by cadmium orange, lemon yellow, cadmium yellow, viridian green, Prussian and ultramarine blue. Next I grab up a palette and several brushes of varying thicknesses along with a large container of cheap turpentine and a smaller one of a higher grade. I believe linseed oil to be my last item, but then I am reminded of the most basic of my staples, a roll of canvas.

With my needs met, I am feeling cheerful as I head for the cashier, a maternal, gray-haired woman in a sweater. The hubbub of the line extends from her toward me in a mix of students totally absorbed in one another. But I am also self-contained, as I stand there dreaming of a successful return to my studio.

Postponed next to the psychology section by an argument at the register, I glance at the shelves, imagining myself intrigued only be-cause of my proximity. I withdraw several books to examine and then I add them to my purchases. Though I feel I am making more or less random selections, I reject several and replace and retrieve the same book a number of times. At the counter, the cashier attempts to engage me with some glib remark regarding our status as coevals among these rambunctious teenagers, but I have no interest and deflect her with a businesslike disregard.

Back at my studio, late afternoon has made the earliest of its irreversible assertions by the time I have cut and stretched half a dozen hunks of canvas onto their hurriedly constructed frames. When I have spread a ground of tinted gesso upon each one of them, some dark, some light, some green, a few like pale halos, I curl up in the corner with the books, hoping that the thinner of the preparations will dry in time for me to try to paint something before nightfall. I sense a shift in the light and look up to see clouds through the darkening window, saturnine masses squeezing from the air the buoyancy with which the day had seemed to abound when I was darting about that college bookstore.

For a while I escape into a deep and soothing sympathy with several middle chapters in one of the books, a paperback by a psychologist named Joseph Antonelli. As page after page turns under my gaze, the basic sweep of the book emerges, the thrust of the developing ideas mounting in my thoughts like the complexity of a tree climbing toward some tantalizing but elusive peak. And there I teeter, there I dangle. On a page where Plato is represented speaking of his allegorical "cave" and Saint John of the Cross is quoted at length regarding his "dark night of the soul," I pause and look into the blackness of the room around me. I am squirreled away in the corner under the lamp I don't even remember lighting. What time is it? I think. But I don't raise the watch I know is strapped to my wrist. Rather, I start backtracking, retracing my steps line by line for several pages until I encounter a blocklike paragraph, where I hesitate. Then, like a stealthy animal, I come forward again, looking for clues in the methodic advance of the sentences and in the gaps between them, seeking a better grasp of the multiple intimations that language and its juxtapositions can prompt into being.

Artists are mentioned. They are described as fretting and complaining over the enigmatic nature of their struggles, the mysteriousness of their work. They are shown wrestling with periods of pointless labor devoid of the slightest inspiration. At such times they feel hopeless, alone, and defeated. With the lengthening of this litany, I grow excited, even hopeful. In their frustration these artists, in Joseph Antonelli's mind, make unsuccessful attempts to change their circumstances. They take trips if they can afford them. They indulge in pointless escapades involving women, alcohol, or drugs. And sometimes it occurs that out of their despondency, a renewed and intense productivity can surge.

Before my eyes, the print squirms, then fades, my concentration diluted in a mist of distraction. I feel that my soul is being struggled for. I see two forces, two lethal and epic arguments. I shut the book. I squeeze it and breathe, as if I'm straining to remove something blocking my path.

Reaching up, I switch off the light. The blackness that falls into the room like coal down a chute denotes the middle of the night. The last few pages I managed to complete contained a discussion regarding boundaries and permeability; "sufficient" permeability was examined, the collapse of boundaries between categories. I am feeling chilled. The existence of flimsy boundaries wavering between conscious and unconscious processes was suggested, and on reflection, these concepts seem a kind of screen between my hopes and me, a kind of lovelessness, a kind of veil muffling me.

Considering a return to the book, which now lies on my lap, I am unable to lift my hand to relight the lamp. I put my fingers to my brow, then slide them to my eyes, but I am arrested by the certainty that I will not like what I find if I open the book again, for the vague, distorted countenance of my grandfather will peer out of the pages at me, a tattered, bearded patriarch with censorious eyes and secrets in his skull.

Getting to my feet, I hear the book thud to the floor. When my toe nudges it, I kick it into the darkness in the opposite side of the cabin. I arrive at the group of canvases that I prepared upon my return so full of hope. When I pull the tiny chain on the light fixture, they are disclosed before me, their grounds like sheets of ice, arrayed against the wall and full of judgments. They gleam with knowledge, as mirrors would if I looked into them. Exactly what they know bewilders me, but like their predecessors, they are bitterly inclined against me. They will repulse me even if the brushes fail to flee my hands. I can feel their resolve, and in the face of their condemnation I lunge to switch the lamp back off.

Returning to my house, I can hear the sleeping breath of my wife and child as I stand outside their doors. First I lean to hers, then his. For several minutes I stand alone in the hall. The furnace comes on with a whine and a rumble, water sloshing in the pipes. A clock is ticking. I can hear my heart. I peer in at my wife. Every minute or so she emits a thin snore. Tobias breathes so softly beneath the shadows spread upon the stuffed animals in whose midst he is nestled that I have to bend quite close to detect the air flowing between his lips.

Descending the stairs, I go to the kitchen, where I pick up the phone and call my friend in the city, but after four rings the voice that answers is recorded, a disappointing technological alternative to the human contact I need. What I am being told is that he has been called away to Europe by an unexpected business opportunity. Through the cheery performance that he has left behind, I detect what I think is the falseness of his hopes. His machine proceeds to try to mitigate my disappointment at his absence by inviting me to leave my name, the day, and time, promising me that I can talk as long as I'd like to. My friend signs off with the genial pledge that he will be back in a month and in the meantime he will be "checking in."

For a while I try to delineate my predicament to the machine. I tell it that things are not better, though there are moments that appear to improve. I tell it about the new paints and canvas that I bought, and then I ask if it's ever read Joseph Antonelli. I start telling it about my conviction that the book would teem with direct references to my life if I read further, but after an ambiguous beginning, I abandon the subject altogether and take refuge in a pause. Acting as if I've changed tack upon the irresistible impetus of a better idea, I emerge from my hesitation, trying to explain about living with my grandfather. But I quickly find that I have nothing factual with which I can flesh out my haunting sense of the forces threatening to pluck me up and bear me off into the unknown. Time, I say, is changing its relations with me—the accepted distinctions are slipping away. Then grief stops up my throat; a gnarled sadness of bygone years. I am left trying to make my point with words like a mouthful of rotten leaves. I have to make up for what I did. That's what I'm saying. I have to make up for what I did. I have to make it up to that poor old man.

I wonder where my friend is in Europe. Europe, I think. I imagine the globe, the map. I see the little books in which one tries to find one's way down city streets with foreign names. No matter how absurd such a proposition sounds, I feel I have to make amends. No matter how illogical such a proposition might be in fact, it has a validity, a sense of necessity. It feels like an opportunity, I say, a fearful opportunity reaching out to me like the claims almost of another lifetime.

Though I don't believe in such things and know that my friend doesn't either, while the answering machine is intrinsically oblivious, still I feel compelled to present them. After all, what do we know about the claims of another lifetime anyway? What could we possibly know since we don't believe in such things? We couldn't possibly know anything significant about them since belief in them would be a prerequisite to the slightest knowledge of them. Our lack of faith banishes them to a realm outside our reach. And yet something is going on and it is inexplicable, so how can any possible explanation, no matter how far-fetched, be categorically dismissed? Why didn't I call the Old Man? Why didn't it occur to me to tell him what was going on? My failure feels like the disclosure of a subtle but dictatorial scheme in which I am collaborating. And then I pause, as if expecting an answer. It's a gap into which anything could rush, panic or ridicule or reproach. I blush realizing the lateness of the hour and how tired I am.

Given the complexity of my silence, the moment extends beyond the machine's tolerance. Hearing a fuzzy yet formal hum, like a stab of mechanistic exasperation, I realize the machine has shut down. I imagine it sitting in my friend's apartment, impartial and untroubled in his uninhabited rooms. The apartment is like a museum without him, things relegated to the site of their last use, trousers on the floor, a book by the phone, a shoe under the couch, an open Cheerios box atop the refrigerator, and the answering machine blinking with my message, like an airplane passing over the night and space between the city and myself. Nevertheless I'm speaking again. I am trying to express what I would have said to the machine had it not cut itself off. My words are dry and raspy, the residue of something from which all the nourishment has been sucked and now I must get rid of what's left.

"Look," I say, "I shouldn't have done it. Of all the people who should not have shot that dog, I'm the one who should not have done it the most. I know that. But—but I had to, or it seemed that I had to. And I— I—" But then the necessary words, the possible words are snatched away in a mass of squirming tendrils whose roots, when I try to trace them, sink away into a silence rank with shame, and the phone moves through the dark until it finds the cradle.

Chapter Four

It is a sixty-mile westward drive to the Murphy place, a farm of hundreds of acres on which Barney was born, and where I'm hoping to find Barney's mother still alive. Even a recent arrival to the area like myself cannot help but know of the Murphys, for their name sooner or later pops into almost any conversation whose concerns are local. Their farm goes back for generations and their bloodline has produced offspring involved in everything from rape to the current occupancy of the county sheriff's office. Now I'm speeding west in my car toward the sector of the county they occupy. The surrounding terrain is lushly woven and fluffed with foliage and open dirt of a robust color. With the sun still high, I'm confident I will arrive before dusk takes it all away.

An hour or so later, vast tracts of undistinguished farmland demonstrate the improbability of my ever locating my goal unaided. The first person I approach is an old farmer on a tractor pulling a wobbling wagon empty of everything but twilight and an odor of chickens. To elicit the information I need, I tell him I'm a journalist doing research for an article on the area, so naturally I have to see the Murphys. It's a mild shock when I hear myself lying in this way, but it's an even bigger shock to learn that I've miscalculated significantly regarding my destination. Twenty minutes later and ten miles to the west, I approach a group of middle-aged women at a bus stop. I claim the Murphys owe me money, and because the Murphys are notoriously cheap, more than a little information is forthcoming.

Back in my car, I set the door ajar in order to feel the rising breeze. Carefully, I examine the fragmentary map I've created on the back of a matchbook cover, a discarded grocery bill, a gum wrapper, and a mud-stained cigarette pack.

Soon I'm driving again, following the lines and arrows from one scrap to another until I'm at the concluding segment, the matchbook cover, which holds the drawing of a tree, a broken fence, and the indication that I should make a left-hand turn.

The tree beside the broken fence is almost identical to my sketch. The waiting road recedes into a diminishing perspective. The moon is up, though it's still daylight. I drive down a road torn and bumpy from years of daily pounding by the huge wheels of farm machinery. To my right a red barn stands with its main doors open. In this gap I glimpse a man in coveralls. The handle of some tool seems to protrude from his hip. Beyond the barn an orange tractor trundles in a barren field, puffs of diesel fuel sprouting from the exhaust pipe that sticks up behind the driver's head like an antenna. A blue truck moves in the opposite direction, and further on a group of men with shovels stab and beat the ground.

Peaked on three sides, the main house towers ahead of me. The front porch sticks out below the most prominent gable, which thrusts directly toward my car shuddering down the road from rut to rut. A sense of foreboding entwines the house, a chill like the effects of a No Trespassing sign. On the porch a twitch of movement snatches at me. It's the door, I realize, having opened and closed. A woman has emerged to stand against the railing. Her ankle-length dress is gray, as is the faded apron she wears and the three-peaked bonnet that seems a miniature of the gabled house itself.

Keeping a respectful distance between myself and the porch, I ease my car to a careful stop. I don't want to appear intrusive. I switch the engine off immediately. Exiting after a second, I stand, stretching my limbs a little, stiff from my hours on the road. When I've managed to close the door quietly, having worked with great concentration, I turn to find the old woman staring at me. I smile, hoping she will ask a question to which I can respond, but the rigidity of her stance makes her position clear. She's not going to start any conversation. We can spend the whole night standing there, as far as she's concerned. I feel icy shards thickening on me, and I look around for signs of wind. I pull my coat tighter, taking the slack out of the belt. The moon seems large and eerily distinct, considering the fact that the sun has not completely set. The air is tainted by a frosty sheen. As the seconds tick by, I start to fear that her silence is based on some intuition about my involvement in Barney's demise. I try to calm myself, advising myself to find a way to speak. The silence is thickening. I'm starting to feel coagulated against the sky, the pair of us like the creations of an alien force layering us in globs of paint. I wave my hand, and my cheeks puff out, my determination to say something bordering on nausea, until at last words pop out, a kind of belch. "I've come to see Saleena. Is she around?"

"What do you want Saleena for? She's a dog."

"I know."

"We don't know where she is. She's too old. She's goin' crazy. It's the wind. I don't know where she is."

"Well, I'm wondering if I might see her. I'd like to get a dog, and I heard that her pups were great pups, and of course she's too old to have any more pups, I know. But if one of her female pups had pups or if they might soon, I'd like you to know, I'd be very interested in buying one."

"We don't sell no dogs. Who told you that?"

"Oh, no. I know that. But I'd take good care of one, you could count on that. And while I was here, I thought I might see her. I heard about her."

"That's what you said. I'm askin' you how you heard about her."

My arm swings out to indicate the sloping forest to the east, where the branches appear to melt into the mists and sunset. "One of her pups. An old man had him. He's over there!" In this melee of color at which I'm pointing, I have the feeling I'm seeing something, looking through the light and color to glimpse something that I recognize finally as the seeds of another painting. This new idea is vague at first, a set of lines, a blast of colors. But from them would evolve a rendering of this moment, this old woman and me—or some old woman and me—the two of us on a porch, like this one below which I stand, but altered for the purposes of emotion and style. I want something intense and sad and beyond the literal. She's singing to me, she's humming while fireflies pop on and off. Our knees are nudging one another, the petal of her hand is in my hair. Beyond us, dynamic alterations in brushstrokes devise a background of fields dissolving in a burning sky.

"This the dog you mean?" she says.

Though her voice maintains a conversational simplicity, I know I'm being ordered to turn and face her. She's standing there with one of the Old Man's posters flapping in her fingers extended toward me, and there's a challenge in her eye.

"This the dog you mean?" she says.

Of course, there are many explanations for how this poster could have come into her hands, many of them innocent and ordinary, and yet the moment feels spooky, it feels threatening, and I want to turn away. I try to hide my panic in a lot of affirmative nodding. "Yes, yes," I say. The Old Man could have brought one by and left it with her, I remind myself, or she could have found one. Another Murphy could have found or stolen one.

Now I am peering into the twilight, and what I'm sensing in this ebbing blaze is the ghostly certainty that the presence of these posters is unnatural. Their proliferation is unnatural. The idea is taking hold of me that they are being spread by uncanny supernatural powers like the ones in whose thrall wolves howl and sparrows veer. The sun has left a lingering film devoid of warmth. Time is slipping its norms, gliding out from under me, like a train veering off the tracks, the common distinctions of past and future and present scrambling. Behind me an old woman stands on a rickety porch. Although I am no longer looking at her, I know she's there. And at the same time that I have an image of her fixed in my memory, I see a third and different version of her ascending through my imagination. I have no idea how she looks on the porch; but in my memory she's bonneted, glaring, judicial, severe, while in my imagination her eyes burn, her lips drool beneath the cruel stab of her nose. It occurs to me that it is because this old woman is once upon the porch behind me and twice in my mind that time is losing its familiar moorings. My feet scrape the dirt as if to find firmer footing. The dusk seems to have been coming on for hours, but the glowing currents appear unchanged, their hue and texture exactly as I remember them from when I first came driving down the road.

Behind me, the old woman says something. When I hear her, I'm afraid to turn. "You got your overcoat on," she says. "It's June. Don't you know that? What are you doing?"

My icy bones grind against each other, and in the fields passing before my gaze, hay is piled in yellow mounds like little huts in a village. Looking into her eyes, I await her next assertion, but then I recognize something that I visually took in minutes ago but that my mind is only now absorbing. And that's the fact that the drawing has been changed again. The handbill that she clutches and thrusts at me is neither the first nor second drawing, but a third. It's another revision, a revision of a revision. Barney's snout has been narrowed and lengthened further, the lines disjointed to increase his forlorn cast. The ears flop forward in dark cross-hatching lines. These ears are bedraggled, tattered, the left one marred by a gash conveyed through savage variations in the thickness of the lines. Penned into the rim of the left eye is the balloon of a tear dripping onto the curve of the snout, which is darkly toned. This is a furry orphan so disconsolate he is unable to hold his ears up, and I'm quite stricken at the sight of him. The urge to rush out and find this dog in the hope of ending his misery is nearly irresistible. But at the same time, there's something very wrong, because this drawing is an insult to the real mongrel, who was defiant, wary, resourceful, wild.

With each revision the Old Man is increasing the amount of distortion in the picture, and with each increase of distortion, the odds in favor of his recovering Barney are going up in one way and down in another. Because, while there is no mistaking the fact that this current version has me ready to race off in search of the lost dog, it's also true that it will have had me looking for the wrong dog. If the Old Man continues on this course, he will enlist more and more people into the hunt, but he will have them ransacking the world for a dog they cannot find. Or one he doesn't want. The more the power of his drawings succeeds in rousing people to look for the dog, the more it sentences them to a doomed quest. If they look for the dog in the poster, they will never find the dog he wants—they will never find Barney.

Now a picture of my own begins to fashion itself, a blur of conception that clarifies swiftly to show the Old Man pacing on his porch as cars swarm into his yard, bringing him dogs. I see his grizzled hair dabbed on thickly by a palette knife. His bearded cheeks are a glaze of gray. On the porch he examines and rejects one yelping creature after another.

The highway is crammed with cars releasing lost dogs, found dogs, kidnapped dogs. I will use bloody primitive tones to depict them, dogs like hunks of ground-up beef, dripping clots of oil. They will be an epidemic of uprooted dogs, the Old Man's deceit conjuring into the world a thousand versions of his delusion. I see the highway teeming with yapping, growling dogs, a steady flow of cars weaving through the madness, and then one car distinguishes itself. The driver is a block of muscle with dirty hair. I whip his figure onto the canvas. Beside him is a woman, and on her lap sits a wide-eyed imbecile of a dog. What will the Old Man do? Comparing this poseur to his counterfeit drawings, will he declare true the lie that his dog has returned? Will he have any choice? Will he even know the difference? And how will I ever invest such a complexity of truth and fraud into the paint?

"What the hell are you thinkin' about?"

It's the old woman's voice and I'm startled to hear her; I'm startled to see her standing there.

"You had one very peculiar look in your eye, mister."

"What?"

"I asked you what the hell you was thinkin' about."

I reach to take the poster from her, and the edges waver as she jerks it away from me.

"Be careful with that damn thing now, you hear," she says, handing it over.

"I'm just trying to see—to be sure that picture is of the dog I was talking about."

"The dog you saw—was his name Barney?" she says, her voice threaded and slowed with calculation. "That's what I'm asking you. And he belonged to an old man?"

"It looks something like him," I say. "It's far from exact, but—"

"He's lost."

"Oh, I didn't know that. What happened to him?"

"When did you last see him?"

"Weeks ago."

"You see him again, you tell us. Or tell Old Man Hampton."

"I will. What happened to him?"

"Now gimme that back," she says, reaching toward me.

"Of course."

"You see all those people out there?"

I look but she is pointing into the dark. Night is gathered thickly all over the ground, as if it's oozing from the soil.

"I got to finish making dinner for them," she says, and turns to start walking across the porch toward the door.

"What about Saleena?" I say.

Giving me a disdainful squint, she disappears through the door, which slams and bounces. "You don't want to see her."

"Wait, I do."

When she doesn't answer, I look into the fields. The wind is making changes in the sky. Black slides under gray and out again. I hope these alterations are an indication of a nearing weather change, an end to the frigid temperatures plaguing me. Mounting the stairs to the porch, I step in the direction of the door. The wood groans and I stop, hoping she will reappear, my back set against the dark where the woman claims hungry people are gathering. "Please," I say.

When her voice floats to me, she seems to be moving deeper into the house, and yet I can hear her say, "If Saleena's anywhere, she's out near the field behind the barn and off to the western side. There's a little woods there. She likes it there."

Chapter Five

How long Saleena observes me before she reveals herself, I have no idea. The barn occupies a basin of worn terrain where the road, after sloping down from the house, veers off into the outlying pastures and fields. Arriving in a distracted state, I seek to amuse myself by kicking a can, and then a stick. After a while I start hurling the stick and running after it so I can hurl it again.

Initially, I mistake her for a cloud's shadow flung down from the moon to sail along the dirt. Unexpected motion occurs at the fringes of my vision. Then the black that I take to be a shadow thickens. My head cocks with inquisitive wonder. Hobbling on three legs, her fur mangy where it isn't worn down to the hide, she's coming toward me. Her left rear hipbone bulges upward, threatening to erupt through her skin, while the attached leg drags along. At first I feel pity at the wear and tear that time has subjected her to. Then I meet her serious, regal eyes, and my sympathy feels inappropriate. Even though her journey out from the shadows is a struggle, her manner leaves no doubt that if she finds me distasteful, she will not hesitate to turn and depart.

Upon the completion of her appraisal of me, which consists of a long and unnerving stare interrupted by a fidget of sniffing, she breathes a moist deep sigh and flops into the weeds near my feet. I sink down beside her. When, at last, I reach toward her, I cast my eyes skyward, feeling bashful. The density of the dark highlights the spherical nature of the moon, its rounded edges smudged with leakage from the hidden side. I lay there looking up, my fingers caressing and kneading Saleena's fur, as if this old bitch contains secrets to be discovered, like a book of braille. A pulsing runs to my palm. What was it I intended here? To chart some dreamy, theoretical pattern backward from my gunsight to this old dog's belly? Tenderly, my fingers glide along the fur beneath which her bones are honed thin. Of course there was a night, or afternoon, of passionate yowling in a field or barn, some roaming young dog from another farm, or a stray from town who chased her, sniffing, and mounted her, bellowing, and left her with a belly rumbling with puppies that popped out in time. I soothe her shabby pelt while the youthful Saleena and a ghostly male dog sail in my mind; their cries echo, the nippings prickle my skin; they frolic in an obscuring lack of light that makes the father indistinct. I try to recall as many details as I can of Barney's physical characteristics. Then I examine Saleena while investigating with an equal intensity my recollection of her offspring. Out of all the factors present in Barney, but unexplained by his mother, I construct the apparition of his father. Poised upon a horizon in my mind, he disappears. I know I will never paint him, though I feel a knifelike need to get him down, and my failure starts disappointment dripping through me. His robust, animal spirit leaves me uncondoned, unendorsed, his powers of flight beyond my embrace.

Turning now to look into the western sky, I see the moon, a white shimmering disk no more than an inch in diameter set in an inky dome arrayed with glittering specks. Lower, along the rim of the earth, large shaggy shapes mark the end of the flatness on which I sit. And while my eyes are registering the orderly scheme of these objects, my mind is trying to transform my understanding into something very different from what I see. The flat disk is actually a sphere, I'm told, and the apparent inch of its diameter is a vastness I could not walk in months, while the light surrounding it has not been generated in the seeming disk, but in a vanished fire whose ceaseless chemical changes send out a wall of light. The black dome is an emptiness that could swallow all the oceans of a thousand thousand earths. The flatness I sit upon is the curved crust of an orb suspended somewhere in that same vacant expanse.

Saleena dozes with her paws resting across my shoes. Rubbing her scrawny back, I slip into a dream in which I'm hungry and I eat. Dripping catsup, I play baseball. I stroke the ball effortlessly, driving it far. I run after it. I catch everything. I go for a swim.

My fingers itch with Saleena's heartbeat. The enchanted painting that I glimpse lying dormant in this moment shows this poor old dog and me curled together in dreamy filigrees of oil. The massive alabaster moon is a strange and loamy surface on which we have settled down to sleep and into which we are starting to sink, as if it is quicksand sucking us in. We're about to vanish when I bolt awake, fear coating me like urine in a wintry bed. Oh, no, I think, wheeling to separate myself from the startled dog. Around me stretches the huge relief of the earth. I have not been snatched from my life. The heavens possess the moon, I see, and I feel relieved and reassured, as if I have just learned that a bloodthirsty enemy has been locked away in prison.

I drive as fast as I can back to the Old Man's field and take up my accustomed position near the harrow, my stocking cap pulled down over my ears. The farmhouse is a shadowy bank, lightless and vague. The Old Man is out, I decide, anticipating a long vigil. Probably delivering posters, or driving the back roads calling Barney's name. High above me, the bleakness parts with a sudden infusion of light.

Looking to the right, I see the Old Man standing there, his shotgun leveled at my belly. I don't know if I failed to hear him approach, or if he was there all along, hiding in the complexity of shadows covering the base of the harrow, where a large number of logs are stacked near the wheels. Moonlight converts his beard of several days' growth into a silvery fungus on the right side of his face, while the left remains obscured. His heels are planted, giving him a bowlegged stance. It was neither sound nor sight of him that roused me but rather a purely instinctual warning that turned me with no specific expectations of what I would discover. He wears a hunter's cap, checkered red and peaked, and his coat has numerous pockets, one of which is bulging with shotgun shells. The bill of his cap casts a band of shadow over his eyes. When he shifts a little, motioning with the gun barrel for me to move to my left, I do what he wants and his eyes are revealed, round and gleaming.

"You're in my field," he says.

"Hello," I say.

"You know whose field this is?"

"Yes."

He jerks his chin at me, his eyes narrowing. The focus of the shotgun shifts a little, reflecting his perplexity, and then it realigns itself. "What for?" he says. "You don't know me."

"No."

"I didn't think so." It pleases him to have been correct about this point. "You got that funny old coat on."

"Yes," I say, watching him closely. Complex thinking has his mouth all wrinkled as if he's sucking on a stone.

"You're wearing that goddamn coat," he says.

"I'm interested in your drawings."

"My father got killed in World War I, so I don't like people sneakin' around, don't you see."

"I'm sorry," I say.

"What're you doin' here?"

"Did you hear what I said about your drawings?"

"They ain't nothin'. I put them up so people would know my dog was lost. You ain't seen him?"

"No."

"He's a real good dog."

"I came over because I saw them."

Though the force of his scrutiny intensifies, the shotgun breech opens for him to pluck out a pair of red shells. His eyelids sag, and then he raises his right arm toward the old house that appears to protrude from the horizon, a sourceless glow behind it. "We can go inside," he says.

After passing through the door, we face a long stairway of worn, uncarpeted stairs, which we start to climb. Beyond the banister I can see several boarded-up doors with furniture shoved in front of them to block off other sections of the ground floor. At the top of the stairs we turn right and enter a second-floor kitchen. After hanging his coat on a hook by the door, the Old Man lights the burner on the stove under a gray old pot with scorch marks clouding the bottom. "Had to seal up the downstairs kitchen," he says. "Pipes broke." He jerks his head to indicate that I should sit on a straight-backed wooden chair, austere and creaky like all the furniture in this room. The cabinet door that he opens groans, swinging at a tilt, the screw that holds the uppermost hinge wiggling. The shotgun leans in the corner, the breech open, the visible chambers empty.

To my amazement, the water seems to percolate instantly, though minutes must have passed. He advances toward me, carrying the pot, his feet shuffling over the grimy linoleum. Curlicues of steam issue out of it. He smiles directly into my eyes. He stands there stirring sugar into both our cups. "You ain't local, are you?" he says as he slowly sits. "People from around these parts wouldn't be comin' around here like you was. Most people steer clear of my property." His inky eyes open into an inscrutable vista.

"I'm fairly new," I say.

"Just moved into this neck of the woods?"

"Well, not too long ago."

"You look a little familiar. Like I seen you somewhere."

"I was in the hardware store the other day. We crossed paths, so to speak."

"I'm tryin' to think when was my last visitor. I don't know when they was by. Whoever they was. I got a reputation, you know. Lot a people don't care much for me. But I don't give a goddamn. People. Everyone of 'em thinks they're such a goddamn particular asshole, when all they are is a shit factory. I seen you in the hardware store. You sneak about everywhere you go?"

"No, no."

"Used to be that people came by a lot. But since I stopped workin' the farm full-time, well, ain't nobody got much of a reason to come by. You a farmer?"

"No," I say. My brain is humming like a high-power wire, stabs of electrical impulse straining to break through barriers in order to facilitate anomalous neural activity, as if new routes are needed to accommodate a growing tide of unprecedented thoughts. My head feels stuffed and pressurized.

He's looking at me intently. "I thought you was a ghost. You been here before, ain't you?"

"I saw your drawings."

"My dog's gone is why I did them. He was stolen. Some bastards from outa state come and done it. Over by Big Toe Valley. That's where they was campin', bunch of no-accounts. So they saw him and threw him into the back of their camper, and off they went, the goddamn sonsabitches. But little did they know about who they was dealin' with. He's gonna be gettin' loose, breakin' loose outa any damn place they think they can lock him up. Their garage or shed or basement. The goddamn fools. He'll just gnaw the rope right through and be on his way, jumpin' out the window that the damn fools will have let open for air. And once he's out that window and on his way, there ain't gonna be no stoppin' him from runnin' back to me."

Above me, a white blur is swimming toward me, taking on increasing definition until it identifies itself as the kitchen ceiling. I am lying on my back on the kitchen floor, seeking to order a number of disparate elements. My head hurts; tears blur my vision. Then the Old Man appears, towering over me, his figure expanding and his face looming, as I realize he is bending down close to me.

"Whatsamatter?" he says. "Have a fit?"

Struggling to understand my circumstances, I determine that I must have fainted. "No, no, no," I say.

"You fell over. You hit your head good."

I'm trying to sit up, an aching bulb of blood thickening on the back of my skull, an excruciating hubbub rattling in my ears. I'm scared, and what I'm scared about is not the condition of my throbbing brain, which feels blasted, its parts in disarray. No, no, what I'm scared about is my certainty that what the Old Man just said is true. That every word he said is true and the dog is not dead. I'm scared that everything I believe about my situation is unfounded. "I have to go."

"No, no. Sit a spell."

"I have to check something."

"You need some rest or somethin'."

Dizziness sweeps over me, threatening to send me back into the blur of unconsciousness. I'm trying to get my feet under me, and it feels as if he's pushing at me.

"What you doin'?" he says. "Where you goin'? Sit a spell, I'm tellin' you."

It's as if I'm drowning and the Old Man is shoving my head under the water. "I have to go."

"But you just got here."

I feel irritated, my voice rising as I struggle to hold back a shout of outrage. "I'll come back."

"All right, all right. No need to get all riled up. I'll cook dinner. We'll eat when you get back. Would you like some roast beef? I can make a stew."

"Yes," I say.

"You didn't tell me nothin' about yourself yet," he yells.

I stagger across the room and step through the door into the hallway. I feel I'm falling down the steps. I have to run to keep pace with my plummeting body. And with every step, I feel more convinced that the beleaguering guilt of my recent days is a delusion. Even in the most persuasive moments of my distress, I was not free of a haunting sense of disproportion, a nagging incongruity that argued against the logic under which I believed myself to suffer. There was always a part of me that felt it was impossible that the death of a mere dog could cause the distraction consuming me. Should I find that the dog is alive, which is what I believe is going to happen, then everything I've thought until this moment was misguided. My inability to paint has no cause, or a different cause. What am I doing here in this old man's house, having been discovered in his field?

At the base of the stairs the vestibule widens. To the left is an archway full of piled boxes. Going to the right would take me around under the stairs, where the rest of the first floor is walled away. But I go straight ahead. I pass over a dilapidated rug whose worn areas have the allure of a trail I must follow to the door, which is curtained with a white gauze infused with moonlight. Imagining that spot in the woods where I have thought the dog's carcass must lie rotting, I now know there is nothing.

When I reach the door, I open it and there is the night. Briefly, things proceed as I expect them to. The passage through the door should bring me onto the porch and it does. After the porch I foresee the vista of the night and pasture and there it is, harrow and all. Beyond the fence, the rising grassland meets the anticipated forest into which I will soon plunge, for I am hurtling toward its shaggy border like a bullet flying toward a dog.

Chapter Six

Quickly, I am deeper into the tangled trees than I would have ever gone had I paused to think. In one instant the shadows are nothing but darkness, and in the next they transform into assailants poking me and pawing me with sticks and leaves. Now I'm wading through snarls of vegetation. Obstacles force me to turn away, and then, after a few steps, I bump into other obstacles, nothing predictable in the pattern of this interference. I feel like a mole, for whom collisions with buried roots and boulders dictate a zigzag course. I don't know where I am. I've turned too many times. The surrounding dark fills the forest like meat interwoven on a skeleton. When I trip and fall, I realize that what I am confronting is my ignorance of forests. They are not all alike. And this is the Old Man's forest, bordering his fields. These trees have been around a long, long time and they are as familiar with one another as I am ignorant of everything about them. For a while it's quiet, except for the commotion I'm making, and then out of nowhere there come a lot of suffering cries and rustling, as if something's killing something in the nearby brush. I see a wave of writhing as the leaves report the mayhem in some lesser pantomimic version of the actual event. Fear comes and goes, distorting my sense of where I am and where I am not, as I seem to puff up and then shrink down with every heartbeat.

I consider going back, but I have no idea which direction I came from and then, as if my predicament is not sufficiently intimidating, the sky and earth conspire to produce a fog. Like a waist-deep swamp, it swallows up my legs. In towering pillars it rises. With so little physical information to guide me, how will I ever find my way to where I'm going? I have to stop and look around, but what I see are differing degrees of darkness. Some I know are trees, while others are rocks. Still others are fissures and banks of air.

Just then the available illumination increases, the lower edge of the moon pushing free of the clouds, and the forest responds with two immediate revelations. To my right are a pair of deer, and directly ahead lies a shaggy mound. It might be a boulder, or it might be a bear. I gasp at the thought, then try to hold my breath. The deer, rattling the bushes like stones in a basket, dart off. But the mound doesn't move. Nor do I, until the light disappears. The shadows are once again my only guides, and I set off, angling around the unidentified mound, my hands stuck out in front of me to protect my face. Gloom is mapped into gloom like the product of an overflowing pot of ink. I feel surrounded by an imperviousness that has no idea of my existence. I feel I have run not only out of the Old Man's house, but out of all human habitation. Who but a fool would have returned here? Who would have ever come back to such a place where vegetation surges in maniacal duplication of its fallen predecessor, which ferments in the rot out of which everything grows? Infatuation with ungoverned fecundity thrives here, animating and devouring every twist and turn in these branches. My will is a pitiful dream. Every leaf and vine and seed and clot of rotting timber is wedded, intertwined, and meshed, and they want me to join them. But I don't want to and I keep walking, trying for stealth and failing, and thinking about my mother, my father, his ghostly disappearance, her ghostly presence. Again and again I see her leaning down above my bed to peer into me, her eyes penetrating and irresistible, my grandmother and grandfather towering behind her, their contours exaggerated in the glare of the hall behind them.

Above me, soaring figures section out the limitless heavens. Looking upward, I cannot detect any part of the sky without the intrusion of these ancient entanglements, their contortions inspired by the effort to engulf one another in an eternal dance of mutually deceiving and aggrandizing generation, whose upshot must be the fumes of chemicals and corruption through which I wade, their powers debilitating. These gnarled trees, I see, with their twisted rotting limbs, own this realm in which I have only now arrived. They are inducing me to disappear—that's their idea—to get me to surrender myself to a repetition of their repetitions. One limb intersects another and turns away. Another limb thickens, broadens, probes. Another limb, its twigs like crippled fingers, twists around itself, shrinking under the aggression of those around it. And everything slinks and spirals. Vines strangle what they can in order to prolong themselves. Skeletons crumble bit by bit. The gloom congeals this place into a single bushy massiveness. It's hard to breathe. Thorns nip my palms; they snag my garments in a dozen junctures, stitching me into the bushes. I feel I have run not merely out of the Old Man's kitchen, but out of the world, out of all hope and civility, so that I no longer exist. A weight and presence slinking up against my brow forces me to hunch my neck and dip my shoulders, crooking my elbows inward, my hands contracting into some cross between stumps and flippers. Now I'm little and hardly breathing, buried like a bug in a bush, thinking about how I'm lost and that I'll never get out. That I'm lost forever. That I'm dead or dreaming—that I'm dead and sentenced to some dreary exile in this wilderness, looking for the body of a dog who isn't even there, who isn't even dead. A carcass that isn't anywhere at all. I could be dead. I could be unconscious. I fell hard in the Old Man's kitchen, slamming my head on the floor. But I'm not. I'm awake, staring at the dark, my fingers seeking along the base of my skull until they find the tender lump where I struck the linoleum, a squishy swelling, like a leech stuffed with blood.

My head is lowering. Though I can't see the ground, I can smell it, a pungency both earthy and chemical. I'm tired. Reaching out, I touch the dirt and feel something reaching back toward me, hauling at me, and I pull away, sensing that this forest is alive. Though it's literal, it's more; though it's trees and dark and night, it has another dimension full of secrets; and it's speaking in a language I can learn to understand if I want to. I have entered into the forest and now the forest wants to enter into me. If I receive the forest, the forest will receive me.

Just then the gloom is altered, an infusion of light transforming the immediate foreground the way two colors mixing create a third, and what I am facing is neither light nor dark, but a glowing haze in which my destination stands disclosed. The formation of craggy rocks backing the plateau in a horseshoe pattern is just as I remember it. In heft and height, the boulders possess a unique contour, a familiar proportion that strikes me as perfectly suited for a dog's memorial. With their gray permanence, the stones of this grottolike enclosure emit a respectful, sepulchral aura as they rise above Barney's resting place. He lies where I dropped him and covered him and then returned to leave him exposed. The delicate curve of his ribs has collapsed now into pieces like a shattered light bulb. His pelt has faded into tufts and strips strewn among a scattering of bones.

In his kitchen, the Old Man worries, I am sure, about his departed dog. He no doubt worries about me, too, his vanished friend. And well he should, for his dog lies rotting at my feet. Never will these scraps and tatters gnaw through a hunk of rope in the first phase of an adventure whose thrilling denouement will bring escape and restitution. No, I'm thinking. It all happened. Just as I thought it did. I am not mad. But instead of feeling reassured, I feel queasy and regretful, as if the Old Man's hopes had been my own. If only I had found his story to be true, my facts illusions. I could rush to him and celebrate my error, help him with the distribution of his posters, and gaze hopefully at the horizon, expecting the dog's return. But how can I go to him now? What can I say? There I would stand, my tongue too occupied with the description of my crime to have a breath for my own defense. He would lose us both again, new friend and beloved dog. When he can have me, at least, if I allow it. Friend with a secret, if I lie. And with me in such a guise he can have his hopes, too, however baseless; he can live awaiting his dead dog's return. There must be a way for me to do these things, to make them possible, a strategy I can devise. If I had time, I would think of one. Yet how can I possibly delay any further, when I have already waited so long that the dog who barked that day is no more than these miserable shreds? A quick report would have been the best response. Then the Old Man would have found a warm and bloody Barney to mourn. What can he do now, presented with this rubbish? Clearly, my faintheartedness that afternoon has destroyed all chances of fair and forthright action. What am I to do? I have no idea.

Exhausted, my head is bowing further. My shoulders sag like stones. I'm trapped, unless my analysis is mistaken. Unless my comprehension is an error. A maze, after all, only appears to have no exit. My best hope, then, might be to hope that all I have so far thought is false. That I am wrong in every thought. A possible, but vexing, premise. Because by embracing it I would have to embrace the belief that I am mistaken, at least possibly, in that premise itself, which must be possibly false if it is to be possibly true, since it consists of thought just like its predecessors. From such a credo would flow the understanding that each and every thought is unreliable. No idea could ever be seen as a stable stepping-stone, as a rock-solid ledge on which to progress toward higher dependable ground. Instead every idea would be viewed as an extension or counterweight to develop or balance some other idea, nothing necessarily true in either. Nothing ever concrete or trustworthy in the whirling world of thought. Never anything clear, never that singular, irrefutable discovery. Never anything but this storm pouring through my brain like water through a cloth, each notion gushing in and out, only to be replaced by another frothing with its self-importance, the entire cycle accelerating until their vanity and velocity turn them all into a futile swirl, like molecules flying away from some disintegrating object.

I hear a ripping sound followed by a crack, and at the same time I feel the resonance of both these disturbances in my head just behind my right eye, as if I've been struck or shot. Then the impact is repeated at a deeper site. Tissue is separating in my brain and I can hear the fibers parting. In the next instant, my head begins to ache. At the base of my skull a gooey condensation shudders, a clump of ideas and cortical tissue giving up a creak and then ripping open. It's like the hull of a ship being gored by a hidden reef. Pressures both within and without are released. I feel an emptiness rushing into my skull. My hands are flailing, my feet going up and down like little hammers. I've fallen backward, and I'm making noises and kicking and squirming, some crucial circuitry in me shorted out, and now my life is firing through me.

I'm bouncing all over the dirt and begging myself to stop, when I'm blinded by an enormous light. It rushes over me, sleek and cold, and I'm squinting into its exploding glare, as shocking as some colossal aircraft made of ice. Only this strange visitor is the moon itself, having come down from its celestial track to settle on the rim of a nearby boulder. Big and round and blinding, its light rolls over me like a storm of snow. I'm lying motionless on my back, my sensibility spellbound. In numerous conversations over the years I have discussed the unknown with a wide variety of companions, and always the people involved expounded upon the unknown as if it were something about which they knew everything, their voices vibrant and cheery, their coffee cups clanking. But the unknown here is different. It is an unknown about which nothing is known. The light of the moon ripples over me, moving my hair as would a wind. The glance it gives me is shocking and full of otherworldly yearning. Oh, no, I think. Whatever this creature wants, I must remain immune. This creature is an enchanter and I must withhold myself. No matter what its inducements, whether voluptuous or threatening, I must resist.

But I can feel unwanted inclinations stirring. The moon, with its ravishing enticements, has found a way to reach into me where it knows each sensitive point to touch. Reciprocal appetites are starting up in me, a taste for lunar perversities, a willingness to cooperate. I can feel myself struggling to resist, but I'm drawn toward surrender. And then my nose flares open to suck in air in ragged chunks. My head goes back, my lips curled as if to encircle the huge orb of the moon. My guts are rushing up with cries constructed of my breath smelling of my belly. I have no idea what it is about me that the moon could want, but I must refuse to give in.

And still it sits there, sparkling with its unearthly inducements. A huge and glowing smear, it shifts and wobbles, and then it lifts without a sign of haste until it is directly over me, where it pauses to make a lingering perusal. The biggest silvery cruelty I have ever seen, it blazes in my eyes and seems to be considering the benefits of staying longer, coming nearer. My repugnance is so violent, I avert my entire body and end up pressing into the ground. What am I doing, howling and having a fit in order to rebuff the moon, when it so clearly enjoys such behavior—when it hovers above me titillated and undeterred? I don't know what it's plotting, but I fear I am ending up viewed not merely as a candidate for its scheme, but as one who is perfectly suited. Especially when I'm howling. But I can't help it. Inches from my nose is a fragment from Barney's ribs, its grainy sheen shot through with light, and I realize that the moon knows what I've done. That's why it's here. To tell me that it knows. With both terror and outrage contending to run me, I spring up for one final heave of defiance that I will hurl into the face of this intractable arrogance above me, which I find vanishing even as I raise my eyes. I see only walls of churning murk around a spinning, shrinking luminescence that grows smaller, like the tail of a tornado, each diminishing loop touched with a glow that is gone as quickly as it is seen, revealing by its disappearance the direction in which the moon has fled.

Now I hit myself with a stick and then I do it again, because I know I want no part of any unearthly project that howling makes you apt for. I keep hitting and hitting, dropping to the ground, as fearful waves are washing over me, for the murk, the trees, the air, the fog are dissolving into something arctic and elemental, and it's seeping into me. It's sickening, unbearable. It's beyond anything I could ever swallow, just a gagging dampness leaking in without a hiss or squeak to fill my insides. I'm alone in the blackest night, nothing around me but the far-flung wilderness. There can be but a single consequence of all this wetness conspiring with my icy nature. Heart and liver, intestine and spleen and colon, it happens to them all. I begin to freeze, until I am like a fish in a refrigerator, turning into fear.

Poor Old Man, I think, and I feel his presence so graphically, I look around. Alone, he sits at his kitchen table—alone like me—the steaming stew he wanted to share turning into a cold reminder of how he has been abandoned again, this time by me, his brand-new friend. Even if he wanted to look for me, he couldn't do it because he has no idea where I am. He doesn't even know where I thought I was going. I just walked out without a word. How worthless he must feel, how sad and forlorn.

And what possible tactic might he use to try to help himself feel better, except the one he's practiced at, the only one he knows, drawing pictures of the things he's lost? He's probably doing it right now, I think, sketching my outline. I see him glancing for reference at the empty chair where I was meant to sit. He didn't know he would ever like me, had no idea, finding me like a twig in his field. Soon my face will adorn the posts, trees, poles, and walls of the countryside. I see him driving around, nailing them up, and as this image clarifies and proliferates, facsimiles of my face raining through the countryside, his dreams of me are filling the spaces I used to occupy. I'm disappearing. I feel lost and imprisoned in some unknown place. A dog in a box in a van. A dog tied up with rope. A dog locked up in a room. He'll die without me, I think. I know he wants me back. I can see him sitting in his kitchen calling out to me, calling my name. And suddenly I hear him, a kind of awful groan infused with the rising tide of the wind, and I'm up and running.

The boulder into which I crash is huge. I reel about, adjust my course, and collide with a tree. Speedily, I have eliminated two directions, and off I go racing in a third. Something massive and prickly cancels that decision but does nothing to defeat my desire. In fact, upon each failure my determination is increased, for discovering again and again the way not to go is a means of sooner or later finding the path I must take. I ricochet off a stony mass, the rebound combining with my own frenzy to send me into a jumble of shrubs that tear at me and leave me screeching like an embattled cat as I find that I'm crawling about in a clear wide field, emerging from the wilds as if from the swirl of a magician's disappearing cape.

Beyond the harrow is the fence, and beyond the fence sits the house, with its windows glowing hospitable yellow. I hurtle toward them, eager to enter, stumbling but keeping my balance. I jump into the air to leap the fence, and then I pause and seem to freeze there, dangling off the ground in a development that, however unprecedented, cannot be denied. Rising from the base of my spine like a lush seed about to flower is an idea that promises to deliver harmony into the forces now disordering my life. In a single stroke whose exact nature and dimensions are about to be illuminated, I will escape the divisive powers of time and sequence, freeing past and present from their separation so that they may unite to melt old guilts and enmities in a fire of present amends. I see myself as a child. I am a child. The image shudders. I am full-grown, the dog sitting on the gleam of my gunsight. Past me plummets my grandfather, his clothing black, his hands outstretched. What did I do to him? What did he do to me? It doesn't matter. For I am about to close a fissure in some wellspring of my life, mending the gap between a pair of perennial and inscrutable opposites. First there was my grandfather, from whom I was divided by his dog. Having lost my father, I lost my grandfather. And hovering in the night, I am asking, Am I to be forever left outside, the banished orphan at the door? Or has the moment come to end my exclusion in these matters of love? It is an illumination, this question, a shock of instruction. In this old farmer and his need I can find and meet my deepest ends, blotting out his memories of his dog with the birth of an affection unequaled in his history. He will open his heart to me, and upon this achievement I will stand triumphant, the natural order defied, my sins absolved, the dog replaced, the heavens and my dead grandfather made again my friend, my father reclaimed.

From this teetering fulcrum to which my thoughts have lifted me, I see my future suddenly revealed, as if it resides in a realm preexisting this moment of discovery, every detail portrayed with a clarity whose perfection is accomplished at the very instant that the entire experience disappears. And with this thought the air lets me go, and I start to fall, as apprehensive and euphoric as a spirit about to plummet to the earth and animate a man.

I hit with a thump. I'm tumbling over and over. When I smash into the beams at the base of the front porch, a reprise of my conclusions coincides so perfectly with the concussion that they seem a single bright bruising event.

Eventually, I stagger up the stairs and enter the kitchen, where I sink to the floor, the worn linoleum clouded with grease stains and smudges of dirt beneath me. I roll over onto my back. Above me the Old Man hovers in a haze.

Chapter Seven

"You're looking a little pale," he says. "You feeling all right?"

I try to smile up at him.

"Maybe you're hungry, huh?"

"Maybe."

"A person gets weak from hunger, anything might happen. Maybe you're weak from hunger." He's prowling the room, picking up a jacket fallen from a hook, moving muddy boots and dirty kettles and pans, sifting through a pile of newspapers. "Food'll be ready in a jiffy," he says.

"Good," I say.

"Can't find the paper. I need something to read while I'm cookin'. Did you see it?"

My thoughts are racing, their speed a startling blur. "I think I did," I say.

"Would you mind getting it?"

I struggle to my feet and turn and leave the kitchen. Behind me I hear his murmur mixed with the sloshing of his big spoon stirring the pot. I hear the clatter of the lid, a slamming cabinet door. Vaguely, I recollect the newspaper lying with a pair of work gloves and an old denim jacket on a bench in the downstairs hall. At a groan behind me, I glance over my shoulder. The empty stairway rises to the empty, dreary hall where the escaping kitchen light hovers.

When I pick up the newspaper from a chair by the door, the house seems bigger. The walls recede into an impression of huge, disconcerting spaces. The ceiling hovers, vast and remote. I climb slowly, conserving energy like a mountaineer, carrying the newspaper as carefully as if it were a flower up the stairs and into the kitchen.

The Old Man stands facing the sink. I observe his angular back, where knotty muscles shiver beneath his shirt on both sides of his spine. I see the wavering border between things that are real and certain other things. They could be real; they want to be real. The urge I feel to place the newspaper between my teeth and cross the room to him with the newspaper in my mouth is a dizzying, exorbitant jolt. My hands dart behind my back, hiding the paper, just as he wheels around, his eyes expectant, his wrinkled hands grinding in a towel.

"Couldn't find it, huh?" he sighs.

When I remain silent, he waggles his head and turns back to the sink, his shoulders sagging. As I start across the room, I know I'm going to do it. I roll the newspaper into a tube and I lift it to my mouth. My tongue dries on the page it touches. The smell is sweetly fresh and I can taste the ink. I sniff the air, breathing through my nose, padding softly, until I'm very close to him, standing behind him waiting. It seems a long time before he turns to face me. He studies me through fluttering eyelids. I see myself from his perspective, and I'm this human being with a newspaper in his mouth. I feel faint, a trembling deep inside me. From some third perspective I catch sight of us both, this Old Man in bib overalls and wrinkled skin standing face to face with this nervous man who has a newspaper in his mouth.

"You found it, huh?" he says.

When he reaches toward me, I watch his hand closely, fearing he's going to hit me, but I don't flinch. Then he ruffles my hair. I feel an electric tingling, as if a minute battery has been implanted in my skull. Beneath his lingering hand, goose bumps spill across me, my pleasure at his touch bursting through my skin. Retreating from my curls, his hand leaves me wistful. I want more of his touch, more of his approval. But he takes the paper from my lips and walks away, returning to the stove. I can smell the stew boiling in the big dented pot. He lifts the lid and peers down through the billowing steam. With the newspaper, he fans himself. "Finish up your coffee there," he says. "Food'll be along in just a minute."

Back at the table, I drink without moving the mug to my lips. Rather, I let my exhausted head bow and I take the coffee on my curled tongue. I make a little mess, and peer up, expecting to be scolded, but his eyes are mellow as he says, "Tired, huh?"

He pats my head and I nod, and together we nearly dip my nose into the coffee. "I knew you was comin' by all those nights. Night after night. Weren't you? Night after night. Standin' in my field. Watchin' me. I knew you was out there. Lookin' in my windows. I been waitin' for you to come closer. I been waitin' for you for a long time, I think."

I watch him pace away to the stove. He picks the cauldron up by its wooden handles and holds it out in front of him, distancing himself from the vapors streaming upward past his face. Backlit by the fire, he appears gigantically thickened with shadow, walking toward me. Using his long wooden spoon, he digs into the pot. The meat plops onto our plates with a wet sloppy sound. "You kept comin' around, I don't know how many times. You hadda know I'd see you. You hadda know I'd be lookin' for my dog. So I'd be lookin' out the window, lookin' for my dog, and so I'd see you. Didn't you know that? Of course you did. Wantin' me to get you. You hadda know I'd be waitin' for you. Sooner or later, I'd get you—I'd bring you in. Ain't that right?"

I am oozing with weakness. I want him to touch me again, to hold me. From a buried wellspring in my guts, a need to have his big arms around me is gushing, as he turns and sits at the opposite side of the table.

With an air of anticipated relish, he takes up his fork and taps it thoughtfully three times against the table. "Let's eat." His huge teeth mash into the brown chunks of meat. From between his lips, juices seep out, squeezed from the meat by his pulverizing jaws. His fork stabs at a scrap that skitters across the plate, until his thumb pins it down so that his fork can pierce it. Brought to his mouth, the meat quivers. "You ain't eating, huh?" he says. A bloody drool trails across his chin, then drops through the air to the plate. When he lifts his coffee in his clublike hand, his cheeks bulge and swell with panicked commotion, as if some creature is squirming to break out. A knobby thumb and forefinger dig between his lips and pull out a thin bone sucked clean of flesh, except for a dangling tissue that shimmers like a string of spit.

"You don't like rabbit meat?" he says. "You ever had rabbit meat before? You a city boy or a country boy? Where'd you come from?"

These questions leave me gaping. Though he expressed himself simply, I've found an arcane purpose behind his words. Any answer that addresses only his literal content promises to be not only inadequate, but unwise. I don't know where I draw this certainty from, but I am convinced of its accuracy. My origins have a sense of irreducible ambiguity. My mind, like a kite broken loose from its tether, is tumbling through a space that has cast all ordinary answers into disarray.

"What the hell's wrong with you?" he says. "Don't you like my cookin'?"

"No, no, it's fine, it's—"

"Bullshit! You're just sittin' there. Don't you like my cookin'?"

The needy gleam in his eyes leaves no doubt regarding the only answer this moment will accept. I must say that I've eaten rabbit meat many times before and loved it every time, but never more than now. In order to do this, I say, "I've had rabbit meat many times before and loved it every time, but never more than now."

"You ain't acting like it," he says in a mocking tone.

"I was daydreaming. I don't know what happened."

"Well, if you like my cookin', you got a funny way a showin' it." He's sort of smiling, the slit of his mouth and the massive wrinkles on his cheeks squirming.

"I've been living in the country most of the time recently," I say, hoping to manage a certain conversational response that will indicate a kinship between us in its main statement while its qualifications roughly reflect the truth.

"Eat some a the leg here. You got a nice hunk of leg there. You got some terrific breasts and buttocks. You got some terrific leg and buttocks there; you better eat 'em or I will."

"Rabbit meat, I love it," I say. "I love rabbit meat, I love rabbit meat." And with each reiteration I feel more positive about what I'm saying and the way I'm managing the moment. In spite of a shaky start, it seems I do have the resources necessary to handle the protocol that governs the Old Man's dinner table. I'm nodding enthusiastically. "I love rabbit meat more than almost anything," I say. I'm talking a little

too loud, and I know it, but it doesn't seem improper even though it
ought to. "You told me it was beef. You were going to make beef, you
said. I like that, too. I was just feeling a little funny. It didn't look like
beef."

His study of me has a quality that could be suspicion; it could be
irony, or even disgust. "Eat it or don't eat it. It's all up to you."

"I will," I say, and haul to my mouth a piece of meat that startles me
with a sensation of movement. My stomach rolls.

"Good, huh?"

"Great," I say, determined to show pure delight, as my stomach
heaves to block my throat from swallowing, but I persist. He chews and
I chew. He nods and I nod. We swallow together. I'm determined to
please him. I want him to view me with pleasure and interest. Is it his
age? Is that the cause? Is it the fact that he has survived so many years,
so many hardships, so many sorrows? All I know is that I want him to pat
me again. I want to feel again that electric delight.

Grabbing up the salt and pepper in one huge fist, he suddenly shouts
and leaves me breathless as he sprinkles these condiments on my head
and then my wrists. "You got that funny coat on and you wasn't in World
War I," he says. "Where'd you get it?"

"I'm cold," I say.

"Cold?"

"Not everybody's cold right now, but I am."

"That ain't what I asked you. I asked you where you got it."

"I know," I say, and laugh, enjoying the give-and-take of our playful
exchange, which, like the opposition in a tug-of-war, is the source of our
enjoyment. "I know what you asked me."

"So where'd you get the coat?"

"No, no, no," I say, wanting to tease him the way he teased me with
the salt and pepper, wanting to follow his example and increase our fun.

Then his huge fist plummets from a yard above the table, crashing
against the wood. "You goddamn sonofabitch! I asked you a question."
Misreading my inability to speak for defiance, he repeats the gesture,
setting our plates and utensils clattering. "I had a friend," he says. "This
was years ago. He was standin' on a street corner, smokin' a cigar. Now
up to him comes this other fella, this total stranger, and he says, 'You got
a light?' My friend says, 'Sorry. No.' The fella says, 'You got a lit cigar in
your mouth, gimme that!' Now my friend smacks him flat in the nose so

---

the blood is spurtin' and the guy is on the ground screaming. My friend starts screamin' too. 'You didn't ask me if I had a lit cigar, goddamn you!' So the fella's gettin' up, and my friend puts his cigar out right on the fella's cheek, and he says, 'And now I don't even have that.' Meanin' a lit cigar."

He's glowering at me, but I don't know what I've done wrong. I'm not even certain how his story pertains to our disagreement.

" 'I was enjoyin' that cigar, too,' my friend says. 'I was lovin' it. I was lovin' that cigar. You bastard, I ought to kill you.' "

Because the story seems to be about not asking the right question rather than failing to answer a question quickly, I cannot draw from it any clear-cut instruction about my offense.

"So you gonna tell me where you got that coat or not?"

But I'm afraid to speak. There is a jeopardy in words, an unpredictable power. They can summon into your life the opposite of what you intend to get by them.

"I almost shot you out there tonight. Did you know I was real close? I coulda, you know. It's my field. I thought I was gonna shoot you. I don't know why I didn't. That's a twelve-gauge shotgun I got there. You was on my land, sneakin' around. I coulda give you both barrels. I coulda turned you into a puddle of shit."

Beneath the table, my legs are trembling. He's glaring at me. All I wanted to do was make him smile, and that's still all I want. He lifts a hunk of meat from his plate and starts to chomp away, his gaze hooded. I have not the slightest idea what he's thinking. He wants something from me. He's waiting for it, squinting at me, and then he looks away, disgusted. I want to apologize. I want to please him, but I'm frightened. How can I try to fashion a workable approach to him unless I know exactly what's bothering him, exactly what he wants? Unless I know what's going on in his mind? After all, in just the last few minutes I misread him several times. I thought he was going to hit me when he was about to pet me, and then, convinced I was going to enhance the fun of our game, I caused this present crisis. His needs are subtle, his moods quixotic. But I can rehabilitate this situation, I am sure. There's a way. Something I can do. Something he wants from me. All I have to do is think of the right thing to do. But what is it? What sentiment, what phrase, will take the danger from this mood?

His features are crushed and stretched as he gnaws away on a hunk of bone. He offers me a mocking smile. His parting lips reveal a sliver of flesh stuck between two stained incisors. I don't want to offend him, or disappoint him, by speaking rashly or inappropriately and making matters worse. Some ill-advised suggestion could crush a happy impulse at the very second of its birth. If only I knew what was going on in his mind. But he seems impenetrable, like a block of granite. Yet I sense a wildness in him, a brutal frenzy that anything might set loose. I'm trying to think of what I've done that pleased him. When I brought him the paper, of course, but I've already done that. He has the paper. I can't do it again. I'm straining for an alternative, my brain full of distress like a bulging muscle.

Then I notice certain aspects, attributes, and observed mannerisms that clearly belong to the Old Man flickering before my inner eye. They're not exactly focused, or exactly what I want, and I don't know where they've come from. They seem to be leaking from somewhere. Following their pattern backward to its source, as one would follow air bubbles rising underwater, I spy a chamber of brain tissue from which they're seeping. In this sphere of thought, I see stores and stores of the kind of information I am hunting physically housed in knots of nerves and cells. There, I think. There I can find what I need. Everything I know of the Old Man is compiled before me, all my deductions, intuitions, memories, conceptions, and observations, every speck of knowledge whether gained through labored study, spontaneous insight, intuition, or abstraction. It's all collected in this pulsing lump, and so I'm staring directly into it, trying to figure out how to take advantage of it, when it breaks loose.

Growing dark and troubled, it shifts, then rises like a rain cloud in total silence, gliding to leave my skull. Without the slightest sense of violation, this opinionated chunk of cerebrations starts to float away, and before I consider what I'm doing, I leap to follow. I cannot lose these riches now. Like some daring captain catching hold of a hot-air balloon climbing through the rabbit fumes that fill the kitchen, I fling myself aboard. Upward I go, enveloped in layers of the Old Man's characteristics and observed deeds and feelings and secrets and wishes, for this portion of my brain is devoted to him exclusively, and I'm merging into it as I go soaring toward the ceiling.

At the table below, my body is slurping coffee and gnawing rabbit bones. Clad in a tattered, ill-fitting winter coat, my body is an appalling sight. Across the table, the Old Man is gaping at my body. He's rambling on about the different kinds of food he likes to eat and those he doesn't, but clearly he's growing repulsed by what he's looking at. He sees that my body is empty, that my body is without character, the eyes glassy, hollow. Sweat coats the skin in an unappetizing sheen that transforms my figure into a synthetic doll of a man. From my special vantage, I see that the Old Man cannot be fooled about how weird I am. He knows my body must be watched with slit-eyed suspicion at all times. Nor will any of my body's eccentric behavior ever be considered a trait to be viewed as charmingly unique. No, no, it will always cause disgust. Which is exactly what it's causing now in me, as my idiotic body spills its coffee, nodding and groveling over everything the Old Man does or says. It is a fraud, a sham, a disgusting fool, trying to fawn and flatter in order to cover its own absurdity. The Old Man knows it, and I, afloat in the air amid the Old Man's opinions and values and judgments, know it. Only the body lost in its groveling appears to have any hopes for its bumbling performance. The hands keep spilling coffee and dropping forks, spoons, knives, bones, as if to make some statement or another.

"Be great when Barney gets back," says my body at the table in a voice like a squealing cat.

I cringe. I want to turn my eyes away from these mortifying events below me.

"Yeh," says the Old Man, across from my body.

"I can hardly wait," says my body.

"Remember how things were before we met?" the Old Man asks.

"Whatta you mean?" says my body, knocking over the salt.

I want to choke my idiotic body. I want to silence that hideous voice.

"I thought my days were over. Now you come along. My dog is gone and you come along. You're a real funny-lookin' critter, buddy boy," says the Old Man at the table. "But we'll have a good time."

And my body laughs, "I know. I know. Oh, well."

"Eat up. We gotta be strong when Barney comes back. He'll wanna go runnin' in the woods. He'll wanna go chasin' things. Like you, maybe. Maybe we'll be huntin' you, huh? Me and my dog, huntin' you. We'll run you into the ground."

"No," says my body.

"What?"

"Please."

"Whatta you lookin' at?"

"You," my body burps, overtaken by a sudden squirming.

"That's what I thought. What's your point?"

My body begins to quiver. The Old Man at the table snorts. In the air, I feel weird and queasy. Fear is everywhere in the room. My body is trying to express the opposite of the distress it feels. Struggling for geniality, it manages a ghastly smile, a kind of gash ripped in the skin.

Leaning forward, the Old Man says, "You look at me when I don't want you to and you might get the surprise of your life. You might run into something very unexpected."

Abandoned to the Old Man's scary gaze, the arms and legs of my body are trembling. The torso is rocking back and forth on the hinge that connects it to the hips. Hovering in the air, I'm straining toward my suffering body, struggling to return, filling with a burst of newborn pity. But I'm restrained; I'm restrained from behind. The weight of my ideas about the Old Man are massive and they're holding me back, the stature of his character, his virtues, his traits, my special theory of our relationship.

At the table, the Old Man hates the flailing hands of the body he's looking at, the sputtering lips, the fearful eyes. And he's right. He longed for friendship and diversion, not this disgraceful blubbering all over his table. Desperately, I'm struggling to descend, flailing like an inexperienced swimmer in unruly tides. My body is so wracked with tics it appears a writhing slip of meat in a skillet. I must get back, I will do anything. I must not be restrained in these heights. I will take what I have learned with me, all of it—it's all too valuable to leave behind— and I will hold it, cherish it, preserve it forever. The way he is so sad, and old. I will let his melancholy fill me; his elderliness will fill me.

"I lost my goddamn dog," he wails. "I don't know where he is."

There, I think. That is the sadness I just felt. It's simultaneously disarming and exhilarating to have his passions afflicting me rather than remaining only in him, for what this moment means is that I can read his mind. I have accomplished what I wanted.

"I don't know what you gotta act this way for," he yells.

Deliriously, my body rocks and starts to pound the table. I'm desperate to fly to its rescue, but still I am restrained. For all my desire and frenzy, nothing alters except the volume of my thoughts and the delirium of my body, which is now pounding the table so wildly it seems determined to break the bones of its hands.

With a swooping gesture the Old Man reaches behind him as if to grab something off the stove. Then his palm comes slashing forward to collide with the face of my body at the table. The sound of the slap is a whiplike crack that sends the head turning, as if it will rotate completely. Only the farthest extension of the body's skeleton prevents total separation, and there the head recoils, snapping back like a ball off a bat.

"I got troubles," the Old Man is screeching. "You stop what you been doin'. You stop this crazy shit!"

Again he reaches far back and swings. The head of the body responds—again there is the frightening crack, the spin and recoil. I'm nauseous in the air.

"I ask you in for dinner, now you're pounding on my table like you got no manners. You got no right to bother me this way. I offered you dinner, some coffee, you wanna break my table. The hell with you."

The angle at which our eyes encounter one another is level. We stare through rising fumes of food. The coffee vapors are white and damp, the odor sharp. A quick glance upward to the tattered plaster of the ceiling confirms that I am no longer hovering there. Of course the Old Man is sad and angry. He is right to feel abused. I feel it also, a disappointed, piercing bitterness and resignation. He has been mistreated, left feeling stunted, abandoned. My empathy with him is extreme, the specifics of his plight drenching me. I am as old as he is, and I am as sad as he is, the qualities of elderliness that I have just assimilated transfiguring me. His melancholy fills me. His immense regret oppresses me.

"That's better," he says.

"I'm sorry. I feel awful." The room is chilly, his eyes are glazed. "Is there anything I can do for you?" I say.

"Of course there is. You know there is. What was wrong with you, actin' that way? C'mon," he says, getting to his feet. He pats my head. "Let's go to bed."

If I've agreed to spend the night with him, I've forgotten that I did it. But it doesn't seem possible. A hurried consideration of the prospect leaves me confused. Perhaps I did agree, but— My wife, I think. Her face wobbles through my mind. She's made arrangements for me to sleep at our house. A room with a big bed and lots of covers. She expects me to do my sleeping there. That's what I expect, too.

"Let's go," he says, and puts out the light.

I'm just about to refuse his invitation—I feel I have to—when I hear a gentle rapping at the window, as if a bird has brushed against the glass. I look, thinking that the Old Man is looking, too. Something multitudinous and white and elemental is all awhirl and falling through the sky. Flakes and speckles are storming through the dark. Millions of feathery particles rise and slide, lowering in one region while in another they billow upward on the wind. The night is giving up some alabaster aspect of itself, a thronging whiteness, every facet distinct against the gleaming sable depths, as if beyond the normal grasp of our senses there lies a celestial landscape of icebergs and now, in avalanche, their mass descends.

"It's snow," I say.

"What?"

"It's snow. Look."

"It can't be snow; it's June."

"It is, it is," I say, moving to the window and pressing against the glass.

"I'm going down. I'm going to see. Somebody's down there throwing things at the window. Somebody's down there."

"No."

"The hell they ain't."

Poised before the open kitchen door, he is irradiated by the hallway light pouring through his clothing to carve the frail outlines of his bones. Stepping out, he flings the door shut behind him.

Be careful, I think. I turn back to the window. The frame groans as I strain to lift it from the sill. Leaning out a little into the open air, I behold a world ravished by gusts of wind alternating with waves of uncanny stillness. As far as I can see, the terrain is disappearing in this cascading substance, which is quite different from what I first took it for. Either I misperceived it initially, or its nature is evolving. Given this moment to observe, I am thunderstruck to see that this blizzard is not gathering on the ground in an even blanket, like a normal snow. Rather, it is accumulating in clumps and fragments that now, because they are near some familiar object like a barn or a tractor, have their size put into perspective. They are gigantic. The smallest is as big as an automobile and each is individual. The only traits they share are their whiteness and their unexpected immensity.

When the Old Man comes striding out, I watch him pause beneath a mound that has the look of a huge bear. He gazes up for several seconds before moving off to look up into a peak of whiteness that suggests the outline of a church. Almost instantly, I find some implication in this image painful, and I turn away. Above me, the sky is canyons of air and ongoing wind and snowfall through which I half expect to glimpse him wandering in some counterpoint to the way he wanders the terrain below. The massive stars beyond the storm are caressed in gauzy halos, and I see that they consist, as do those fallen clumps among which the Old Man prowls, of particles fused together. Now the air through which I view this spectacle takes on a sheen of magnification, and assisted by this power I understand that each ingredient holds a clue to some absent aspect of itself. I feel a fluttering in my stomach, as if I have been elevated then turned upside down. In this disrupted state I can hardly see, yet I manage to spot the Old Man beneath a gargantuan mass that appears to be an arctic tear rising in an epic curve above him.

And, of course, he's right: It isn't snow. It's his soul, his banished, disconsolate spirit, from which his stellar sadness has flooded out to tumble through the frigid reaches of the night, and now he wanders about within it, puzzled and humble, turning to call up to me in a tiny voice that does not reach me with its meaning intact.

"What?" I yell, and he calls again, but I can't hear him. It's something about how impossible it is for snow to have come in June.

"I know!" I yell. "I know!"

Leaning out the window, I feel a mix of compassion and superiority as I watch him prowl about among huge and glacial manifestations of his own inconsolability that he, strolling like a widower in a graveyard amid the tombs of strangers, has mistaken for snow.

"Snow!" he snorts, disgruntled, scornful.

I stare at him, my heart made tender by what I've learned, my nose pressed into the night. Of course I'll stay, I think. Of course I will. "Hurry up!" I yell down to him. "C'mon! Let's get to bed."

Chapter Eight

When the Old Man returns to the kitchen and denies the presence of the snow, the shock I feel makes me mute and sullen at first. But after a minute or two my disappointment, emboldened by bitterness, will not let me hold my tongue. I had anticipated a bond of intimacy and wistful amazement at the mysterious beauty of the night we were sharing. Once I start to argue, I leap quickly from sadness to outrage that he should be so callous about such a special event. But then, in the midst of a phrase meant to blast every possible drop of merit out of his position, I find myself interrupted by a sudden sense of insight into the reasons behind his denial. It's a weird, almost violent experience, a little like someone shouting in my ear. But it's actually the expression in his eyes that enlightens me, a glaring need, a flash of desperation. It's his grief that we are arguing about, after all, not mine. That's what I'm seeing. It's his inconsolability, and it's arctic and immense and in many ways unnatural. That it should fall from the heavens to lie throughout his yard is evidence of unparalleled heavyheartedness. His need to reject such an occurrence strikes me now as not only understandable but inevitable. It's his susceptibility, the depth of his kinship to this suffering, that demands that he deny its existence. There's no way for him to accept it. And once I see this, the words just stop in my mouth. I back off from my argument, grateful that I've had such a revelation. There's nothing really at stake for me, anyway. I know what happened and how it's made me feel. I don't have to force him to admit that his misery has spilled from the polar reaches to which he exiled it.

"No, no, no," I'm saying, "no, no, no." I'm trying to reassure him, because my abrupt change seems to have left him uneasy. He keeps insisting on making his point. He keeps pacing to the window and looking out. "Get over here," he says.

"I don't have to. You're right."

"Just look."

"You're right."

He stares at me. "I'm right."

"Yes."

"There ain't no goddamn snow." The action of his brain is grudging and heavy, like the revolutions of a cement mixer behind his eyes. "Then let's go to bed," he says at last.

Turning, he steps out the door, and I hasten after him. He's just about to depart the hallway when I catch up, and he throws a wall switch as we sweep around a corner. The house goes black. A flashlight blooms in his fist. The passing walls show plaster rippling behind wallpaper printed with larkspur. Intermittently, the light strays upward to uncover streaks of ceiling. When he stops, he has brought us to a rectangular gray of a door. Peeling paint dangles off the panels. I try to see his face, but the light stops at the level of his shoulders. As he turns the porcelain knob, the hinges squeak and wobble. The room resists the light, and the air is stale, the overall effect like that of a long-abandoned mine shaft.

"There," he grunts, as we enter together. The sheeted figure of a little bed appears before us in the sweep of the light, a bit of wreckage surfacing from a sunken ship. "I got things to do," he says. "I'll see you later." Now he's retreating past me. I'm hoping that he will give me the flashlight, but I'm hesitant to ask.

"I'll be up for a while," he says.

I nod, and he presses the door shut, leaving me in the dark. Reaching out for the wall, I start feeling around, trying to find a light switch. Through the walls I can hear him moving off. As I begin undressing down to my underwear, I'm trying to find the bed, hoping it will reemerge when my eyesight has adjusted. The Old Man seems to be wandering around all over the house. At one moment I hear him in a nearby room, and a little later he's nearly out of earshot, the sounds of his whereabouts a faint scratching. With my arms extended before me, I find the bed and paw the covers back just enough to squeeze in. The sheets feel stiff over my naked legs and chest. I'm certain I'll never sleep. The bed receives me with several whines. I pull the blankets up to my chin. It's a narrow little bed and the frame feels like brass. The mattress sags at the middle into a crevice that draws me down, wedging me in. Still I hear the Old Man moving around. Drawers slide open and then wheeze closed. At one point, his footsteps approach my door, and I think he's going to enter, but then they trail off into the vast anonymity of the house, where their last sounds are characterized by a descent, as if he is going down a lengthy set of stairs.

I want to call my wife. I wonder if the Old Man has a phone. I want to tell her what's happening. I imagine getting out of bed, moving in the hallways, finding a room, finding a phone, dialing, talking to her. It's all a little vague and I don't exactly hear myself, or know what room the phone is in, though I have the impression of a library with tiers of crowded bookshelves forming all four walls.

The musty odor persists, heightening my sense that I am in a mausoleum. I want to turn, shift a little in my bed, but I feel inhibited. The stuffing of the mattress has collapsed and I am sunk and restrained in this fault, as if the taut crisp sheets are a set of rules I dare not violate. I feel caught in the impression of a stranger's body in this stranger's bed. Whose? I wonder. The question floats about unanswered, a kind of derelict.

Just then a swath of eerie luminosity comes creeping upward to release a stain across the ceiling. The white plaster above me is sprayed with cracks that mimic a wilted flower. Over them moves a slash of shadow projected from the slit between the windowsill and a lowered shade, a crack like a gleaming knife blade. The moon was absent when I entered, but now it's pressing toward me, seeking access through the walls. I can feel its ravenous longings, its flagrant nature spellbound by its own caprice beyond all possible regulation.

I want to tell my wife that I don't understand how I got to the place I'm in. I want to tell her that I need to start over. Or at least I need to understand how I ended up where I am, lying in this bed in the Old Man's house.

When a toilet flushes close by, I'm startled. Then the outline of the door glows, and the door swings open, the hall light flooding in. Clad in a nightdress, the Old Man seems a tall and angular woman. In the swelling illumination, I spy a huge double bed on the far side of the room. The click of a switch in the hall reinstates the gloom, leaving me blind in the violent contrast of the dark that replaces the glare. The door thuds closed. I hear him shuffling about, but I don't acknowledge that I'm awake. My desire to go unnoticed is so extreme, it feels like a hand squeezing my throat. When he pauses, I worry that he can see me in the murk, though I have no idea where he is. I hear groaning springs accompanied by a sigh, and I imagine him sinking into the depths of the big double bed. Hoping to go unnoticed, I breathe at last, but I feel as if I'm doing something criminal. For a while, he flops about. At first the air goes in and out of him with a hiss. Then he starts to sound like a snarling pig. He is so old, I think, so tired, so unhappy. Just then he stirs, and his grumble seems accusatory, as if something has annoyed him, as if I've annoyed him somehow. I tense, seeking paralysis as a way to deference. How? What could I have done? I was just lying here thinking. Unless my thoughts disturbed him? I hope not. It's unnerving to consider that he heard my thoughts. But after all, I snatched his out of the air, so I know it's possible.

And with that acknowledgment, I am suddenly grimacing like a man on a rack, my self-censure twisting the wheel tighter. By admitting that I violated the security of his head to steal his thoughts, I've just committed a terrible blunder. And I've done it at a most inopportune moment. If he hears me now, he'll be furious that I was fooling around in his head. And he could hear me, because that's what I'm thinking about. That he can hear my thoughts—that he in fact did hear my thoughts a moment ago and one of them disturbed him. Now I groan, clenching my teeth with reproach, for I've done it again. My every thought on this issue flirts with disaster. I must stop. I command myself not to think at all. But quickly I face the difficulty of such an ambition. The command itself is a violation of the law it wants to institute. In a worsening state, I see the impossibility of emptying my mind and still figuring anything out. My only chance is censorship, the strictest possible censorship. And I must manage it deftly at a point before my thoughts have become words, for if they're words and he hears them, he'll understand them. I must sort the permissible from the banned at a level inaccessible to that part of my consciousness to which he is attuned, and at which I normally operate. At the same time, in order to mask what I'm doing I must fill my mind with happy, positive, genial things about how nice everything is, like a kind of buoyant static. At least until he sleeps. Once he sleeps, I can try to consider the truth and make my real plans. If our minds merge then, he will not know it, imagining that he dreams, mistaking my renegade ruminations for an invention of his own, less familiar parts.

Nearby, I note a baby's crib, the vertical bars standing just inside their shadows. The sheets, the blanket and pillow are all in place. Beyond the crib I detect the outline of another single bed sunk in the shadows. I cannot help but speculate that there must have been a time when the Old Man's family was large.

That's when I notice that his breathing has changed. I listen to him closely, like a prisoner listening to the sentinel who blocks escape, and it seems he has slipped away into a less agitated state that could be sleep, though I can't tell for sure. After a while, I give a little kick beneath my covers to test if something minor will disturb him. Several minutes go by, and then I experiment again. I wait and then I cough. He gurgles; he takes a breath. Nothing in his comportment appears disturbed by my activities, so I determine that it's likely that he's deep in sleep at last and it's possible for me to begin to move.

Sitting up, I tiptoe from the room. Despite the care with which I tuck the door into its frame, the tiny click of the lock is startling in the silence. I hover in the hallway, holding to the emptiness like a mountaineer to icy handgrips. My hope that the Old Man didn't hear me is wrestling with my certainty that he did, while my eyes are struggling to adapt to the dimness. I don't know where I am in the scheme of the rooms. We left the kitchen in the dark. At one corner, we went up a little. At another juncture we made a brief descent. Now I'm sneaking about, my hands crawling along the wall like insects to guide me.

Pressing open a door, I squint into a backdrop made entirely of clothes. Clumps of undergarments like piled plates rise on several shelves, and below them are racks of hanging things, rustling with my presence.

A little later I push back another door, which resists but gives slowly, operating on a spring. Behind it I find a room filled with furniture in piles.

My next foray shows me the silhouettes of a pair of big armchairs. Light through the window streams over a phone on a little table. I pull down the shade to blot out the moon, feeling anxious as I grab the phone. The walls are tier after tier of empty bookshelves. It's a room quite like the one I imagined when I first determined to call my wife, only in that one the shelves were full.

"Hello," I say when she answers. She sounds awful, groggy, her words as thick and labored as the speech of a drunk.

"Who's this?"

For a second or two, I'm confused about what response would be the most appropriate.

"Who is this?" she demands. Her sudden expulsion from sleep has left her with a raspy thickness clutching at each word.

"It's me," I say. "I thought I should call you."

"Where are you?"

I try to explain. The Old Man, the neighboring farm. I refer to the dog. I try to keep the cows as a kind of footnote, but it's difficult. I want to ask her how she could have cared about the dog and not the cows. The cows were scared, the cows were unhappy. Their own bulk, when contrasted with the diminutive stature of their persecutor, served to heighten their humiliation. Still I know it's wise to keep everything as sketchy as possible, while making it clear that these matters are significant. I want her to understand that I will amplify them later on at the first feasible moment. My stifled work needs mention, as does my need for some central but elusive knowledge. I try to get through the first few sequences in a rush, working to stitch my life together in a loop of facts for her. But the selection process is confusing, and it's discouraging trying to determine what to leave in and what to leave out.

"Goddamn you," she says.

"What?" I say. I'm realizing that her slurring is not merely the product of someone unable to fully lift herself up from sleep. She's actually drunk.

"You're having an affair, aren't you," she says.

"What?"

"You're having a goddamn affair, aren't you."

While I'm hesitating, trying to grasp her meaning, she says, "Who the hell are you fucking? You're fucking somebody!"

"No," I say.

"Oh, for God's sake," she says, "and then you have to call up and insult me."

I don't know where to begin to address the full range of her misperceptions. I don't know whether it would be wise or not to mention the power of the moon and woods, which I have discovered, the transubstantiation of time, the miracles of rejuvenation lying dormant in our sensibilities, their vibrancy mistaken for dreams, and without these subjects I'm bewildered about how to make my points.

"You're such a bastard," she says.

"I just wanted to let you know I was all right."

"As if I should fucking care. How can you do this to me? I don't understand. In the city I had friends. I have nothing here. What do I have here? Answer my goddamn question."

I'm looking around. My head is turning to the left and then back to the right. There's nothing in the dark except the dark, I know, but I feel the presence of something huge and alien, and my certainty regarding this presence is increasing, as if inhabiting this hour there is a dark that is not the night at all, but something else. It might be the Old Man, I think, knowing that it isn't, that it's bigger, far more dense, and that there is this bidding in it, a summons, both personal and authoritarian, but seeming to allow the option of denial; and yet there is an urgency in it, and also—subtly and hard to discover at first, but once detected, unforgettable—there is this mad ardor like the obsessive crying of a lover. My wife is talking about the cows, and how she's been feeding them, and she's sick of it. She's got blisters on her hands from heaving straw in to them, and she's sick of it. She's sick of filling the water tank.

I want to tell her I'll help her out, but I can't. I want to tell her I'll call her later, but I can't. I'm running. I'm thrashing into the hallway and back to my room, and the dark is after me. It knows the house, it knows the corridors, and it's whirling with desire, like a spinning pool in whose magnetic circles I'm caught. I can feel them pulling at me and swirling around me. Even though I run as fast as I can, it stays right with me, this terrible whirling dark; even though I find the room and rush in, pressing the door shut, the darkness passes through the useless screen of trembling atoms of which the wood of the door consists, hanging there on its hinges like a sheet of air.

Plunging across the room, I fall into bed. I drag the covers up over my face. Something terrible is going to happen. It may already have started. I feel that I'm moving, that I'm being transported, that this dark has got me and it's wrapped around me. I'm fainting with fear, falling away. The air feels remote and thin, each breath something I have to strain and fight to get. My wife, I think. The swoon into which I'm sinking is like the lid of a gigantic box shutting down on me with a rumbling sound. The natural elements have made some unnatural alteration. Something's coming. That's what's happening. Something terrible and violent. Some devastation. Flood? Ice age? What will it be? I can feel its approach, and in the scope of its foreboding it seems a cataclysm. In the rising magnitude of its rumbling symptoms, it seems apocalyptic. Fire bursting from the earthen bowels. Serpents and rats, disrupted from their lairs. The sea shall lose its rhythm. The earth shall rock upon its axis and stagger through the starry night. And what malevolent contrivance can deliver all this but earthquakes? And not one to rock a little Chinese city, and another to make the Indians quake, but an epidemic, so that the whole broad circumference of the globe is shaken. Volcanoes lie beneath the oceans, and when the sea floor sinks, they tilt and roar. Continents rotate like titanic ball bearings in response to distant urging. I see them heaving toward one another in geological anxiety, huge slabs of earth and piles of rock bursting up from underground like deadmen from their graves. Seas are awash across my stomach, and I am convulsed from side to side. Africa is careening to collide with rumbling Eurasia. Lions roar. Apes and orangutans cling forlornly to their trees. The Alps, in all their angular immensity, rise up like snowmen on a teeter-totter. Below me the sea floor is sinking and above me the Old Man is hovering, wavering. Like a drowning man coming up from the depths of an icy country pond, I see a high and distant glasslike surface through which I burst. He's a weird, weird old man, I think. "What are you doing?" I cry. He's yelling at me. His hands are pawing at me, it feels as if he's licking my stomach. "You're slobbering," I yell. "What are you doing?"

"Who are you?" he groans.

"Me."

"Who?"

"Me, me, me."

"It's you!"

"I was here for dinner. You had me for dinner."

"It's you!"

"Remember? You forgot who I was, I guess," I say.

"No, no."

"What were you doing?"

"Saying good night."

"Oh."

"I enjoyed having you for dinner. I wanted to tell you. We didn't say good night. I thought that was impolite. I thought it was rude of me. It's my house."

"You were licking me."

"It's up to me to say good night first. It's not up to you."

"I didn't mind. It was all right."

"Well, I like to be polite. People get mad at you when you're rude."

"I wasn't mad."

"When people are mad at you, they always keep it a secret. They have to. So I didn't want to be rude to you and not say good night and have you mad at me."

"I wasn't."

"Mad at me for waking you up?"

"No."

"Tell me if you are."

"I'm not."

"Any secrets?"

"No."

"You don't have any secrets?"

"No," I say. "None."

"Then get out of my bed."

"What?"

"Get outa my bed, you ain't ready yet."

I fling my arms out, feeling wide rumpled spaces of blankets and sheet. He must have carried me to his big double bed as I slept. Or when I came back I jumped into his bed by mistake.

He laughs. It's a big laugh, like nothing I have ever heard before. The size of it is overwhelming, so huge that I feel the entire room is shaking, every nail and bead of plaster and the bed and me with it, all of it shaking. Then I realize he slapped the headboard of the bed with one big hand, so uncontainable and unfamiliar was his laughter. It's strange to him, I guess. Next thing I know, I'm laughing along with him, as if to help him learn about it, and I'm learning, too. It's all such a big surprise, I nearly vomit. It's like when you trip. You're walking along, and suddenly you fall to the ground and you scream. You're walking, then tripping, then falling and screaming.

"See you in the morning," he yells. He's still laughing. So I better get at it, too, or I'll get left behind. I make sure I'm laughing. He's leaving now. I watch him sail across the room with his laugh now thin and high and a little like singing or gagging. Who can tell? We're both so excited.

"I'm gonna sleep somewheres else I can get some rest without you botherin' me," he says, laughing, a sound like an animal hooting in distress or effort, as he passes from the room. The hall light slashes in at me, only to be shut away by the closing door. After a hushed and breathless second there comes a metallic click, like a coin in a slot. It's the sound of the tumblers falling. He's locked the door, he's locked me in. My heart balloons into my throat. Simultaneously, it manages to hammer at my ribs like a jagged rock. This is just his indirect and gentle way of telling me that he desires more than anything in the world to keep me safe. I want to scream, *What are you doing?* But I can't because I'm overwhelmed, as if the room has sprung a leak and there has come rushing in, wet and sappy all around me, love. So many sweeping, towering waves of it, I am sopping with my passion for this great and wondrous old man. Love is everywhere. It could be an ocean. It could fill the room, the heaving, throbbing that I feel of love; I want to scream it: love, love, love, as a drowning man might gasp, *Glub!* More love than a person with a normal capacity and taste for it could ever bear. The room can hardly stand it. The floors and walls are creaking. In a lesser person, there might be shrieking, as it fills and fills me, and fills the room, until it seems there must be a bursting. It's a room to drown in, such a preponderance of seething, savage love. My heart stops; it hovers in my chest, and that's it, I think, I'm going to die of it.

Then tears erupt from my eyes, and breath slams from my nose and mouth. I don't want the responsibility. I don't want to have seen his arctic grief and inconsolability. Poor Old Man, I think. I know his dog is dead. But I can't stop the tears. I can't stop the fear. I don't want to have this tremendous power over him, the ability to shatter his hopes at any moment, the means to perpetuate them, to extend and amplify them. I don't want it! I don't want it! I don't want to know about his polar bitterness and rage, the sense of monolithic slabs of havoc barely restrained in the deeps of space above my head, their rumbling presence threatening annihilation if they are ever released.

And suddenly I start peeing. Just peeing madly, all over everything, peeing and peeing, urine gushing out of me and coating me, so thick on every part of me that I slide right out of bed and hit the floor. Water is rushing out of me in all directions. But it doesn't matter. I'm crawling toward the window. Having buried the dog in the woods, I must go again and this time I must bury the burial place. I know what I am to do. I must go to the woods and bury the burial place and make him happy.

Yes, I say to whomever I'm listening to. For I am receiving orders, and duty-bound, I listen, my body frozen at attention. Where there is no corpse, there is no crime. Dreamily, the voice goes on. And nothing shall be discoverable through even the most determined of investigations. This burial place shall seem to any passerby a natural site composed of rocks and dirt and shrubs and weeds, its design the result of wind and rain and time. The pebbles, twigs, and rocks and shrubs will appear so perfectly random that not even I who will have deployed them will recognize the buried truth beneath the deception of this camouflage should I pass by again. If only I can find the window, I'll be on my way.

My orders, it seems, have reached completion, and I feel advised to expect nothing further; and then, in what could be mistaken for a total silence, I hear a distant murmuring. It demands that I move closer, and it is into the final echelon of clandestine proceedings that I go, where one descends to reach the heights, and nothing but pure intelligence and cunning operates, spinning schemes in countless coils, one of which is winding around my ankle as another moistly strokes my throat, and still there remains a revolting length of slime to slide across my brow, as I am licked and sucked and tasted and nearly swallowed, for this is my initiation, this is my incorporation, after which I must make it honor's worst violation to go too far back in memory's terrain. Who's talking? I ask, and I am told that it must be known that every reconnoitering patrol has confirmed that only betrayal and corruption result from such questions. Only fiends and monsters lie across the boundaries being established in this midnight contract, which like a fearful apparition must be succumbed to, its strictures swallowed, the entire episode digested and banished from all possible recollection. No dark summons shall ever be allowed to lead to an uncomprehending but fixed obsession with the wilds, an inquisitiveness regarding night and undergrowth and trees. Nor shall the slightest trace of this conversation survive, not even in a ghostly form, vaporous and vague.

Having found the window, I nod, looking into an utterly lightless sky, a colossal and formless space. Hanging out into the dark, I let go. I'm happy. But it's a funny happiness; it's odd; I'm filled with it, but there's a peculiarity to it, something unnatural and strange, as if it's someone else's happiness filling me.

I'll have to hurry back and wash the pee sheets out, I think, the way I wet them in my excitement.

Soon, I know, I'll hit the ground.

BOOK TWO

Something Monstrous on The Loose

Chapter Nine

In the morning, I wash my face with water poured from a white porcelain pitcher into a matching basin. Sunlight dapples the edges of the dresser on which these items stand, alongside a neatly piled towel and washcloth. I splash my face, then pat my cheeks and brow dry. The mirror above the dresser reflects my gaze back through a diagonal crack that bisects the faint imprint of a dozen roses snarled in the glass. My countenance is both familiar and strange. I remind myself of someone I knew intimately once, but now, through the passing of many years, I have been impoverished in some elusive way that exiles me from what I remember.

Because I don't have a cup, I lap a little water, squish around a rusty-tasting mouthful, and spit it out. I dress, quietly, overcoat included. Expecting to have to knock and yell to be let loose, I'm amazed to find the door unlocked. In the hall, I look in one direction and then the other, pondering the complexity of the house. My recollection of the night before is a hodgepodge of shadows and blasts of light.

Once I begin moving, the rooms I chance upon are an odd assortment. The first three appear to have been shut up for years. In each of them, the furniture is shoved into a clutter in the corner and covered with a dustcloth. Descending one floor, I enter a sunny space crowded with wicker porch furniture. The neighboring room is crammed with cardboard boxes and suitcases, old lamps and clothing in piles. The garments of men and women mingle with those of children. Infant booties and knitted caps are stuffed into a corner shelf on top of dresses and tiny trousers, a sad unkempt tangle.

Some minutes later I turn a corner, bound up a short set of stairs, and tug open a squat door with a surface identical to the walls around it. Crouching down, I step into a wedge of stifled air beneath a roof so low I can't stand erect, my initial interest turning into unease. This attic is a lair of collapsing space drilling deep into the house like an animal's burrow, and I sense an offended secrecy lurking in its innermost recesses that presses me back. In the momentum of this retreat, I go down the stairs.

A sitting room with a partially open door is ahead of me, several stuffed chairs inside. I'm walking toward them, intending to take a moment's rest, when I cross an intersecting hallway and down its narrowing lengths I spy the head of the stairway that leads to the front porch. I know the kitchen door is beside it.

Seconds later I am looking in at the Old Man. He's seated at the table fully dressed and reading his newspaper. When I walk in, he gives me a casual glance, then retreats into his reading. Though the atmosphere of the kitchen, with its lingering scents of foods and garbage, makes me aware instantly of how hungry I am, I behave with restraint, sniffing but standing still. I feel compelled to regulate my behavior on a basis of deference and patience. It's gratifying to see him so engrossed in the pages of the paper I gave him. I want to do it again—give him the paper the way I did. If the paper is delivered, it will arrive late in the afternoon. I'll do it then. Though the smells are tantalizing, I know better than to disturb him. I know, also, that rooting around to feed myself would not please him. He turns a page, and I cock my head as if he's said my name. But he doesn't glance in my direction. The morning light is spreading through the air on sparkles and leaping circuits, turning the room into a seamless pool of radiance. Contentedly, I sag against the wall, the sensations of the day casting a spell into which I gaze. When I feel the sudden crisp fact of his attention, I look to find him pondering me. I have strayed into a dream. Like a whistle, his interest snaps me back to the present, and with this change come waves of hunger.

"You sleep this late every morning?" he says.

"No, no. What time is it? Is it late?"

Producing a pocket watch from a slot in the front of his overalls, he stares at it intently, as if reading his palm. After a moment he chuckles, then snorts, "Eight twenty-two. A.M."

"Well," I say. "I'm usually up by this time."

"Yeh?"

His tone is largely sarcastic. Still, it's possible to take his question as real, so that's what I do. "Oh, yes. Usually," I say.

"Nothing in the paper about the goddamn snow," he says, and shoots a sidelong look at me that is both a challenge and a mockery.

"Well," I say. "There wouldn't be."

"No, there wouldn't be."

"No. Of course not."

"Because there wasn't any."

"What about the dog?"

"What about him?"

"Anything in the paper?"

"Not a word. Why would there be?"

"I thought maybe you advertised."

"No need," he says.

"Right."

"He'll be home soon," he says, starting to smile. Or at least his lips are squirming around.

The harmony of our exchange is tugging the edge of my mouth out in a grin. It seems. to me he's letting his approval broaden, too, as the satisfactions of this moment appear mutual. The furrows darkening his brows have their origin in past calamities, I know, and they have nothing to do with this present moment. Snow falls through my mind. He turns back to the newspaper, and I am left there, awaiting a clear-cut explanation of his wishes regarding me. I sag back against the wall.

When he faces me a little later and nods, I have no idea how much time has passed, but his approval generates once more a surge of that electrical and dreamy goodwill bolting through me. Among the thoughts flickering in my brain, there are some that I recognize as my own, while others have qualities that identify them as his, my consciousness a staticky hybrid, our separation overrun. In a moment, I think, his interest in the newspaper will fade; he will turn and gesture for me to take a seat opposite him. I wallow in the sweetness of this fuzzy merger of our sensibilities, a sleepy contentment overtaking me.

Thoughtfully, he folds the paper, and I watch him as he sits there, staring ahead, his posture so focused that I feel the compositions of his mind must stand before him with a definition more compelling than the real objects in the room. His brow is crumpling up in worry, his eyes freezing behind an anxious gleam. When he moves to speak, I lift my head.

"Did you have a good sleep?" he asks. Suddenly he faces me, and I'm stung by the force of his eyes.

"What?" I say.

"Were you comfortable? I mean, were you comfortable?"

Is that what he's been sitting there worrying about—the adequacy of my accommodations? To see that he is so insecure makes me sad. "I slept great," I say, eager to reassure him. "I don't think I stirred."

With a snort, he seems to consult an invisible conspirator, whose opinion on the current issue quickly confirms his own. He nods, then shrugs. The disdainful smirk that he casts in my direction knifes past my friendly hopes. I feel belittled by the smugness of his glance, as if I have made a shameful error and he is right to humiliate me. But before I can ask him what I've done, he says, "C'mon. Sit down, why don't you? Take a seat."

Moments ago, I saw this offer coming, and with its appearance now my anxieties start to fade. I pad across the room. I still feel a little unsafe, but I expect my confidence to fully return. When I reach the table, I'm surprised by the fact that I don't stop. I continue on impulsively, walking past the chair he indicated. It's weird. I know what I'm doing at the same time that I'm startled. Wariness tightens up his posture, his eyes fixed on me. This instant of perplexity fills us both with suspense. Then I'm settling onto the linoleum at his feet, and I'm looking up into the wonder of his response. His bewilderment is dissolving in an onrush of satisfaction, a babyish glow. "I see," he says. He reaches down to fluff my hair. My blood heats up, my nerves sparking with happiness. A raspy rumbling of pleasure emerges from my throat as our eyes meet, his smoldering, mine darting away, shyly. "Well, well, well," he says. Leaning back in his chair, he shakes the paper open again. I'm lying with an increasing slackness drawing me down onto the floor, my limbs melting. In seconds, I'm going to snore. He stares into the air above the pages, which are settling slowly toward his lap, as we surrender to the narcotic enticements of this mood. I await his fingers in my hair.

"All right," he says. "Let's go."

His words enter the drift of my thoughts like an alarm clock into a late-morning snooze. He's getting to his feet and striding toward the door. I'd thought we'd stay for hours. But already he's gone, the speed of his departure creating a vacuum in which I am confused. Clearly, my ability to foretell his whims and moods lacks a certain sophistication. I can hear him thumping down the stairs.

I arrive in the upstairs hallway just as the front door swings shut below. By the time I catch up with him, he's halfway across the yard headed toward the barn, which I take to be our destination, a typical weather-beaten red structure into which gray streaks have been dyed by years of exposure to wind and rain. Just as I get even with him, and settle into his stride, the door ahead of us startles me by swinging open. A large angular man with white hair in knots fills up the gap created by the parting slabs of wood. He wears bib overalls and a stained denim shirt, and his scabby skin sticks out in filthy swatches through tatters at his knees and thighs. The Old Man grabs my arm, veering to the left and dragging me off on a course that will take us wide of the barn. "Don't pay no attention to that sonofabitch," he snarls.

Hovering in the parted doors, the glaring stranger snorts to gather phlegm from his throat. He spits a heavy clot of mucus down onto the hard dirt at his feet.

"Ain't he somethin'? Don't worry about him. What a sight. Hard to believe we're related, huh?"

At the same time that I'm struggling to match the Old Man's pace, I'm looking back over my shoulder, my attention fixed upon this newcomer, as if he is a blazing light.

"I bet you don't believe he's my brother, do you?" the Old Man says, and then he growls. Something in his own words seems to infuriate him. I have to start to trot in order to keep up, my arm aching in his reckless grasp. Making no attempt to disguise the lethal enmity in his heart, he says, "If you're worried he might come over here, you don't have to. He ain't gonna do nothin', and he ain't gonna say nothin'. And don't make the mistake a thinkin' he was in the barn workin' or doing anything useful. That's where he lives. You wouldn't believe the things he said to me; my momma had a big gold-plated clock and it was supposed to be mine. But that sonofabitch over there—that crybaby sneak—he took it, and acted like he didn't. He hid it at first, and said he didn't have it. And then he admitted that he did have it but it was his, he says. Momma give it to him, he says, the dirty lyin' bastard. The SOB. He ain't worth the pig shit it would take to drown him. Well, I let him have it. I give him a piece of my mind. So we had the worst row and there ain't been a civil word between us since. Which is how I like it. Which is just fine with me. I threw him outa the house into the barn, and that's where he's been livin' ever since, and he can live there until he dies. It was three years and twenty-nine days ago and I wish it was a hundred years. You look like you got somethin' to say."

"No."

"Sometimes I'll just cuss at him and really give him what for, but he don't ever say a word to me. Now there's the chickens."

Straight ahead is the chicken coop, a three-tiered shed of wood and wire situated on a barren little patch of dirt strewn with seeds and chicken shit enclosed by a fence. In filthy clusters, a number of hens are gathered around their stinking water bowls. Others dance and scratch the dirt. A few take note of our approach, their heads cavorting like the tops of worn-out toys. In a clucking fuss, several scurry into groups from which, for unknown reasons, they erupt, their futile wings flailing. As we arrive, he says, "Now, go get us one."

"What?"

"Go get us a goddamn bird!"

Still confused, I look at the chickens, then back at the Old Man, my face scrunching up with question.

"You goddamn idiot." He jerks open the gate to the pen and shoves me in. Three of the nearest birds erupt into the air while several others react with a mix of desperation and stupidity that sends them bumping against my feet. Am I just supposed to grab one? And if so, which one? Turning to the Old Man for advice, I discover him stationed at a tree stump in the nearby sunlight, sharpening an axe. He spits, the moist glob of his saliva deepening the black of the whetstone, and the axe starts to grind to the accompaniment of his grunting. I am startled when he looks up to leer into my gaze. His thick lips are a pair of moist worms forming his pronouncement: "The big one," he says. "The big one with the funny look in her eye. Over in the corner there. Got a look in her eye like my brother's got in his eyes. Let's eat that one." With his forefinger he designates a chunky chicken dopily obsessed with picking up grain near the fence. "Bring her over here. And hurry the hell up, if you don't wanna take her place."

As I cross the pen, I feel a wave of aversion walling up the air through which I have to move. The chicken flutters and hops. I approach slowly, getting within a yard before I start to reach for her. But then she springs straight up, squawking and scaring me as she shoots past my hands. I lunge. She is plummeting back down. I catch only a couple of the spray of loose feathers through which she falls. Her fellows scamper off in every direction but the one she's taken, as if they know that the Old Man and I have come to pluck her pretty body free of feathers and gnaw her limbs. We want to fill our bellies with gas. We want to fill our brains with dreams. Frustrated at her escape, I snarl, incensed that she should think herself above our aims. Scampering off, she seems to grow disoriented, tottering into a post. After a rebound of several steps, she falls on her side and lies there, her breath pumping in woe-filled spurts.

I'm crouching, my shoulders humped, my arms extended, my hands curled like a noose. She has her own priorities of seeds and hopping, a wish for eggs and dozing on dainty nests of straw. Dreamily, she lies there, as if to neutralize her jeopardy by ignoring it. Then she bounces to her feet and starts eating. She's in the corner of the pen near the roots of an old tree. Even as I bend to take her, her head keeps stabbing down to pluck up seeds, and when I snatch her from the ground, she doesn't even look at me. With her huffing body caught between my palms, I bear her across the pen. Using the tips of my fingers, I stroke her head and throat. I can feel her despair, the spooky expansion of her apathy overtaking her like an eerie drug. With each heartbeat her resignation overwhelms her further, her appetites a retreating dream.

Ahead is the chopping block stained with antecedent gore. Beside it the old farmer stands with his axe. "You know what to do," he says.

It's like a dream whose logistics I have implemented often and routinely. I didn't understand them then, nor do I now. But I know how to stretch and lock her neck over the blood-drenched wood. The Old Man hums a tune. To the rhythm of his own voice, he swings the axe whistling through the air in a series of practice strokes. He seems to think he needs to hone his abilities for a complex task, and when he's finished, he sighs. It's hypnotic when the blade is finally rising for real, a measured prelude. With a whoosh and a blur, it falls, and the chicken erupts against me. I fling my hands back, as if she's supernatural, having somehow survived our brutal machinations. Off the body races, like a hysterical snowball spitting blood. I look away but meet the chicken's head nestled in my palm. Just as I realize what I'm looking at, she winks. The pupil, vanishing from view, returns and then goes out while I glimpse the unfulfilled impulse of a smile evaporating from her gaze and beak. Ten yards off, the corpse, a scarlet muff, has come to rest near a dandelion growing beside the remnants of a fence. The soiled, tattered corpse is inert except for the blood sliding from the stringy socket of the neck.

Red-faced and short of breath, the Old Man is gazing at me. His head keeps twitching to the left with an involuntary expression of delight. It's obvious that he's eager for me to share his response, and so I start to imitate his mannerisms, shaking my head a little from side to side. I purse my lips in emulation of his almost carnal satisfaction.

Then something subtle but crucial changes in him. Because my senses are fixated on him, I am instantly engaged in trying to solve the mystery of this new desire flickering in his eyes. What does he want? It's agonizing, as if he has his hand on a vulnerable part of me so that he knows he can hurt me if he wants to. "Fetch," he says.

Looking down, I see the knot of the chicken's head in my hand, its eyes coated in a dimming mucus, the vacant pupils as glossy as plastic.

"Fetch!" the Old Man snarls.

I look at him, and realize that he's talking to me.

"What the hell's the matter with you? Get that goddamn chicken over here before I kick your ass."

I yelp, racing off to grab the chicken, and gallop back, presenting the dead bird on the platter of my palms. He nods, but seems largely distracted. Simultaneously, he meets my eyes. It's disorienting. His attention feels threatening. To the degree that I have obeyed him exactly, I have stimulated a sense of far-flung, embittered ruminations. Is he remembering Barney? Is he missing his dog because I am such a paltry substitute? I look to the sky, wondering if it's going to snow. But the air is clear. And while I know it would be misguided to categorize this moment as happy, I feel a certain weird approval, however perverse and paradoxical, swirling around us.

"Let's go," he says. Grabbing the bloody corpse from my hands, he sticks it into my mouth. Then he strides away. I'm going to gag. It's a lot of feathers, an alien intrusion into the moist intimacy of my tongue and palate. But after my immediate revulsion, the vile aspects of the sensation start to diminish. Blood is leaking into my mouth, a heated sweetness, which accompanied by the gamy stink curling through my nose reminds me of my earlier hunger. My breathing begins to rumble. I start swallowing the blood, feeling old appetites glutted, new ones kindled. I clamp my teeth, crushing the feathery mass to produce a further hemorrhage, and then I go running after him, dripping chicken blood and chicken gore and breathing through my nose.

Chapter Ten

As he steps onto the porch, the angle of his body alarms me. His posture rebukes me because I'm lagging behind. I respond with frenzied scampering. But I have been negligent and he wants me to know it. "Get over here!" he snaps.

When he opens the door I slip past. Above me, the kitchen emits a glow, and I hasten toward it. The old man moves me along, bullying me up the stairs. With a quick peek over my shoulder, I hope to spy a bit of evidence in him from which I might infer his next desire. But the gleam of his eyes is ambiguous, his concerns intense, their nature undisclosed. I race ahead, turning into the kitchen, where I pick the carcass from my mouth and try to catch my breath. Blood spots the filthy linoleum. I pry feathers and grit from my teeth and gums. My hands are grimy, my trousers stained. I hate it when he looks at me that way, so full of reproach and disappointment. I hope he won't look at me like that when he comes in. And then I realize that I've been in the kitchen for several minutes now without him, and I turn to the doorway, expecting to see him standing there. But the door, which I left open, shows only the fragment of the hall visible through it. When the next few minutes pass and he still fails to join me, my unease gets bad enough to start me pacing about. I end up at the sink, where I turn the water on and wash my hands and face. Using a nearby window as a mirror, I try to fix the mess of my hair. With every passing second my anxiety is getting worse. I see it reflected in my face. I feel it stirring in my fingers. Finally worry takes me over, and I plop down at the table, my head in my hands. It's obvious that my decision to come into the kitchen was wrong. He's pursued a different course than the one I took, thinking I was anticipating his wishes. Now he's off somewhere in the house and I have no idea where. I have no idea what he's doing, or what he wants from me.

Jamming the chicken back between my jaws, I head for the door. The hallway provides several dim alternatives, corners and corridors branching off into other corridors full of other doors and corners. After a moment's hesitation, I have a sudden instinct for the way he's gone. It's my nose, really, a sharp sensation. In spite of the stench of chicken guts and feathers clogging my nostrils, I feel I've discovered a significant scent, and I hurry off along the hall, pursuing the odors of oil and metal, the penetrating aroma of machines.

Traveling on through several twists and turns, I enter a hall that feels unnaturally narrow and then I'm in a wing I've never seen before. Sensing something behind a door whose cracks exude the presence of tools, I pause. I peer in carefully. Abruptly, he emerges from the shadows. With his next move he grabs his shotgun. He's stuffing into the open barrel a pair of red and brass shotgun shells, either of which could be my doom, and his scorn is a wall that isolates and intimidates me. I want him to look at me, but he doesn't. I need at least a clue to what he's thinking. He doesn't give me even a sidelong glance when he says, "I thought you knew what you was doing."

Our disappointment was identical. I want to explain, I want to apologize. The barrel of the shotgun keeps lining up on me, even though he's absorbed in other activities. Now he's strapping on a knife in a sheath. We suffered from the same illusion, I want to tell him, and I step sideways, trying to slip out of alignment with the barrel, but it follows me. He looks up. I meet his eyes, hoping to express an emotion that is large and sincere, one that conveys the regret I feel, but what bursts out of me is high-pitched noise as I try and fail once more to elude the gun. He's aiming it at me, smiling down the sights.

"Just put the goddamn chicken in the kitchen where it belongs," he says.

"Right," I say. "Now?"

"Goddamnit!" he shouts, and I jump from the room. I'm running down the hall when he shouts after me, "You're wasting time!"

As I skid into the kitchen, I'm nervous and hurrying and my ankles tangle. I go tumbling into the table. A metal pitcher springs into the air, clattering against the wall but spilling nothing because, luckily, it's empty. I pounce on it to silence it. I'm afraid he's going to come raging in the door. I want to put the chicken where he wants it, but scanning the room, I have no idea where that is. I settle for a wild guess and throw the carcass toward the sink, where it lands with a splat, the white porcelain misting scarlet.

That's when I see the clock on the wall. It's almost noon. My wife, I think, and I see her stormy face. I've been away from home before, but never like this. By now she'll have awakened to my empty place in the bed beside her. I'm scared that my continuing absence will affect her like a diatribe with every phrase an insult. She's mad at me the way it is. When I started hanging around outside the Old Man's house, I could feel her burgeoning jealousy. That's why I went in secret. Now I've been with him all night long. Her face and words, as I imagine them, are incensed. She's furious. I should go home right now. Or else I should never go back. If it weren't for my little boy, I could stay away. But if I don't go back, she'll be embittered and crazy, having been abandoned by me, having been insulted. Not only will poor Tobias be deprived of my companionship, but he'll be facing her enmity alone, as if he's not only my miniature but my surrogate. Tobias, I think, and I feel I must escape. But I don't move.

Something hard and painful rings against my skull. I yelp and duck too late. A shotgun shell is sailing off toward the pots and pans in an arc that will deliver it short of the sink. It hits with a clang and rolls, spinning, until it ends up pointing at the Old Man, whose knobby shape fills the doorway.

"You gotta wake up," he says. "You're off in the clouds. Every time I turn around, you're off in the clouds. I tell you to do something, you're off in the clouds. You like getting hit on the head? Fine. You don't like getting hit on the head, you better wake up. Understand?"

I nod, rubbing the tender swelling in my hair and hoping my manner of solemn understanding is enough to appease him.

"What the hell's the matter with you?" he bellows. "Can't you do anything right?"

"What?" I say.

"We ain't done yet, that's what. We got work to do. Now let's get going." He stomps across the room to the door, where he wheels, as if he cannot believe I have not moved. "What the hell are you waiting for?"

My search for a response leaves me conflicted and alarmed. Sooner or later I must tell him that I have a wife, a child, a house to return to. But I fear the effect these facts will have on the tenuous balance of our relationship. There's no way that he will manage graciously the realization that I am not his exclusively.

"Goddamnit, let's go," he says.

I feel hopeless when I start to talk. "Sure, that'll be great," I say. "We'll go for a walk and then do whatever else you want to do and when we get all that done, it'll be late afternoon, I guess."

"What the hell are you talking about?"

"Well," I say. "Well, I just—I—" My thoughts are bouncing off one another rather than coalescing in a purpose.

"Didn't you hear me say we gotta get going?"

"Yes," I say, "but I'm just saying, I'm just saying, that after that—after that—if it's okay with you, I'll have to go home."

"What?"

"I mean, I mean, I—"

"What'd you say?"

"What?"

"What'd you say?"

"I'm talking about later on. Much later on. And—"

"But what the hell did you say?" His shoulders are hunched, a growing threat nested beneath the frozen surface of his eyes.

"That I have to go home."

"What are you talking about? What the hell are you talking about?"

"I have a wife, you know."

He's marching toward me.

"And a son. I told you. Didn't I tell you?"

"What the hell you talkin' about?"

"I thought I mentioned it."

"You damn well didn't."

"I meant to."

I want to duck and cover up my head, but I stand there, smiling sickly. He starts to circle me, his manner stealthy, as if he's stalking me.

Watching him closely, I say, "So you see, that's what I'm getting at. *After. After* we get everything finished here, and only then, only after we do everything here—everything you want to do, everything I want to do—well, then I'll have to go on home, and see how things are there."

"So you're not moving in?"

"Excuse me?"

"I thought you were moving in."

"Oh."

"Or are you?"

"Well . . . I mean, I wasn't. I . . ."

With his body pulled up to its full height, he moves with a heavy, pompous gait back toward to door. "It's probably just as well. Probably wouldn't have worked out. Goddamn. Shit. Piss," he says. "Goddamn. Shit. Piss." The room is filling up with bitterness. Loneliness. Rejection. I feel his bleakness, even as he grumbles in some throaty celebration of his ability to endure punishment.

When he departs the kitchen, the room actually darkens, as if his sentiments are a batch of storm clouds. I know he expects me to follow, but ambivalence suspends me between a set of misgivings and a desire to obey. His footsteps pound down the stairs.

I feel I have been left in some desolate part of the world. The front door slams. I can't say I decide to bolt after him, but the passing seconds threaten me like the onrush of angry footsteps, and suddenly I'm running down the stairs.

Emerging from the house, I see him at the edge of the porch. His skin is mottled with a bridled passion that rises like a pox, leaving him flecked and pale, his eyes unfocused.

My lips are numb, my words a heartsick hubbub as I run toward him. "Don't worry. We'll get everything done," I say. "Just everything. And Barney'll be back today. I'm sure of it. He's on a back road by now, that one over by the Murphy place, I bet—by that big tree, the one behind the barn, and he's getting ready to—"

"Shut up. You don't know shit. You wouldn't know your ass if you looked at it in a mirror." He strides off the porch, and I go with him, keeping close this time. At the fence, he leans against the top rail, his hands wringing one another as he stares out into the pasture. "We got the goddamn chicken for us, but what we gotta do is get somethin' good for Barney. He needs somethin' too, you know. So he has a nice nourishing dinner when he gets home. Then I don't give a shit what you do. Go *home*," he says, twisting the word as if it's a curse. "Go *home* to your goddamn *wife. Please.*"

The scorn with which he perverts these normally wholesome words compounds my anxiety. "He'll be home soon," I say. "I mean, if he got loose when you said. I mean, that was—"

"Barney?"

"Yes."

"A lot you know."

"I mean, he's been loose for a while, hasn't he? So he's probably taking a big rest over near his mother's house. Somewhere over there. Out by the barn, that's where I mean, that's a nice spot. The Murphys' place. He's taking a little nap just before he comes the rest of the way." I'm babbling, and the Old Man is glaring at me, his eyes like knife blades seeking to open my skin in little slits so he can reach in and poke and paw my innermost parts.

"What you talkin' about?" he says.

It's almost as if my arm points itself, swinging out to indicate the forest's perimeter, where scrub brush and dwarf pines mix with weeds. "Barney!"

"What?"

"Barney!" I yell.

"Barney?" The word has a plaintive thrust off his tongue. He seems to choke.

"Behind those bushes."

"You saw him?"

I'm pointing at the bushes. "There! There!"

We are both transfixed by the greenly woven growths parting before the onrush of a muscular, earthen color. The wind, moving the tips of everything, prompts a sound like water in a creek bed. Brittle stems are crackling with heavy footfalls. Longing rips its way into the Old Man's eyes and then it fills his voice: "Barney! Barney, come!" he shouts.

Flecks of wavering brown appear to be an approaching canine commotion. The intervening screen of shifting greenery undulates, then
stabilizes. The russet mosaic that could have been fur stands revealed as
a clump of dying leaves on brittle branches.

Filled with my own sense of loss, I turn toward the Old Man. I want
to share the disappointment I know he must be feeling. The shotgun is a
blur streaming toward my face. Pain bites into my cheek like a set of
savage teeth. The bones of my jaw groan, a bell-like resonance rising
through my brain.

"That ain't him, you goddamn tease!"

Wobbling to my left, I miss a step. The ground races up, slamming into
me and hurling me down, sticks and brittle hunks of dirt gouging me.

"How come you wanna be a crazy mean person who's gonna tease me
about Barney bein' where he ain't?" he yells. "I hate bein' teased. I hate
it. Don't you have any goddamn decency, to tease me about that?"

I'm careening about in weeds and vines, like a fish in a whirlpool. I
can hear the Old Man yelling, but he seems so remote and vague, it's
hard to care about what he's doing. Having gotten to my feet, I try to
stagger out of reach of the ground tilting up to crash into me once more,
a blow that leaves me face down, my head tingling like a sleeping foot.

"Don't you just lay there, you little bastard."

Searching to see him, I discover a burst of sunlight above me, with his
figure smeared across it like a haloed scarecrow. "What the hell you
cryin' about?" he says.

"I thought it was him."

"Just stop cryin'."

But how can I explain, how can I make him see? How can I describe
the poignant deprivation that I feel. Something precious was just lost.
Whatever I glimpsed and then doubted in the weeds was confirmed
once he began to shout in welcome. Briefly, we shared a prelude to the
reinvigoration of our barren world with the return of trust and honor
and courage and faithfulness, all those virtues thought lost forever.

"Let's go," he says. "I shouldn'ta hit you with the gun butt like that.
I'm glad I hit you but I shoulda hit you with my fist and not the gun butt;
I coulda broke your jaw."

I groan, trying to speak, the hinge of my jaw a sickening ache. What I
want him to understand is that it doesn't matter that nothing emerged
from those wavering weeds. That nothing emerged is not so important

as what nearly came. Because what nearly came was wondrous, it was
astounding and uplifting.

"You see this stick? You see it?" he says. In his fist he holds a three-
foot length of tree branch thickened with periodic knobs like turkey
necks. Slowly he waves it before my eyes. "I asked you, do you see it?"

"Yes."

"What are you shakin' about?"

"I'm cold."

Back and forth goes the stick.

"Take a good look. I'm gonna be carryin' this with me from now on.
And when you do one of the wrong things you do—and you do more
wrong things than any damn fool I ever seen—I'm going to hit you with
it and I'm gonna hit you good. Now let's get going. You see this stick?"

"Yes," I say.

"You ready to get goin'?"

"Yes."

"So move!"

"Where?"

He pokes me with the stick, and I yelp.

"To get some food for Barney, you selfish bastard, that's where. To
shoot a goddamn rabbit, buddy boy." He stabs the stick into my ribs. He
slaps the knobby side against my legs.

"All right! All right!" The end gouges into my stomach and the side
bites my thigh.

"So move it, then, goddamnit."

My hands are fluttering about in front of me, trying to anticipate his
next point of attack. "I don't know which way to go."

"Where do you think a rabbit is, you jackass?" His big arm springs out
to indicate the woods.

"All right!" I say. He jabs me in the ribs. I lunge several hasty steps
toward the wilds, wanting to get ahead of him, to get out of his reach,
but a wave of weakness starts to drag me to a stop almost immediately.
I'm dropping to my knees. When I see him striding past me I close my
eyes. I cannot face the dark for long alone, and I have to peek. He waits a
few yards ahead of me, squinting back. Beyond him stands the forest.
Oh, no, I think.

"I got my stick," he says.

He might as well be telling me to go into a pit of vipers. He's coming toward me, raising the stick. My legs are wisps. The forest is oozing evil. Depravity crawls along the vines weaving around the phantoms disguised as trees. Dark eyes stare out from the welter of these coils. I almost hear the voice whose strictures filled my mouth and throat last night with prohibitions against this place. I don't dare go in. I was forbidden in the night. "No, no," I say. "I—I—" The stick jabs into my stomach and I see clearly that these are not the words to make my point.

"We're goin' in the goddamn woods!" he shouts. Suddenly he starts to pound me, flailing away against my legs. I try to fend him off, I try to retreat. When the stick cracks, half of it goes flying out of sight, the rest remaining in his fist.

"Please!" I cry.

"Shut up! I'm warning you." With the clublike fragment he smacks me in the head.

"We can't go in there!" A harrowing edict prohibits entry to these wilds and I must protect the Old Man, who doesn't know the recklessness of his desire. The tangle of limbs, I want to tell him, the confusion of leaves, the incessant alteration of rot and burgeoning—these are an evil that must not be trespassed.

Crashing down, the club feels heavier, harder. I reel off and attempt to avert a fall by stepping straight up into the sky before I slam on my back against the ground. We can't. We shouldn't. I'm crawling to escape him. Like a man climbing up a cliff, I'm hauling myself over the level ground, grabbing rocks and roots. "No," I yell. "Monsters! Fiends!"

Crouched above me as if to pounce, he follows along. His club and heavy boots smack against my limbs and skin, blows so numerous they lose their individuality, merging in a haze of pain.

Now he grabs my hands. He has a rope. A stick is thrust behind my back and through the crook of both elbows. My hands are stretched across my stomach, where he starts lashing them together. "No!"

"Shut up!" he screams. "Barney's gotta eat."

"Don't you hear me? What's wrong with you?" The rope is running round my waist and out again to my hands and then on to him, where he's looping the end over his shoulder and turning to stride off. "Oh, don't," I cry. "Stop!"

"Shut up!"

Kicking at the dirt for leverage, I try to fight but I am overruled by his ferocity. Head over heels I am sent tumbling, my fall forcing him to drag me crawling and rolling along the ground, struggling to regain my feet.

He's laughing wildly now. "We're going in!"

Ahead, I see his legs, his big black stomping boots. Through the dust raised by our commotion I see our destination. The bushes and the trees, in their accumulation, are a darkening cloud beneath his roaring voice, and the forest is an onrushing storm.

Chapter Eleven

"Now you just calm your goddamn self," he tells me.

The rope encircles my belly and snakes off to wrap around the grooved and grainy trunk of a massive oak. My hands are still bound before me, the stick in the crooks of my elbows. I lie amid roots, one of which appears to overlap my thigh.

"And get yourself real clear about one goddamn thing, because if you don't, you might just find yourself stuck out here forever. Then you're dinner for whatever godforsaken creature might come along and wanna eat you. Are you listenin' to me?"

I feel I'm going to explode with the intensity of my attention on him, for clearly my life depends on my understanding him exactly.

"You wanna run around with me," he says, "and visit me and be with me, you gotta be able to go into the woods. You can't go into the woods, I gotta tell you, you ain't gonna be no more use to me than piss on a boot."

Straightening now, he seems enormously tall as he turns and steps away in a move that I realize is the first in a series that will bear him off into the wilds, leaving me. I want to stop him, but my urge to protest is crushed back by my fear of being hit again. He's leaving me, and he's woefully unprepared. He'll die, I think as I watch him blend into the layered leafage, the shifting vegetation closing over him as would the ocean on a sinking body. I'm trying to be obedient and be quiet but the terrible cries I'm struggling to restrain keep leaking out in tiny squeals. And then just when I think he is gone, he bobs back into view as if the depths have repulsed him for one last tantalizing glimpse and I can't stop myself. "Come back," I cry.

He vanishes in a lengthy flurry of branches and leaves. His footsteps are the last I know of him. Tears roll down my cheeks. I take a swipe at my snotty nose with my shoulder, wondering where he's going and what he intends to do. Above me, the matted foliage reduces the sun to a bubbly sheen, like grease in which the greenery is cooking.

I should have made a better presentation of my argument, for his sake as well as my own. Even if I didn't exactly understand what was happening to me, I should have tried to warn him with clarity instead of surrendering to all that blubbering. Now I'm trapped, and he is wandering about, his every step taking him deeper into jeopardy while he imagines himself safe, while he imagines himself occupying the innocent forest that he, in his ignorance, conceives this place to be. I know what that's like. I know what it's like to think that way. I can recollect a time when I believed that ditches, caves, owls, and birds were nothing but themselves. Holes were a consequence of burrowing animals, or rushing water. Trees, boulders, shrubbery, pebbles, sticks, all exhibited a mindless natural order. But now, I have another awareness, a haunted vision. And more unnerving even than its content is the overwhelming shock and violence of its onset. I didn't know what was happening to me, but at the forest's edge, this force rose up like some mysterious giant to fling me down and leave me shaking on the ground. I saw that every leaf and twig was alive and watching me, incorporeal powers swirling in the trees.

Looking off in the direction that the Old Man went, I hope to see him coming back. But nothing human meets my eye. Spears of shadow are lurking there and merging with massive leaves in the creation of a fleshlike tissue that heaves a sudden breath and turns to look at me. I press my face into the dirt. I beg myself not to look, but then I do. I see the aftermath of a malign invisibility disappearing behind a nearby boulder. Something was there, but now it's gone. Above a brooding stump jutting out of moss and mud, a spooky phantom hovers, waiting to sneak up on me. Then a shape in the nearby shadows sighs, and I have to get away. I start to crawl, but the rope stops me, making me feel faint. I sink to the ground, my face in the dirt. The lurking thing, whatever it is, slinks closer. I feel its presence gathering over me. Soon its jaws will close on me and I'll shriek, my body shredded in some alien appetite. Like the chicken, I think, remembering the swoon with which terror overwhelmed her, a drugged and sickening transformation beginning to conquer me. It's more a falling away into a faint than any routine entrance into slumber, but unconsciousness is an irresistible force. I welcome it, my mind filling up with a rush of images that leave me sniffing and snorting.

Startled, I'm staring at the dirt. Something hard and sharp is digging into my hip. I see a big black boot. Looking up, I find the Old Man dropping down onto one knee beside me, a dead rabbit draped over his thigh. Entrails seep out a seam along its mangled side. The bloody stink, so close to my nose, is gamy and invigorating, moving me to sit up.

"You ready?" he asks. When I just stare, his brows narrow, his lips tightening with irritation. I emulate him as best I can. About the time I reach the stage where I'm shaking my head disgustedly, he chuckles and unties the rope from the tree. He raises the loop encircling my belly until it is a noose about my neck. My heart presses against my lungs so that it's difficult to breathe. He thrusts the dead rabbit into my hands. "Now you take care a this, all right? This is your responsibility." I accept the rabbit with its leaking intestines. I clutch it to me as I would a beloved toy. He's wrapping the loose end of the rope around his knuckles, and when he's finished, he turns and heads off into the forest's depths, drawing me along in his wake.

Around my throat, the pressure of the rope is like the climactic turn in a long and compelling argument. I can think of little else. Because he is unfettered and free to set our course, he maintains a headlong pace. My pinioned hands impede my balance, but I manage to keep my feet while hanging on to the rabbit. His enthusiasm for his plan, unknown to me, blinds him to the increasing tension his bursts of speed are creating in the rope leading to my neck. The cumulative effect is the steady reduction of my breath, and I'm debating whether or not I should alert him to my growing discomfort. But every time I decide to speak, a burst of inhibition flings a picture of him at me, his eyes full of rebuke and scorn and disappointment that I failed to understand him, that I failed to trust and obey him. But suddenly I'm coughing, desperate to breathe. He spins to face me, just as he did in my imagination. His eyes are glaring and he hisses to shush me, his fist a wavering threat. I respond by nodding, a fidget of agreement. I tighten up my throat, determined to ration my breath. My head above the noose is blank, as if I am a newly minted infant. Whatever he wants to tell me, I'm a receptive space.

But then the predictable levels of the path are broken by an intruding mound. I lose my balance. I'm stumbling, staggering. He lunges on, and I hit the ground, scrabbling to follow, but I can't, I'm wedged between two rocks, I'm strangling, kicking and squealing. I can feel his rage rushing back at me, and I try to fill my eyes with apology and self-reproach as he rips me to my feet, his fist clutching my hair, the look in his eyes as horrifying as a house on fire. In this smoldering, I see that he knows absolutely everything important there is to know. "You better start to pull your own weight, buddy boy," he says. "Or I'll leave you out here. I swear I will. I'll tie you to a tree and leave you here. You can learn it the easy way, or you can learn it the hard way. I don't care which. But you are gonna learn it."

Then he marches off. I'm trailing along as close to him as his own shadow, unable to think of anything but his eyes as he spoke to me of what I had to learn. And suddenly I see how my first interpretation of these events is all wrong. Stunned into hysteria at the edge of the forest, I misunderstood his reasons for entering the menace I foresaw. Given the magnitude of my distress, I could only understand his reckless desire to rush into the woods as a form of ignorance. But now I see another possibility, something strange and hard and enviable in his heart.

Without even looking back at me, he tugs the leash, ordering me to pick up the pace. I can no longer deny the obvious truth that the force moving him to drag me along like this is more complex than mere cruelty or ignorance. He didn't really have to bring me with him. He could have come alone. And then I ask myself: What does he expect me to learn? Does he face the dangers of this trail because he believes himself capable of defeating anything that might dare to attack him? Is that what he possesses—is it strength and courage? And are they what he's trying to teach me?

Behind some bushes near a lake he lashes the rope to a fallen tree.

With a stern look, he bids me to be quiet and settles down against a nearby log. I hold the gory, stinking rabbit to my chest. Under the admonition of his steely gaze, I struggle to subdue my panting along with my excitement. When I succeed, he grunts and turns away. The mist above the water is a spangled haze. I can smell everything. I lie there chewing on the edge of the log.

Two ducks leap up to penetrate the mist and dart across a wedge of pinkish light. They speed toward the sun, which pulsates in a remote and mottled sector of the sky. On my knees, I watch the Old Man elevate his gun. The barrel slides along the sky. I see him press the trigger. The explosion and the aftermath lift the weapon and tilt him backward. I cover up my ears, but I have to watch. A swirl of force envelops one of the ducks, dragging it a yard to the left of its intended course. Then it plummets, disappearing into the water. I am standing up. I can hear the muffled honking as the duck flails away, sending up a spume. The legs kick but the head doesn't lift. The neck no longer works, while the wings pound. It must be horrified to drown, I think, I know I would be. But when the Old Man looks at me, his eyes are filled with a strange ecstasy I know he wants me to share. Does he hear the flailing of the drowning duck? If he does, it pleases him.

"Go get it," he says. He winks at me, and I know enough to wink back. He lifts the noose from my neck, unties my hands, and shoves me toward the shoreline. I place the rabbit on a flat rock near the water's edge.

It's difficult to swim through the dark gray surface to the bobbing body of the duck. Sticks bump against my chin, and I haven't taken the time to remove my clothes. Arriving at the soggy floating corpse, I grab it and stuff it into my mouth. I have no choice if I'm going to have both arms free to swim. A clot of tiny tail fluff sticks to my teeth and I try to spit it out, feeling as if I'm going to gag. Even more discomforting is a big feather adhering with its ribbed fluffiness to the roof of my mouth.

Above the splashing of my awkward struggle to keep afloat and manage the duck, I hear the Old Man yelling. With some effort to lift my head and perceive him through the foam, I see him, blustering up and down the shore. He's waving his arms and bellowing. My first fear is that one of the dreaded forest phantoms has assailed him, and my arms start to speed me to his aid. Quickly closer to the shore, I am able to hear his cries.

"That's not a very good stroke!" he yells.

Realizing that he doesn't like my swimming, I attempt immediate adjustments, lose the duck, and in my flailing sink the corpse with a swat of my arm. I dive to seek the little body in the murk, but I can't find it. I'm cold, and the underwater is too dark. I rise and discover that the duck has bobbed to the surface, where it rises and descends on the swells of my commotion.

I try a sidestroke and hear his muttered comments. "He can't do anything right. That's a ridiculous way to swim. I'm leaving."

"I'm coming," I cry after him, losing the bird as I speak.

"Bring the bird."

"I will. I will."

Lifting myself out of the water, I pounce and snap at the feathery carcass, infuriated that it has managed to frustrate me as much as it has, embarrassing me in front of the Old Man. I clamp my jaws so fiercely that my teeth clink and bounce off bone. To free my eyes of dripping water, I shake my head, and I reverse my posture in the waves to try the backstroke in hope of his approval.

"What are you doing?" he screams at me, and of course I can't answer. My mouth is stuffed. Yet I do my best to wave. A stick comes sailing over and smacks my foot. Then a rock sends up a spume to the left of my head. "What do you think this is, your goddamn vacation?" I hear him roar.

When I clamber from the water, I'm as drenched as an old pile of clothes just pulled from a washing machine. I shake myself as if I'm having a fit.

"You're getting me all wet, you idiot!" he shouts.

I try to make amends, offering the bird on the platter of my palms.

"You swim like an old lady. You carry the goddamn bird, and don't get me wet."

I hug the duck, looking around at the fearful trees, and in their shadowy shifting and hissing I see both the terror and the simplicity of his lessons. You have to learn to live in the woods no matter how much you fear them, no matter how strange they are, no matter how sick they make you feel. You have to live surrounded by the curses and the tangled mysteries of the dead, the living, the dying, and all the while you have to ignore them, treating them and the feelings they engender as if neither exists inside you, as if nothing exists inside you.

"And just stop your goddamn shakin', all right?"

Reducing my frenzy to a series of repressed tremors, I gaze adoringly at him. In the last few hours, I feel I have come to know him in a special way.

"You gonna run away anymore? Or you gonna come along like I want?"

"I'm gonna come along and do what you want," I say.

"I don't have to put this rope on you no more, and you'll just come along. No more fussin'. Right?"

"Right," I say.

He fits the noose over my head and adjusts the knot carefully into place against my throat, his eyes probing me. "I don't believe you," he says, and he tightens the knot. His gaze is dense and complex, an icy draft sinking through my skin so that my insides shiver. I know I dare not presume to grasp his purposes. I don't dare imagine I know the content of his heart.

"I don't want to lose you in the woods," he says. "How you feel?"

I try to speak, but I only smile, a sensation in the moving tissue of my face like breaking ice.

"You ain't a bad boy. You're a pretty good boy. Ain't you? Even if you can't swim for shit. Huh? You're a good boy. And don't forget the goddamn rabbit!"

"Oh, no," I groan, looking around to retrieve it.

"You was gonna, wasn't you?" He puts his thumb and forefinger around my nose, and squeezes. A burning bubble of sensation lunges into my throat, where it breaks apart, one half dropping into my grumbling guts, the other erupting in my brain. I'm jumping and yelping as we head off. If I were him, I wouldn't trust me either. I would tie me up. I would control me just as he is, using a rope to rub like a warning against my Adam's apple, a reminder that he could kill me at any instant.

The sunlight on the air is giddy, a fractured mosaic hung in particles amid the wavering leaves and branches. The play of these elements across my senses has a magical, lulling effect on me, so I'm floating along in a pleasant stupor, when suddenly something happens and it's as if I've heard a peal of thunder, the ground quivering under my feet.

I falter and start sniffing and looking around, feeling panicky for no reason I know. The Old Man jerks at me, without even glancing back. The rope gouges my neck. I stagger on, but I keep looking and sniffing, trying to locate the cause of my escalating alarm. And then I see that our route is taking us past the tree to which the Old Man bound me when we first came into the forest. The place feels spooky. The spot where I lay alone feels haunted. It's weird and unnerving. The dark, foreboding air is inhabited by something like a curse or hex, something phantasmagoric that seems to have once belonged to me, and it's seething and embittered, a kind of entity like a ghost, enraged and suffering and lurking in the trees. I feel confused. It's something essential and invisible and deeply personal, an entity amputated from me and forsaken in the trees. I feel lost and I want to be closer to the Old Man. I want to touch him, to have him touch me, but he strides on, his shotgun cradled in the crooks of his arms. His boots are dark as is his hunting cap. He wears black trousers, a black jacket, and an inky streaming scarf.

Ahead of me, a veil of foliage parts and I glimpse a pasture on the other side, a sunny vista that vanishes from view behind a rush of leaves folding back to seal away not only the patch of green and sunlight but the Old Man, too. He's disappeared, and I feel left behind, like the thing I myself abandoned—an outcast left to die and haunt the wilds. Then the rope snaps tight. It jerks me through the bushes, and the noose is suddenly precious, a necklace emblematic of our connection, my salvation.

Bursting into the pasture, I discover that in the spacious meadow open to the glittering afternoon the Old Man is a colorful abundance of greens and browns and gunmetal blues.

Lifting the noose off my neck, he pats my shoulder and twists my ears. Though I find myself glancing back toward the enigmatic wilds, I feel nothing. I know that place within me like a squalling infant that abhorred the woods has been left behind like a petulant, bothersome child. But it's not an absence, this nothing that I feel, not an emptiness, it's something heavy and cold.

"What the hell you dreamin' about now?" he grumbles.

I elevate our trophies, butchered rabbit and droopy duck. He nods approvingly. "Go on home!" He kicks me, and I'm scampering off down the sloping pasture toward his house. Like a gigantic orange, the sun teeters on the peak of the roof.

"I'll see if Barney's back," I shout.

Chapter Twelve

After depositing the dead rabbit and duck in the sink with the chicken, I scoot back to the hall and up a set of stairs. Somewhere on the third floor, I stop and stand watching dust motes falling through the air. After a few minutes go by I lie down on the floor and continue to watch the dust motes. They fall and fall. I don't know where Barney is, but I don't think he's here. When I finally return to the kitchen, I find the Old Man at the stove. He glances at me, then returns to the coffee he's preparing in a pot.

"I saw a shadow I thought was him in the hallway on the second floor," I say. "It looked just like him for a second."

He snorts and lifts the old pot, and the coffee he pours flows past the chipped spout into a blue ceramic mug. Several spoonfuls of sugar follow, and he stands there stirring. He crosses to the table. Sitting down, he sinks into a meditation so absorbing that I feel alone. At the sink, I run a glass of water.

"He ain't here," the Old Man says, after taking a sip of his coffee.

"I thought maybe. You know, maybe he was. I wasn't teasing."

"I'm sure you weren't."

"It was like it was running when I came around the corner," I say. "This shadow. I thought it was him. But it wasn't."

The nasty underpinnings of his expression, which isn't really a smile, make me uncomfortable. "You don't have to worry," he says, and the modulation in his tone reveals a little more of his worrisome mood. He appears benign, but I feel reproached. "It was fun to watch you runnin' around the house lookin' for him and I know the house is empty," he says. "That tickled my funny bone just a little, don't you know. But you was gonna look or bust. That gimme a couple a good laughs. I enjoyed you makin' a fool outta yourself. Where you think he is?"

"What?"

"Where you think he is?"

The faint rapping surprises us both. Originating off to my right, it makes me look in that direction, but nothing that I see hints at the nature of the noise. When I turn back to the Old Man, his eyes are slits, his fingers poised on the table. He bounds across the room and into the hall.

"What?" I say, darting after him.

At the top of the stairs, I wait while he descends to the vestibule. With his forefinger, he nudges open the curtains covering the glassed-in upper half of the frame. "Hmmmm," he says, and flings the door back.

"What?" I say. I'm rushing down to join him. On the porch, a middle-aged man and woman are waiting, the burden of a black fretting cocker spaniel shared between them, the man with his arms under the fluffy torso and hindquarters, while the woman holds the head.

"You the people lost the dog?" says the man. He looks from the Old Man to me and back again.

"We don't mean to bother anybody," she adds, her smile ending up on me.

The Old Man sweeps his gaze over all of us, his eyelids trembling. He steps out onto the porch, and I'm right behind him. Clad in coveralls, the man sucks on a battered pipe, while the woman wears a pale print dress and has a kind of flowerpot hat perched on her white hair held flat by a melee of bobby pins. The dog is quivering, its mouth panting, the eyes morose. The impression of wanting to escape that the creature conveys is more a result of exaggerated yearning than any real act of struggle.

"We heard you people lost a dog," the woman says.

"I lost a dog," the Old Man says.

"You put up the posters? You the one?" The man is talking to us, but he's angled sideways toward his wife, as if checking his words against her expression.

"That's why we come here," she says.

The spaniel keeps shifting its gaze between the Old Man and me. With some regularity, it glances up at the man and the woman, clutching it. Though the dog seems equally attentive to all of us, I feel there's something different, something excessive when its eyes meet mine. I feel imposed on and resentful as the spaniel repeatedly turns to me with its cloying, sickening expression.

"We saw them drawings on the road, and we think this little fella is the one," the woman says. She prods the dog's face toward the Old Man, using her palm as one might use a spoon.

The Old Man takes a step closer and then he turns toward me. I'm expecting him to speak, but he whirls instead and rushes into the house, slamming the door. Through the window, I see him flying up the stairs, leaving the four of us gaping after him, as the dog begins to whine.

"What's all this?" says the man to the woman.

She shrugs. "Beats me."

As the two of them turn to me, demanding an explanation, creaking sounds emerge from remote portions of the house. The man and woman both grumble, their perplexity and indignation a matter of sighs and shrugs and annoyed remarks, while the spaniel gazes up at me, panting. I hate the fact that this obsequious cur believes that I will respond to it. The beady little eyes implore me, hoping to turn me, through steady insistence, into an ally. With my back to the door, I confront the dog and the challenge of the people who brought him. I narrow my eyes in a confrontational grimace, intending to protect the Old Man should they try to enter the house. I want them to make no mistake regarding my unflinching loyalty to him. I want to leave no doubts about the magnitude of the blind faith with which I endorse his every whim.

"You know what's goin' on here?" she asks me, but I refuse to answer.

"This is downright rude," says the man, and I tense my body, crouching forward in a show of defiance.

Then a distant scratching evolves into rhythmic footsteps approaching along the second-floor hall, and the Old Man comes thudding down the stairs. The door bangs open. His brows are tight with concentration and he clutches one of the drawings, his head bowed as if to memorize each dot and line.

I am startled and intrigued by what he's doing. I don't know what I expected, but it wasn't this. I glance at the visitors, who are regarding the Old Man expectantly, but he is oblivious. He's as mesmerized by the poster as we are by him. Examining the drawing, he suddenly wheels to the dog in their arms. As if the fluctuations of his concentration govern us, we all do the same. But it doesn't last, and he looks away. For the next minute or so he gazes off at the clouds, fretting, while we remain locked on him, awaiting the conclusion of his struggle. He groans and thrusts the poster in front of me. "You think it's him?" he says.

"What?"

"Is it him?"

"I don't know."

The resemblance between the handbill and the spaniel is strong. Across the wrinkled paper, the ears flop forward in a set of despairing smudges, while the dog in the couple's arms has ears collapsed in a sprawl. Both the dog and the facsimile have woe-filled expressions. Even the saccharine balloon of a tear, rendered amateurishly in the drawing, is matched by a clot of mucus in the bloodshot eye of the dog, to which the woman points with a maudlin assurance. The spaniel, responding to this finger in his eye, sniffles and recoils.

I look at the clouds, and I sway from foot to foot. The pattern of the wind is visible in the rolling vapors. Spinning with a raw impulse that catches me off guard, I emit a groaning sound that evolves into a growl as I charge to the door and into the house.

"Where the hell you goin'?" the Old Man yells.

I hate that goddamn idiotic pooch with his droopy ears and plaintive eyes. I hate him begging to be allowed to come live with us in our house. I slam the door. The way the Old Man is working to determine whether or not this insipid beast is Barney is infuriating. It's an insult. This powder puff who can hardly stand on his own feet is a disgrace. If being lost has turned Barney into this sycophant, this conniving, useless beggar, I want nothing to do with him. Throw him out, I say. The fact that the Old Man is giving this imbecile serious consideration is demeaning and degrading. I'm so mad I want to rip the spaniel's hair out, I want to gouge his eyes, burn his ears, drive nails through his toes. I want to hurt that dog or scream. But of course he's outside and I'm in here, running up the stairs. And they'd protect him anyway. I'm sure they would. Just my luck, I'm going nuts, and nobody around to hurt when I have to hurt somebody. Anybody! And then I trip. My ankles hook and over I go. The house spins around and around. I'm banging, grunting, bouncing down the edges of the stairs to the bottom, where I stop. Breathless, I lie there in an aching tangle as the Old Man's head pops in the door above me, his voice falling through my dazed consciousness. "What in God's name are you doin' in here? I need you out here for a second. Is it too goddamn much to ask?"

I'm dizzy. Because of the weakness engendered by the violence of my fall, I'm having difficulty getting to my feet. I think I'm up but he's cursing at me, accusing me of stalling.

"Now get the hell out here," he says, and disappears.

It takes a while, but eventually I reach the door and step out. I find the three of them crouched on the porch stairs with the trembling spaniel and the drawing positioned side by side, so the dog appears reflected in a bleak, wrinkled pool of paper.

"Look here," says the Old Man, and he reaches to seize the pup by a paw. As the dog starts squealing, he places the paw directly over the figure of the equivalent foot on the page. "There's a major thing in the paw here. Don't you see it? A big difference."

"What?"

"Just look."

"Yeh?" says the other man, bending close. "What?"

"Look at the last pad there and the way it goes into the toe."

"I don't see no difference."

"It's right there."

"I don't see no difference. What difference?"

Leaning in as if her contribution might settle this dispute, the woman declares, "They look the same to me."

"Are you serious?" the Old Man whines.

"It looks like him, I think," says the other man, and then he faces me. "Don't you?"

"No," I say.

" 'No'?" She spits the word at me. "You don't? Really?" She can't believe her ears. She's shocked and seems to hope to disprove my assertion purely on the basis of a disdainful glare and a haughty tone. "How long is it since the two of you have seen your dog anyway?"

"What are you getting at?" the Old Man snaps. His body is taut as he glares into her innocent pose.

"I was just asking a question," she says, feigning amazement at his tone. "I was just wondering how long he's been away. That's all. How long you've been without him."

"I just have this feeling," the Old Man mumbles.

"I mean, we wouldn't have brought him if we didn't think he was yours," says the husband, sounding exasperated that he has to declare something he finds obvious.

"What about the difference in the foot?" the Old Man says.

Opening her mouth to speak, the woman makes herself the focus of our expectations. Coyly, she hovers there, our desire to know her mind increasing as her silence lengthens. When she finally manages to speak, her manner is that of someone making a very uncertain suggestion. "Maybe the drawing's wrong," she says.

"What?" the Old Man says. Like a runner stumbling to the ground in the midst of an arduous race, he seems confused by the point at which he has arrived.

"Sure," the husband inserts.

"You think the drawing's wrong?" the Old Man asks.

"Couldn't it be?" she smiles, as if her concerns are strictly theoretical.

"Wasn't for that foot thing you'd recognize him, right?" says the man.

"Forget about the foot thing, why don't you," she says. To her it's an obvious solution.

"I just got this feeling," the Old Man groans.

"What feeling?" the woman says.

"This feeling. These feelings." He's clearly besieged.

"But what are they?" the man insists. "Tell us."

"I don't know." His voice is whiny and threaded with a shrillness I've never heard from him before. Turning to escape their onslaught, he faces me. "What do you think?"

"You're asking me?"

"I can't tell if it's him or not."

"You want to know what I think?"

"I mean, it looks sorta like him, but—"

"Of course it's not him! For God's sake," I groan, my words laden with scorn. "Of course it's not him. And even if it is, who cares? If this sniveling piece of shit is Barney, I don't want him."

My tone strikes both the Old Man and the spaniel like a physical blow. The Old Man looks at me as if he's never seen me before, as the terrified dog issues a dribble of urine, staining the edge of the drawing. We all recoil.

The woman snorts in mortification. "Goodness' sake, he ain't even housebroke."

"That's right," I say. "She's right, you know."

"That's disgusting," says the man.

"I mean, you should have trained him," I snarl, and the scorn of my assault finds the Old Man unprepared. He expected help from me, not this loathing in my voice. He's standing there looking at the piss on the floor. "I bet you didn't train him at all, did you?" I say.

"What?"

"Look at that! Pissing on the stairs. Pissing on the drawing! Did you train your goddamn dog? You have to train your dog! It's your responsibility! That's why you lost him. Don't you know that? If he's gone—if Barney's gone—and you didn't train him, which you didn't, because he is gone, isn't he—he is gone—then it's your fault, and you know it. You should have trained him! You should have trained your goddamn dog!"

The Old Man's eyes petition me, and I feel the claims of mercy, but I want something else. I want to taunt him, to torment him, to get his goat, something weird and outraged rising up in me. "I mean, dogs have to be trained. Why didn't you train him?!"

Backing away until he hits the door, he's glowering at me, but it's only a shadow of his normally imposing rancor. Weakness lights up in his eyes, goading me on. "If you'd trained him, he'd still be here and we wouldn't even have to be looking at this idiotic simp, this piece of simple shit—let alone trying to decide whether to let him move in with us or not. Who cares? I hate him! Is he Barney? It doesn't matter! You should have trained your goddamn dog, and then you never would have lost him!"

His frozen expression is preliminary to a shriek, yet what erupts is silence followed by a weak whimpering voice. "You're gonna run away, too. I know it. Goin' back to your goddamn wife! I know what you're thinkin'! I know what you're gonna do!" Reaching behind him, he flings the door open and rushes back into the house.

For an instant I teeter on the verge of pursuing him. I lunge into the hall, glimpsing his figure flying up the stairs. But before I take another step, I find my intentions canceled by a set of insurgent, aggressive priorities. I pull back and slam the door with a loud bang. Shaken by the sound, the spaniel starts whining in a constricted way, as if someone has a rag over its face. I turn and step toward the three of them. I pronounce, as might a judge, my icy verdict. "We don't know this dog."

"No?"

"No."

"Wonder whose he is," the woman says.

The dog is drooling and scraping its tail back and forth on the step.

"Damned if I know," says the man. He puckers up his lips in an exaggerated show of worry. "We thought he was yours."

She sighs, offering a wistful little glance at me. "You folks must be just plain heartbroke."

"He's not ours," I tell them.

"We'll be on our way then." She nods.

"Nice afternoon," the man says, bending at the waist in a jerky little half-bow. Behind him, the woman takes a step backward. The spaniel, huddled by the drawing on the porch, continues to emit a terrified hum. The man and woman are walking away as if the dog's no longer their responsibility. They amble toward their car, a dilapidated station wagon with the rear window shattered, the back door on the left-hand side bound shut with wire. His hand is on her shoulder, delivering a congratulatory pat, when I scream at them, "Get the hell back here! You ain't leavin' this garbage here. This goddamn garbage."

With his palms spread wide to demonstrate his lack of any further involvement in this matter, he complains, "He ain't ours."

"You brought him here, you get him out."

"We just found him," says the woman.

Squealing, the spaniel begins to bump against my leg.

"He likes you," says the man.

I throb with a sickening jealousy. I turn my foot and thrust the toe into the spaniel's trembling ribs, driving him toward the stairs. "But I hate him," I say. The dog goes into a whirl and collapses into a pile of despairing fur. "Get him out of here. We don't want him here."

From the back seat of the car the man snatches a gunnysack. The woman, studying me, nods, her smile disappearing in a leer. The spaniel defecates on its rear feet, and the woman's expression transforms into a mockery of a pout as the man hands her the gunnysack. By the time she gets the bag open, the spaniel's front legs are clenched in one of the man's thick hands. The hanging dog spins its head, belches, farts, and swoons over the bag. The hind feet go in first, followed by the belly and the head. Looking around, they start picking up stones. The woman hands them to the man, who drops them in the bag. With every thump, the spaniel yowls and the bag erupts with a fit of agitation, scrabbling around on the dirt.

"And clean up that dog shit," I say.

The woman gives me an annoyed smirk and says, "We was gonna." With the edge of a piece of wood, she scrapes the turds onto a hunk of cardboard, and then, keeping the entire mess at arm's length, she dumps it into the bag. Meanwhile, the man has located a gray, jagged rock about the size of grapefruit. He peers into the bag for a second, aiming before letting the rock drop. After the thump, the moaning escalates and never stops. He pulls a hunk of twine from his pocket and binds the top of the bag shut.

Before me, they're walking toward their car. Dragging the bag along behind him, the man glances at me and says, "You have a nice night." When she turns back, I see a river surrounded by a silent desolation in her eyes, a glowing nocturnal landscape. Through the water of the river a gunnysack sinks, rotating slowly as it descends, twitching with something that struggles inside it to escape.

Before me, the engine of the car is running and the man and woman have closed the doors. As they drive off, the car grows smaller until it seems to have never been at all. In the west the sun sits just above the tips of far-off trees. When the car disappears, the entire landscape is perfectly inert and silent except for the murmuring wind and the shivering leaves.

Chapter Thirteen

I find a note on the kitchen table. The contents, rendered in large shaky letters, order me to remain in the kitchen until the Old Man returns. The savage underlining of the final phrases have ripped the paper:

. . . I wanna find you sittin' at the table. I don't wanna have to go lookin' all over creation to find you!

Determined to do as I've been told, I settle down at the table. But the Old Man's absence, along with my growing guilt about the way I attacked him, will not let me rest, though I keep telling myself to try. I don't know why I yelled at him. It was those people and their stupid dog. They caused it. It was that other dog, it was his fault. That's what I want to tell the Old Man. That's what I want to make him understand. As soon as he comes back.

Out the window, the diminished sunlight appears to have taken on a metallic, wintry tone. I'm dreading the coming night and worrying that he'll never return. That's what's really bothering me. Why should he ever come back, after the way I treated him? No matter what the note says. I'm the reason he ran away.

When I find myself pacing by the door, I realize that I left my chair without even knowing what I was doing. I should go look for him. I could do it in a second, but if I do, I will be disobeying his clear-cut orders and risking another offense. Furthermore, rushing off could create the exact opposite of what I want, as I could easily end up far from the kitchen at the moment that he returns here. That's a definite possibility. But its predecessor is equally possible, in which he never comes looking for me. I don't know what to do, stalking around the room. I don't even know if he's in the house or out somewhere in the fields or barn. The fact that he wrote a note would seem to indicate that he departed the house, and yet I feel that's not the case. The one thing I'm certain of is that I can't go running around outside the house in a blatant disregard of his command that I wait in the kitchen. Not that I know what I can do.

I'm like a man tied to a pair of opposed and straining horses. My misery is growing larger, its debilitating effects starting to dwarf the foreseeable disadvantages in any of my imagined actions. The untried option of setting off to look for him will not let me alone, and suddenly it seizes me, overwhelming me with its impulsive, dark appeal. Consisting mostly of anger and rebellion, it shoots me out the door.

I've little to go by, and I must do something. Instinct takes me to the third floor. After prowling for a few minutes, I feel certain that I hear him moving about behind a closed door. I stand outside warily listening before I risk peering into the room that awaits me. It's crammed with sealed cardboard boxes. But he's not there. There's not a trace or scent of him.

Descending a creaking set of stairs, I arrive in a corridor where the walls are blue, their borders carefully edged in white. The doors here open onto rooms of varying sizes, each containing at least one neatly made bed. But of course he's in none of them. In a wing I have no recollection of ever having seen before, I enter a space full of sedate furniture tastefully arranged. Against a glassy expanse of windows framed by lacy curtains, an upright piano has the impact of a square and stolid piece of sculpture.

The house is much more vast than my anxiety to find him permitted me to remember at the moment I decided to set out on this search.

More and more I feel as if I'm prowling a wasteland whose complexity defies exploration. When I return inadvertently to the spacious formal room with the piano, I reinspect every corner, as if the Old Man is such a hazy presence that I could have overlooked him during my first visit. He's not here, I think. He's not even in the house anymore, I think, as I peer behind the piano. Then I feel a chill and turn to see the oaken door through which I entered. Something is warning me that the door is about to slam and seal me in. I run toward it, knocking it open and racing down the hall until my panic and the maze of the house shoot me down a set of stairs that bring me face to face with a dank, cobwebbed wall. Feeling tired and confused, I drop to my knees, striking something metallic. My examination reveals a handle. I am crouched upon a doorway embedded in the planking of the floor. When I tug on the handle, the floor swings open and what emerges is an updraft of black, clammy air. Somehow my frantic wandering has delivered me into that part of the first floor that was shut away behind boarded up doors and piles of furniture.

Squinting, I attempt to pierce the darkness by concentrating. When this fails, I enter my hand, feeling for a light switch and remembering a dream in which I probed a similar murk. Leaning into a crack that seems to open into both memory and my immediate surroundings, I find the stony walls are held intact by moss-laden cement. I take a careful breath. At last my foot settles onto the first stair and then there is another. For a few steps I advance tentatively, but then I'm speeding up. The steepness invites rapidity. The dark rises as would the blackest water, and I hear the sounds of warring rats coming from the distance. I hesitate, wondering if I should retreat, but I am drawn on beyond my own power to decide, going down like some natural object governed by gravity. Distinguishing first the sobbing and then the sighs, I realize that this racket that I took to be the rage of rodents is the human clamor that accompanies human tears. The stony resonance of these buried caverns amplifies each cry. In the exaggeration of this emptiness, the grief I am approaching sounds huge. The echoes are producing echoes in a storm of choral havoc. I reach the last step and set off toward a plume of illumination hovering in the almost solid dark that fills the distance.

Sliding sideways, I find a wall, I advance cautiously but steadily toward the light, until I arrive at a corner where a wooden beam rises in support of the craggy ceiling. There the vigor of my stride evaporates. I can't believe what I've come upon. In the light that is focused about a hundred feet in front of me diluting a small portion of the gloom, numerous drawings of the dog are wavering in the air above a broken wall. Some pivot slowly from the ends of strings. A few are fastened to the walls by nails pounded into the structural beams or jammed into cracks between the stones and mortar.

Ducking to my hands and knees, I steal forward, aiming at the waist-high pile of rubble lying along the line of the original wall. To my left, other sections have collapsed, and through one of these flaws I see the white tangle of the Old Man's hair. He's bent forward, pulled into a hunched position, and he's moaning. I lower myself onto my belly and keep advancing, the shock of my circumstances like a drug injecting my brain with a weird stasis, which is strangely unpleasant because of the excruciating speed at which my heart is racing. I just keep crawling forward, trying to ignore this weird discomfort and to remain oblivious of the chips of brick and stone gnawing into my palms and knees.

When I reach the wall I'm less than thirty feet from him, but I'm crouched so low that the piled debris makes it impossible for me to see him. Slightly to my left the ruins taper into a gap. Inching to that point, I peek into the grotto and see that he is crouched over a desk, rocking back and forth and groaning. Seated on a straight-backed chair cushioned by a blue pillow, he stares down, his massive fingers clutching a pencil. His mouth is open, his stomach pumping like a bellows, each blast producing an anguished sound as the pencil twitches back and forth over the page of a large sketch pad. The garish green shade of the standing lamp above his head shapes the light around him, while the spill falters against the dark surrounding.

I'm paralyzed, kneeling there. Though I've set out to comfort him, though I wanted to apologize, this is a private rite at which he mourns, a kind of chapel in which he adores, and I know I don't dare show myself. The decent thing to do is to tactfully depart. I feel sordid, my presence a transgression, but I cannot move.

Instead, I inspect the length and breadth of his sanctuary, as if to memorize its secrets. On the battered desk several boxes of graphite pencils stand near a box of chalks, a set of charcoals. A drinking glass contains a compass, a scissors, and numerous stomps for blending charcoal. Near his feet lies an open box of watercolors. A wall cabinet holds more pencils and numerous pads of textured paper. Several books on dog anatomy lie in the corner, where he must have thrown them, the pages crunched and tattered. Everywhere the storming canine pantheon of countenances expands around him. Some are skulls. Others are full-fledged portraits. There are delineations of a kind of supernatural dog engaged in multiple poses at different ages. In one, fluctuating lines combine with rubbed accents to climax in a dark mask. I see a galloping brute about to vanish in an impression of filtered light managed by erased tones and an obscuring of the edges. In a wistful portrait, changing line widths create a sense of feathery lightness. Shadowy emotions are suggested by crosshatched lines. There are detailed versions of his eyes and nose; there are explorations of a paw, and several attempts at abstraction that, in their lack of development, suggest that they were abandoned. A few are modeled dark to light. They vary in size from the dimensions of the standard sketch pad to the sweep of banners draped across the wall. My mouth is dry from hanging open. Innumerable as stars, they fly around him. In crushed balls, they flow across the dirt of the floor.

Then suddenly his bellowing stops and he bolts erect. I fear that he has discovered my presence. But then I see his eyes are closed. The straining wrinkles around his mouth make clear his effort to calm himself as he lifts the sketch pad and moves it out at arm's length in order to gain a new perspective. His eyes open slowly, and his lower lip begins to tremble. His teeth flash against the gaping pinkness of his tongue. He cannot choke his feelings down. The savage way he leans forward convinces me he is about to hurl the drawing aside, but instead he slams the sketch pad down on his desk, reaching out to grab a box of carbon paper. With heroic determination he assembles a pile in which blank white sheets alternate with inky carbons. What could it be, this drawing that he's preparing to trace and copy? It must be yet another revision of his poster. Something based on his encounter with those people and the spaniel? That's what it probably is. It must be. What else could it be? I don't know, but whatever it is, the fact that it can stimulate such emotions as those I have just witnessed makes me want to see it. But I would have to get closer, and I don't dare. In fact, I should get away right now. It's almost as if my desire to approach him magnifies my need for flight, the power of the temptation filling me with aversion. Inching any closer would almost force him to discover me, exposing me to his legitimate outrage and punishment. Besides, I have to pee, and I'm sweating so fiercely I feel I'm coming down with a fever.

Before I know I've made a decision, I'm slipping backward the way I came. The corridor is long and dark, and his cries diminish with my every step, his heartbreak continuing with no more premeditation than his breathing. I know the portraits of the dog that hang around him shake with his exhalations, but neither the vaulted stone above him, nor the heavens beyond, nor the paper icons of his vanished love respond to his grieving. In time, his lamentations seem so small I could once again mistake them for the cries of warring rodents. Though it's a struggle to climb the stairs, whose descent was so swift, I manage finally with a determined heave to go from the cellar's blackness into the ground-floor light. After the briefest pause to catch my breath, I continue on, hastening up the shaky set of stairs whose accidental discovery brought me to this point. I want only to get back to the kitchen, where I hope to rest.

But when I finally fall through the door, the agitation I wanted to leave behind awaits me. It seems to pounce upon me as I enter, as if generated by the waning afternoon light spread upon the plates and spoons and the pale sink top. I cannot escape the cruelty of my behavior on the porch. I see an elusive but irrefutable connection running from the Old Man's suffering in the basement back to my invective, my inexplicable attack about his failure to train his dog. I cannot look at the ceiling without a facsimile of his misery intruding in a thousand forms. How could I have insulted him that way, knowing as I did of his disenfranchised suffering hovering in its exiled state, like icebergs in the heavens? To act the way I did was not only unkind but insane. It was madness to berate him like that with those monstrous snows poised to fall at the slightest provocation. Didn't I almost die already, when earthquakes nearly crushed me in his bed? And now I not only know of the dangers that his displaced passions pose, threatening to crash upon the world in an avalanche of arctic emotion, but I have seen his underground grief.

Just then the momentum of my thought is interrupted by a distant sound. I freeze and listen for an instant, but no further evidence arises to clarify the nature of that first banging. At the table, I start to sip cold coffee from the Old Man's mug, trying to return to the issues I was examining. But then it comes again, a repetition of the initial noise, only silence doesn't follow it this time. Rather, the sound comes again and again, growing louder with each repetition, as if someone has shut a door and is now trudging up a set of stairs.

Leaping to my feet, I realize that he's climbing from the basement. I want to escape, but I know I don't dare run away. I have to be here. I have to be here waiting when he gets back, just as his note first ordered me to do. From the mounting volume of his steps I can tell he's getting close. I scan the room, and somewhere in the rotating array of objects I find a plan. I'll just be absorbed in some normal activity when he arrives. That way I can achieve a kind of safety, or at least neutrality. If I appear to occupy a state of neither innocence nor guilt, whatever happens next will be completely up to him. He will have to make of me whatever he wants. He might not even notice me.

From atop the refrigerator I take a big red apple. Next I hasten to the table, where I pick up the newspaper. Plunging my teeth into the pulp, I open the paper and turn the pages until I stop at a black-and-white photo of an overturned car in a field, and just then his footsteps sweep into the room, marching straight up to me.

A strange white cloth rushes past my face. Something collides with my back and I'm being toppled off my chair. When I slam into the floor, I say, "Hello?"

"Shhhhhhh!"

Pressed down on my back, I feel the cloth tightening around me. Daylight is a halo through the weave of the fabric, like the sun behind a density of cloud. Somewhere on the other side of the cloth a pair of big broad shoulders and the bulge of a head are shifting about.

"Don't worry," he says.

"What?"

"Shhhhhhhh!"

But the voice is strange. If it's the Old Man pawing me and trussing me, something's happened to him. He's come down with a cold, or he's hoarse from all that screaming in the basement.

"That's a good boy," he says. Panic turns my blood to ice, because it isn't him. I don't know who it is, but someone else has grabbed me. Up to this point, my docility has been based upon my belief that I was involved in another of the Old Man's eccentric needs, but now I am frenzied. If it isn't him, who is it? The people in the van? Is it them? Having stolen Barney, have they come for me? Is it death? Is it death whose grisly hands are closing down on me?

"No," I scream, and with a heave, I start to fight.

"I want to help you."

The voice is pleading, but I drown it out with a howl. The hands recoil; I feel them weakening as I grow wilder, snarling, my teeth seizing the cloth.

"Wait," he says. "Wait."

But my response is maniacal, and I bite the cloth. My head flails back and forth, rending the fabric clenched in my teeth while my fingers are moving toward the hole.

"No," I hear. "Please."

With my hand stuck through the flaw, I give a brutish bleat, both my arms erupting sideways. Spittle stains the air, and the veil parts in a blur of light and ripping sounds, and I come bursting forth to confront the cowering figure of the Old Man's brother falling backward from my upheaval. He collides with the wall and then the refrigerator. There he halts, his hands upraised in front of his face like those of a woman of great refinement positioning a fan, around which he peeks. "Don't hurt me," he pleads. "Don't hurt me."

On the linoleum floor lies a sheet tangled in tape and ropes. I grab these things up and throw them at him. "What'd you think you was up to, tyin' me up, you sonofabitch?"

"No, no," he squeals. "I was just tryin' to help you. I was just tryin' to help you get away."

"Whatta you talkin' about?"

"We gotta get away."

"I don't wanna get away."

"I need some food," he moans, his head bowed to demonstrate his subjugation while his eyes slant up with his petition. "I gotta have some food."

"What was you plannin', damnit?" I shout, and raise my hand, threatening to strike him.

He shrinks from me. He flings open the refrigerator door, which he steps behind to create a shield between us.

I rip the barrier from his grasp, disclosing him to full view. He is stuffing his pockets with leftover food. "I just wanna get out of here, you got nothin' to worry about." Snapping up half an apple in one grimy fist, he uses his other hand to collect a mound of rabbit meat. Both hands plunge into his pockets, then dive to ransack the shelves for cheese and bread. He digs his filthy mitt into the gravy, then snatches a milk carton and throws his head back and guzzles.

"What the hell are you doing?" I shout, reaching to pry the milk from his grasp.

"Nothin', nothin'," he says, stepping backward, skulking toward the door. "I ain't doin' nothin'. I'm gettin' outa here, that's all. And you oughta, too." Milk dribbles down his chin. Twisted over, he manages to bow in homage to me while maintaining a steady upward glare, and all the while he continues his retreat and gnaws on the apple. "Believe me, I know I'm dirty. I live in the barn. But you gotta hear what I'm tellin' you." Suddenly he seems to feel I'm threatening to grab him, for he flings up his arms protectively and yells, "Just let me go! I didn't mean no harm. I'm goin'. I'm goin' tonight. You don't have to worry about me. We gotta get away. We gotta have help. Believe me, it's horrible, what's comin'. Believe me. We gotta."

Framed in the door, he spasms, overtaken with an attack of shakes that threaten to shake him to the floor, but he resists, struggling to remain upright. His triumph ushers in a weird and startling equanimity. Every detail of the room feels peaceful and suspended and expectant, and out of this stillness, whose effect seems to enhance him the way a floodlight would, he speaks in a voice of calm authority. "I meant you no harm," he says. "I meant you no harm." Leveling a massive forefinger in my direction, he says, "Run for it."

Although addressed to me, his imperative appears to give him the guidance he has been awaiting, and he whirls from view into the hall, leaving the door open. What follows is the patter of his feet floating away below me. The closing of the downstairs door has a faintness that bespeaks the use of extreme care. I hear him cross the porch. The floorboards mark his passage with a sequence of squeaks.

Assuming he has entered the yard, I rush to the window, where I spot him on his way to the barn, and he is hunched over as if to make himself inconspicuous, a tumbleweed that is wafted finally through the open door.

Chapter Fourteen

How crazy of him to think that he could do that, that he could steal me. He's lucky I didn't tear his hand off when I came out of that bag. What's he doing now? I wonder, and I concentrate my gaze on the walls of the barn in the failing sunlight. I imagine him trying to pack for his journey. But what could he have to take with him? I see him rummaging through straw and cow shit, digging behind loose boards where rats and mice live. What would he find to take with him? His shame, a change of dirty clothes, his treachery, his lies, his stink, the food he stole. That's what.

Thinking I'm done with him, I turn from the window, and I'm appalled by the state of the kitchen. The refrigerator door is open. Milk is spilled on the table and linoleum. An apple core lies dripping on a chair. The tangled sheet and knotted, tattered tape lie on the floor. Crumbs along with gravy stains are everywhere. If the Old Man notices, he'll have a fit, and how can he fail to notice? I'll end up taking the blame for what this goddamn idiot did!

Slamming the refrigerator door, I run to grab the sheet in order to wipe away the trail of milk stains and grease leading from the refrigerator to the kitchen door. As I drop to my knees and start to scrub, my anxiety escalates. I'm certain that the Old Man will arrive to catch me in the act of cleaning up, and my effort to rectify things will convict me of being the one who caused this mess. From his point of view, why else would I be working so hard to eliminate the evidence? I could try to explain, but why should he believe me? He thinks his brother is too afraid ever to come in the house. And given my rude behavior on the porch, a disturbance like this will seem completely in character. Now I'm racing about, and the harder I work, the more my concern heats up. Looking for a place to dump the sheet in which I have the entire mess collected, the top knotted like a bag, I rush to a cabinet beside the sink and fling open the door. I find a shadowy cavity crowded with pots and pans. Clearly it's not a good idea, and I turn away. Next I am gazing into the corner waste can, the lid sprung open, the sheet descending. But then I recollect a large metal garbage can sitting along the outside of the house.

Down the steps I gallop, feeling observed and pursued, until I manage to rid myself of the entire mess, throwing it into the rusted aluminum barrel and slamming the lid shut. I'm free and safe at last. Looking around, I see no one watching me. My relief, and the sigh that expresses it, are huge, and with their completion I find I have to take an enormous piss. The need I felt in the basement has returned with a burning urgency. Amid gasps, I barely get my zipper down before my urine is rattling against the wall and hissing into the dirt. How absurd of that old fool to think he could interest me in his crazy ideas. I want to scoff at him and laugh, but it nags at me a little that I didn't attack him when he insulted the Old Man the way he did. I wish I'd ripped his hand off. The fact that he saw me as corruptible makes me feel slightly insecure, a reflex indignation coming to my rescue and leaving me glaring at the wall inches from my face.

At last my pee dribbles to a stop. Exhausted in the wake of so much stress, I stagger to the porch, where I collapse into a state of instantaneous and consuming relaxation. Like an undercurrent in an idyllic pond, my weariness draws me down, my tongue lolling with the first taste of sleep, from which I intend to arise invigorated in just a moment, after just a little rest.

Though my eyes are open, my stare is blind and so I am utterly without a context for the noise that's breaking over me. My arm aches. I'm scrambling. I have been hit by something, or bitten by something that seems to consist of sounds. Before my blinking eyes is a curious picture, the details bouncing due to my batting eyelids. The Old Man's brother, having come out of the barn, is running up and down along the remnants of a dilapidated corral fence. But the voice I'm hearing is not coming from his direction; it's coming from behind me, and its qualities are those of the Old Man's, as a big boot penetrates my field of vision and settles on my forearm. "Want me to kick you again?"

"What?"

"I thought you run away." Towering above me, he is glaring down. "Don't pay no attention to that fool runnin' up and down over there. I tole you!"

"What?" I say.

"I come into the kitchen. You wasn't there! I told you to be there, you wasn't there!"

"I came out here to sit."

"And I told you not to pay any goddamn attention to my brother! Didn't I tell you?"

"He wasn't here when I first came out."

"Didn't you get my note?"

"Yes, I got it but—"

"And it said to wait in the kitchen, didn't it?"

"Yes, and I did. But I got restless. I just was waiting here."

"But it worried me when I didn't find you in the kitchen. I figured you was gone, and I wanted you to do an errand for me. Look at him running up and down over there. He's a goddamn fool! Did he try and talk to you?"

"No."

"You sure?"

"Yes."

"What'd he say?"

"Nothing. Nothing. How are you feeling? You all right?"

"I'm tired. I'm tired, goddamn you. I hadda look for you. I looked all the hell over. I got an errand for you. You don't make life easy, you know. You ain't exactly helpful."

"What's the errand?"

"What, goddamn you?! Goddamn you to hell!"

"What'samatter?"

"Whatta you care?"

"You said you had an errand."

"That's right."

"What is it?"

"Somethin' I want you to do on your way home. You think you can manage that?"

This reference to my departure startles me. "What?" I say. I hope I appear no more than simply conversational in my interest.

He is staring at me, like a man who's caught a thief. "You gotta go home, don't you?" he says.

At the thought of leaving, an undeniable pleasure is radiating through me. I can feel it and I know that to let it show is indiscreet and somehow risky, but my effort at repression produces a series of twitches rather than the wistfulness and regret I think might please him.

"That's what you said, ain't it? You gotta leave me. Can you at least do somethin' for me on the way home, goddamnit!"

"Sure."

The scowl that distorts his features trivializes every other anger I have ever seen. I glance at the sky, thinking of thunder, thinking of snow. At the sudden step he takes in my direction, I raise my hand to protect my face, though simultaneously I realize that his violent stride is not aimed at me, but at something off to the side and behind me. Awkwardly trying to convert my gesture into an adjustment of my hair, I turn to discover him running down the steps and storming toward his brother.

"Get back in that goddamn barn, you sonofabitch!" he screams, flinging his arms around and stomping his feet. "You think you got the right to just run up and down like that? Get in the barn where you belong. Mom ain't around to save your ass no more! Get out of my goddamn sight before I get really mad!"

As I hasten up to the Old Man, his brother is cringing toward the door, which he apparently finds repulsive. He makes his entrance grudgingly, dragging the big door shut behind him, the hinges grinding as the bottom gouges the dirt.

"Take these," the Old Man says, marching past me.

I turn, reaching to receive whatever he's offering. Near the house, he's grabbing something up from the edge of the porch. Into my out-stretched hands he places a paper bag, the end folded down and taped shut to create a parcel, like an elongated phone book. When I see the opulent gleam in his eyes, I respond with a tingling in my arms that seems to melt the bones. I feel gooey and spookily thrilled, because somehow I know I have just been entrusted with the handbills whose tormented creation I witnessed in the basement.

"You take 'em," he says.

"Yes," I say.

"These are new posters."

"Yes." I'm excited; I'm awaiting his next pronouncement eagerly, but he falters. With his lips parted for the breath to fund his rising sentiment, he says nothing. His expression turns pained, and though it might be thought that he is confused about the appropriateness of his ideas, I recognize a residue of the agony that possessed him in the basement. Leaning close, I want to help him. "What?" I say.

"You'll do that for me, won't you?"

"Just tell me what to do."

"We gotta replace the ones are up. Somethin's wrong with the others. They ain't workin'. You replace the ones are up wherever you see 'em on your way home. Put up the new ones. The new ones'll get him back. I know they will. Then you can go *home*. To go see your goddamn *wife*. To leave me and just go. Ain't it what you want?"

I'm filling with an inestimable relief at the thought of my own little bed, my house, the yard, the doorway, my wife and little boy.

"So get goin'."

"Right now?"

"Ain't that what you want?"

"I have to."

"So do it! Go," he says. "Go." But his resentful tone, laden with contradictions, maims the freedom he appears to advocate. Though he stands before me, I feel as if he has turned his back, or disappeared into a dark corner. By the arcane and threatening complexity of his real intentions, which remain unacknowledged, a negativity is generated, a mystery that holds me like a riddle I must answer, a problem I have to solve.

"You gotta get goin', don't you?" he says.

I stand there, staring.

"So get goin', damnit," he says.

"I really must," I say, and it comes again, the sense of imminent liberation, as if I am already galloping down the road, my prerogatives my own. I find myself unable to prevent the happiness of this future moment from entering into the sadness we presently occupy.

Wistfully, he turns away, looking off down the road to contemplate my imminent departure. Together then we are left behind, as that paradoxical moment confronts our present unity with my future absence, our future separation. I am filling with a sense of pain and mourning not altogether native to me. Forlornness is permeating the air. My head is cocked to stare up at him. "What's wrong?" I say. "What's wrong?"

"Nothing's wrong."

"I feel like something's wrong."

"Nothing's wrong!"

"I mean, I don't have to go just now. Just this second. I mean, you're the one who said I should go home right now."

"It's what you want, ain't it?"

"Yes, but— Well, yes, but I mean, if there's something more I could do before I left, I could stay a little and do it. That's what I'm saying. I could take a couple more minutes."

"It's nothin' important."

"What?"

"It's nothing important, I said."

"But there is something—there is something? What?"

"A game. It's just a game."

"A game?"

"Barney and me used to play it."

"It's a game you and Barney used to play?"

"It'd cheer me up a little, you know. But I don't wanna make you late."

"Don't worry. What is it?"

"He'd just run. I had a bunch of rubber balls. I'd throw 'em at him. He'd dodge 'em if he could."

"I could do that. I mean, not as good as Barney, of course."

"You wanna?"

"Sure."

"Maybe it's too late, though. It's gonna get dark quick now."

"No, no, no. Let's do it."

"You sure?"

"Yes."

"I'll go get the balls; they're just up on the porch."

As he heads up the stairs, I'm looking around, drifting in his wake. He's right about the light. The sun is down and night is coming on fast. We'll have to hurry. He's halfway across the porch when he whirls to face me. Disappointment has distorted his features so severely I feel he has donned a gruesome mask that both exemplifies and caricatures regret. "Oh," he groans, sounding as if he has been kicked in the stomach.

"What?"

"I don't have the balls down here," he cries. "I put 'em away when Barney got kidnapped."

"Oh."

"They're way up in the attic."

"Well, go get 'em! Or tell me where they are. I'll go get them."

"We don't have time. It'll just make you late."

"I'm already late."

"No, no, no," he says, descending the stairs, "there's no point. I mean, if I go up in that damn attic, lookin' around for where I put them rubber balls—I was upset, you know, I don't know where I put 'em— they could be anywhere—you'll be waitin' out here forever."

"But I'd really like to," I say.

"Well, if you really wanna give it a try, we could use this dirt here."

"I do, I do."

"If we use this dirt, you can sort of see what the game's like and if you like it." He's indicating a mound of uprooted earth. Piled in chunks, it resembles a huge beehive.

"Well, if you think it'll work," I say.

"We couldn't really do it. We'd just sorta do it." Carefully he selects several clots and hefts them in either hand. "Maybe," he says. By studying their weight he seems to measure their value; his fingers probe their texture. He nods to me, the twinkle in his eye glistening with delight. "All right," he says.

I'm anticipating a kind of euphoria, a happy resolution to our dilemma, a playful finish to our visit, when the first hunk of dirt comes speeding from his whiplike arm. As if hypnotized, I watch it smash into my thigh. Numbness shoots from my hip to my knee. I squeal, looking at him with shock, expecting to find concern in his eyes, but I am met by a bullet of knobby earth whose path I try to slip too late. Careening off my brow, it crumbles and I yelp, only this time my cry is blurry and woozy and I start wobbling about. His laughter seems to arrive from a remote, inconsequential place.

"You better get running, you bum! I'm winning two to zero."

I feel like puking. I want to sit down. "Wait," I murmur. "Wait. It hurts." Emerging somewhat from my haze, I glimpse the onrush of a third object, trailing a thin spray like a rocket. I flinch and twist and the trajectory just misses my nose. "Didn't you hear me? It hurts," I cry.

"No, it don't," he says.

"Honest. It does, it does."

"No, no, no."

"Get the balls."

But he's aroused and fanatical. Either my cries, or the fact that I ducked trying to avoid his throw, has challenged him. Suddenly he's energized, his enthusiasm so blinding he doesn't see how we need to modify the game. He's too excited. He's bent to the ground, scooping up an armful of dirt. I'm on my knees, trying to breathe to keep from throwing up. Both his anguish in the basement and the lassitude that threatened to overwhelm him as my departure approached are gone. With a whoop, he comes running toward me. If I wanted to cheer him up before leaving him, I've certainly succeeded. Smirking and agile, he is hurtling across the little gap between us, grinning like a madman.

"Wait," I shout, but he keeps coming. I don't dare stand there another second, for clearly the thrill of the game has derailed him, routing every other consideration from his mind.

Sprinting for cover, I find there is none. I'm in a yard. Smacked at the base of my skull like a fish with a hammer, I feel my knees go numb. I give a throaty cry, to which he responds with a shout as he mistakes my sob for a combative shout. But before I can correct his misunderstanding, he roars and flings another missile. Unable to remove myself from the onrush of this blur, I hunch my shoulders and spin to turn my face away. A ricocheting blow slants off my spine into the back of my head. Tears spurt from my eyes, and I hurl myself off. His sight is keen, his arm dexterous. With a wail, I try to create a kind of diversion by cavorting in unpredictable directions.

"You win," I'm shouting. "You win, you win!" As I peek, he's studying me, measuring my patterns and speed in order to predict my moves and be sure to hit me.

"Don't quit," he shouts.

"Get the balls!"

The throw that follows is whistling and uncanny. He has put all his calibrations, weight, and pride into it. Nothing but my eyes have time to turn, while my hand sacrifices itself to the full concussive insult of the rock he's flung. My brain flashes white, while such a deadness leaps through my arm that I am convinced my skin has opened near the elbow and all the bones slipped out. I squeal and run about in circles. I can hear him laughing, and the sound is shrill.

And suddenly I'm thinking about that newspaper and the way I delivered it to him. If only I could do it again—if only I could do it now, he might remember my value and how much he likes me. The fact that I saw several discarded editions in the garbage can when I dumped that mess from the kitchen now strikes me as fortuitous, a blessing. I'm trying to get to the house, intending to grab a paper and stick it in my mouth and run to him, reminding him of what I mean in his life.

Flinging aside the lid, I plunge in my hand and come up with a fistful of newspaper. It doesn't matter whether it's out of date or not, it's the idea that I want, it's all symbolic, all a reminder. The missile that cracks my butt at that instant is like a giant's meanspirited, sadistic slap and I turn, stuffing the paper between my teeth. I start to run toward him, hoping to save myself. However, I can't see him, because everything that passes before my view is unfocused by the moisture in my eyes. The images of whirling sky and deepening dusk might or might not reflect what is actually around me. I cannot speak because my mouth is full, and every time he hits me now, I scream through gritted teeth. I'm running and hoping it's toward him so that he cannot miss the meaning of what I'm doing.

When the paper is ripped from my teeth, I see that he's standing next to me. Like a monster in a dark room, he screams and threatens to hurl a clot of dirt at me from less than a yard. I whirl and flee, struck again and again in the back.

Not only does he possess skill and experience at this game, but he's filled with a maniacal need to win. Ineffective in my every defense, I end up waving my arms like a comical bear attacked by a horde of bees. I don't know what else to do but keep on running, which is what I am doing when a stunning idea makes me scream just as a rock impacts my leg like a knife. But the bloody contusion on my thigh is nothing compared with the pain of the suggestion that the Old Man is barraging me with taunts and rocks because he wants to hurt me. Because he likes to hurt me. That can't be the reason behind all his galloping about, all his vigorous pleasure. This is just the way he plays and I must learn to enjoy it just as he does. I have to learn the fun of it, because that's what he wants. I'm sure of it, and to demonstrate my certainty, I squeal, "Whheeeeeee!!" as I'm hit in the shin and my leg goes out from under me.

Next thing I know I'm begging and weeping, even though I more or less agree with his assertion that I'm exaggerating. He kicks me and mocks my squeal with an imitation all his own. As I am writhing on the ground, more blows rain down. I cannot fend them off for all my flailing.

"How you like the game?" I hear him call.

I want to beg, but I don't. Muteness seals up my mouth like stitches, a surge of disorientation flinging me about as an irrational exhilaration explodes in me, blasting my priorities and beliefs apart. Swallowed up in spiteful celebration, my agony becomes a barking triumph as I pummel the ground, screaming, "It's great! It's great! What the hell you standing around for, huh? What are you waiting for? You getting tired?"

"Not likely," he shouts.

"What'samatter, you getting old?" I roar, electrified by my audacity. "I'm gonna knock you on your ass, you sonofabitch!"

"Oh, yeh? That'll be the day!" My relish of rebellion hurls me to my feet and I run off, flying into anarchy. Sprinting toward the sun, I'm hit in the arm. Wheeling, I have not taken one full stride when a barrage of blows hammers me along my rib cage. Impelled sideways, I cannot breathe, pretending that my fall is really a dive onto my belly, where I glimpse a lumpiness exploding in a gyre inches from my nose. "Missed me," I bellow, taunting him as I scramble up to my feet, trying to make the throbbing leg I'm dragging behind me look like a result of my desire to hop.

"How come you're limpin' if you like this game?"

"I'm not. You're blind."

"Not blind enough to miss a goddamn critter as slow as you! You run like an old woman! You pissant! You piece of dog shit!"

I am laughing and shaking my rear when I realize the incredible, humbling scope of his accomplishment, for without a doubt, he has done it. We're having fun, the both of us shrieking with laughter as he pelts me, beans me, sprays me, and topples me again and again. It's wild and free. Even his brother has been drawn from the recess of the barn to glare enviously at our camaraderie. I mock the contemptible fool by grimacing smugly in his direction, and then I pirouette and leap.

The sudden silence makes me curious. The gray of the distant sky is flecked with scarlet. I'm lying on my back, and the liquid that I'm sucking off my lips is blood oozing from my nose.

"I stung you good," he says.

His vague and bulky figure against the inky heavens appears to be a creature dissolving at its edges. I reach upward, half expecting him to disappear.

"You didn't even see that one coming, did you?"

"Yes, I did."

"How come you didn't duck then, smart-ass?"

My memory of the event that dumped me here is like a watercolor wash in which the specifics are slowly emerging. The Old Man nailed me square in the mush; that's what happened, and I fell, woozy and ridiculous, and now I am about halfway back to consciousness. He's hovering above me, fretting over the fact that he hurt me as badly as he did. My nostrils and throat are thick with gore. He's very worried. I can feel how upset he is.

"We better get going," he says. "It's too dark to keep on playin'. I'll start missin' you more than I hit you."

This is just his manly style of apology; it's the best he can do. But I know what he's really feeling. In better light, he would never have made the mistake of picking up stones and hurling them at me. Had he been able to detect my exact outline, he would never have hit me in the nose. That's why he's feeling so badly. "It's all right," I say. "Don't worry. I'm okay."

"You got to do that errand for me, remember? I mean, you're gonna still do it, ain't you?"

"Of course," I say.

"Well, if you don't get going, you won't be able to see where the old posters are. You'll never get 'em changed like I need 'em to be."

"I better hurry."

"You got me too excited with the game. It was a dumb idea to play it anyway. You ain't any good at it. You run like a duck. It's so easy to hit you, it's boring. All you did is make me feel worse about not having Barney around. And on top of that you made it get so goddamn late, you'll never get these posters up tonight."

"Yes, I will."

"Here," he says, presenting me with the paper bag of posters. "Now get the hell out of here. I gotta get 'em up, 'cause I gotta get Barney back. You understand! I was thinkin' maybe if you stayed, it wouldn't matter so much. But you ain't stayin', are you? I get lonely, you know. I gotta get my dog back. And these are gonna do it, these new ones." As I'm struggling to my feet, he grabs me by the arms, his big fingers wrapping around my biceps like cables. "You come back if you want, but only if you got your mind made up and you mean to stay. You get sick of your wife, which you will, don't you come runnin' back to me unless you got your mind made up, you understand? You come back again, you're comin' to stay. I'll be here. You understand me? I hate a goddamn tease. That's what I'm sayin'." His big hands release me and he kicks me. "Will you get a move on, goddamnit!" As I back away, he keeps kicking at me. "I don't know why I got to put up with such a goddamn good-for-nothin' worthless pile of shit as you."

"I'll take care of everything for you," I say.

"I ain't gonna hold my breath countin' on the likes a you. You got shit for brains."

"Don't worry," I say, adjusting my grip on the posters, trying to impress him with my seriousness.

"Don't worry?" His eyes are wide with disbelief, my offer of reassurance striking him as outlandish. "Worry is the only damn thing makes any sense with the likes of you. Now get the hell out of my sight. And don't come back unless you mean it. Don't tease me, you sonofabitch. And I don't want your goddamn wife comin' around here screechin' at me because a you, either. You understand me? That'll be the last goddamn straw in this old man's life. You keep her off my back!"

"I will," I say, struggling to get to my feet. I hug the posters close and start off, and it seems to me that I'm lucky he plays with me at all. Considering the way I endlessly annoy and disappoint him, I don't know why he does it.

Chapter Fifteen

Out of the corner of my eye I can see the Old Man's brother lurking in the shadows just inside the barn door. In the deepening dusk, he's barely visible, and yet I know he's watching me. I can feel his cloying, disgusting need for recognition, like a beggar's, as I hobble past him. I refuse to give him what he wants, surrendering not even a glance in his direction. Instead, I embrace the Old Man's posters as a sign of my allegiance, a manifestation of my rejection.

On either side of the road the dirt is scribbled with shadows and shapes of thick, towering pine and dwarf pine and saplings and shrubs no bigger than cats. The sky is a luminous inky haze, a diluted surface, the depths vague.

I'm trying to understand the sense I have that these events were somehow forecast. It's as if everything that's been happening I've anticipated for years, though inexactly. From the door where memory opens to find me toddling down a hallway to start off toward this present moment, I see myself as somehow awaiting the arrival of an old man in order for us to live out these hours together. Not this Old Man exactly, but someone old and superior. Who can deny secretly pining for an ancient escort, a mentor, an elderly guide?

I'm looking back the way I came. The road retreats to the fading house misted over in the dark. And suddenly I'm running, as if I've just remembered a dangerous mistake, such as leaving a pot on a flaming stove.

I've only traveled a short distance from the house, so I get back quickly. I sneak up close and peer in the window, feeling like a criminal. Partly, I'm just concerned that if he spots me, he'll fly into a rage because I'm supposed to be off doing his errand. But I need to see him. I had to come back. The poignant ache governing me takes its power from a sense of loss as graphic as if he has been eliminated from the planet. Nothing but the actual sight of him can refute the anxiety threatening me.

He slumbers in his chair, his arms like hanging ropes, his stillness so extreme that only the pulsing of his belly declares that he's alive. He wanted me to stay so badly. I know he did. It was awful how distressed he was, how badly he felt. How badly we both felt. But I had to go, and I still do. I have no real choice. But at least he's there and he's alive. At least he's old and he's mine.

When I turn from the window, resolved this time to begin my journey and complete my duties, the sky has been swallowed up by a stormy blackness. What was horizon now appears a part of the air. The visible details of the night have been overwhelmed as I dawdled at his window.

I'm trying to hasten along, but I can't even see the ground. How can I possibly replace all his posters in a dark so dense? The hand I am raising inches before my face appears a ghostly blur. I should have brought a flashlight. No other light can possibly help me at this hour except the moon. And that's something I'm better off without. Remembering the hunger for intimacy with which that lunatic shone upon me, I think I should be grateful for the perfection of this gloom. I want to forget about it if I can, disowning and repudiating everything that happened that night between me and the moon, that lustful monster with its sordid, shameful advances.

If only I'd asked the Old Man for a flashlight, I think. I'm wondering if I dare return now and ask him, or look for one. I know he has them. Also, I think I need more specific instructions about my task. I need a modification of my original instructions, or an alternative, something better adapted to my circumstances. I feel somehow I have muddied his directions, losing details essential to what he required. If only I'd asked him to repeat what he wanted when I was back there. But he was sleeping. I could have woken him, of course. I could go back and wake him now. I'm wavering, my stride timid and nervous against the growing weight of my confusion, and then I just stand there. I don't know what to do.

First I hear a massive growling, and then light suddenly surrounds me in a surge that is pushed from behind by the onrush of a mounting rumble. As if borne upon these waves of thunder, the Old Man's head and shoulders bounce into view beside me. Before I have the slightest idea of what's happening, red lights float at the center of a billowing sail of incandescence ahead of me, and then I realize that he has just shot past in his pickup truck. Now the taillights vanish. In their place erupts a beacon, which I recognize as headlights. Faltering, I stand stock-still, as if this radiance is encrusting me in ice.

Without letup, the engine throbs and roars, and then slashing into it comes the punctuation of a slamming door. Footsteps grind the gravel. I clasp my posters. I wait with squinted eyes and a broken smile. My conviction that the approaching figure must be the Old Man can barely survive the assault of a spooky horde of inferences, warning me of otherworldly creatures and dangers.

"You got those posters yet, or you lose them?" the huge old voice demands, as if the rippling light is speaking.

"What?" I say, perplexed because I have my arms wrapped around the posters. The silhouette before me dances against the explosive headlights.

"You lose all the goddamn posters, or what?" he growls.

"No," I shout. "See?" I hold the parcel out, hoping to emphasize my diligence and devotion.

"What are you doing? Are you lost? You're lost, ain't you? You don't even know which way to go to get to your own goddamn home, you goddamn ignoramus?"

"Sure," I say.

"Then get going!"

I start to run.

"That's not the way!" he roars. "You don't know the way!"

I whirl and sprint in the opposite direction. Because of the contrast between the surrounding blackness and the blaze of his headlights, I'm blind. But I plunge ahead, until I trip. I don't know what I've hit. It feels like a foot. I skid along, yelping and banging my ear, skinning my neck, my shoulder and thigh.

"What happened?"

"I'm okay," I shout.

"See, you don't know. That ain't the way," he yells disgustedly. "You say you know it, but you don't. I knew you didn't when you took off. Gonna just run around in the dark, ain't you, and get lost and be out all night long so your wife is furious at us both, ain't you, and all the while you won't even get a single goddamn poster put up. I gotta do everything myself, don't I? You shoulda brought a flashlight."

"I know."

"But you didn't, did you?"

"I didn't think of it, and then you were sleeping, so I couldn't ask you where it was."

"So it's my fault! Is it my goddamn fault? Is that what you're saying? Is everything my goddamn fault!? Here!" He thrusts a hammer and a sack of nails into my hands. "You forgot these, too, you jackass! You wouldn't know your ass from a hole in the ground."

"What?!" I say.

"You wouldn't know your ass from a hole in the ground if I was pissing in it."

I scrunch my eyes, struggling to understand his remark. The literal content seems comprehensible only as a metaphor, though a flush of shame heats my cheeks.

"Let's go," he says, and vanishes, his footsteps crackling gravel in the direction of the headlights.

I'm trying to decide whether or not he means for me to join him in the front seat, when I hear the truck door bang closed. Bolting off toward a juncture just behind the origin of this sound, I hope to climb into the rear of the truck. However, the engine growls, revving with a rush of gas, and the phantom shape of the truck sails away. "Wait," I cry. "I'm not aboard." But he doesn't hear me. With a yelp, I dash off in pursuit.

Down the road we go, the truck leading me into the starless sky. It takes a while for me to realize that he has decided to assist me by showing me the way rather than giving me more instructions. As I follow along behind the bouncing taillights, I'm trying to breathe deeply and conserve my energy. Around me the dark has an almost material impenetrability even as I glide through it, uncovering gradually, as I grow more attuned to the phenomenon around me, a velvety sensation streaming over me.

"There!" the Old Man shouts, and I see his arm jutting out of the cab toward a gnarled old leafless tree where a shadowy poster flaps like a scab of skin. I run and do his bidding, ripping down the old poster and nailing up a new one, hoping that I've got the right side of the picture facing out, because in the intensity of this dark I can't really see.

When the truck departs I stumble after it, my head bowed forward into the mounting wind. A storm has rolled in. Gusts are plummeting out of the heights in tumbling slabs. Chilled, my skin is glazed with goose bumps, and I have to cinch the belt of my big coat around my waist, the hem rapping at my knees. When he indicates the figure of a telephone pole rising through his headlights, I race over to it and remove the poster and hammer up its replacement. The dark is so thick I can't see my hands six inches from my nose, but I do his work as best I can. When his booming voice demands my return to the truck, I obey, sprinting back. Off we go, the truck slipping away before I arrive, so that I have to struggle after him.

On we drive and run, something complex and wild governing the details of our enterprise, something enigmatic and mathematical manifesting through us, as the new posters subtract in my arms while the old ones increase in the back of the truck and the force of the wind escalates. The posters that I remove beat against my hands, resisting my aims; they flail to escape me and I fight to rip them down. I have to concentrate like a sailor in a gale, toiling to stabilize each new sheet against contending winds, for this night is like a tossing ocean. Clouds sweep inches from my face, leaving me with the feeling that I am somewhere high above the ground. I work in one new place after another, yet each seems essentially identical to its predecessor, with my task the same and the winds ever-present. Wherever I was last, I feel I still am, dealing with posts and trees and walls of different sizes and textures. I pause on porches. I flail away at barn walls, telephone poles, the shacks of strangers. I pass through barnyards. A creek is swum, a gully jumped.

And then the first traces of predawn gray find me on a hillside beneath a muted vista. Below me is a familiar community of houses. On the horizon the Old Man's truck is about to reach the vanishing point, the green of the metal like a splash of pollen enfolded in petals of dust. Upon the completion of my task, he has left me standing here with our little town below me as a reference point. A short walk will get me home. Yet I am not moving, for something I never noticed before holds me riveted where I stand. The houses below me are all exploding. It's a gradual process, unfolding in mesmerizing increments. Rings of pain are leaping out the windows. Loops of anguish like loops of the most ferocious light are radiating out into the vestiges of night, and not a house is exempt from this phenomenon. It's pain, but it appears to be a species of light and it comes in spirals out the windows. Motionless and tilted forward, I watch the lassolike arcs of incandescence revolve in a rising cluster of shimmering gyres that peak and then peel back, crisscrossing with one another like links in a chain of flaming anguish. And from this spectacle I know something I never could have known before. From the dominion of this hill, I can see that human life is impossible. It cannot be lived appropriately for it is covert in its most essential elements and procedures. In all its central points it is unknowable, its secrets impervious to every investigation and formulation, no matter how rigorous and sincere. What could I have possibly known before this moment, I ask myself, what could I have possibly known before I saw these wheels of pain and the way, like havoc crying out, they spin through all the houses? Every task and issue, every chore and obligation that is imagined to be a priority each day, the urgent duties and desires, are all nothing but a veneer. They are nothing but the most superficial reflections and misapprehensions of these hoops of pain that lie concealed beneath every breath and thought.

It seems only seconds before I'm peering down upon the roof of my own little house. I must have been walking and thinking for a while. The sun is about to appear now, its arrival forecast in a leaking slice along the eastern mountains. While the elevation of my present site is not so impressive as that at which I stood above the town, still I have a certain vantage from which I am looking down, preparing to descend. Just then it happens. Pain comes looping out the windows of my little home like a string of diamonds. That pain I saw transfiguring those strangers' houses is spilling from my own. It rises in a coil from the windows toward the sky, in whose fathomless lengths it appears to falter, bending gracefully and solemnly, ebbing in its vigor as it curls backward, sweeping down, its overall impression like that of an unnatural rainbow of a single burning hue. I know my son is slumbering in the cold recesses of dreams he has no chance of understanding. My wife, unconscious, snores and paws the air to fend off bleak and fuzzy intimations.

Light is everywhere, rushing in thin streams revealing its protean, fluid nature. I swipe my hand across my gaze, seeking to clear the air through which I'm attempting to peer, and inadvertently my gesture puts before my eyes the fact that I still hold one of the posters. In my fist, it's squeezed into a knobby tube. I'm about to fling it away when I realize that I don't know which one it is. It could be one of the old that I spent the night ripping down. Or it might be one of the new ones, whose contents I've never seen. In the basement, I feared to go close enough, and during this night, though I spread them around the countryside, they were hidden in the dark. As I unravel the twisted folds, I remember the anguish of the Old Man's struggle to create and copy this drawing, and my curiosity is mixed with a bleak concern.

It is clearly one of the new. I press the paper to the ground and try to iron out the creases carefully, as one would tend a precious antique document. The written information has been left out. There's no description, no promised reward. So intense is my concentration that I am disoriented for a minute and must, like a man recovering from exertion, pause to breathe. I look away and then, after gathering myself, I return. The immense and jagged teeth yearn for carnage; they ache for ripping and tearing. Jutting out in bulges, the fangs distend the lips into a snarl. Drool oozes from between the gums. The eyes are radiating pools of arrogance and vanity. Nowhere is there a hint that the consciousness lurking behind them is one that might respond to appeals of reason, appeals for mercy, appeals for sanity. The graphic elements are all violent slashes, crazy smudges, savage inky blows. These are the eyes of a despotic egoism aglow with a depraved appetite. Like a rabbit who has heard a high hawk screech, I want to run but I have no escape. I scan the little valley that contains my house and then return to this frightful conjuration confronting me with the truth of my most ominous prophecies of last night. As I lay in my bed, I feared that something dreadful was happening, that something terrible was coming. This is a nightmare document. It is a Wanted poster. Something monstrous is on the loose.

BOOK THREE

The Moon Has Its Way

Chapter Sixteen

To arm myself, I retrieve my Marlin lever-action .30/30 rifle from the basement niche where it has been hidden. The wood and oiled metal glide from the leather case with a hiss. Cocking the mechanism open, I gaze into the darkness of the empty chamber and find my disquiet unabated. In town, I go to the sporting goods store, where I purchase a Smith & Wesson .38 Special revolver with four boxes of hollow-tip shells and a 60 × 40 telescopic sight, along with additional ammo for the rifle. While filling out an application for the pistol, I'm told I won't be able to take the handgun with me until after my application has been processed.

It pleases me to imagine this procedure, the tiers of bureaucrats passing documents around, their eyes dim behind glinting spectacles, their approval delivered with nods, scratchy signatures, and rubber stamps as if they recognize the necessity of my armament. Far behind me, they cower from the dread I am preparing to confront. Havoc, unquestionably, is loose. Gun barrels and the brass of bullets, binocular lenses and compass cases shimmer with mayhem's light, as do the salesman's predatory eyes. A compass could be useful, I think. One could get lost, and not know the way to go. North, I think. To know which way that one way always is. North. There would be one stability in my life at least.

I'm closing the trunk of my car over the rifle, the scope, the paper bags folded down on the boxes of shells, when it occurs to me that, as prepared as I am, I am not fully prepared. I head back into the store and buy a hunting knife with an eight-inch blade along with a machete, several flares, and three army surplus gasoline cans. Staring at the compass face, the tiny numbers and symbols of direction, I feel a violent stirring. Though my eyes are captivated by the compass, I know I will refuse to buy it.

"Want one?" says the clerk. He thinks they're great, the look in his eyes so foolishly eager.

"No," I say. I turn away and start to grin. Walking from the store, I am daring the universe to just try and lose me. That's the dare. Just try. In the hardware store, which is my next stop, there are more compasses displayed on a shelf behind glass, but they fail even to tempt me. I pick up several hundred yards of rope and head on home.

Contrary to my expectations, my wife has been pleasant since the morning of my return. Making no reference to my absence, her mood has been cheery and cooperative. A number of her offhand remarks have seemed designed to communicate the idea that her gratitude at my reappearance is enough to cancel any need for recrimination. It's not so much that she states such a position as it is that, among her many comments, there are some that invite such an interpretation. I am relieved, yet puzzled, because I have prepared a fairly elaborate story to explain my physical condition, if not my activities during the time I was gone. I'm fairly battered and bruised, my body full of welts and scrapes, which I intended to account for on the basis of my having tumbled down the side of a cliff while walking in the nearby wilds.

But she seems to lack even the slightest curiosity regarding anything about me. While I'm grateful not to be interrogated, this indifference on her part feels false, and there are moments when I catch myself worrying that her placidity is a mask, a ploy to cover something else. And if I'm correct in this concern, what's she covering? Perhaps her easygoing manner is calculated to put me off guard. Perhaps it is her intention to lull me into a trusting state in order to spring her interrogation on me when my defenses are down, my vulnerabilities exposed. I vow to remain vigilant against such dissimulation, even though my wariness appears unfounded, as she approaches to hand me a cup of tea. I know she has to have her suspicions, her grievances, her veiled intentions. She was growing snide and unreadable before I left, increasingly irritated at my moods and accusing me of indulgence in the majority of my interests and actions. Now I've been away for twenty-four hours, and we argued on the phone, I think. I'm certain that I called her from the Old Man's house, even though the image of our exchange has a tenuous and unstable form that situates it in a realm neither definitively memory nor imagination. Though I could ask her to help me sort out my impressions, I don't dare. To admit my confusion would risk reigniting the acrimony that, in my sense of things, characterized the moment.

In the middle of the second day after my return, we go shopping at the grocery store and have a pleasant enough time filling two carts and giggling at the coupons she has collected in order to save a dime here, a quarter there. Later on, I doze a little watching television before dinner and she awakens me by flicking a piece of string under my nose.

At dinner that evening I glance up from my spoon just as Tobias wanders past the door to the living room. He looks disheveled and distraught, dragging a blanket. I watch him appear and disappear, and then, after a moment during which I contemplate my recent actions and unavoidable neglect of him, I resume my meal. Munching peas, I say, "We're not doing so well with Tobias, are we?"

"I think you should speak for yourself," she answers, shooting a smug little twist of superiority into her tone. She's smirking as if she knows a secret.

"How's he doing at school?"

"Great."

"Is he?"

"He made the cutest card for Grandma and sent it to her. It was all elephants and fuzzy flowers. She wrote him a letter saying she loves him. Want to see it?"

"Isn't he going to eat with us?"

"What?" she says, her surprise colored by a playful determination not to be tricked. "Of course. Why do you ask?"

"He should eat."

"Well, I know. I don't understand."

"What?"

"Your joke."

"What joke?"

"C'mon."

"C'mon what?"

"Your joke. What's your joke?"

"I didn't make any joke."

"He sat right in the chair across from you. I mean, for goodness' sake, he ate—let me see—well, everything you're eating. Peas and carrots, hamburger and mashed potatoes."

"What?"

"Why are you teasing me?"

"He ate?"

"Yes."

"You're saying he ate?"

"Just a minute or so ago, for goodness' sake. You saw him. You had to. He was right in front of you."

"Right there?" I say, pointing with my knife toward the empty chair across from me. I can find no sign of anyone having eaten, no plate or fork or stain. "I don't remember. And it's so clean," I say, indicating the table.

"He's neat. You know that."

"Of course. Yes."

"And then he took his plate, and he put it and his knife and fork away, and wiped the place clean where he'd been. I mean, just the way we've been trying to teach him. Isn't that nice?"

"Yes," I say.

"I think so."

"He was right here?"

"Ohhhh, c'mon," she twitters. "Stop teasing me."

"I must have been thinking."

"What about?"

"I don't remember."

"Must have been very interesting. But then you've been very distracted recently, don't you think?"

"Yes, I have," I say. "Well . . ."

"Are you so distracted, you don't even know that?" she giggles, making sure I can't miss the neat turn she has given our exchange. "Must have really been some very interesting thing you were thinking about that hard," she says, the jaunty surface of her laughter breaking open under the pressure of her scorn.

"Oh, yes," I say, and nod. When I try to smile, my face hurts. My stomach rolls like a flopping fish. I feel as if the muscles of my face are creaking. So cumbersome is my suspicion, so oppressive my anxiety, that I lack the means to shift the slablike sections of my cheeks. Their leaden heft drags at the flesh I would shape to reflect a jovial state that I lack completely.

"What'samatter?" says my wife.

"Hmmmmmmmm?" I say. "I'm not feeling too well." My hope is to deceive her with an excuse of physical discomfort. Or if I can't deceive her, at least I can stall a little until my misgivings are reined in and covered by a glaze of perfect trust. "He was right there eating, and I didn't see him," I say. "Isn't that amazing?"

When she smiles and shrugs in a tolerant acceptance of my annoying and habitual distraction, as she sees it, I push a brimming spoonful of peas into my mouth. I chew with dramatic little sighs, beaming my appreciation at her. If any part of my inchoate alarm and suspicion is correct, the facade behind which I'm trying to operate is essential. From now until I've cleared up certain nagging inconsistencies, I must act with perfect vigilance, a cloaked equivocation. I don't know how to understand the strange facts gathering in number and fearful implication at our table. Am I to believe that he eats but I don't see him? He eats but no evidence marks the place at which he was seated?

When she sighs, I'm smiling at her, but my heart is icing over. The accumulating discrepancies demand that I posit the existence of a scheme to explain them, a malevolent scheme—that she is trying to harm Tobias. And then I see more clearly the idea around which my mind has been circling, the frightful thought I've been resisting—that she is implementing, in nearly undetectable stages, a systematic strategy whose aim is diabolical, that she is trying to starve little Tobias to death, that she's trying to kill my little boy. However outlandish and scandalous at first sight, the embrace of this idea delivers a steadying effect on a widespread array of puzzling factors. Looked at through the prism of this plot, numerous irrational and discordant details start to fall into place, their sudden cogency arguing strongly for the validity of the notion, however implausible its superficial appearance. At its deeper levels it has a shocking sense of epiphany as it makes compelling order of things that previously had seemed trivial and unconnected. It transfuses life and purpose into the eccentric, the paradoxical, the casual. First, she must appear generally happy and content day after day. Second, she must make me think that she likes me, when I know she has reasons to be furious. Third, she will convince me that my little boy is eating when he isn't. Fourth, she will make me think I am so preoccupied I cannot see what's going on right in front of me.

Such a plan will doom him, rendering me helpless to protect him, for how can I rescue him from dangers whose existence I've been seduced into ignoring?

At the kitchen sink where I've gone to deposit my table setting, my worry, which is still largely theoretical, finds itself fired into concrete form. His dirty dish and spoon and cup lie in a pile he is too short to have made. The logistics of his tiny height and little limbs could not have moved these items to where they now sit, unless he raised them as high as he could and hung them over the sink and dropped them, and then the plate and cup, both ceramic, would have broken. No, no, only she could have placed them there. In bleak wonder, I'm gazing down at her cruelty displayed in kitchen china and cutlery under the dripping faucet. The kitchen feels like a wheel upon whose spin I've been set awhirl, clutching the edges of the table, as I return and settle down across from my wife, the both of us smiling.

"Will you help me now?" I hear her say.

"Of course," I say.

"Good."

"Do what?"

"It's time for Tobias's enema."

I nod as if this is the task I expected. I clap my hands in a show of enthusiastic readiness. I must be as resolved in my developing deceits as she is in her routine machinations. My one advantage lies in her ignorance of the fact that I have discovered her scheme. As long as she believes she has me fooled, I can hope to find an antidote to her macabre plans. "Yes, of course," I say. "I'd be glad to help you. Let's get at it."

"I think we better." She's at the sink, filling a teakettle. Then she heads to the stove. "He hasn't had a decent bowel movement for days."

"Really."

"Not that you would have noticed, given what you've been up to."

"Well, actually, I did notice," I say.

"Really."

"I was going to mention it."

"I'll be right back." She casts a slightly deprecatory glance over her shoulder at me as she slips out the door.

Depression is numbing, a transfusion of despair as debilitating as cement, and I start to pace, hoping to resist the need to sink to the floor. The fact that I must appear to countenance her abuses, that I must convince Tobias that I am aligned with her against him, sickens me. I taste the desperation, the abandonment I know he will feel. I want to oppose the things I just declared myself eager to support. I can't starve him and then suck what little nourishment he might possess out of him on floods of water, I can't do it.

The flash that fills the room startles me. It seems a breath of light, my wife standing at its source. She is in the doorway to the living room and the hole behind the lens of the camera she aims at me is shuttering closed like an insidious peephole in a wall, intruding on me. What secret has she snatched? To whom will she show my unguarded face, my poor expression? In this amputation of my countenance clues to my inner life may stand revealed, my private strategies exposed, or at least hinted at. My features will be robbed of all context, all flow and flex-ibility permitting her to study me without the slightest protection for hours, using even a magnifying glass to scrutinize my peculiarities, the hapless symptoms of my interior spread upon my cheeks and naked in my eyes.

"I saw this program the other night," she says, "and it made me want to take a picture of each one of us every day. Won't that be nice? It was one of those nature shows, a blooming flower, this time-lapse photogra-phy, I think it's called. Imagine if you had a photo of yourself each day, one a day for years. Wouldn't that be amazing?" She's clicking the lens cap back on the camera and fiddling with a knob. "Do you mind?" she says, inserting the camera into its vinyl carrying case.

"No," I say. "I don't mind."

"You look like you do."

"No."

"Good. Go get the enema bottle," she says, smiling.

I grin at her, my cheeks like glass. I'm staring at the zipper sealing the camera away in its black paunch. This image that she has stolen could prove my undoing if she uses it to figure out what's going on behind my eyes. Unless I find a way to steal it back. Like a robber, I think, I could come here and take a number of things.

In the bathroom, I grab the enema bottle from the towel rack beside the tub. Hastening back to the kitchen, I find her waiting with a simmering teakettle in her hands. I unscrew the cap and elevate the gaping rubbery mouth toward her. As she tilts the teakettle, the water arcs in a curving gleam between my hands. Steam rises up to faintly obscure the conspiratorial whisper passing back and forth between our eyes.

"Now we'll have to add some cold," she says, moving toward the sink. "We don't want it too hot."

"No."

When we enter the living room, Tobias looks up from the puzzle he's trying to put together. Studying our approach, he tenses. Too late, he tries to run. We grab him and fling him screeching to the flowered carpeting. While I pinion him down, my wife inserts the Vaseline-drenched tube into his resisting rectum and then elevates the bottle high into the air as though to celebrate her triumph. All the while she croons an off-key tune of melancholy consolation punctuated by his sobs.

When the ordeal is complete, he staggers around like a dizzy drunk, his belly bloated, his lips distended with loathing at his failure to prevent our violation. In all the world, for all his cries, there was no one to help. I hear him grunting, growling, and spurting like a hose in the bathroom for a long time. I watch television, holding hands with my wife. Tobias totters off to bed, an infirm, whimpering wreck.

When she complains of drowsiness a little later on and wanders off toward our room, I stay in front of the television for another hour, waiting. Then, carefully, I pack a little lunch in the kitchen. I gather a loaf of bread and as much cheese and fruit and as many bottles of juice as I can fit into a plastic bag emblazoned with a smiling toothbrush, a happy razor, the logo of a town drugstore. Stealthily, I make my way to his room, and like a mad and romantic hero abducting his beloved from the bedroom of her home in a deep and unexpected night, I lift him from his bed, my hand pressed upon his mouth to stop his screams as I carry him into the immense and lightless vista beyond our door. Protecting him with a blanket against the chill, and comforting his frailty with tender little kisses, I bear him into flight. Down a slanted, tree-laden unknown we dash. With menace undoubtedly at large, I must maintain a constant surveillance, watching out for every tick and twitch in the dark surroundings. Tobias is small, yet I sense significance in him, its existence exuded in a kind of vibratory halo ringing him in which I want to submerge myself. He is a web of infinite promise, dainty, pesky, as light as a bag of air, while I am downcast with my memory of the cruelty I helped inflict on him.

I don't know where I'm going, and I wander about until I recollect a cave beneath a nearby hillside where I once saw little boys at play. Wearing cowboy hats on their tousled heads and wielding several pellet guns, these little boys shot an ill-fated blue jay from his tree and left him flopping in the dirt.

Until this moment, I've been galloping about among the trees and shadows without a plan, other than my desire to protect Tobias. Settling to one knee, I take a series of restful breaths as I chart a course and then set out upon it, stepping carefully to make certain my feet tread the precise pathway of disordered rocks, clustered bushes, and fallen blue jay that I have devised in my mind. It takes a while to find the blue jay. After another moment or two, I spot the inky opening I seek.

The cave is huge, but the addition of a tiny fire adds a semblance of cordiality. The farthest influence of the flames probes the magnitude and exotic shape of the cave, as each flicker summons previously unseen crags into existence at the edge of an ongoing blankness. I will burn her camera, I think, and I will do it soon. I will burn her film, I will scald her memory raw until it hasn't got a trace of me. Scorched and shrinking wisps float across my mind.

Tobias and I are huddled together, and I am working to nourish him with bits of bread, hunks of cheese. As he chews, his manner is timid, incredulous. When I pour juice from a bottle to his lips, he neither refuses it nor drinks. He seems to await the cruel trick that will rob him of this sustenance in the same way he has been robbed of everything else. The juice dribbles from his lips, staining his chin, and I have to dab with my sleeve to keep him clean. I hold a slice of orange over his mouth and squeeze, forcing the juice to drop onto his lips. Only at the very end do I glimpse a trace of gratitude far off in his eyes. Like a dazed animal reawakening, he seems dismayed by the prospect of his own consciousness. He wonders if he dares return to life. Giving up a little sigh, he can't keep himself from slipping off to sleep, his delicate skeleton caught in the nest of my arms.

High in the changing light where the fire paws like a straining animal, there is a rock with a tip of crystal on which a bit of water distends until it falls in and out of illumination and lands on Tobias's brow. He is my miniature in hair, texture, and color, in spindly arms and calves and thighs. In the glistening of this liquid bead, I sense the existence of a vital shimmering within him. It seems to glow from in his brow. I start to rock him back and forth. Peering into mirrors, we never see the reflected radiance of this intuition, but only the poor meat in which we've been sentenced to wander about amid the highways, super- markets, old roads, cars, people, our lives.

I make a pillow of the loaf of bread enclosed in its plastic bag and fit it under his head. He has a webwork of bones, expanding as he sleeps. I put my hands on him and try to feel him swell and change.

Sometime later, after tucking the blanket around him, I sneak out of the cave and back toward the house, intending to find my wife's camera and steal the film. I can't bear the thought of my face cut off from its life and used as this specimen for her to study, turned into this window through which she can peer into my innermost being, as if a hole has been cut into my body so she can watch my organs functioning.

But on the road that climbs from the pasture to our house, I stop. Ahead of me, a stranger is loading the cows into the back of a cattle truck. Up the hill behind him, the silhouette of our lightless house stands against the pale night clouds. The man is in his thirties, a rugged- looking farmer, his clothing and boots filthy, straw caked into clots of mud melded into his clothing. When I ask him what he's doing, he glances at the house, then back to me. I expect to find him a little leery and unnerved, but he's perfectly calm. In fact, he's amiable and chatty as he tells me that my wife sold him the cows. As far as he's concerned, I should be pleased, because she got a damn good price. If he notes my agitation, he ignores it. When I ask him where the cows will be living in case I want to visit them, he laughs and tells me they'll be living in the truck until they get to the slaughterhouse. Then he chortles and gives me a playful shove with his shoulder, as if we're a couple of cows ourselves, bumping about for sport.

Two of the cows are already in the truck as he heads off to collect the other pair, and I grab hold of a chain hanging over the side, step up on the wheel, and climb into the back. Peering at the broad wedge of their brows, I try to see the knowledge I know they have of me lying somewhere beyond the moist placidity of their eyes. They feel almost holy to me, as if we have shared some primordial test and survived. I give them each a pat, and then a hug. With a lot of disgruntled snorting, the last two climb the loading plank, urged on by the farmer, who leans into their haunches, shoving. Then he jumps down and waits to slip the gate into place as I continue my farewells. When I hop down, he slams and locks the gate and offers me a cigarette, but I don't smoke. He lights up, the glow of the tip like a spark in the wind as he walks around to the cab.

When the truck is gone, I stand there in the dark. Wild things other than us are of course loose in the night. Everything is looking for a place to hide. Suddenly, I'm worried about Tobias and the way I left him alone in that cave. I hasten to my car and take the rifle, the knife, some ropes, and gasoline out of the trunk. I run to the cave. Though I'm not sufficiently armored to fend off the most savage and unrelenting of attackers, at least I can show a warlike spirit sufficient to deter the common criminal, the common prowler and thief, and if they aren't deterred, I can kill them.

When I find Tobias still sleeping, I lie down, snuggling close. I rest my fingers below his nostrils to follow the intake and release of his breath. He stirs so slightly it might seem he has not stirred at all. For a time I recline like this, feeling comfortable, and then, without a movement or thought that might have served as a warning, I am transported. If it is sleep I enter, I go without the slightest recognizable transition. My consciousness merely changes. In a twilight of several levels and fantastic specificity, I take note of the altering light and the manner in which details blur and disappear like steam off glass. Speculation and reflection are a mounting spiral and I find myself borne along upon the proposition that there are thoughts that we notice and others that we fail completely to attend to, though they may be of the highest order— though they may be of the most crucial consequence—such as the one I am now detecting with a sense that it belongs to someone other than myself because it is nearing completion as I spy it.

When I open my eyes I'm in my bed. Checking quickly, I find that tiny Tobias snores peacefully down the hall in his own little room. Moonlight falls in a narrow glare like a sword blade across his brow. I pull the shade as if to save his life, and hasten back to my own sheets. My wife, I think. My child. They are locked in a deadly struggle, and I am his only hope. To save him, I must stop her. She has already dispatched the cows to their midnight execution. There is no one else to help him. Only I can do it. I must confront her. And I must do it soon. Yet I must be careful to proceed upon a flawless basis. Ineptly performed, confrontation will not only fail to save my little boy, but it will betray the one advantage I now possess, which lies in her sense of superiority regarding me, her ignorance of the fact that I have discovered her deadly aims. Should I fail to conquer her—should I not disarm her in a single stroke—I will stand exposed before her powers, I will fall victim to her poisons, my defeat sentencing Tobias to extinction in her cruel hands. To avoid such a possibility, I must prepare. I must commit myself to a relentless self-instruction until I am ready to attack with such a lethal expertise that she must succumb. I have to train. I have to research. I must acquire a perfect familiarity with confrontation in its every form, so that when I face her, I will have the ease that arises from absolute mastery. But how? How am I to do this, how am I to acquire such virtuosity? There is only one way. I have to practice.

Stretched out like a moonlit marble effigy of myself on my own bed, I feel my wife shift beside me, and my brain is a haunting shimmer like a crystal from whose hidden core an eerie, primordial signal is flashing, like a summons from another world. Other women, I think. I will practice on other women. I will learn to confront my wife by practicing on other women. In order to prepare to confront my wife, I will have to start going out on dates.

Chapter Seventeen

Because it is still so cold and seems it will remain so forever, this desolate, unalterable November, this winter of tragic permanence, I decide to go to a bar and pick up a girl.

Resulting from this decision, there are other decisions and actions that follow. I go to my closet. I stand. Some time goes by. I have thoughts, my lower lip curling up as if I am sad. What could be the source of this sadness? It could be something I don't know, or even something that I will never know. I stand before my closet. I put on a stocking cap, along with my big old coat, the cap as black and ragged as my loneliness, the jacket as long as my knees. The scarf that I loop about my throat is a comforting noose made from the wool of a lamb. In the space between my cap and my jacket collar and just above the scarf, I put on a face that will appear gnarled by the wind; a dirt face. Nothing else will do in a bar where girls are to be picked up.

In the mirror, my face hangs like a head shining through a window in a wall: I look insane, and I smile. Girls like that. I yell very loudly as if to scare someone who isn't there. I'm starting to have fun already.

In my car I drive very carefully, following the white line that divides the road in two equal halves. Though I am attracted by the prohibited left-hand sector, though I am enthralled by the field beyond the fences, I do not veer out of my proper lane and off the pavement to plunge bumping and thumping into a collision with whatever it is that might be out there hauling at me.

In the first bar, everyone is dressed in an oddly elegant manner, an off-putting amalgam of casual and cultivated vanity. I am ill at ease. No one wants to talk to me, so I walk smugly from one end of the room to the other just to make clear to everyone the disdain and contempt in which I hold them. With a haughty show of scorn, I stride out the door to my car. The parking lot is all dust and flying gravel with the effects of my departure.

In the next tavern things are far more to my taste, because everyone is dirty. They all wear filthy, oil-stained coveralls or ragged jeans or big tattered plaid shirts. The music here is so loud it resonates in the bones of my head, and everyone is yelling. People drink with big long gestures and knock each other off chairs or throw fistfuls of food at each other. I gulp down several glasses of bourbon. When two of the more boisterous occupants pull my hat over my eyes and throw me against the wall so hard the nearby pinball machine tilts, angering the man playing it, I'm overcome by a fit of laughing. The man playing the pinball misinterprets my giddiness, imagining that my pleasure is because of his misfortune. He throws his beer at me, glass and all. It's just then that I recognize the undeniable fact that, though this place might be wild and fun-filled, there are no girls present. And that's what I came for, after all. Quickly then, I depart, dripping beer from my hair and blood from my nose.

In the next night spot and the one after that and the one after that, I keep on drinking. Sometimes I buy two drinks at a time and guzzle them in a rush, pouring them down my throat with the same hasty dispatch I might use to dump something vile into a toilet. Every now and then I yell. People seem to like me, though they don't know what I'm yelling about. When they ask me, I yell again. Girls are in some of the bars I go to and not in others. The girls I see are all the same in some ways and each very different in a lot of ways. I'm amazed by their similarities as well as by their differences. Also, the number of them is amazing to me. In some bars they're everywhere.

I go to more bars and drink in all of them, and in every one of them the jukebox is taxed to the limit, the squealing intensity of the treble an insupportable load, the base bludgeoning the apparatus until it shudders at the verge of disintegrating like a light bulb under too much voltage. The voices of the singers and their passionate sentiments and stories beat about in my head like eyewitness accounts of some cataclysmic series of events, whose aftermath has left these stupefied survivors buried in their fantasies and memories, telling and retelling the anecdotes of their nights of love and sex.

Some girls talk to me, and others merely stare. A few walk away rudely. It doesn't seem to matter that I'm smiling and swaying to the music. There are always more bars to go to, and more girls, and more to drink, and the same music. Somewhere along the line I begin to listen very closely to the music. In the narratives unfolded by the mooning voices, in the lyric and heartfelt reveries of loves discovered and lost, in the ecstasy and bereavement of passions aroused and spent, hearts enraptured and broken—in the incessant repetition of this single tale, I begin to hear an exact description of the events I have been living through this very night. I cannot find the girl I'm looking for. And as I focus on this rush of sentiment strung upon the melody now winding through the smoky light, I suddenly realize that what they're singing about is me. This song is about me. As was the song before. All the songs are about me. Each one of them is a song about my life.

Needless to say, I'm shocked. This discovery leaves me reeling. I totter about the bar swaying into chairs and bouncing off tables and into gruff customers, one of whom shoves me with such force that I careen off the front door, against which another person, whose face I never see, slams me again and again. Someone else is screaming, "Throw him the fuck out." It's a high female voice.

"I'm all right," I yell.

For her rejoinder, she has nothing whatsoever to contribute.

"So what?" I say, while this ferocious, sinewy person I still can't see keeps banging me against the door. Somebody else says something, and then a lot of people say a whole bunch of things. I wish I knew what was going on. I'm trying to figure it out, but I can't. And if they're hoping to explain things with all their shouts, all their brash, rude caterwauling, they're more self-indulgent and vain and petty and stupid than I thought.

Soon I'm wandering the parking lot outside the bar, upon whose roof a big green cat stands outlined in neon light bulbs against the sky. As I stare into these feline, lascivious eyes, I note it has begun to rain. Drops are pouring through the kitty's curvaceous shape.

Looking up, I see the moon demurely masked in lacy clouds as if to embellish and incite further perversity to fall and drench the already wanton night. Out from this harsh lunar surface pours snowy light. Coupled with the rising wind, it shreds the lower clouds into a netted substance like a whore's stockings. Anything might happen in a night like this. It's wild, this night, and full of music. Oh, the music. My sad music. The rain has me smiling. The weather has been like this lately: unpredictable. Seasons rushing out of nowhere. Time seems to have lost its regulatory powers. Light collides with dark, and rain comes suddenly and violently, like an outlaw with a gun. Such forces feel criminal, brutish, anarchic, like lunatics with knives.

The rain storms through the outline of the neon cat, like atoms flying from its disintegrating shape. Around me strangers scurry to their cars exclaiming at the weather. Those who note me no doubt think me drunk, attributing my wandering in the lot to the fact that I have misplaced my car. They seem startled by the rain, by the low-cast clouds falling to the ground in an avalanche of fog, by the sudden thunder. Haven't they noticed the eerie cold? And the music? Weren't they listening, didn't they understand? Amid the grind and grumble of their engines firing into departure, tires fling up sprays of gravel to rattle through the chunks of melody that come as the bar door opens and shuts, emitting patrons in pairs and groups. High in the brain of the cat a neon bulb ruptures with a hiss, and almost simultaneously the door to the bar is left agape, allowing the music to rush upon me, a sustained and potent outpouring. And in every turn of phrase, in every chord or reprise, whether lustful, or debauched, or lyrical and sweet, what I hear is that it is all fated. Cars splash past me, headlights sweeping me from head to toe, the repetition of their glare informing me that I'm involved in a rhythmic event, a dance of retreat and advance, like a sea swell, a process of coming and going. The woman I am to find must hide, and I must look. Or so the music sighs as the story is retold with drums and squealing guitars and harsh, high voices; I am destined to find the girl I seek. The universal laws of revelry and liquor and musical theology are at work, having ordained my search so that, in the helpless and provident spirit of this night, she must be delivered to me. I can relax and laugh. As the hymns predict in the orgiastic parables they depict, the cosmos is obligated to bring her forth before me so that in my fated way I can confront and lose her. All I need to do is keep on looking.

Chapter Eighteen

A daintily curtained lamp stands on the end table behind her. The emerging glow irradiates the mixed browns of her hair, endowing her tough and sensual features with a sense of haunting delicacy. She wants me to eat something. She is considering what it might be. She is trying to decide what clothes I should wear. She doesn't like the clothes I have on. She drinks several sips of wine and beams at me, bursting with the affection that her smile suggests my presence has roused in her to the total exclusion of every other feeling.

Above her adoring eyes, the brows are bushy. Her tender emotions swallow me like a warm bath, and as I luxuriate in these lapping waves, wariness commences, a stinging tightness in the soles of my feet. My toes claw inward as if to grasp my place on the floor. That her eyes and eyebrows can provoke such apprehension indicates a fault in me, because her manner is so loving. Still, I'm no longer really looking at her. The details of her presence are a blur, so removed have I become, so muted in my layered introspection. I urge myself to return to her, to focus quickly and with a forceful objectivity.

Just then, the wrinkles below her eyes swirl and transform, as if tiny snakes are squirming off within them to find further concealment in the crevices above her cheeks. Now her eyes are hooded while she smiles. I encounter her mouth, where a knot of vehemence is fading. The geniality that rises in its place is an artifice, and her jaw is jutting out at me in a threat of physical assault. Frustrated rage slides upward from her mouth into her cheeks, as if these wrinkles are electrical channels. I start to retrace my way back to her lips, intending to check their content once more. But I'm in such a panic that I can't follow my own wishes. Part of my focus is lost in pursuit of the aggression that beset me from her jaw. But this menace has already melted away. Just as her vehemence has fled her lips. High above her cheekbone, the skin is clotted with a bulge of resentment that subsides and retreats through a series of ripples shadowed by several dangling curls of hair, until it hides just above her ear, disguised as a minor contour.

Like a man who has seen a ghost, I'm left with a haunted relation to the commonplace. Out the window, the night is deep. Intense but aborted thoughts break across my mind like startled fish. Their departure necessitates other vague cerebral constructs, a flow of neural activity producing impressions and theories, words and their counterparts. But it's all discordant, jangling, like a traffic jam. The room is carved into fragments of light and dark; I'm sitting in the corner with a pile of shadows muffling me, that's all I know, like the fur of some black beast pulled over me.

She's pacing through shards of lamplight in the center of the room. Bearing a tray of food, she's walking toward me. At the coffee table, she stops. There she bends and arranges the bread and milk and sandwich meat, the condiments and quart bottle of Coke, two bottles of beer, some glasses. We eat, we chat. When she starts away, the disembodied upper half of her hovers near an unlit fireplace, and I must remind myself that she has legs. Struggling to hear the sounds of her feet, I wonder if she is tiptoeing. I sink backward into my wedge of gloom. When she explains how amazing she found my appearance in the bar, how weird and stimulating and perfectly suited to her wanton, iconoclastic mood, she's not entirely visible. Her head and torso are blotted from view, presenting me with the sight of her lower extremities shifting about, no apparent mind to guide them. I tell her that she must come closer so I can see her better.

Of course she's delighted by this sign of interest, her response tinged with a throaty satisfaction, a carnal tickle. Of course, she's been keeping her lustful feelings hidden, trying to make me fret and beg, granting me hints, compelling me to guess at her secrets. Is it too much to ask that I be allowed to know what's going on? I'm in a room. She's in the room, that same room. Now she begins to speak in such an enticing tone that I recoil instinctively from the feathery spell of her voice. At the same time, I'm struggling to appear calm and a little blasé. She's smiling as she talks, as if I amuse and please her, and every passing second is magnifying the impossibility of my desire to resist her. Each new word and gesture envelops me a little further, looping me into a yearning to obey her, an overwhelming appetite to acquiesce to her slightest suggestion, my brain inoculated by a druggy lust whose nature makes my own thoughts dull and trivial compared with the miracle of her every murmur and shrug. The timbre of her voice is lyrical. I experience myself as less and less, her lushness pulling me deeper under her expanding charms into which I'm dissolving.

Just beneath the surface of my face, where I am hidden, I have to try to fight. Just beneath this sheet of skin there are muscles, and I start to tense them. Exactly where my interior rises to meet the world, I'm struggling to protect myself from the force of her effects. Veins and blood vessels are interwoven with fibers and membrane, and I am straining to constrict them until the tension squeezes a deadness into them. I need a second face inset between my skin and skull, a kind of shield injected at this point, like a mask of glass only harder, as permanent as diamonds and devised just below the docile, doughy flesh of my chin and guileless nose and cheeks onto which I will impose whatever premeditated expressions I need to project into the world while I survive behind them, hiding, secretive, cowering, unknown and unknowable, sequestered and unassailable.

She's babbling away. What a chatterbox she is. On and on she goes, convinced by my performance that I'm listening. Duped by my invention, she believes that we are connected by the exchange between her words and my facial expressions. So she yammers on, smiling at me, while I experience my expressions as an alien sequence of shudders, like the spasms of a frog I'm squeezing to death in my fist. My face, convulsing with its rote responses, is estranged and despicable, just like a squirming frog dying in my fingers, a slime of fear and treachery contaminating me, filling me with disgust at my lost integrity, my

cowardly surrender. Amid these thoughts, I'm retreating even further
into bitter plumes of hate, and I ride them, feeling coldly disenfranchised and resentful.

Looking out from wherever it is I have come to, I see the tiny flicker
of a question perplex her lids and fingers as I draw the hunting knife up
out of the sheath in my boot and force the tip slowly into the wood of the
table.

"Ever see a knife like this before?" I say.

"What? No."

"It was a little uncomfortable in my boot. You didn't know I had it—I
was going to show it to you at the bar."

"I like a man who carries a knife."

I'm amazed by these words. Her conviction that she can endlessly
beguile me seems to have no limits, and I wonder what it will take to
crush it from her. I want to laugh and my face does something, I make
some noises.

"A gun or knife," she says, looking off around the room, trying to find
the door, the window. "For protection."

"You live alone?"

"Why?"

"No reason," I say.

"Oh."

When I have stripped her and gagged her and blindfolded her and
tied her down, one arm to each side of the radiator, one foot to each of
the front legs of the heavy oaken chair I have dragged over from the
opposite wall, I feel it is time that I begin to express to her some of my
deeper, truer feelings, and they are more violent than I could have ever
anticipated. Chairs fly about the room, lamps flash on and off, the bulbs
shattering with the detonation of my feelings. Pictures waver on the
wall and crash to the floor, and the plaster and paint crumble, fragments
raining down. The noises I make are scarcely human, yet since I am
making them, they must be human. Normally they would be attributed
to some other kind of creature than a man, but these are norms that
should be revised because I am a man making these noises. She lies on
the floor, a pitiful tangle of terror and ropes and rags, her breasts spread
by the pull of gravity, the pitted and bumpy buds of her nipples cowering in submission and supplication as I touch them. Now gravity begins
to pull at me also, and the situation is becoming dark and grave,

enormously dark, enormously grave. Things will, I know, get grimmer, grittier, and even more somber and hazardous, sooner for her than for me. I feel the yearning of each planet for its own mass and all it contains, along with all other planets and their responsive masses. We are desired by one another. We are desired by everything. When we get too close, things happen. The force of gravity is dangerous. Anything that gets too close can suck you in with a thick, dark immutability.

She seems to have grasped the fact of the existence, if not the nature, of my inner monologue, because she suddenly wants to talk to me, to tell me something. She starts to moan and squeal, and it's all about her life, I'm pretty sure, and it's interesting enough, though difficult to hear because of the rag stuffed in her mouth and fastened there with a slice of rope. She was of course born somewhere, her parents having migrated from a different place. They moved to the little town where she was born for reasons that were a mix of whim and economic necessity, arriving just days before her birth. When she was old enough, she went to school and did well in certain courses and not so well in others. There was a lover, a first heartbreaking boy, from whose effects she never quite recovered and in whose wake a deep and unresolved antagonism developed between her and her parents, because somehow they seemed culpable in her loss. Still she went ahead and got a job and then after a while moved away from that town, having grown bored with her job and weary of her dissension with her parents. She married someone else but she didn't love him. So she got a divorce. Married again. Then got divorced again. One husband smoked cigars, the other cigarettes.

Strangely, with all the speeches I am prepared to make, I say nothing. It's all interesting enough, I think, and I attend her closely. At the same time, I'm speaking to myself about the clothing she will demand that I wear soon, the pilot's cap with earflaps and a strap to bind beneath my chin, big rubber boots with clumsy buckles, mittens pinned to the arms of my jacket, big woolen socks and dilapidated shoes and corduroy pants. Next she will tell me to smile all the time and to say that I love everybody, absolutely everybody. She will be planning lengthy dinners and when I should talk and when I shouldn't.

It's hard to understand her because of the gag. Still I decipher enough to find her behavior truly pathetic because it exposes the terrible desperation she feels just because the moment appears to involve death for her. Glimpsing her own imminent—how shall we say it?—

departure, disappearance, ego-loss, body-loss, breath-loss, life-loss—
she has become so frantic as to seem graceless and debased.

I can feel tenderheartedness signaling for my attention, but it's not
really very strong. I try to listen, as she talks on and on, because I know
that's what she wants, my gaze fixed on her, my manner placid. But I'm
not really listening, I'm just sitting there. And suddenly I see how—
because of my new invention—the snarl of gleaming scars just beneath
the skin of my face—I can spend hours with people and they'll never
know what I'm thinking. From now on I can live safely inside myself. I
can talk about the weather or any little problem such as what time we
should meet for dinner, or what kind of activity we should plan after
dinner or after work, or what's needed from the grocery store—we can
settle the question and dispatch one or both of us off to perform the tasks
our conclusion has determined necessary—and all the while the other
person will never know that, as we are talking, I am thinking about
killing them. They will never know. I will barely know. What does it
matter if I am ignorant of the thoughts underlying the thoughts I'm
thinking, the words I'm uttering, as I smile at the people to whom I'm
speaking? Butchering multitudes, I will grin. The heads will roll. I will
chat. I'm simply tired of holding my breath. That's what it comes down
to. I've been holding my breath for a long time, and I can't do it
anymore. Everyone I meet just wants me to hold my breath. Now I'm
going to let my breath out. Standing over this woman, I'm going to
breathe. Looking down past pity and anger and disgust, I feel humiliated that my alternatives have shrunk down to the pathetic few I see.
But the time has come for me to breathe, and I'm going to do it. I'm
going to take the air in and let the air out, for the opening has been made
in her side eight centimeters up from her hipbone and four inches to the
right of her belly button—a slit just wide enough, as she rolls in her
bonds and an assault of emotions alien to any she has ever known.
Unprepared by history, she thrashes as I slip into the wound and begin
loudly to practice the confrontational lessons I must learn. Now I'm
roaring, and she's screaming. This is not what I wanted for my life. I
can't pretend it is. She thrashes, crying out because she's no more than
what I make of her, and I am gaunt and gnarled, squeaking and sobbing
in time with her pulsing as she grapples in her bonds to free herself from
her own gore. But I am hooded and horned within a skin of rubbery
scales. Are my nostrils not flared? Smoke pounds in the tubes of my

brain. Who am I that the moon has given me this moment? Who am I to have flown out of all boundaries and returned with permission for this act?

She has never been treated this way before. Nothing has prepared her. Not kindergarten, or grade school, not dating or necking with boys in the back seats of old cars in alleys and side roads. Not Sunday school or fucking the long line of fuckers she has fucked. Not the food she has eaten. Not the beef or potatoes or beans or chicken or chili has prepared her. Not the polio shots, not the tetanus shots. Not the standing in long lines in supermarkets reading gossip magazines. Nothing has prepared her.

Breathing in her sweat and stink, I feel I own her innermost parts, as if she is magically mine, and I see that the burning core of her experience at this moment, which must be understood as "terror," is fueled by the fact that she has no idea what's going on in this room. She has no idea what's happening to her. As if she ever did, with her pathetic little blackboard of an identity scribbled on the feeble tablets of her brain: "I am Sally. I was born on March 18, 1952. My father is . . . My mother is . . ." What is this "I" she raves about, this "my," these "I wants," these "my feelings"? She has said to herself, "I was born on March 18, 1952, in Tomahawk, Indiana," just as she said it to me, as if it meant something. But what is this "I"? And what does it mean for this "I" to be "born"? Out of the limbs of her mother, the puddle that contained her plopped out. Was that the birth of the "I"? Where was it at that instant? And where before? No, no, she has been in a mystery all along, but never before has she glimpsed it. From the beginning a mystery hidden in a mystery. Only now with my knife I have pried it open like the lid of a can in which, for an instant, she has seen the contents of her life like a person looking out from the rim of the planet where she teeters on one toe at the edge of a black nothing, the cosmos like the opening into an unknown hole.

She steps off. It's a long fall. What else can she do but howl? It's all beyond her. It's all beyond me. Knives are beyond me. Her crying is beyond me. She is looking where I have no desire to look. Nor would she, had she any choice. She's looking off the rim of the planet and this is not like looking off the edge of the table down to the floor. This is not like looking off the roof of a building at the street below full of vehicles and pedestrians. And though I'm with her, though I'm right beside her, my state is very different from hers. I cannot see what she sees. But her face, which remains before me and from which I'm incapable of removing my eyes, is a kind of mirror, reflecting the vision she's meeting. Her expression, full of minute and unusual changes, is a distillation of her experience. The speculations, the new theories and principles she's struggling to grasp are blazing in the heat of her facial expressions, the moist blush of her skin.

Like a man putting on spectacles, I lean closer, and through the intensity of my stare I begin to perceive a simulation of the eternity into which she is gazing and entering. And she wants me to see. She's working to make me able to see what she's looking at. Her face, inches away from my gaze, is a periscope into time, and I am attentive. No, no, I am devoted. Obsessed. I hold her head between my hands as a man might hold a crystal ball. I am gentle, my fingers in awe of her, my eyes narrowing, for I am squinting into an intolerable glare. Inches beyond my fingers the eternal is occurring. My fingers are upon her skin, which is layered over bone behind which dangles the magic matter of her brain where the infinite has come to visit in whatever form it comes, which is what I ferociously want to see. My stare is intent and savage, and then the intention alters and the force quadruples into a fit of staring so violent I fear the windows of the room are going to shatter. Due to her glimpse into the eternal, which is, no doubt, ephemeral and inconclusive, her face shines with sweat, her expression an ashen translation of the harrowing events she is contemplating at an excruciating proximity. Every nuance of her changing countenance contains an inner event of such impact and pressure that I find myself beginning to groan with tenderness. And though "tenderness" feels strange and unwieldy, it is all that suits my newborn emotions. Though "worship" is useful, and "affection" has merit—though "adoration" might beg for consideration—my state escapes them. In this instant, my interests are narrowing at a dizzying rate down to a single subject in all the universe and it's her. What I want to know is what she thinks. No more guessing, no more desperate conjecturing on the basis of the gleam in her eyes, the fluctuations of her mouth or mood.

My fingers are advancing to remove her gag. Timidly, with reverential expectation, I want her to speak and I await the marvel of her first pronouncement, for she is at the very center of this singular spellbinding event. From this pivotal vantage, her utterances will have the far-reaching value of the wisdom that comes to one such as herself who, occupying the bone-wrenching and convulsive blackness that must mark her departure out of time, manages to send back a message to the mortals she is about to leave behind.

"It hurts," she says.

The gag is in my fingers. My fingers having tugged it from her mouth, where they jammed it earlier. "What do you mean?" I ask.

But before her response can reach her mouth and become a sound for me to absorb and comprehend, I've retreated across the room. She shouts at me, outrage and accusation and some other, unearthly emotion distorting her voice and clotting her features. I bounce off the wall; my backbone throbs, and I must struggle to resist the distress urging me to my knees, a weakness arising not from my collision but from the effects of her voice.

The sudden rapping at the window shocks me. I look and listen but there's nothing there to see, not even the trees. Then the moon hurls itself at the glass again and again in streams of ice. Behind me, the woman's voice is barbarous and animal, a blur of begging and fear and hatred and mourning, and it's raising this excruciating feeling in me, bringing it up from some unknown part of me, this unbearable, unknowable feeling. I'm backing toward the door.

"Don't go," she cries. But I know she's going to leave me if she gets the chance. I can't stand the thought. I can't stand her voice. It leaves me feeling battered. I spin from the room and through the kitchen and out of the house and across the yard.

The moon awaits me in the woods, burning with a snowy light. The heavens are smeared with angular, frosty strips. The moonlight rages in carnal vibratory surges that fall in rhythmic strokes producing bumpy layers all over my skin in such a rubbery profusion that I feel scaled. I fall upon my knees, a broken disciple to this light, surrendering. I can't help it. The rushing vapors of the moon are hurled from its core like thunderbolts from clouds. In hammerblows they slam against me, beating on me just as they beat on the heads of other men all over the earth, who grit their teeth and moan, abhorring the visions awash in their brains, for which they take sole responsibility. They consider themselves governed by a singular consciousness, an autonomy they call their individuality, and so for what is horrid in their hearts and minds, they blame themselves. When it is the moon. When it is the moon slamming on their heads and filling their eyes with hideous sights. When it is the moon, the chanting, pounding symphony of light encircling them with its lunatic shimmering and the calamity of its cries. It's the moon that sinks the vessel whose helpless helmsman guides its hull into roaring rocks. It's the moon that casts men into alleys where they snarl and tear at each other's flesh with sticks and broken bottles. It's the moon that urges the woman down the carpeted hallway to the window and out with a baffled cry into the cool black air, her nightgown flapping.

I'm crawling on my belly through a thicket of low-slung evergreens. The dew-damp ground is hard and rough. Piercing the uppermost branches, the lunar forces fall like shards of glass. I grunt against these successive impacts, struggling to advance, and then the nearby bushes thrash and rattle. Though I look too late to catch sight of the cause, I see a dozen wavering branches. I hear the dying rustle of fleeing footsteps. But it's from a deep and animal intuition that I draw my interpretation of what I've just witnessed, the rush of an unseen intruder through the trees. Someone has just run by me headed for the house. I rise to follow, a risky enterprise considering the ongoing bombardments of the moon. I run as best I can, stepping into dips and inclines, leaping over a pile of rocks and then a stack of logs.

The house, in spite of several additions over the years, remains the spiritual descendant of its original eighteenth-century architecture. Everything about it strikes me as strange, as if I have never seen it before. Built in the early 1800s, it's a conscientiously tended home, the paint looking smooth, the shrubs manicured, the flower bed weeded. A warm glow of lamplight filters from the ground-floor windows. Ahead of me, the figure I have been following is gone, having disappeared into the house. Who is it? I wonder, just as a moonbeam slams me like a sledgehammer, depositing me onto my knees. Far more clever than I am, the intruder is safe inside; he's sophisticated and swift, having negotiated the dark with miraculous ease, while I'm staggering about in his wake, under the barrages of the moon.

Against the side of the house, I press myself into a pile of shadows, trying to hide. Now the moon bursts from the heights drenching me, and I start to shake, the atmosphere around me transforming into a frosted mist.

Peering in the window, I see the woman lying as I left her, only now her attention is no longer riveted on me, because I am no longer there.

Instead, she's transfixed by something else. She gazes off at what must be the newcomer, the stranger, who has replaced me in the room, and from a hidden vantage he displays himself before her. She seems stupefied. She stares helplessly, like a baby spellbound by a rare and fulfilling sight. What can it be that is so wonderful about him? I want to see him. I want to examine him.

But when I try, I cannot, for the frame of the window blocks that part of the room in which he preens and performs for her. Encircled in a ring of his most captivating charms and desires, she lies there, her dreamy interest pouring out of her toward him. Her body is so slack, she appears resigned to the ropes in which I bound her. She looks almost contented, as if she's surrendered all hope of escape, settling for the enchantment provided by the stranger. She seems to be conserving her energies and trying to bring whatever comfort she can to her weakened limbs. Her head is cushioned by her shoulder. Her mouth is open, her lips drooping as she gazes with a kind of innocent expectation toward the stranger just beyond my perception. Childlike, she awaits his instruction.

Dismayed, I look off from her. Throughout the room, the moonlight has a quality of gentleness, a soothing feature absent in the woods. A feathery gloss is being added to all the shapes in the room, blurring corners, softening angles. I see a ledge above a fireplace. On it stands an empty wineglass within whose shimmer wavers a tiny moon complete with pinpoint craters, craggy valleys, miniaturized peaks, and infinitesimal sparks. Pressing my face against the cool pane of the window, I see that this little moon and I are sharing an identical experience, the both of us isolated in a translucence of glass, hovering across from one another.

Then I see the woman lift her head in response to a sign that only the stranger could have made. No one else is here except the three of us, and I have not moved. Abruptly, the atmosphere burgeons with clues to the approach of something charged and significant. It's going to happen. I can see it coming. In the drifting cloud that I glimpse through the window in the opposite side of the house, I can see that it's near. In the lamplit cone of dust trembling through the room and in the icy touch of the wind crawling on my neck, it's clear. In the mournful cries of a far-off owl and in the tear-smudged cheeks of the woman—in the trembling of her bare feet, whose movement is no longer directed by the wish to free herself but by some neural or muscular tremor—in all these things, it is declared that the next few minutes will be different from anything before them. I am sweating. I'm cold. This is not what I wanted. This is too awful. Were the stranger to venture one step forward, I would see him, and then I might be able to measure the magic in his glance whose unnatural power is enough to bring this woman to the point at which she now lies, considering leaving her body to join him, because that's what she's doing.

I want to flee the window. I want to move to one whose angle will focus me on the corner where the stranger stands, weaving his spell, working his sorcery. But as I start to move, I lunge back. A pair of contrary possibilities will not let me go. I'm worried that, even if I do move in order to see him, I will just end up staring into a different empty corner because the stranger, abundant in guile and perversity, will have altered his position in a diabolic harmony with my own. He doesn't want me to see him. I don't know why, but he doesn't. In all probability, I would gain no advantage by moving though I would run the risk of missing some important development in this event rushing to its conclusion before me. Her ultimate response to the stranger, which I yearn so desperately to witness, might easily occur while I'm journeying from window to window. There I will be, looking in from my new vantage onto the aftermath of her surrender, having forfeited the opportunity I now possess to scrutinize at least one of the two participants in this weird and compelling encounter.

But to my utter shock, as I force myself to penetrate the mists of my own bedazzling thought, the climax has transpired unseen before my distracted eyes, leaving nothing available for me to observe except the fact that she's gone. Her body is empty. It's over. I have lost her totally.

In addition, an automobile is arriving in front of the house. This fact is undeniable on the basis of the throbbing, wind-like roar and the headlights sweeping across the yard to my right. Shimmering beams burn through the shaggy trees, melting the shadows off a gnomelike shape to reveal a startled owl, whose wings erupt like an opening cape.

Initially, I feel intruded on, interrupted, and my disappointment is strong. And yet these feelings are dwarfed by my alarm at the sudden surrounding silence, as if the occupants of the arriving vehicle are trying to trick me into believing that they are not there. The lights, too, are gone. Am I supposed to imagine that I saw only the passing of a falling star? No, I think. Not only am I positive a car has arrived, I know that it's a Buick, and it's as black as swamp water, a very old model with high fenders accenting its nearly square design, and it's delivering a number of scary occupants.

When I turn, the vista of the night spreads before me full of occluded areas that alternate with empty stretches and clusters of trees. The air and light are a sea of sparkling variables, while the ground is covered by a sheen of moonlight like an inch of ice. The diamond-hard mask beneath my face is vexed, a meshed and aching numbness about to transmute from living tissue into an inanimate, chemical substance. And this old woman in black is getting out of the Buick, and her dress has a collar buttoned up around her neck, and she wears black gloves and shoes, the pale orb of her head hovering above this inky foundation adrift over the frosty, glowing ground.

I don't have a chance. The stranger is gone, having fled the scene, using his expertise in deceit to steal off with everything vital in the woman. So whom else can this weird little group be coming to accost but me? I'm the only one here. What else can this old woman be doing but stalking up to get me, to interrogate me? She will want to know what happened here. She will demand an accounting, as if anyone could account for such an occurrence when thoughts flew in and out of the room like savage beasts who left nothing but the havoc of their unnatural deeds, such as the blood deepening the definition of the cracks on the floor near the remnant of the woman, who is acquiring a statuesque stillness appalling in its grandeur. Anyone would run. I can't deceive myself into believing that my accounting might gain the slightest sympathy from such grim judicious types as this old woman and her entourage, who are now trudging toward the front door of the house, having disembarked from the Buick to wade through the moonlight flooding the yard. Her face is featureless, and it pulses as she walks. Her thoughts are pressing against the sides of her head and they make it swell like an expanding balloon, and she has these companions, who are angular in every way, all lines and degrees, and their skulls are cubes and they have these numbers scribbled on their brows and cheeks, and while she interrogates me, they will stand behind her with these numbers on their faces changing and pertaining to me while she sits in a big wooden chair with armrests of carved mahogany sea serpents, clenching her fingers as she commands me to explain everything, charging that I must account for my behavior.

I tumble down a steep slope, my trousers ripping as I slide to a stop and lie there, taking my first deep breath. I can race on forever in such a night, if I don't get tired. I can sprint until I fall down and can't get up anymore. But I can't account for my behavior. I would only end up creating additional inexplicable behavior, for which I could be ordered to account. I might satisfy the old woman, but I could not account for my behavior. I could only concoct stories. Better to dash off now that the Buick has arrived, better to flee. I could light the house on fire, and I could run, as I am now, but I could not account for my behavior. Only old women like swirling mists claim one can, stalking through the moment and pointing behind them to their assistants with numbers on their faces, as if their tally is proof.

In the wild woods with only the animals for companions, I come upon a ridgeline overlooking a clearing. I cannot escape unscathed from events such as those I have been a part of. A toll must be exacted, a reckoning that will proceed with me into the future. The moon has had its way with me; the wind has had its way. I want to go home. Below me, the ground appears infinite and white, as if I have been lifted to the lunar surface. For an instant I believe I am no longer on the earth. A creek wiggles through the hoary ground like the first fissure of a quake about to rip the place apart. On either side of this crack, two trees stand, their branches stripped of foliage, each fork and joint articulated with drastic clarity against the whiteness. The narrowing roots flow out from the trunks and plunge down into the gleaming ground, as receptive as a field of crushed glass. The branches that rise into the air appear to also spread across the flatness below in a complex scrawl of interwoven streaks, the shadows duplicating their elevated counterparts.

A man lying on his back and staring upward is small. The stars are countless specks gathered in spirals and far flung in swirls. A man might think himself to be looking up into the heavens, or he might imagine himself to be reclining high in the heavens, looking down from the stars. It's hard to tell up from down in such a setting, where shadows of branches mirror the shapes that spawned them, flawlessly. One could never account for one's behavior in such a place. One could only pour kerosene all around the sides of a house and right up to the gas tank of the Buick and flip in a match and then run, determined not to get caught.

Let the universe go about its business, I think, lying there. I will go about my own. And it seems that my business at this moment is the stars, their number and variety, and so I start to count them. I see isolated stars with fuzzy edges. I see stars in pairs and in crowds. There are cities and families and wanderers, and I count them all one by one, sitting up and pivoting my head along a level axis, until I'm stopped by a massive burst of brilliance.

Dominating the horizon out of which I've run is an enormous star that appears freshly minted, bursting into existence at this very instant. The blend of joy and gratification I feel at this spectacle is instantaneous and keen, but in no way incommensurate with what any amateur astronomer would feel were he to witness such a genesis. At the base of the distant wilderness, a newborn ball of fire is ascending, a licking gaseous clot whose most unusual and original characteristic is its color. It isn't silvery like all the other stars. It's scarlet and orange flung about by a melee of arcing tongues. And in the giddy excess of this moment of discovery, I feel it is a star of my creation.

Chapter Nineteen

Coming down the stairs into the kitchen, I button my flannel shirt and zip my trousers. After putting on my army greatcoat, I fill a kettle with water from the tap, which sputters twice before sending a steady flow rattling into the spout. I turn on the gas to ignite the front right-hand burner, where I place the kettle. At the cabinet, I locate the jar of instant coffee with its cheerful red label and unscrew the lid, then transfer a teaspoon of the grainy contents into a yellow mug decorated with the decal of a golfer. When I notice that the water in the sink continues to run, I turn the faucet off just as the silhouette of a cloud passes over the morning sun and marks the wall with the form of a turtle. My trip to the refrigerator to look for some milk is interrupted by the whistling of the teakettle. I grab up a hot pad to protect my hand, and the steaming water I pour from the kettle into the cup turns instantly black.

When my wife arrives in her blue robe, she studies me from behind an ostensibly civil expression struggling to mask its darker undertones. The result is an eccentric grimace, her face muscles pulling in contrary directions. "God, I have a headache," she says. Bloated little pockets surround her eyes, turning them into slits. Her skin has an unhealthy lack of color.

"You were drinking last night, weren't you?" I say, nodding.

She thinks for a minute before replying, "I had a couple of drinks. How come you have that idiotic overcoat on?"

"I'm cold."

"I don't remember what time you came in."

"Want me to guess what you're thinking?"

"Don't ask me stupid questions, please. I haven't even had my coffee yet."

"I made some instant. It's very good."

"Who cares? I hate instant. Why are you looking at me like that?"

"Like what?"

"It's the middle of June and you've got that goddamn coat on."

Tobias wanders into view, dragging a blanket down the stairs. He's visible through the open kitchen door. Blond and thin, he's struggling to button his shirt as he staggers in to join us.

"Are you cold, Tobias? Your father's cold."

"I'm not cold," he says.

"Your father's cold. It's the middle of June and he's cold. I don't know why."

"I don't know why either," I say.

"You look so stupid in that big coat all the time."

"I don't like being cold," Tobias says. "But I'm not."

"It's not that I like being cold. I just am. That's why I'm wearing the coat. But the coffee's warming me up."

"Where were you last night?" she says to me in an offhand manner that belies her searching glance.

"Do I have to go to school today?" says Tobias. "I don't want to. I don't feel good."

"You were out late last night. Where were you?"

"You were sleeping when I got in," I tell her.

"I know that."

"Passed out, really."

Tobias flops into a chair, his shirt closed but several buttons out of sequence. "Sally, from next door to James's house, keeps spitting at me at school. It makes me sick."

"Is that why you don't want to go to school?" She seems offended, shaking her head. "That's not a good reason. I don't even want to hear about such a reason," she says.

"She spits at me all the time."

"Well, you have to go to school," she says, scowling at me. "Isn't that right?"

"Yes," I say. "We'll talk to your teacher."

"Mrs. Melltz likes her better than she likes me."

"It doesn't matter," my wife says. "You have to learn to put up with these things. To cope. That's part of what school is for. To learn to cope. I'm going to drop you off at school and then do the shopping before I go to work."

"How's work?" I say.

"If you tried it, you might know," she says.

Before I can fashion a retort cutting enough to convey a fraction of the resentment I feel, I've bolted into the living room. The dilapidated old couch welcomes me, and I'm glad to have actual wooden walls between myself and the vindictiveness I know she is spewing all over the glittering kitchen. I can hear her slamming cabinet doors and pots and dishes, and I decide to ignore her by reading the newspaper, which is lying all over the flowered carpeting, as if the pages have exploded.

On my hands and knees, I begin returning the paper to its original organization. Sorting pages, identifying numbers and sections, I pause to stare at the photo of a large man pointing toward distant mountains. Who is he? I wonder. A nearby column of text refers to an escalating number of rabid raccoons. But the grand, tawny face of this man immortalized with his elegant gesture into the mountains is not pertinent to raccoons. The photo I'm looking at is unrelated to the words I'm reading, and I catch a whiff of cryptic significance emerging from this dissonant juxtaposition. I'm rooting around, trying to find a photo of the raccoons or the start of the story about the man and the mountain. I'm leafing pages, discarding and rearranging, when the pace of my actions slows before the emergence of a startling fact. There's something unique and illuminating to be gleaned from the examination of an opinion or sentiment while one is ignorant of the event to which the text is referring. Even more informative are the consequences produced by the random assignment of any picture to any statement. Such mismatches are metaphorical, poetic, magical, their effects electric.

Now I'm crawling about tossing the sheets of paper I thought to order into increasingly innovative connections. Faces gaze moodily out at me, as if uneasy with their unfamiliar context. This is the puzzle of the world, and the secret I have found is that the order is in the disorder and the more I scurry about the more I understand the way in which things commonly considered to be independent actually share a relevance that only increasing the chaos of their relations expresses. From the mouth of the sedate and formally attired politician, murderous sentiments flow. The jolly corpulent housewife speaks of space conquest. The burned and ravaged child pronounces on the perfect recipe for sword-fish. A one-armed hobo with clothing like a rain of rags gestures to emphasize the essential point of his philosophy of child rearing. The wild-eyed, thick-necked outlaw with his tattooed biceps shining through the tatters of his T-shirt declares that strip mining must be stopped.

Turning a page, I feel in the company of a greater truth than mere reporting can accomplish, my critical faculties so refashioned that I am dissatisfied by the depiction of a conservative politician in a conserva-tive suit pontificating on foreign policy to a bespectacled prime minister from England. Scooping up all the papers I can manage, I elevate them toward my face like a kneeling priest raising hallowed objects. Then I throw them. What I want is to see! And to see now! And if not the brutish beast of wisdom, then at least some sign of him, the totems that must arise where he has been, or is about to be.

The airborne sheets fall past me at different speeds. One still rises as the others are in full descent. I watch them, awaiting their next dis-closure. The last to touch down is a rough ball that wobbles to rest beside a relatively unwrinkled double sheet. Several inches along the border are folded up, forming a kind of backdrop for a quarter-page black-and-white photograph of a bearded motion picture actor best noted for his capacity for playing sad sacks. Standing on a rooftop in an urban setting, he gestures across a vista of newsprint toward another photograph, which, when I see it, startles me.

Though I may have commenced this enterprise in playful innocence, I must now proceed with daring. If not an exhibition of wisdom, this unexpected photo certainly contains a kind of truth, for what it displays are facts. A charred and fire-gutted house crumbles. Smoke twines upward out of embers still smoldering. The remnants of the chimney teeter over the scorched waste of a sofa near the shattered half of a dining room table. This rubble seems an ancient ruin, an archaeological find unrelated to the local case of arson and murder depicted in the text of the article, whose impersonal tone meets all the demands of reportorial convention.

Bowed over on my knees in order to read, I'm like a civilization into which inimical data has been introduced. I'm looking down at the tiny black words spread like particles of poison over the page. What am I to feel in response to what I'm seeing? Am I to revise my beliefs to accommodate this photo and these words? I feel that I am—I feel that I am to alter my point of view. But how? Before I can even begin, I will have to determine exactly the principles and choices and events that shaped my past. And how can I be certain that the forces I discover are actually the ones I'm looking for? What if my history is dominated by cunning, deceit, and malevolence, while I declare it a matter of sincerity, honesty, compassion?

I tell myself to address bravely, or at least stoically, the rigors I am now facing, for they are testimony to the importance of my project. They are barriers shielding a fortress that I must breach to get the treasure. Led by my icy intellect, my fierce opinions and savage theories will be warriors breaking through the walls to drag the truth before me. Maintaining the judicial impartiality of an archaeologist pursuing footprints through a jungle, I will search every inch of my past until I understand the significance of this moment, probing even the murk of my own prehistory, if I have to, where I will find that I disappear. I will wheel into the opposite direction, the future, where I will find that I disappear. And at this juncture, the fossil of my skeleton ending up a sketch of chemicals on a rock, will I learn the lesson that such desolation demands? That something basic in my premise is in error—that first of all there is an assumption and second of all it's in error. By inference, the study of one's life is the study of the larger, all-encompassing chronicle, but both are folly because there's nothing really there. That's what I learned this morning. It's just a cascade of events, a flux of light, a storm of sensation, but no story, no proper sequence to be recovered should the course of things have become twisted—no epic tale to be a part of, no inherent progress, sequence, history, no elegant and brutal pageant unfolding to the denouement of destiny. There is just me kneeling here clutching and balling up sections of newspaper while my thoughts, my postulates and questions, collide and reshape themselves.

I let the pages drop, hoping to discard along with them a certain murkiness gnawing at me.

"Please don't expect me to clean this mess up," my wife says.

She's behind me, and I don't have to turn to see the disgust in her eyes.

"What are you doing?" she says. "You're throwing the papers all over the room."

"You really shouldn't talk to me like that. In that tone," I say. "I can see what I'm doing. You're the one who doesn't know what I'm doing."

"You're not fooling anybody."

"What?"

"Oh, the hell with you," she snarls, and storms from view.

I'm trying to do something; I'm struggling to understand something. I go down to the basement but hover at the entranceway, peering into the moist dark. Back in the kitchen, I open the door and look out. The green of the landscape rises into the bleak sky, which seems to curtail the light and color like a lowered windowshade.

Eventually I enter the attic, a cramped, low-roofed room. Cardboard boxes are piled on top of old chairs; there are trunks and suitcases, a radio with yellow, dusty tubes. Sunlight radiates so fiercely off the rafters it makes the wood seem smeared with gold.

"Why did you come up to the attic?" she says.

I refuse to look at her, hoping that my rudeness will compel her to leave me alone. I'm infuriated that she's followed me. For a time I stand glaring at the wall, while her continuing presence is registered in the heat of her breathing on the back of my neck. I turn, squinting at her. "I just came up here to look for something, and it's none of your business. It's a personal matter."

"Listen to me," she says.

I turn away and start shoving boxes about.

"I'm thinking of moving back to the city," she says. "I'm suffering. We both are. And there's no point to it—I don't know what the point of hanging on is—it's only getting worse."

I'm lifting old clothes from the recesses of several cardboard boxes. I feel I'm about to come upon a significant misplaced item.

"I mean, what good does it do to pretend?" she says. "We should separate for a while. I can't bear it here. The woods, the woods. I hate it here. I mean, I thought when we moved—and I think that you thought it, too—that when we moved, we might find a way to—I don't know what—salvage things. But it isn't working. You're miserable. Look at you. You can't work. I mean, marriages fall apart. There are worse things."

Memories dance in the dust, prompted by my disturbance of these garments. I'm feeling awful, discovering baby clothes once worn by Tobias and old trousers that were mine in happier days. I see a scarf that I remember once provoked a pang of love as my wife flung it casually about her throat one night as we strode from our apartment onto the city streets to hail a cab and go to a movie.

"I know you've found somebody here," she says. "You're out all the time, out at night—behaving so desperately. It's sad. I'm sad for both of us. I mean, I know you're having an affair and I don't really—I mean, not really—blame you. But you're suffering. I'm suffering. You owed me, I thought—I mean, I had affairs in the city—I didn't think you knew, but obviously you did. I mean, when you came up with the idea of moving up here, I realized that you did know and you were trying to defuse it all. I mean, I thought—I think we both thought that coming up here, getting away from those people—it doesn't matter who—I think that we thought we could start anew. But it isn't working. You can't say that it is. No one could."

"Do you remember the night we went to that movie, it was a children's movie, but we didn't know it until we got inside and it started?"

A pained expression flies across her face. She's staring at me out of a desolation moving through her like a hook.

"You wore this scarf," I say, gesturing with the scarlet blur of the cloth. It whispers in the air.

"Fond memories are no help for us. Don't you know that? We're beyond that now, for God's sake."

Closing my eyes, I feint toward the wall, then spin in the opposite direction, which takes me past her as she steps backward, looking startled. I'm almost out the door.

"You're going?"

With each succeeding instant I am falling deeper under some eerie influence buried in this room but unloosed by her words and my rummaging in the clothes.

"I'm sleepy," I say, and go, leaving her behind me, stunned and mute but railing away in silent condemnation. I can feel her spite and abhorrence following after me like so many miserable henchmen dispatched to badger and degrade me.

In the bathroom, I pee and then wash my hands and face. I head for the living room, where I plan to clean up the newspapers. I want to eliminate any and all legitimacy in her complaints. Her assessment of our marriage has provoked an anxiety in me, like a scalding metal worming through my stomach. This encounter has shown her capacity for trickery to have disarmingly subtle variations. The sentiments she managed to rouse in me in the attic were soft and nostalgic. Now I look up, and she's in the doorway studying me. Then she raises her camera, aiming it directly at me.

"Not now," I say.

The flashbulb flowers, a bulge of light that fills the room.

"I have my project," she says. "I'm not going to give up everything just because you've decided to ruin our lives."

"What project?"

"My photography class. That's what. If you have to know. That's the project I'm talking about."

"Liar."

"You're the liar."

Her indignation propels her back into the kitchen. I'm standing there with my arms full of newspapers, which I transfer across the room just as I was planning to do before her interruption. I place them neatly on the end table, patting the edges even.

Passing the kitchen on my way upstairs, where I hope to rest, I glance in and see her seated at the table, bent over a notebook, a ballpoint pen jutting from her fingers. The book's blue cover is open, the white pages ruled by fine black lines. I freeze in the doorway, trying to remember whether or not I anticipated her doing this, or something like this— taking pictures, writing things down, gathering evidence. I feel that I did. I feel that in the next few seconds she's going to turn to me, smiling. She's going to point the pen at me, flexing her fingers, and then she will rise and come closer and pat my hair, as she asks, What are your plans for the rest of June? I need to know your plans for the rest of the month.

"What are you doing?" I say.

She acknowledges me with a disgusted glance, the turn of her head managed on a grudging pivot.

"What's wrong with you?" I say.

Suddenly she begins to scribble, her head fixed intently, her shadow concealing her endeavor. In a vigorous flurry, her hand races across the page and back again. "Just go to sleep if you're going. Didn't you say you're going to sleep?"

"No."

"You did too."

"What are you writing?"

"You said you were tired and that you were going to bed and then you went downstairs and messed around with the newspapers."

"What are you writing?"

"None of your business."

"Is it about me?"

"No."

"You're taking pictures and you're writing things."

"It has nothing to do with you."

"I think it does."

"Of course you do."

"What is it?"

"I'm taking a class in photography and I'm supposed to keep notes, too, about some of the things I take pictures of."

"But what are you writing?"

"I'm trying to understand what's happening to us."

"You can't."

"I'm trying. *Trying*. I used the word very consciously. I didn't suggest I was getting anywhere. Just go to sleep, why don't you. It has nothing to do with you, really. Not really."

"You don't know what's going on inside of me."

"I never said I did."

"You don't know what I'm thinking."

"What?" Her attention is riveted on me. I've clearly struck a nerve. To dramatize the outlandish nature of my remark, she sets the pencil down and amplifies the disdain of her stare. "It's not about what you're thinking. Everything is not about you, you know. It's about what I'm thinking. I have my own ideas, you know. I have ideas. I can write them down if I want to. They're my ideas. And I can write down what I think. And what I think you're thinking. I can do that. Or what you say. What we say. What you wear. I can write those things down and try to understand them if I want to. You wear that overcoat. I mean, you act like you're cold. You pretend you're cold. Just let me alone."

I try to imagine her purpose. I must understand the function of this document in her overall plan. Having turned away in a reflex compliance to her chiding, I hear her laugh behind me, but I continue to move away. I hear the scraping of the pen point accelerate. She's writing about me. She's writing down her thoughts, assumptions, theories. Her memories, all prejudiced, unreliable, false. She's misquoting me, misinterpreting my every move, misrepresenting me with some invented phantasm of her own construction. But why? What does she hope to accomplish by this preservation of our deeds and actions?

In the living room, I check to make certain the newspapers are all still in a neat pile. I will burn her journal, I think. I will burn those photos. When she isn't looking. Someday I'll get them and burn them. I can't now. But later, when I have the chance, when I have the strength. But I'm too tired now. The fire rises in my mind, pillars of destruction wrapping around her squirming journal.

I topple into bed, my overcoat still weighing me down like a coiled beast against whose overwhelming heft I flail. I paw at the buttons and the belt, but I cannot break free. I'm asleep before I hit the pillow. Vibrations run through the clustered cells of my brain, setting waves trembling. I drift through a grayish darkness growing darker. I blink my way across a vista of confusion toward a nearing bank of consciousness, a kind of gleaming shelf upon which sits the realization that I have been asleep and now I'm waking up. I lie there for a while, deciding to rest a little before sitting up on the side of the bed to begin my day. Little do I anticipate that when I finally sit up on the side of the bed, I will realize, as I do, that I am still sleeping. I sit there, my feet on the bedroom carpet, my hands in my lap. How far will I sink into this night before my reasonable, objective, discriminatory mind can pluck me out? Each dawning I encounter delivers an ominous tinge to my understanding of where I am and what is possible. With each illusory awakening, I am being lured into a more complicated fabric of dream. Each comatose interlude delivers me into a further awakening in which I sleep: I am being passed from level to level as if from one giant to another by the beings who, situated one below the other, oversee all slumber.

Chapter Twenty

I want to start a new life. Before the day is out I must change my habits, everything I can, my point of view. The situation is critical. At the edge of my bed, I sit with my hands around my shins. I press my nose between my knees. My mood is one of impinging devastation. Though I can't locate or specify the fount from which my dread flows, I feel lost. Like some faulty part of a huge and otherwise magnificent machine, I feel condemned and on the verge of expulsion.

My fingers are squeezing the skin on my leg. As I watch their movement, I see that I'm being diverted from the reorganization I want. I'm sinking deeper into the state I want to escape. Rising to my feet, slowly and carefully, I coach myself to start simple. I will take a shower.

The water is hot, beating on my shoulders and back. It dribbles down my spine. In the gathering puddle at my feet, it splatters. Sometime later I start to shave, laboring to avoid my eyes in the glass. When I peek, having cut my chin, I duck, for the countenance hanging in the steamy sheen is stern, judicial, unforgiving. I stick a wad of toilet paper onto the bloody welt, and then, as the feeling that I'm going to puke rises up in me, I scurry across the room to my bed.

Lying down, my dripping body soaks the sheets. I'm fighting to determine the first and most important of my goals. It's hard, like looking into a snowy glare. I need a list. I want to do what's right. I want people to like me, and to know I'm working hard to set things right.

A little later I descend to the kitchen, where I boil water and make a cup of instant coffee before settling with a notepad at the table to begin formulating an agenda. That's what I need. The unease in which I woke this morning has convinced me that I dare not venture from the house without strict guidelines. I must have an orderly and detailed description of my tasks, a sequence and a timetable. For the best results, I should estimate the time necessary for each task and then allot a few extra minutes. The most useful sequence would be one drawn from the natural order of the various buildings to which I must travel to perform the unrelated deeds whose unifying factor is my well-being. Rather than trying to find a pattern inherent in the tasks themselves, I'll progress according to the locations of the places I need to visit. Such a method suggests that I start at the church situated about a mile west of where I live. The ruddy brick walls support the rising steeple, a silver dome and cross.

Sitting in my kitchen, I watch the pencil fidget in my fingers, drawing doodles and designs and leaving words adjacent to numbers. Scudding clouds reduce the morning sun to a grimness like the unhappy hours twilight can seem to bring, and looking out the window, I worry that all hope for the rest of my life depends on the fulfillment of my scheme.

The church door opens to let me enter, and I move at a reverential pace, my urgency coiled beneath a willed restraint. Sunlight streams through the painted glass emblazoning the images of the saints absorbed in their endeavors. They kneel; they implore the heavens; they beatifically suffer arrows; they commune with birds and squirrels. I know that going to church normally involves companions and a ceremony, the priest or minister conducting a service for a crowd, and I regret their absence. I close my eyes and bow my head and hope I'm praying. I have the pose exactly, my eyes lowered, the palms of my hands pressed together, the fingers pointing up. If a pose is praying, then I'm praying, even though my head is empty. There's mainly a stillness modified by a slight hissing and muttering. Glancing at my watch, I see it's time to go.

On my way up the aisle, I detour to a tiny altar in the corner. It's hewn from rich brown wood and covered with a lacy cloth, like frosting on a chocolate cake. I drop eight pennies and three quarters into the collection box and light a devotional candle. Kneeling again, I beg for help through every pore, my tissues straining. The pulsebeats in my temples resound like little hammerblows chipping away at my brain.

When I reach the street, I regret the emptiness of the church. No one knows that I have prayed and given money, that I've been to church. No one has seen how hard I'm working. I hasten to my car and slam the door. I start the engine and check my list. I button my coat against the chill.

At the drugstore in the center of town I buy half a dozen newspapers flown in from a number of nearby major cities. It's the duty of every citizen to keep abreast of world affairs, I know. With the fat and boisterous saleswoman behind the counter, I chat a little, as neighborly people like to do. I will scour these pages when I go to eat my lunch later on. Having a newspaper to read when you're alone in a restaurant is an ordinary, reassuring thing to do, a sign that one is at ease and self-possessed.

"Come again," she says, as I turn to leave.

A beggar in ragged trousers, a seedy coat, and shoes so dilapidated that his toes stick out is staggering about beside my car. His presence seems to justify the imposition of a minor revision on my schedule. After moving the planned stops at the restaurant, the Salvation Army, and the library to later slots, I advance the item "Charitable Donation" up to the present. For several minutes I offer this dottering creature a lengthy explanation whose point is how much I understand his plight. I pat his shoulder and hand him three dollars. Good people give to the poor, I know.

Eight blocks west, at the Salvation Army dumpster, I drop off the four shopping bags of clothing scrounged from our attic and basement. At the finish of this task, I am stalled by a dizzying rush in my blood, a sickening, pointless commotion that leaves me woozy. I feel almost drunk and hope that my discomfort is nothing more than a signal that the time has come for lunch.

The diner, *BIG GUYS*, in which I've spent some pleasant hours in the past, is located at the opposite end of town. I drive with the car windows open, hoping that the air I gulp will refresh me. Seated on a corner stool, I select two of the papers and place them on the counter, ordering

coffee, toast, and scrambled eggs. The papers are a bizarre and unnerving harvest of accidental mayhem. Airplanes are raining from the sky.
Over Nova Scotia, one Cessna hit another. In the cloudless heights
above Nebraska, a commercial flight plummeted four thousand feet
before leveling off with an elderly woman dead of a heart attack inside.
Just west of the California coastline, a helicopter vanished in the waves.
As I turn the pages, they emit a whisper, a ritualistic hiss. Cars are
shown to be no more trustworthy on the road than the planes were in
the air. From one end of the continent to another, collisions of every
possible combination erupt and then, as if having left some aspect of
havoc unexplored, they reoccur. Locally, a school bus slams into a tree.
On the entertainment page, movie advertisements are an array of guns
and knives, suggesting disaster. The sports pages announce broken legs,
shattered knees. Teams smother one another or go butchered from the
field. Buried in secondary paragraphs and parenthetical clauses I find
vows of vengeance and carnage.

The obituary page intensifies my hallucinatory state. The black-and-
white columns interspersed with little pictures are a macabre array.
Faces range in age from the glowing gaze of a child to an old man whose
eyes seem set in a brittle shard of ice. I feel as if I'm looking at an edifice,
a kind of wall, and each report is a window in a building, each story and
accompanying photo the final tally for some human being's life, and one
by one these lighted windows are going out. A doctor vanishes. An
architect falls. An ex-governor departs his state. A chemist dissolves. A
judge, along with an innovative entrepreneur and a physicist, all slip the
scene. Who will tend these families? Who will do these jobs? Is this an
ordinary day? The widow of a famous dancer steps out behind her
vanished mate. A boy of twelve is destroyed in the car driven by a
drunken teenage girl, the both of them naked. A drowned hobo is found
enmeshed in willows at the shoreline of a pond. A woman, recently
divorced, is murdered, her house set aflame at the edge of a small town
less than a dozen miles away.

I look up from my reading. I glimpse the ceiling. A sheen of fluores-
cence off the tubes of light sends my gaze glancing out the window. In
the afternoon declining there, I half expect to spy hordes of souls
scurrying through the overcrowded sky. With my toast and scrambled
eggs before me, I sit and stare.

At my elbow a man turns to his companion and says, "The price of damn near everything is enough to make anybody go off their rocker these days."

"The weather! The weather," mutters someone in astonishment.

"The weather's just goin' through a weird phase, that's all. That's all."

"Well, I've had enough of it. It's nuts."

Is it possible that I am not alone in my preoccupations? Is it possible everyone has madness and the weather on his mind? I pay my bill and exit into the day, feeling anxious. Clouds, collected in a lowering mass, are muffling the light in a leaden drift along the horizon. At the corner, where I pause to button up my coat, I freeze, startled at first and quickly alarmed. A stranger, a tall young man in a blue pin-striped suit, is darting across a well-tended lawn across the street. He disappears behind a white frame house. On the porch, an empty swing sways in the breeze. The shutters on the windows are green, and I'm thinking, Deadly events must have a deadly agent. The speed with which that stranger scooted out of sight tells me this could have been the flight of a fugitive, his elegant garb and youthful figure a ploy to obfuscate his dark, hideous nature. Could he be the one haunting our lives and dreams, the cause of all the disasters in the paper, the force behind all our troubles? Like some diabolical hypnotist, could he have put us into our individual enchantments long ago, leaving us without a clue to the truth of our terrible condition until this instant in which I glimpsed him and wondered who he was, this stranger? Is he the stranger, the terrible stranger? Have I been hypnotized? Is everyone in the world under a hex? He's fleeing me, leaving me.

I'm searching through my pockets for my list at the same time that I'm trying to focus my analytical faculties on the troubling possibilities I've found. My stomach feels full of air and fear, a sensation like icy gas. My hands are pawing about, as if on their own accord, as they rotely dig into my pockets. When they lift the list before my eyes, I barely recognize it. It feels annoying and intrusive, a kind of bolt of static scrambling my immediate concerns. Next on my schedule is the bank. I breathe deeply, struggling in the contradictions of the moment. I have to sort my priorities. I have to reconnect with the logic and merit of my detailed itinerary. Even though the whereabouts and identity and activities of this stranger are burning questions, I have to remember that these guidelines in my fist were established to shepherd me through exactly the kind of tangled circumstances in which I'm now struggling. The reason that I made this list was to protect me from the enticements of whim and impulse, so they could not drag me off into some venture whose powers would lie beyond my ability to resist or anticipate or comprehend, because that's where danger lies for me and I know it.

Were it not for the restrictions of my list, I would be gone already, having raced off around the corner of that white house, chasing that stranger. I would be over there out of sight, pursuing a course whose only basis was my failed attempt to defuse the storm of conjectures prompted by his passing. But I'm not. I'm here where I belong, managing to do what I set out to do. And I'm relieved, even though I'm panting with the effort. The prudence in the idea of my list leaps out at me with undeniable clarity. Because of it, I'm doing what I should—what's good for me—what I set out to do. I'm going to the bank, where I have important matters to attend to. I have responsibilities at the bank. I have accounts.

The teller, a woman wearing glasses and a brown pantsuit, examines me, and though she's very sad, she smiles, her muted mood like a disturbance in the air between us. To test my new theory on the universality of our concerns, I say, "Isn't the weather mad today? It's crazy."

"Sure is," she smiles, adding a little flurry of genial twitches. "And our air conditioner is on the blink, too. Wouldn't you know it?"

"That's a break."

"Not the way I look at it. But everybody's a joker today, so why should you be an exception?"

"It's just that everybody's concerned with the same things from different perspectives, don't you think?"

"Except we're the only ones with our air conditioner broken. Anyway, can I help you?"

It's as if she's sensed the urgency underlying my need to do my duty at her bank and she's trying to hasten me along. "Well, yes," I say, feeling grateful for her help. I know that succeeding at such an ordinary task as banking will inculcate the ordinary into me and me into the ordinary, which is what I want. I ask for all my papers, my records, and she looks at me compassionately.

"You mean your 'file,' " she says.

"Yes. It's my file I want," I say. "You're right. Thank you."

The seconds pass slowly as I await her return, and then I hasten to a large table, where I settle myself and begin studying my accounts. When the numbers begin to confuse me, I try to remain calm. The codes slink back and forth, withholding themselves from easy access, something occult peering out of them. The numbers on the papers, which represent the world of money in my life, rise off the page and float about and rearrange themselves in columns of their own shifting invention.

I try to will them back to their original order, concentrating as if my mind can coerce them. I have responsibilities to take care of. I have a son. He needs schooling. There's a mortgage on our house. I'm a landowner, a citizen. For a long time, I sit at the table on which my documents are spread. I slip into a haze of thought that I find consuming and consoling, a kind of misty commiseration in which I sink, as if I have been swallowed in the muck of someone else's sentimental concern for me.

When someone taps my shoulder, I look up into the disgruntled, jowly face of the burly bank guard, who appears to have just awoken from a deep sleep: "Closing time," he says, rubbing his bloodshot eyes.

"I'm finished."

"You been sittin' here a long time."

"I had a lot to figure out."

"Yeh, but you been here a long time. Never saw anybody do that before."

"Never?"

"Most people are in a hurry."

"I was in a hurry. I just had a lot to do."

"Hope you got it done."

Returning to the teller, I move with haste, wondering what took me so long.

"You been here hours," she says, chuckling.

"I had a lot to do."

"Time to go home."

Outside, the late-afternoon light is interlaced with somber clouds. As I step from the building, I know that the bank guard and teller have moved to a window to peer out at me, their ongoing interest trying to confirm or disprove the suspicions they're feeling about me.

I stuff my hands into my pockets and eliminate all hesitation from my stride. I know better than to give even the briefest backward glance in their direction. They will see me marching purposefully across the lot. I want them to watch me climb into my car, put on my seat belt, and then, with a degree of caution exactly suited to my circumstances, drive off. The unease my overlong stay has aroused in them will be erased by my calm behavior. They will think I'm regular. They will consider me ordinary. They will think I'm fine. But I'm not. I'm desolate. I'm lonely. I'm shivering. With nothing more on my list, I don't know what's going on. With nothing more on my list, anything might happen.

At the outskirts of town I pull onto the shoulder and cut the engine. I open my window and determine that the whispering sound is the wind in the field. Looking out, I see the grass that wasn't crushed by my arrival rising up around my tires. Looming in the east, the dark throws itself at me, tightening my breath. A rumbling that might be thunder is the approach and passage of a monstrous truck and trailer, and rushing in the opposite direction, a car shoots by, the driver obscured except for his hands lightly resting on the wheel. Who's that? I think, my fearful certainty that it's the same young man I saw just before I went to the bank sounding an irrefutable note.

I start the engine and hit the gas, and my vehicle shoots up from the inclined sod onto the pavement. The tires, freely whirling in the grass, catch hold with a jolt, catapulting me down the road, the rubber squealing.

The velocity of my quarry, combined with the time it took me to react, has given him a significant head start. Silverish in color, his auto drops out of sight some hundred and fifty yards ahead. The dusk is deploying inky swells throughout the waiting landscape. A glance into my rearview mirror shows me a bloody sunset like a whirlpool. I look ahead, then back at the mirror, where a huge wild eye burns in the glass.

At the peak of a distant concrete bulge, the reappearance of my adversary demands a burst of speed from me. The stranger and his silver car have sounded a major chord, and in response my heart is racing, my nerves sparking. The road sweeps on before me, narrow and straight. Stomping the gas, I plunge into a valley and then up the following crest. But I can no longer see him.

For half a dozen miles I race on, my panic held in check, fences blurring by on either side. Cows attend me, mournfully. Sheep pose on the ascending curves of grass-laden hills, a gory color seeping up at their feet as if something bleeds in the soil. I can feel the earth rolling under the wheels as it turns away from the disappearing light in the east behind me. The dark is deepening everywhere. I turn my headlights on, but he's nowhere to be seen. He's gone. Slowing down until I've nearly stopped, I turn into an ill-kept dirt road cut into a field, intending to reverse my direction. My headlights flash over a dilapidated wheelbarrow leaning among the stalks of corn. I swing back onto the road determined to retrace my course. I switch on the radio, and the impersonal yet charming newscaster informs me of a fire in a hospital where the helpless burned. At the site of an earthquake in a tiny country I've never heard of before, he says survivors are reported digging toward the diminishing cries of buried children.

Flicking the dial to escape this macabre litany, chance lands me on violins, rising in ethereal splendor, and just then a cornfield ahead to my left blooms with a gigantic, conical illumination. The stalks shimmer. They glow like X-rayed bones. Out from their midst comes a rushing wall of light, which I recognize, after a heart-stopping instant of violin-saturated confusion, as the advance of an automobile. Across my path the plunging beams strain to the limits of their wattage. Extending from the front of the car like two huge poles, they drill a pit into the dark into which the luminescence pours. Directly in my path, the silver car pauses, a shiver running through its metallic flanks, as if the engine has stalled for a millisecond. With a roar, it springs forward across the road and into the tract of corn to my right. My own headlights crash into the reconstituted dark with nothing to reflect them. To my right the silver car is a tremulous scarlet, snaking off like a torch flung down a well.

Braking, I retreat and wheel to the right. Ahead the taillights cavort. What seemed a solid wall of corn is penetrated by the surprise of a narrow road. The music on the radio is mounting in a tangle of sophisticated passion. Though I'm driving with all the skill I can find, the silver car is lengthening its lead, unleashing speeds I cannot match.

When we leave the dirt road and leap onto an interval of concrete, I hope to make a gain. I grind the pedal against the floor, but all I manage is to keep the position I've established. Though the violins are in a climactic frenzy, their ambitions enhanced by the support of cellos and the thunderous approval of drums, I fail to close the gap. The car is little more than a metallic blur when it suddenly seems to leap back toward me. With such abruptness that both right side wheels rise off the road, the vehicle veers to the left and vanishes beneath the shredded shadow of a willow tree. Even though I start to pump the brakes right then, I almost miss the turn, squealing and downshifting.

Entering the same gateway that he took, I find a road full of potholes ascending the erratic terrain before me. I will have to be less aggressive here. In these rutted twists, I could easily break an axle or drive into the ditch. Straining to see to the very limits of my headlights, I am startled when I exit from the lane of dense, intertwined limbs. Suddenly I'm on a gravel driveway headed directly toward the gigantic ruins of a house. The silver car is nowhere to be seen. I tap the brakes and start to halt. A scorched wooden beam slanting upward through the beacons of my headlights begins to teeter at the center of the rubble. With a rumbling slowness, it slides through the air, attaining a furious speed in the last inches of its fall, so that the ground quakes with impact, as does my car. My heart begins to ache, like a tooth with rot squeezing through its nerves. Smoke billows from the ashes to envelop the fireplace and its half-fallen chimney, the only structures remaining. From the shadows beside the broken wall where the smoke is dissolving in the dark, a figure is emerging. Skirting the border of my headlights, this phantom blooms with a bulb of illumination that must be a flashlight aimed at me. Certain that I am watching the approach of the driver of the silver car, I fear I have been lured into a trap. But I sit there, fatalistic and interested. Crossing my spellbound gaze, a man appears in my headlights and then vanishes behind the glare of the flashlight aimed into my car, but it's not who I anticipated. Upon responding to the rapping at my window, I stare up into the glare, whose abrupt removal leaves me looking into the belligerent eyes of a policeman.

"Lemme see your license and registration."

"Of course," I say. I turn off the radio and do as I've been told.

"What are you doin' here?"

"What?"

"Sick bastard."

"Excuse me?"

"You're about the tenth car tonight. People," he says, disgustedly. "This is private property."

"Did another car just go by?"

"I was in the woods takin' a leak. I hadda take a leak. I come out, you were here. You better get goin'. Don't you people have no respect for the dead?"

"I do," I say.

"Then get outa here. The body ain't here no more, anyway."

"What happened here?"

"You don't know, huh?" he says, meaning to mock me for reasons I don't understand. "Then what're you doin' here?"

"I got lost, I guess."

"Don't you read the papers?"

"Of course," I say.

"There's some lunatic runnin' loose."

"Everybody's worried," I say. "The weather's been crazy, too." I nod, looking about as if to find evidence of the madness with which we are all concerned.

"I haven't noticed."

"And the prices. We were talking about it at the diner," I say. These points of agreement please me, as we touch upon our common themes of weather and insanity. "It's everywhere," I say.

"You better get out of here."

Beyond him, I glimpse other figures moving in the surrounding forest. Their flashlights flicker like the tails of fireflies. From a group of nearby evergreens, a tall angular shape is breaking loose and gliding toward us. Behind it moves an utterly contrasting form, a rounded blob stuffed under a policeman's hat.

"Just get going and keep going," says the man at my window. "The driveway loops around and will take you right back out. Just follow it."

"All right."

"And don't come back."

"No," I say.

I drive off slowly. My mood is somber. The scorched timber and crumbling brick, the ashen tatters of the couch, the coals on the floor, the half-burned sticks will occupy a section of my memory indelibly. Although I arrived in my pursuit of the stranger feeling hopeful, even optimistic, that I might catch him, I am leaving feeling haunted, and more than a little disconsolate.

Back on the paved roadway, I increase my speed and reach to switch on the radio. But at the touch of the dial, my fingers rebound from the prospect of drawing additional horrors down from the airwaves and into the radio's crystals and speakers. Where there are evil consequences, I think, there must be evil agents.

Along the road, the trees waver. Behind these brutal deeds whose evidence has pursued me through the day, there must be a brutal cause, I think. In my rear window sits the burning silver of the moon.

When I halt on the driveway alongside our house, I switch the headlights off and note that the ground-floor windows contain a cozy warmth. As I climb from my car, I'm eager to enter, hoping to find dinner cooking on the stove, the hearthlike shimmer and banter of the television in the air, my wife bustling around in the throes of domestic frenzy, my son at play. Springing up the stairs to the back porch, I open the door and find them screaming. At first I think their confrontation is a prank performed to tease me. I'm certain they will transform with a show of glee when my distress is extreme enough. Her fist, mottled and shaking, is knotted in his hair, and her eyes leak a kind of venom. "You don't know what he said to me!" she screams.

Tobias is wailing, his little body quivering as if the fingers on his head are firing electric stabs of current through him.

"It was awful; it was so awful, the little beast."

"What?"

"You've got to give him a spanking! You've got to!"

"What did he say?"

"Just spank him! You've got to! He's too big for me!"

"All right." She drops him on the floor. He's frantic, his legs splayed out as he flails to escape, but his panic has made him so uncoordinated, he merely beats the linoleum with his fists and scrapes his knees, as might a fish gouging dirt with its fins. When I seize him by the shoulders, he squeals. If I have alternatives, I don't know what they are. For his sake and my own, I have to seem her ally. I must deceive her. Besides, I know that the husband obeys the wife in such circumstances. The father beats the son. Though this situation is not on my agenda, I avert my eyes while my free hand leaps to loosen my belt. Just as I whip it from my pants, he erupts from my grasp. I strike out, hitting him in the face. On the floor he groans. I drag him to a chair and fling him across my knees and hold him there, his buttocks stuck up at my face. Rearing back, I smack my hand down. When he starts screaming, I start to scream just like him, all the while looking at her to keep the count as my hand crashes up and down. "Is this enough?" I yell.

She shakes her head, her eyes offended by my ignorance.

"How much more?" I cry.

"Just do it."

I'm using both my hands. My elbows hum, the bones filled with weird vibrations. The muscles in my shoulders ache. His voice has vanished, swallowed in a guttural gagging as might rise from the struggles of a stopped-up sink.

"Now?" I yell to her.

"No!"

I pound away.

"All right," she says.

My release is instantaneous. He goes tumbling to the floor, his constricted throat emitting a hissing noise as if he leaks. In spite of my best efforts to avoid his eyes, his outraged glance finds and blasts me.

"Thank you," she says.

"Sure."

"Where are you going?"

I'm headed for the door. To be away is my only goal, to escape his blubbering, the twitching of his little heels.

"Could you go to the store for me?" she asks.

"Sure."

"I need things from the mall."

"All right."

"Wait," she yells.

"What?"

"You need my list."

"Yes, of course."

Behind her Tobias lies on the floor, his limbs aquiver, his gaze the hollow-eyed stare of the mortally ill.

"Good-bye," I say.

"He deserved it."

"I know."

I shut the door, and run for my car.

Chapter Twenty-one

The jangling turns me to look at the pay phone located in the shade under the artificial hemlock tree. Even though I intend to keep on walking deeper into the granite extravaganza of the shopping mall, I stop and stand there, looking at the phone. I'm attracted by the maze of corridors ahead of me, the coruscating panes of glass into which hordes of shoppers stare, spellbound by desire. Overhead a skylight holds the moon shedding a bluish wash, the lunar craters like insects impacted on the surface, a halo ringing the circumference in a web.

My hand startles me, leaping out to snatch the phone and slam it against my ear. Now my thoughts disintegrate and I am examining the air for the power that moved my hand. My wife's voice is saying over and over that she loves me. "I love you," she says. "I love you, I love you."

For the first few seconds I experience her strictly as a voice in my head. Then, almost as an echo, I hear her speak aloud. So similar is this second manifestation to my inner preview that a veil of confusion falls over both versions of her speech. In a further complexity, a subterranean echo haunts her words with a kind of nattering hum.

"I mean," she says, "why don't you believe me?"

"I do," I say.

"I can tell by your tone you don't. Come over."

"What?"

"C'mon."

"Now?"

"Please. I want to see you."

"I have to go shopping."

"Stop teasing."

"I'm not."

"Just stop it."

"I just want to know what you mean. Do you mean before or after I do the shopping?"

"What?"

"I'm at the mall."

"Who is this?"

"I have your list. Is that what you're calling about?"

"You aren't Bobby."

"What?"

"You aren't Bobby."

"No, no, no. I'm your husband. I have your list. I've been looking for the things on it and I've been looking in some of the windows."

"Oh, for crissakes," she says.

"But everyone's doing it. Everyone's doing it. Everyone's looking in the windows."

"Who is this?"

"What's wrong with you? You sent me here!" Perhaps she hangs up because she detects the fury that's subverting the civility with which my manner is held together, the inflections, the ideas, the words, the tone. When I hear the mechanistic insult of the dial tone, I realize she's gone, she's hung up, and everything falls apart. It hurts. I grab my head. My heart is in there—it's beating in my brain. Erupting from a sunken chamber, passions fly, shedding the levels that once repressed them. I look into the cavity of my torso, where my liver, my lungs and kidney, my heart and glands are shaking, their surfaces infected by a widening field of cracks. I seem to be disintegrating and I begin to scream, but like a survivor buried underground. Nothing reaches the surface. I make no actual sound. I bang my fists on my head and, turning, discover half a dozen strangers standing nearby and staring at me. The fact that they've interrupted their errands because of me is alarming.

"There's something wrong with this phone," I yell, hoping to approximate a sort of communal, neighborly concern. "There was somebody on it. My wife, I think. But I wouldn't use it, if I were you. I couldn't really hear her."

From the flow of shoppers streaming in both directions, a man and woman and then a pack of teenagers veer off to join the cluster already eyeing me. At the forefront of this crowd, a large man in a brown vinyl jacket, his chubby legs stuffed in jeans, directs an ominous gesture disguised as a shrug at me, his jacket crinkling as he heaves his shoulders up. His disapproval of me is drastic, even though he tries to hide it. He would punish me if I were at his disposal. He considers me unruly, a troublemaker.

To escape his scrutiny, I pivot, only to encounter the approach of a little band whose doughy faces are somehow intrinsically allied in spite of their apparent variety. They exude both titillation and aversion as they stare at me.

The individual desires that brought all these people to the mall are being displaced by the discovery of an obsession of which they knew nothing when they left their homes. They want to look at me. Facing me, they hiss and murmur. Elbows nudge nearby ribs, provoking automatic smiles. From their increasing mass, these people are drawing a deepening satisfaction whose degree of pleasure seems somehow determined by their number in relation to the distance that separates them from me. They guffaw, sharing a confident interpretation of the moment, their homogeneity growing into an all-embracing agreement among them, a kind of doctrine of the mall in which they are the perfect examples of the way life must be conducted, while I am found repellent and faulty, I am condemned. Their whispering little coalitions reject me, for I live in some other way than they do, their repudiation as degrading as hurled dirt or spit or concrete or shit. By my position as outcast I demonstrate the privilege of their circle, and they beam at me, gratified by my deficiencies.

Then suddenly aflutter, like a flock of birds when one member decides to fly, they begin to point at me and yammer, some turning and shouting to summon stragglers who are still gazing into the diamondlike luster of the display windows.

I don't know what to do. They scare me. I want to leave, but I feel there's something I must do first, that there's something begun between these people and me that must be resolved. If only I had my list, I think, I might know what to do. I can remember it as I drew it up this morning, a piece of paper, lined and written on and folded and stuck into some pocket of my clothing. I'm looking for it unsuccessfully, and now I start looking harder, my hands diving about and tearing at my pants, plunging over and over into my pockets, but I have only my wife's list requesting toilet paper, scrub brushes, paper towels, more film.

People who are tall and fat intermingle in the crowd with others who are short and thin. Some are tall and thin and still others are short and fat. Some are male, many are female. There are young and old and middle-aged people. Predominantly, the shirts the men wear are rectangles of a single color with buttons that are mostly closed, though a few have no buttons and are imprinted with fanciful designs. Hair is long and neat when it isn't long and tangled, or short and neat or short and tangled. A large number of men wear similar-looking blockish garments with hunks of patterned cloth tied about their throats. This kind of garb has a name, but I can't remember it. I used to know it. I still know it, I just can't think of it. Among the women, the majority have printed fabric dropped over them with a hole cut for their heads to stick out so they can see to get around and find their way here to stare at me. And more and more of them are arriving, stirring the mix of their colorful clothing into an autumnal blur.

The rich red on my hands is blood, I realize, as I tenderly investigate my nose. My head aches from my manic pounding. I hurt myself worse than I realized when I hit myself with the phone.

Scanning the first wave of faces, I try to smile. Beyond them are the display windows ablaze with miniature floodlights dramatizing the virtues of the mannequins whose demeanor and fashions, I suddenly realize, are largely the prototypes for the crowd. With their blank eyes and tranquil poses, these statues are paragons of dress and decorum, and even, in a subtly managed way, of emotion. Occasionally I see it happen, the way these gleaming influences work. Someone in the crowd grows confused or worried and he looks around at his companions, but eventually he turns for help to the mannequins in the windows, facing away, sometimes for seconds, sometimes for minutes. When he returns, his uncertainty is gone, his posture transformed by arrogance or ease or vanity, depending on the instruction he received, something painted and plastic in his eyes. But I'm alone and unaided. In the walls of glass and people surrounding me I go unreflected. I have no one to look to for help or advice or assurance. I'm just this cloud of blurred gestures hunting for my list, my arms groping into my pockets and pulling them inside out over and over.

"He belongs in isolation," I hear, though I can't determine who's spoken in such a resonant, impervious voice. But that's exactly where I am and I know it—in the "ice" of my freezing life—in the "oh" of my cries—and the "lay" of where I will soon fall, before the "shun" of the world's repugnance.

"What?" says one of the crowd. His tall angular form is covered by a plaid jacket and blue jeans, and his thinning reddish hair has been plastered forward over his balding pate. "What did you say?" he says. He's stepping toward me.

I try to glimpse the brain behind his eyes. I see a shy and furtive creature peering out. What does he want? Desire has put him into motion. Behind him the crowd is rearranging itself, like pebbles in a pile, the people sliding around until they fill the space he left, and then they settle down, soothed by their restored symmetry and by the hum of heartbeats all around them.

Staring into the blue of the man's eyes, I glimpse a befuddlement very similar to my own. In his smile, I spy a concealed sadness that starts to squirm with embarrassment the instant it feels the force of my interest. Now that he's separated from the others by some distance, he impresses me as quite different from them. After an uneasy moment, he looks back at the people he's left behind, then returns to me. When his shy and tentative manner manages to direct a friendly nod at me, I decide to speak. "What's going on?" I say.

"You mind if I ask you that?"

I whisper a few words to invite him nearer.

"What?" he says.

"I think we've met before—haven't we met?"

"What?"

I keep on whispering. "I think we've met. Where did we meet?"

"Not that I know of."

"You look very familiar. Do I look familiar to you?" I lean close to him, very close, and I'm thinking loudly, You don't have to admit it. I know you can't admit it in front of these others. I understand. But if I'm right and you know me as I feel you do, nod twice.

Though a pulse of unease surfaces and retreats in his eyes, there's no doubt that he nods, while stepping back several paces, and then he nods again.

"I knew it," I say.

"I don't think so."

"But if you didn't remember, you wouldn't know," I say. I'm doing my best to make him feel at ease. The fear in his eyes, so much like my own, seems to affirm his grasp of my situation, which is to some extent his own.

"I have a very good memory," he says.

"So do I," I tell him, unable to quell my growing excitement.

"And you remember me?"

"Yes. Absolutely."

"You've been doing a lot of very funny things here."

"Just joking."

"You punched yourself in the face with the phone."

"Pretty funny, huh?" I bang my right fist into my right eye, followed by my left fist into my temple, and then, in order to climax the matter with a daring finale, I slam the flat of my right hand against my nose. The startled look he fakes is quite convincing. "Go ahead," I advise him. "Laugh. It's okay."

"You live around here?"

"No."

"Where do you live?"

I can hardly keep from laughing, my pleasure is so excruciating. I want to hug this friend with whom I share an old and inexplicable connection. But I restrain myself, because I am aware of how embarrassing it would be for him should I allow the longing in my arms to encircle him in front of this crowd for whom he must pretend an affection while faking a total lack of familiarity with me. Yet I cannot keep myself from hopping up and down, my buoyancy at the rewards of our simple conversation feeling so completely irrepressible.

"I really don't know you," he says.

"I know!" I yell.

We are talking with a coded subtlety that only the deepest of friend-ships can engender, our intimacy sheltered from the boorish stupidity of the crowd behind him.

"These people sent me over to see if you needed some help," he says.

"I know."

"I really don't know you."

"I'm glad they sent you over."

"They're thinking of calling the police."

I burst out laughing at the perfection of our exchange.

"You're hopping up and down, you know."

"No, I'm not."

"You're acting crazy."

"So are you."

"I don't want to talk to you anymore."

"I don't want to talk to you, either," I say, giddy at the ingenuity of our ability to understand each other no matter what we say. As he walks away, I want to stay very near to him because I want to study him and emulate him, and so I duplicate his every movement whether it's a long-legged stride, a flurry of twitches, a woeful shrug.

Ahead of us, the crowd, in its array of mannequin-inspired poses, begins to waver. I note a nearby fountain spuming twin arching sprays of water. When my friend whirls to face me, he grimaces, so I grimace back at him. He pushes me and I push him. He looks away from me and shrugs; I look away from him and shrug.

"Get away," he says.

"Get away," I say.

Arriving at the edge of the crowd, I feel welcomed and relieved even though they are alien to me, because my new friend's going to guide me. By imitating his every mannerism, I will ingratiate myself with the rest of them, winning their approval, rousing an undeniable acceptance. Soon I will be assimilated into their harmonious confeder-ation, our entire assembly studying the spot I used to occupy. But I will be gone. I will have been removed from my loneliness and scorn. I will have been incorporated into their companionship. My happiness at this thought is strong, my feelings overwhelming. Like the innocent bride before her beloved, I look toward the ground, my shameless pleasure at my adoption by these strangers humbling me, and I close my eyes.

But a sudden dizziness sweeps me. Though I fight it, I can't resist for long. I have to look around and pant in order to escape its pressure.

I'm staring into a colorful shifting shape that takes me several seconds to identify as the flowing figures of the crowd reassembling themselves. Apparently having disbanded, the many parts are returning to the whole. Only they are not around me as I expect to find them. They are far away. Gazing through the splattering fountain, a misty partition of bubbles and spray, I see that I have been abandoned. My newfound friends have walked away and left me. The instant my eyes were closed, they made my emotions into an opportunity to sneak off from me, like criminals in the night.

Now I stand with my back to the framed and shiny mannequins seated in their perfect kitchen at the gleaming Formica table, the exact site where I joined the crowd. But the crowd is over by the pay phone. They're milling around across from me, their attitude as cocky and smug as a band of insolent thieves. No wonder I am dribbling snot all over myself.

From the insult of their eyes, I recoil, whirling away. Before me a hallway appears, diminishing to a slot of glass filled with a rectangle of star-filled night. Catapulted by the presence of these traitors at my back, I leap off, hoping to leave them behind, hoping to escape.

In the rhythm of my stride and in the direct access I have to my freedom and the night, I sense a cloudy shape, an idea full of emotion but ephemeral, the passing shape of something. Wavering into focus, it has a brief impact. Sprinting now, I start to see that the events leading up to this moment were not the unrelated autonomous acts I took them for. Appearing random, they were the minutiae of a vast and fortuitous scheme. Concealed in my suffering over the crowd's abandonment were the seeds of my liberation. In order to fool those people, I had to fool myself. It was not their community that I wanted when I entered their ranks. It was access to this hall. What I wanted was the night awaiting me, the swaths of light swooping back and forth beneath the stars. Hidden codes and signals directed my behavior, as if I were receiving orders from the moon. I walked to the crowd and shut my eyes. Like a dog submitting to an irresistible summons, I turned and bounded down this corridor toward my freedom.

Ahead of me glass panels in gunmetal gray doorframes reflect my approaching figure. Beyond this specter, headlights spangle. There I am, the perfect model of myself, my glassy image enshrined in stars and other streaming beacons. I am my own ideal, my own perfect mannequin. My shirt is bloody, my eyes serene, my stride as graceful as a lover gliding to his beloved. Flowing out behind me, my shirttail flaps like the cape of a hero who, having survived a great hazard, is delivered beyond the reaches of his foe to win the maiden of the tale.

As the door arrives, I stretch out my hand to touch my face, and when I press on the bright impression of my ear, the shape of me swings away, opening into the night, and there remains only the real me, galloping into a dark that sizzles with stars. Cars, which I recognize as cars despite the undulating currents of illumination through which they coast, are traveling in every direction. The overhead lamps hover above the excess of light escaping from the mall, their blend an uneven glow probed by the shifting headlights of the cars.

A maroon Oldsmobile with Pennsylvania plates and five teenaged occupants glides past me. I reach and stroke the fins. In the distance I see my own car wedged in among the many other autos aligned as if for sale in this huge parking lot. Although nothing I see indicates that I am pursued, no clattering footsteps or angry shouts, still I know the mob I left behind me is racing after me, and soon they will burst from the door.

Fumbling in my pockets for my keys I find coins and peanuts, an old sock, a tattered ticket stub. My fingers pass through the lining and strike a metallic jumble, like a knife blade or a bullet. Ahead of me a shadow floats through the interior of my car as I withdrew my keys. I feel a premonition, dark and visceral, whose implications keep me walking, because suddenly I know that someone is lurking in my car. My sense of approaching danger has a blunt, disorienting impact. Those who sought to trap me in the mall could have easily observed my arrival and identified my car. The entire ruckus by the fountain could have been a ploy to flush me out. That which I thought was the trap could have easily been a lure to maneuver me into the real ambush here in the desolate parking lot, where I would be alone and unobserved as I fell before the lethal skills of the assassin in my car.

I look behind me, seeking a place to hide. With the haven of my car forbidden, there's nowhere to go. Shoppers, both men and women, glide about the concrete expanse of the lot, some advancing up the stairway to enter the mall, others descending from it. The headlights of half a dozen cars flow in different directions, leaving a netlike after-image in my eye, and I feel I'm about to be trapped in a similar crisscrossed snare.

The car cruising up before me blinks its headlights out, the wheels veering into a space just a little ahead of where I stand. I've been aware of this blue Camaro for a long time now. Minutes ago it passed from the main road to the entrance off to my right. As it prowled the crowded lot seeking an available space, I watched it without knowing why. Now the car door is opening to release its occupant. A quick survey of the area behind me reveals that the bloodthirsty mob is about to emerge and storm across the pavement, where presently almost no one stirs. A few cars are herded together at a distant corner of the concrete, their radiant webs encircling a green trash dumpster. Close by me, the lot is empty.

The driver of the Camaro is female. I see that she is young, yet this is not the most important thing about her. What's important is that she's arriving at this instant. It's her sense of timing, her punctuality that is exhilarating, far more exhilarating than the thin suede coat she wears over a plum-colored blouse stitched at the pockets with maroon thread, and I see how her breasts puff beneath the fabric as if each meaty mound contains a dozen furry mice who breathe. I want to congratulate her on her punctuality, and begin to move forward, my steps banging with a giddy resonance on the concrete. Though I failed to catch sight of her eyes in my first glimpse of her, I trust that I will find their hue and size appealing, their glint and shy retreat delightful, the harsh assertion of her glance a revelation of the passion that lies behind her reserved manner. Having climbed from the car, she stands there looking back into the interior through the half-open door. By the soft slope of her buttocks, as fluid as warm water in a sack, I know that her eyes are intelligent and strong, her will formidable. Though she's not yet aware of my presence, she will recognize me when the moment comes. Something at her center hauls at me. Our imminent meeting is governed by rules whose inevitability equals the force and grace of a mathematical equation. I seem to fail to even touch the ground. In the gray of the foaming sky, the moon peeps out. Like numbers fated to a certain sum, we equal the intersection of this rendezvous. We are lines and we are geometrical. With our cars and lives, with my wife and son and this woman's intelligent eyes, with our struggles and travels, our buttocks and hands and breasts and slacks and pants and ears and thighs and handkerchiefs and everything that led us here, we have reached the cumulative point where we must meet.

"Hello," I say.

The minute she sees me, which is just when I want her to, she begins to express her surprise. I stop her by seizing her by the hair and slamming her head against the dashboard. I tell her I love her, I love her, so she won't feel too badly as I slam her head again and again into the dashboard. I'm the one she was waiting for, I tell her. That's why she parked here. At last, to both her relief and my own, she goes to sleep.

"I'm your date," I tell her. "You knew you had a date tonight, you just didn't know who. I'm the one you've been waiting for. Neither one of us knew until just seconds ago. That's the way blind dates are," I say. "That's why they're so exciting."

To help her sleep more deeply and comfortably, I shove her down onto the floor on the passenger side and cover her with her coat. "I'll drive you home," I tell her. "We'll talk about it there." In her purse, I find her billfold, and I thank her for telling me her address as I read it off her driver's license and turn the ignition to start the car up with a voluptuous roar.

It's quite miraculous the way we end up in her house. I try to be alert and conscientious regarding everything that occurs, wanting to acknowledge and savor every detail. Yet the moments fly. Chaos overwhelms me with a startling and abundant rush. I know her every wish, though the jacket tied around her head obstructs the means of communication with which we are both most familiar. Yet her sounds, muffled and garbled, have all the subtlety of a new language that is ours alone to share, and in this exclusivity there is an intimacy that exceeds the range of common conversation. Messages are everywhere. They fill the room just as they filled the night as we drove, the asphalt sending through the rubbery tires a sinuous longing upon whose hiss we rushed down the four-lane highway. Other vehicles swept past, emitting coy whispers and groans as if there were no longer enough air to sustain a world lost in such exertion. Light glanced off the heedless fenders, and our eyes were dazzled. Curvaceous corners were rounded. Darkness, swelling out of alleys, rushed past. Stretches of countryside rose up around us, full of aroused and swaying fields of grass. Trees rubbed one another, lost in an undulating incitement they had no power to withstand. Branches and leaves reached out, spellbound at the brink of contact like prying tongues and fingers longing to torment each other. Impatience and appetite governed the tumescent sky, where the wind possessed the silken clouds, their secrets melting in its roaring demands for satisfaction.

In such a night as this we were helpless, my date and I. I moaned in a strange and uncensored way. I caressed the wheel, and felt a response. On the floor, my date was mewing, her feeling overwhelming her. I sought to call to her and calm her, but I was so lavishly tantalized that I managed only hoots and howls. As if released by my example, she started screaming. I reached to pat her and reassure her that I would not forget her, and I felt a jolt of passion in her arm. The coat swirled like the folds of a flower on the surface of a pond. The volume of her cries increased. To encourage her surrender to this orgiastic night, I roared along with her, and pressed my foot down on the gas and felt the car nearly burst as the tires sang out, tearing at the concrete.

Had there been anyone at her home upon our arrival, what a lot of explaining she would have had to manage, bringing me back, the two of us so sick with lust we could hardly walk. Of course no one was there, and she knew it or she would never have invited me back. It was only to tease me that she made me lock her in the trunk of the car and then prowl the perimeter of her darkened little cottage. Somewhat elevated, her house looked down on a little lake bedazzled with luster pilfered from the moon and spread in thousands of hatch-marked lines upon its surface, like a plate overflowing with splinters of glass. Pine trees stood like bushy-haired elves all around this glowing oblong. In some of the windows into which I peered to see the uninhabited rooms, the lake was reflected. In others, the forest was a clotted smear. Turning from the house, I saw the heavens rising in an inky veil, while the pond below seemed an enormous diamond, uneasy in its earthly setting.

Carrying her in through the front door, I filled with wonder as we crossed the threshold, her heartbeat flickering against mine, her body trembling like a bag full of birds in my arms. Setting her down in the corner, I undressed her, but I left her hooded.

Now her jacket, bound with my belt at her throat, makes her a faceless nude shuddering as she lies at the brink of a familiar but forbidden dream, hoping that I will know the way to guide her past the limitations of identity and the restrictions of reality. She expresses herself in timid, birdlike noises, and I step away and start to move around the room.

I look out the window. Only moments ago I was looking in. But I'm not there any longer. I can see her car, isolated on the empty terrain, no other hints of civilization visible as far as the horizon except for power lines along the road winding away. When suddenly her cries grow louder, I race back, alarmed that something is harming her. Though naked, she sweats, her body skimmed with a gloss like the face of the lake in its lunar glaze outside. I shake my head in disbelief at the heat that must smolder within her. I'm padded in layers of sweatshirts, sweaters, flannel underwear, and my thick old coat, yet I am cold. I'd like to speak to her about this inner ice but I feel mortified. Everyone dislikes someone who is cold all the time. Still, I'm tempted to explain myself; I'm on the verge of trying, when the mysterious hood of the jacket strikes me as a mask over a mask, a facade over a facade, for what does the human face ever reveal except its deceit, employed as it is to conceal the truth most of the time, to distort and hide the genuine content of each moment.

And yet, as my fingers trace the tangle of the knots and rope with which I have secured her, I want to see her eyes. She shivers at my slightest touch and I feel a kind of nostalgia, a sense of having been robbed. I feel I'm no longer looking down at the body of someone new to my life, but at the memory of an old friend, an old lost friend for whom my affection is large—and now in this cottage, where the wooden walls strike me as the walls of memory, I am staring not at a woman but at the specter of a friend whose face I can't remember. How did I get here? In the numbness of my innards, the ice constricts. Grabbing a blanket from off a shelf, I cover her. I can't bear the way I feel much longer, worrying about whether or not she's someone I once knew intimately. I want her to be who she is. I remove the jacket from her head. She has a face. I'm looking at it, and I don't recognize it. I've never seen her before tonight. It's clear. When she sighs and slips away into a kind of unhappy sleep, I have no need to rouse her and make her speak in order to verify her particular existence. I don't know who she is, and I don't know who I thought she was. I don't want her looking at me, and I use rope and cloth to bind her eyes.

Out the window, the lake appears as lustrous as the diamond it seemed to be. The world has placed this effulgence there to honor this woman and her relationship to me, this massive shimmering beside our little cabin, our nearly bridal chamber. For we are indeed wedded in ways that neither of us understands, and the earth, whether we recognize it or not, is a ring. Yes, I think. The grip of my reverie tightens, then grows slack and lengthens and dissolves.

I'm seated on a footstool in the corner, shadows blanketing me. I rise through them slowly, ending up on my feet. I seem to be waking up, my heart buzzing as if I've just been startled out of a deep slumber. I'm wondering about the stranger. Has he come? Was it his arrival that woke me? Did he shake me? I seem to feel an alien presence, the squeamish discomfort that comes from being spied upon. And as I search about, hoping to discover a key to his hiding place somewhere in the room—as I look out the windows trying to find a sign of his approach through the visible night—I notice for the first time the numerous musical instruments arrayed on sections of the fluffy carpeting and on some of the furniture. It's bizarre that I didn't see them before, and yet I have no memory of their existence. I was preoccupied. But was I that preoccupied? Or is it possible they were delivered while I daydreamed? Perhaps I actually slept. On the flower-printed couch angled across a shadowy corner, where one would expect pillows, I see a trumpet, a French horn, and a trombone in a nest of golden brass. A black streak, a brassy curl, and a silver wand lie side by side on a rectangular table adjacent to the couch. When I've stepped a little closer, I identify them as a clarinet, a saxophone, and a flute.

Transcending my surprise, I no longer let the shadows fool me. Instruments are everywhere. A violin and a cello are crisscrossed on an armchair in the corner. Behind them, a bass fiddle rises up, leaning against the back of the chair, so that these stringed instruments seem three old fellows gathered together, the wood of their frames a uniform burgundy. A kerosene lantern stands atop a nearby desk, and from the base an electrical cord squirms off in the direction of the wall. The switch brings forth a cone of white light. Atop the desk, a gray-blue swirl of feathers sticks up from an inkwell. However, this quill, when I lift it up, ends the slotted tip of a pen. Great care has been invested in the mood of this place, the selection and order of these objects intended to evoke the easier pace of an earlier time. Hints of the preindustrial era combine with an invocation of scholarly attributes.

Along the top of the desk three neat piles of paper form a horizontal row, the staves and bars used in the composition of music covering their surfaces. The pile on the upper right is filled with musical notations, while the sheaf on the left waits in unblemished readiness. On the top two sheets of the middle pile, keys have been inked in and notes set down, until they stop at a point about three-quarters of the way down to the bottom. At first glance, the third and fourth pages of the pile appear duplicates of their predecessors, except for the broad black X slashed across them. However, a closer examination quickly reveals that the apparent correspondence was an illusion, because a set of subtle variations was developing in the latter stages, the number of these divergences increasing as the cutoff point was approached.

These are the pages of a musical composition, I see, in which the composer, after encountering some difficulties, struggled through several drafts before rejecting everything that had been done. This is an unfinished musical creation. And the whispering thought that accompanies my realization suggests that this composition may go unfinished forever, unless the garbled cries and scraping I hear across the room are the ingredients and inspiration for its fulfillment.

I turn and the sight I encounter contains, within its literal nature, an evocative power. The woman is there, the pillows, the ropes, several of the instruments spread over the fluffy beige of the floor. But lurking in this pictorial display is something new, something unknown announcing its cunning presence. Implications invite me to approach them at their source, where they exist just outside the reach of normal perception, the grasp of the rational mind. I have seen trombones before, and I have seen tape and rags. Violins have chanced across my view. Trumpets have been played, squads of sprightly musicians parading down the street. I've seen women. But in this room and night, their unexpected juxtapositions have generated an energy in whose effects ordinary objects radiate with enigmatic contents. Trumpet and trombone lying golden on the couch—violin and cello on the chair—saxophone and gagged, blindfolded woman on the floor—drums in the corner, halos of cymbals hovering in their midst. These objects pulse with implications that, however frightfully near and tantalizing, remain unintelligible, like the knowledge that languishes in the mind of a brilliant amnesiac.

With frustration and yearning, I beg the secret to step forward but nothing changes except that I start to sweat. The concealed significance will not present itself, nor will it let me forget about it as it keeps coaxing me and washing over me in sticky, invisible waves. Why have I been brought to this point where I feel addressed by this thing reaching out to me from an inchoate otherworldly realm in which it remains unknown? The allure is voluptuous, its power equaled only by its inscrutable nature. Is it the stranger? I think. Is he here, refusing to make himself sensible to me?

I am crumpled in a corner, my head against the side of a large armchair. My effort to breathe produces a thin wheezing. Saliva dribbles from my mouth to dot the veiny back of my hand. I'm staring at the pattern running through the stitches of my skin. I feel that I can't move—that I will never move again, and then suddenly I'm rising up and falling to my knees in a stiff and resolute posture of devotion. Startled by my own transformation, I seem to be enacting instructions. When the immutable will not move itself, there are ceremonies to appeal to it, begging that it shift and stir. When the insensible refuses to deliver itself in rational forms, there are rites to urge it forth. There are incantations, evocations. I have the means. I have the instruments and the woman.

I start to pound the drum, hoping to initiate the transaction I seek, but I feel clumsy and inept, and I stop. Impulsively, I start to worry about what I'm wearing. Then I feel insecure about the suitability of her attire. Dashing into her bedroom, I emerge with an armful of clothes. I stuff her into a swimsuit cut high at the hip. The geometry of her body expands the elasticity of the nylon. Bold slices of rainbow curve to embrace her, and I note the shadowy firmness of bone extending out from her crotch into the sweep of her thighs. Shading deepens the swell of her breasts, above which the straps disappear in the ends of her disheveled hair.

Again I address the drum, my hands fluttering like wings against the skins in an instinctive maneuver whose rhythm I hope will open up the unseen world of the air, some dormant power of second sight rekindled in me. I look out the window and see the blazing circle of the pond as white as the moon, and it seems I'm being drawn into it, that I will be ingested, that I'm plummeting through the intervening spaces into this blinding, insubstantial surface of gleaming slivers. I run to the door and lock it, but it's too late. I'm gone. The moment has dropped me out into a phantasm of the moon devouring me. I grab the trumpet and blow, but nothing answers. I rip her from the swimsuit and try a floral print kimono with a black bikini bottom. Tied at her breasts, the sash falls between the lapels, which open on a wedge of belly, a slice of pinkish skin. I grab her shoulders and scream. From the saxophone I manage to provoke a pathetic whine, followed by a dozen discordant squeals. At the drums, I thrash away until my shoulders ache. Yet when I pause to breathe, the room remains empty and all that speaks is the woman, her garbled cries like those of little animals. I shred the kimono and rend the pants before I deliriously force her into a pink shirred-sided maillot splashed with blues, the accompanying wraparound skirt draped from her shoulder to her thigh. Though inappropriate, I know this will have to do. After adding bracelets to her wrists and ankles, I tip a box of jewelry over from above her while standing on a chair. Rings and earrings, pearls and trinkets cascade through the air. Where they land, they lie scattered in the folds of her scarf, the crooks of her elbows, the indentations on either side of her pelvis. A scarlet ruby shimmers at the side of her mouth; a pearl dots the cleavage of her breasts; an opal decorates the cloth that covers up her eyes.

Now all that remains for me to provide is the ceremony, the music, the fire, and the blood. From the table, I grab the knife, my gesture stirring the sheets of the unfinished composition waiting there. Briefly captivated by these lines and dots, I wonder if I am to complete and play these notes to create the element missing from my rite. Is it blood and songs and screams and death alone that will charm the stranger? Whatever the original intention behind this creation—whether it was conceived as a cantata or fugue or symphony—in my rendition tonight it will become a requiem for everyone in this room.

Her muscles are exact, the soft summons of every indentation an opportunity for me to attempt to slice away those finely established definitions that divide duty from cruelty. I will walk the thin line of amorphously contrived distinctions between cosmetic and cosmological surgery, where beauty is the issue, and truth, too, as the knife probes to deftly separate meat from meat in order that the essential matter may be uncovered. Beauty must be cut in order that beauty may be found. In cosmetic surgery it's only vanity that's served. But in cosmological surgery, the skin is the veil to be lifted in order that the mesmerizing enthrallment inherent in all flesh may be discovered and examined, its overwhelming powers dispelled.

Blood makes the trumpet slippery, but I press my lips together and blow. From within the vibrating, brassy tubes, piteous bleats emerge. At the drums I pound. With the sticks I hit my face and then the resonant skins of the drums, as if they are covered in fire I must put out. Running to the saxophone, I bite and wheeze, prompting a set of grievous notes that fill me with a bleak emotion.

Panting, I search every corner of the room for a sign of the stranger, but nothing hints at his presence or approach. I run to the composition on the sheets and scribble some notes before racing to the trumpet, where I begin my round again. Soon the squeal of the violin is amended by the trumpet's shout. After the cello weeps, the saxophone sobs its melancholy. At the center of the room, where I have gathered my instruments, I rush among them until their individual expressions collide. I learn to pump the bow on the violin while huffing on the trumpet. I flail at the drums while plucking at the cello. I see the diamond of the pond burning through the window. I scream and spit into the horn. I hurl the drums; I clutch the saxophone; I cough so much I gag, clawing the cello's strings. My foot rattles at one of the drums. I start wheezing through the trumpet. Louder, louder, louder. And then I'm getting it. I'm on the brink. I blow, I pound, I wheeze and shriek. Music storms the battered air. I sense which instrument should follow which and when the drums should have a thundering voice followed by a whisper. I know the tempo and the rhythm. The music has a mounting power. I think the room is full of echoes, like a cavern carved out of stone. It's a kind of avalanche of noise tumbling over me, much more than I could possibly be producing. Sound is generating sound. The notes, once born, have powers of self-perpetuation and procreation. Still I must puff and pound. Before me stand the drums. Beside me lies the violin. Hurtling through the air, the saxophone is startling. What's left for me but screaming? Everything else is noise and whirling! I blow, I gasp, I wheeze. And then I stop, but that which I have initiated continues. It is out of all control now, a cacophony around me, a cataract of noise in whose spumes I'm trying to shout for help. But I am being impelled in bursts that are either the inspiration or consequence of some superhuman expression preempting the event I have begun, for what encircles me now is anarchically awhirl so that upon each revolution of this vortex I am pushed to a further, less tenable ring in the centrifugal force taking over with a sickening velocity and then, to my horror, I am let loose. I have been discarded. I am where I have never been before—beyond what I ever thought to venture near—beyond all human reference and reciprocity. I am cast away. This is banishment. Exile. I have been flung out.

Chapter Twenty-Two

"I need guidance," I tell him. "I need help."

"Well," he says, beaming, "we could go to my house."

"I'm very confused."

"Want to follow along with me? We'll have some tea. It calms the nerves, you know. Herbal tea," he purrs. "You need a friend," he purrs. "Do you drink a lot of coffee?"

"I do. I really do."

"I have a back porch. It's a beautiful setting. We don't have to talk. Unless you want to. Do you know what you'd prefer?"

"In what?"

"Whether to talk or not."

"I don't. Not really."

"Well, we'll see when we get there."

"My life has just—it's not what I hoped for, or ever intended. It's just taken a turn, it's veered—I mean, that's what I mean—it's just veered off in some unacceptable, terrible direction I don't want anything to do with."

"We could study vectors."

"What do you mean?"

"You said 'veered.'"

"Yes. That's what it felt like."

"We could study vectors. They might reveal something of what has happened to you. The 'veer' to which you referred."

"I see."

"I have some wonderful books on vectors and their implications. Beautiful books. Beautifully bound. Elegant books, elegantly thought out and written."

"Do you think it might help?"

"First we could have some tea. Do you like tea?"

"I don't know. I mean, I'm not sure."

"So that will be the first thing we do, then. We'll go to my house, and we'll have tea. We'll try to see what you feel about tea, and I'll show you my book on vectors and we can see whether or not it's worthwhile regarding your veer."

"I mean, it's taken me so far away from what I intended for myself, so far from where I thought I was going. What I thought I was setting out on. I was going one way, and I thought I would just keep going and then, you know, I started some of the things—you know what I mean—I did some of the actions that led into the veer, and initially it seemed they were going the way I was already going—that they were a continuation, a progression. But it turned into this whole other venture, veering off and me with it, and everything from that point on started to happen in just this completely undesirable, harmful, awful way."

"Well," he says, "first we have to find out about the tea. We'll have a delightful situation on my porch. It's elevated, outdoors. The chairs are very comfortable. Big armchairs. I take them in and out depending on the weather. Nothing to distract us. We'll sit and sip the tea. I'll do nothing at all to influence you. You can report to me your responses. We'll record and measure your responses. We'll evaluate our measurements and find out whether or not you like tea. I'm talking about herbal tea, of course."

"I don't know if I like it or not."

"That's what we'll find out, then. Isn't this a lovely walk?"

"Yes. It's strange though. Moody. Haunting."

"The trees are my favorites. So green. A very unique green, don't you think?"

"And so orderly. It's amazing how they're so neat. It's as if they've been arranged."

"They're cultivated. Oh, there's my house."

"Where?"

"There," he says, pointing. "Isn't it beautiful?"

"Where?"

"Don't you see it? I always feel so happy to see it."

"No, no, I really don't. There's only the trees—I mean, it seems to me you're just pointing at the trees and— Oh! Look! It's in the trees. There's a doorway in the trees."

"I wondered when you'd see it."

"The house is in the trees!"

"It is in fact in a hillside. It's delightful. The trees, as you see, are on the hillside."

"The house is built into the hillside."

"There was a natural underground cave. I merely elaborated. I excavated and expanded the subterranean spaces that were already there, already hollow, already cavernous. Then I decorated and moved in."

"It's amazing."

"I'll make the tea. And while I do that, you can read about the vectors."

"All right."

"Or perhaps you want to rest first. Take any chair."

"They're gorgeous."

"Teak."

"And so comfortable."

"You see, the thing is," he says, "that every body must persevere in its state of rest or of uniform motion in a right line unless it is compelled to change that state by forces impressed upon it. That's the law. So perhaps the particular veer your life went into was due to other forces impressing themselves upon you?"

"Like what?"

"I don't know."

"What forces?"

"I don't know."

"Be careful with the tea. It's very hot."

"All right."

"Do you like the smell?"

"Let me taste it."

"Sip it slowly. It's hot."

"It's very hot."

"There's no need to rush. Do you like it?"

"Yes, I do."

"How much?"

"What do you mean?"

"How much do you like it?"

"A lot."

"Keep sipping."

"It's very good. Very, very good."

"So you like the tea."

"I do."

"Two 'verys,' you said, right? 'Very, very.' "

"Yes."

"Well there you are, you see? We've taken care of that one."

"Yes. But what was that you said before? You were talking and you said—"

"About the tea?"

"No, no. The law. Some law."

"Oh, yes, I said, 'Every body must persevere in its state of rest or of uniform motion in a right line unless it is compelled to change that state by forces impressed upon it.' "

"I see."

"It can be said that you were moving along, were you not? Your life, I mean, was proceeding, going forward, was it not?"

"Yes."

"As a wagon might upon a smooth road in a state of, so to speak, uniform motion. Just going forward, proceeding."

"Well, yes."

"That's how it seemed to you."

"Up to a point."

"That's what we're talking about, trying to identify. That point—the point of your 'veer.' "

"Yes. Of course."

"The law states that if you were in a state of uniform motion, then you would have continued in a state of uniform motion if no external forces acted upon you. You would have continued in a straight line."

"What do you suppose it was?"

"What?"

"The thing that hit me."

"Did something hit you?"

"Well, something must have."

"I wonder what."

"I don't know."

"Did you pick up speed?"

"What?"

"In your veer. Did you accelerate?"

"I think I did. It seems I did. Because first of all I was in the time and place I thought of as 'now.' And suddenly I'm here and that's all there is, there's just where we are now."

"You mean, here and now? Where we are?"

"Yes."

"That's now."

"Right. And between 'now'—and that which was once 'now'—but is now 'then'—there is only this blur, which is certainly how things might appear if I were traveling fast."

"Well, there you are."

"So I feel that I did accelerate, and in the blur—well, in the blur there are things, or events, in which there are people and things and animals, and both these people and things are doing things and animals—and I'm one of them, one of the people doing things. In other words, things are happening—and I'm involved—but it's all a blur. Can you help me? I need you to help me."

"Well, we're talking about vectors, aren't we?"

"You said there was a book."

"Many books."

"On vectors."

"Would you like to see one?"

"But first could you just go over it again?"

"You mean, of course, from the classical frame of reference; the mechanical view of phenomena, as we've been doing."

"I don't know."

"Because it's only from that perspective that the law we have been discussing is known to exist."

"And the law is that 'Every body perseveres in its state of rest or of uniform motion in a right line unless it is compelled to change by forces—' Wait a minute! Wait!"

"What?"

"*Compelled?*"

"Yes."

"Is that appropriate?"

"It's the closest approximation, in my opinion, that language can devise to express the precise nature of the law."

"Because, you see—if that was the nature of the events of which I have no recollection, except the blur I spoke of . . ."

"Yes?"

"Well, if that was what happened to me and I went off on this veer, this vector, because I was *compelled*, according to the law, then I would have had no choice. If I was *compelled*, in the true sense of the word, I would have had no choice."

"Not according to the law."

"So it wouldn't have been my fault then. It would have just *happened* to me."

"The law is very specific: 'compelled' or some equivalent is always present in any language by which this concept is expressed."

"And you said something about a wagon? I want to get that straight."

"In the speculation?"

"I'm not sure. I just remember you said something about a wagon."

"In the speculation on the law, I referred to the wagon of uniform motion, which of course cannot be found in reality or in any actual experiment, but nevertheless—"

"It can't?"

"No, no."

"Why not?"

"It's very useful, though."

"For what?"

"In regard to thinking. Indeed, it must be utilized in our thinking. There's little choice, really, and frequently it does lead to an understanding of real events or experiments. For example, if we think of your life as a wagon on a road, or a stone thrown from a tower, then we can begin to—"

"A stone thrown from a tower!"

"Excuse me?"

"I'm just saying that seems more accurate. Of the two, that seems the more appropriate to my life."

"All right."

"I mean, a rock flung out from a high huge tower, just hurled out and falling—that seems a much more apt representation of my life."

"However, it is far less useful in our circumstances, because it is actually quite difficult to conceive of such a falling stone as free of all external forces. It is far easier to imagine the wagon free of such forces, however hypothetical both cases might be."

"I don't want to cause a problem. I was just—"

"I could go along with your wishes, of course, but I have to admit that I would prefer to continue with the wagon as the image by which we attempt to exemplify your life. Because to imagine a wagon advancing in uniform motion is at least possible, however impossible such an actuality might be."

"Could I have some more tea?"

"Say when."

"When."

"So what we have is the little wagon of your life advancing upon this absolutely level road, its propulsion a synthesis of all the influences that have to this point been imparted to it, and at this point you were doing what?"

"What?"

"When things changed—what exactly were you doing?"

"You're asking me exactly what I was doing?"

"It would help."

"I don't know exactly."

"You can't remember?"

"No. Not really. Not exactly. Is that a problem?"

"No, no."

"I could try and remember. I could—"

"It's all right."

"You're sure?"

"We'll just go on. So there you are, doing something, going along in your little wagon, the uniformity of your progression firmly established. Now let us imagine, for example, that you are given a push from behind. What would happen? The obvious, of course. You would go faster."

"Would I veer?"

"No, no. Straight ahead."

"Well, that's not what happened. Because my course altered. I went off."

"Just try and follow what I'm saying, all right? Don't get impatient."

"I'm sorry."

"Now if your wagon were assailed from the back by some force, it would speed up; and if it were assailed from the front by some force, you would have slowed down, stopped, or gone backward, depending on the size of the force, which is not what happened either. Is it?"

"No. It was more as though I was struck from an angle, sort of off to the side—like I was running and something hit me, so I veered. It was as if I was ambushed, shot in the back of the head."

"My point exactly."

"That's not what you said."

"The series of ideas I am presently making are only the foundation for the later points, which, when we reach them, will pertain quite clearly to your experience. But if you fail to attend these issues now, you will encounter the later points still impeded by your current ignorance."

"I see."

"In other words, the concept to be established is simply that your life would have continued to roll along in a state of uniform motion had it not been influenced. Therefore, since it failed to perform as expected without influence, it must have been influenced. In other words, it is the alteration in speed *and* direction, the alteration in the velocity of the wagon—or in this case, the 'life'—that testifies to the presence of an external force."

"You're saying that there had to be a force."

"According to the law. The clue is in the change in velocity. The change in velocity is easily detected, impressing us, as it does, as different, and inarguably revealing the presence—through its effects—of a force. And so, as far as our question, we know by the very fact that you 'veered,' as you termed it, with your speed changing, that there must have been another force involved, however undetectable it must have been in every other way."

"Well, I did veer."

"That's my point."

"But as of yet, unless in my impatience I missed it, you have not described the kind of effect I underwent. You have mentioned advancing, retreating, being brought to a standstill."

"The reason that I have not yet mentioned the kind of phenomenon with which you are concerned is that we have to this point devoted ourselves exclusively to linear motions, which are, in themselves, far simpler than the phenomenon you experienced. My strategy has been to approach the more complex issue via the simpler avenue. Curves and their understanding are our true goal. Curves are the true mystery to be grasped. It is along curves that the great planets prowl. Curves are the heavenly inclination. However, the study of curves cannot be approached unless we first skirmish with a prerequisite set of difficulties, which is what's perplexing you. Yet I'm certain we can manage."

"I hope so."

"Now just suppose that the wagon of your life is proceeding as we have established it. It's moving uniformly along a perfect road when a force impacts upon it from an angle that is neither directly in front of, nor directly behind, the wagon itself. What happens in this instant is a consequence of several distinct elements—namely, the original uniform motion, the direction of the impacting force, and the new stage of motion subsequent to the cessation of the impacting force's application of influence. Speed before and after may or may not remain uniform, but direction will have been altered."

"I will have veered."

"That's one possibility."

"But there are others?"

"In fact, I think a more comprehensive view of what happened to you, a more exact terminology, might be found in the concept of vectors. You see, vectors are the tool by which we understand motion as it occurs in nature. A vector, often represented by the sign of an arrow, is a motion consisting of a certain magnitude and direction. When one observes the curving movement of something, such as a particle moving through nature, it is moving as it does because it is under the influence of other forces. Now, if something happened to those forces and they vanished, then that would be the point at which the particle would simply go off in the direction into which it was headed at that instant, and this is a tangent, which is what I think happened to you."

"A tangent?"

"Yes."

"I went off on a tangent?"

"You went off on a tangent."

"Not a vector, but a tangent?"

"Right."

"I went off on a tangent."

"Yes."

"I was going along, and the forces around me vanished, so I veered."

"No, no. Something struck you, as you describe it, from behind and you veered. Then that force vanished and you continued along on your tangent."

"Oh."

"See?"

"So it's like this thing hit me, pushed me, and then vanished without me knowing what it was, even."

"Exactly."

"But if it was this thing that turned me—this thing that turned me with a push—if that was what happened—I mean, what was it?"

"The thing?"

"The thing pushing me—that thing. I mean, why did it hit me? What is it? Where did it come from?"

"Well, there are a variety of explanations we can consider, one being that it was on a uniform line of motion itself, and then it simply intersected with your line of motion, with your life, resulting in your change of direction."

"But where did it come from?"

"Well, it could have been moving along for aeons in another direction—near to you or far from you—even moving parallel to you, until some third force collided with it, so it was altered regarding direction, and this alteration impelled it into you."

"So it went off on a tangent, too—"

"Very possibly."

"It veered, and then I veered."

"Or it was on its own course and simply at this point intersected with your wagon of life. A second alternative—this is regarding your acceleration—a second alternative could be that with your change in direction you were brought into a new relationship with some other power in the realm of gravitation—some other mass. In other words, if your tangent was initiated near some object to which your mass was thrust closer so that it must be more powerfully attracted, then the hauling of this gravitational force would increase your velocity. By your tangent, you could have been nudged into a field of gravitation that had previously had a negligible effect on you. Your acceleration would then increase due to the effects of this new gravitational force once your tangent brought you into its reach."

"Do you think that's what happened?"

"It could have."

"And if it did, then what was the something that hit me? Or what was the force that vanished? And what is the thing that's attracting me even now?"

"You mean specifically?"

"Yes."

"I don't know."

"What do you think?"

"I'm talking theory. I could speculate. But I don't know."

"This isn't helping me."

"I'm talking theory."

"I thought you knew, I thought—"

"I mean, you could have jumped."

"Jumped?"

"Yes."

"Jumped?"

"In classical thinking, motion behaves just as we have been discussing, but in other theories, such as quantum theory, from which these ideas have been banished, motion is no longer seen as an ongoing sequence of fixed but changing points. In other words, the idea that describes motion as a flow of points one after the other has been discarded, and in its place the concept has been established that particles get from place to place in a haphazard manner. I mean, they go from one point to another without going through the middle area at all. They jump."

"So I could have jumped? That's what you're saying?"

"Yes. Though that's not exactly accurate. More precisely, these particles are in one place, where they disappear, and then they show up at another place. Could that be what happened to you? You just went from Point A—which we have to this point taken to be your life as it was before you 'veered'—and then you, so to speak, 'jumped' to where you are now. And the 'blur' to which you referred is your experience of your 'jump.' And now you're here. In other words, you've simply gone from one place to another, appearing and disappearing without going through the middle, a blur in between."

"There was a blur. How would that work?"

"Appearing and disappearing in the manner of a particle. Without going through the middle."

"So you think I might have ended up where I am, having left where I was but without in fact passing through what I take to be my life, my history. Is that what you're saying?"

"Is that what you want to do—explore the relevance of history? We could."

"Would it be useful?"

"Isn't it possible that through the study of other events—by means of a thorough scrutiny of the lives of other men—you might find similar experiences to your own, and in these lives you might locate a prototype, an explanation, at least hypothetically, for the phenomenon perplexing you—inasmuch as you might create a model of your own life based upon the lives of others, a paradigm invented from their behavior out of which you could generate a solution to your problems, a mode of behavior to extricate you, or console you, to aid you somehow?"

"You mean, I could do what others have done?"

"Exactly."

"Like who?"

"We would have to study. And as we studied you'd see which lives pertained, or struck a chord, and which didn't. We could then concentrate on those particular examples. Whom would you like to begin with?"

"I'm tired."

"You look tired."

"I am tired."

"Perhaps you should rest. My daughter's waiting for you, for this opportunity. If you want to go see her."

"What?"

"She's waiting."

"Who?"

"My daughter. She has everything prepared. Just go down the hall. To the door at the end of the hall. See the door at the end of the hall?"

"Your daughter?"

"Go ahead now."

"You want me to go see your daughter?"

"That door at the end of the hall. You don't have to knock. Just go on in. She's waiting."

"This is what you want?"

"Of course. I'll see you later. I'll see you in the morning."

"All right."

"Good-bye."

"Good-bye."

"Hello."

"Hello."

"Oh, you look so tired. Ohh, look at you."

"I am tired. I'm very, very tired."

"I've been waiting for you. I was so worried Father wouldn't send you to me. I've got dinner ready. I hope you like it. Why are you looking at me like that? You're embarrassing me."

"I'm sorry."

"Sit down. What would you like to drink?"

"Tea. I like herbal tea."

"I love herbal tea. It's my favorite."

"It's mine, too."

"Are you hungry? Be careful of the soup—I just poured it. I don't want you to burn yourself."

"It smells great."

"Be careful."

"Mmmmmmmm."

"Not too salty?"

"Not at all. Ohh, I'm starving, really. I'm famished."

"Take your time. I made it all for you."

"And the beans, and the rice. And the vegetables."

"They're steamed."

"I love them, and the noodles, too. The noodles are delicious."

"Don't eat too fast. I don't want you getting an upset stomach."

"Me neither."

"You're making me very happy."

"I am?"

"I can see in your eyes how you mean exactly what you say. What a sweet smile. You have such a sweet smile."

"No."

"You do. Would you like some wine? It's white. Do you like white?"

"Thank you."

"I'll have a little, too. But not too much. It goes to my head. How do you feel?"

"Better. Actually, pretty good."

"You're not tired anymore?"

"Well . . . No, I'm not."

"I thought you were soooo tired."

"I was, but I'm not. I'm not. I'm feeling wide awake, actually. I feel excited, actually."

"You could take a hot bath. I've run the water. And then we could go dancing. Would you like to go dancing?"

"Dancing?"

"Please."

"I don't dance very well."

"I could teach you."

"Where would we go?"

"We could drive to a wonderful place I know. Lean forward, I'll wash your back."

"The water feels wonderful."

"I have clothes for you, too. Beautiful clothing. I want to hold you. I want to go dancing so I can hold you. It's all beautiful clothing, don't you think? And just your size. I had so much fun picking it all out for you. Shall I wash your hair?"

"It's dirty, that's for sure."

"Close your eyes. If I hurt you, tell me. You smell so good."

"It's the soap."

"No, it's you."

"I'm feeling better."

"Let me dry you off now. Stand up."

"I'm feeling better and better."

"Here's the clothes. Pick whatever you want to wear."

"You pick, okay?"

"I love these. I mean, these trousers and this shirt. And there's a jacket in the closet that will set them off so perfectly. I got so excited when I saw it, because it will just highlight the color of your hair and skin. Your eyes will look so deep and soft set off by this shirt. Why don't you put it on, and the trousers, too, while I get the jacket."

"Where are the shoes and socks?"

"Oh, I've been looking forward to this. I've been waiting for you."

"What?"

"Haven't you been waiting for me?"

"You've been waiting for me?"

"Haven't you been waiting for me? I've been waiting for you."

"I certainly have been waiting for somebody."

"Me."

"I think I have. I feel like I've found somebody."

"Me. Me. C'mon. I'll drive."

"Oh, look at the stars."

"I love the stars. And the planets. Do you know which ones are the planets?"

"No. Do you?"

"Of course. I know them all. All of them. Their names and speeds, their exact locations."

"Teach me, will you?"

"Later."

"Now. Point one out."

"I am Venus."

"What?"

"Come along. I can't wait any longer. I am your heart. I am love. I am Venus. Come along. Let's go out onto the dance floor."

"Remember, I don't do this often."

"Shhhhhh."

"It's so dark."

"Don't worry. Please. Put your arms around me. That's good. That's right. Good. And just lean into me, and follow. Yes. So sweet. That's right. You're getting it. You're good. Oh, I love you. I love you. I am your heart. I am your love. I am Venus. I am Venus. I am Venus. Venus, Venus, Venus. Come with me."

"Where?"

"Shhhh."

"Where?"

"Just follow. That's right. Now stand there. Shhhhh. Just face me here. Face me. Let me love you, let me love you."

"What?"

"I am Venus. Your heart, your love."

"What, Venus? What, my heart? What, my love? Oh, my love."

"Shhhhhhhhhhh."

"Who are you?"

"You're so sweet. Don't cry. Ohhh, don't cry."

"I can't help it. I love you, I love you."

"My dear one, my love, my heart."

"My Venus, my love."

"Now?"

"Oh, yes."

"I love you."

"Please."

"Oh, honey."

"Who's knocking? Somebody's knocking."

"It's Father. Don't worry."

"No."

"It's all right."

"I don't want to stop. I don't want to stop."

"He's waiting."

"I don't want him. I don't want him."

"Just open the door and go. You have to go. He's waiting."

"No."

"He's waiting. You can come back."

"I love you."

"I love you. Come back. Forever."

"I'll come back."

"Good-bye."

"Good-bye."

"Good morning. Good morning."

"Hello."

"I've been thinking that perhaps a brief time spent musing on thermodynamics might be of some profit in our quest. After all, should you drop a cup of tea onto the floor, the liquid flowing out in all directions, the form of the cup smashed to smithereens, you would not expect the pieces to recollect into their original cup form, the liquid to reverse its course and reenter the cup, the cup then to spring back up to your hand, would you?"

"No."

"It would seem unlikely, wouldn't it? It would seem impossible. And yet the first law of thermodynamics does not forbid such an eventuality."

"It doesn't?"

"No."

"Are you sure that it doesn't?"

"I thought that might interest you."

"It does."

"I thought that might interest you, though I didn't know why."

"Well, my life—I mean, my life—under such circumstances, my life might be refashionable to what it was. I might be able to go back. It would be possible for it all to be returned to the way it was."

"No, no, that's not possible. I don't mean to—"

"But the cup! You said the cup— I want to go back like the cup."

"I don't see how."

"But if it's not forbidden by the law, and you said it wasn't, why couldn't I do it, why couldn't it happen?"

"Though not forbidden, such events nevertheless do not occur. This irreversibility has little to do with the first law but rather seems inextricably bound up with the probabilistic behavior of systems consisting of a sizable collection of subunits. For example, if you had three coins in your hand and I compelled you to put those three coins into a hat with three other, identical coins, the odds of you retrieving your original three coins with your first three selections would be one in twenty. Not impossible. Difficult. But within the realm of the possible. However, if you were compelled to place those three coins into a hat with a thousand other identical coins, the odds in favor of your retrieving your original three coins with your first three choices would be almost nonexistent. Though possible, of course, the probability would be so slight as to demand that it be ignored. You could work away for decades without ever getting those three coins in three choices. In other words, if we unsettle an ordered arrangement, the likelihood is that it will become irreversibly disordered. In other words, every change leads to greater disorder. In other words, disorder increases."

"Are you saying I can't return to what I was?"

"According to the second law, you—"

"But I thought you—"

"According to the second law, such a return to the original order would be a complete accident. It could only happen accidentally, which would mean it was not a return, but something new. If new order is to be established, it must be in the disorder, out of the disorder. Only artificial facsimiles of the original order can be devised."

"Then it's hopeless."

"Certainly your life must necessarily be viewed as a system comprising a greater complexity than three coins in a hat. Or would you say that you and your life are no more complex than three coins in a hat?"

"I don't know."

"How many coins do you think are in your hat?"

"I don't know."

"A vast array of subunits make up your life, events such as thoughts, feelings, sensations, other people, memories, fantasies, et cetera, et cetera, don't they?"

"Yes."

"Consequently it is impossible to imagine that you and your life are not subject to the rules governing the probabilistic behavior of systems."

"So I'm just off on this tangent, speeding up, just hurtling—"

"No, no, no, you wouldn't be speeding up."

"But I am."

"Not in the situation we've been—"

"But *I am!*"

"Well then, perhaps the force that impacted on you hasn't disappeared and is propelling you. Or you may have been knocked into a gravitational field whose powers of attraction were previously of little or no influence on you, but now they are hauling at you with irresistible results."

"But what is it? That's what I want to know."

"Your acceleration. We're talking about your acceleration."

"No, no, I mean, gravitational field of *what?* What gravitational field? I mean, what force? What's pushing at me?"

"Well, that's actually quite difficult to say. In astrophysics it is currently believed that the mutual gravitational attraction between various masses is governed by the magnitude of those masses and the distance between them. Consequently, it must be seen that everything is affected by everything else—the shifting of one remote, unseen, and unconsidered object such as another planet or some far-flung unseen galaxy—perhaps even undiscovered galaxy—will cause a modification in the normal routine of all other objects in its reach, including the earth and everything on it, of which you're one of those things."

"Planets? You're talking about planets?"

"Yes."

"Planets could be affecting me?"

"Is it not your experience frequently that something mysterious, some distant convergence, or a hidden addition or subtraction in a sector of existence of which you are in no way conscious—that this hidden occurrence produces an alteration in your behavior, your experience of yourself and the world around you? Suddenly, for no reason you can name, your natural powers of intellect are overwhelmed, your powers of foresight and proportion dismissed?"

"Sometimes I feel as if the future is hopeless—a vista I have no desire to inhabit."

"Exactly."

"My thoughts seem like the thoughts of someone else, someone who has no interest in my welfare. It's awful."

"I mean, life is a gravitational field. Life is a gravitational field. As are guilt and love. Guilt is a gravitational field. And hate and hope. Love is a gravitational field. Hate and hope are gravitational fields. Your past is a gravitational field. Your future. Some other person. Ghosts. Ghosts are gravitational fields. People are gravitational fields. Living people. Dead people. Hate. Envy. Envy is a gravitational field. Hate is a gravitational field."

"I'm starting to feel depressed. I'm feeling very depressed. I feel—"

"Do you want to talk about depression, about clinical psychology? Psychology is a gravitational field. Love, envy, rage, rancor—all are gravitational fields. By translating certain applicable terms from the

field of physics to that of psychology, we might delineate your difficulties insightfully."

"Things have been happening. Terrible things. Inexplicable things. I
thought you could help me."

"I am."

"No, no. Dreadful things. I've killed. I've killed."

"We've already dealt with death, with thermodynamics, with en-
tropy."

"But I want to stop."

"But you are doing these things. It's you who are doing them. You are
doing them, and if you're doing them, well, then, you are doing them
and you'll just have to keep on doing them, as far as I can see. The law
states that every body perseveres in its state of rest or uniform motion in
a right line—in your case, this 'veer' or 'tangent'—unless it is compelled to change that state by forces impressed upon it."

"You're saying I'm doomed to do these things—that's what you're
saying."

"No."

"It is. You're saying I'm fated to do these things, sentenced to do
them, damned to do them."

"Unless some unknown force intervenes. Unless some force impresses itself upon you! And you are compelled to change."

"What unknown force?"

"I don't—"

"Some unknown force could intervene? What force?"

"The law doesn't say."

"But some unknown force could intervene! And if it doesn't, I'm
doomed!"

"According to the law."

"What force? What force?"

"It's unknown."

"But it could save me! What is it?"

"The law leaves that up to chance."

"But what does it say?"

"It doesn't say. It's up to chance!"

"I could appeal! I could appeal to it! What is it?"

"Where are you going?"

"Your daughter!"

"Not now!"

"Your daughter, your daughter! I've got to see her."

"Listen to me!"

"You're telling me I'm doomed. You're telling me I have no hope."

"Don't go through that door!"

"I have to see her."

"NO!"

"I have to!"

"DON'T!"

Chapter Twenty-three

What I enter into is the night. It is a vaulted gloom inhabited by layers of shifting dark. Depth and definition dissolve and reappear, ceaselessly transforming beneath the domed twinkling of the stars. Under this moody spangling, I run. I don't know where I'm going. The road before me is a streak of gray climbing over the swelling ground. I hear my footsteps repeating in the dirt. Flight, in my current condition, appears indistinguishable from ardent approach. Retreat could be advance. Run where I might, I'll go where I must, for my stride is empowered by fate.

Ahead, the moon is a pockmarked orb haloed in lacy swirls. Lower on the horizon, clustered fragments of clouds are animated and emotional. Scablike particles join with pitch-black petals in a tumultuous fabric and I am fixed upon a veiny indentation, a darker curlicue that threatens to break open, gushing forth to fill the world with the otherworldly substance that, now constrained, makes the bulging sky so black.

I run quite quickly, with an oddly buoyant gait. But then, I've lost a great deal. Among the many things I am without, the first that comes to mind is hope. Every sense that I ever had of optimism or self-determination has lapsed. I am malleable and adaptable, initiating nothing. Fear has gone away, and so has shame, while rage, though available, makes a thin appeal. I have found myself doomed to conclusions and actions I can not resist. Tears are running down my cheeks. My knife is in the bag I lug. I have my tangle of rope and rags and scarves and hats.

Looking up, I find a shifting shape, like a demon in a cocoon, his stormy tail rising into spooky realms. What lies within those swirls? What terrible birth grows hidden in those depths? What law, natural or unnatural? What dark instruction? My next commission?

Throughout the length of the horizon, bruiselike lumps are proliferating, one among them more conspicuous than all the others. That darker curlicue I noted previously has grown even more ominous, swelling up and threatening to burst. Pressurized from within, the expanding orb has a translucent surface like the pupil of an eye opening onto the world, something dark and brainy peering out. The edges stir with blood and around it rolls a current of purple thickening with the growing stress behind it, until the sky starts to split, the panoramic darkness shaking.

And then what bursts forth to the accompaniment of the most gigantic silence I have ever heard is the morning. Out rushes a level disk of light, a plate of diamonds turning over to spill. Raining down upon me is light. In its tidal sweep, this storm of sunshine reveals everything. It's daybreak. That which I sensed as struggle, assailing me with its impression of blood and wounds—this was the war between night and day. From its outcome, cows are emerging, and weeds and grass and trees and horses are advancing out of shadowy clefts into fields of grass, a world of distinction afoot, adrift, alive.

I pass the rusty remnants of an abandoned car whose rear window frames a large squint-eyed rat lying on his side. Beside me the fence posts are crowned by a line of blackbirds backed by bushes beneath a sky of newborn reds and blues. My legs lift and pound; my heart gulps down my blood, the rushing air pumping my lungs, feeding my muscles. I'm going somewhere fast. It's ahead of me. I'm going straight. And as the road veers to my right, I turn without a second's doubt. I am on a line, and my line is fate. I am headed for where I am going.

I span a little bridge over a flashing creek. On I go, the grass wavering as I fly by. With undefinable wonder I cry out, causing some robins and blue jays to spring up from a pine tree for a better look at me. Their wings produce a clapping sound and I feel that, as they rotate above me, my appearance pleases them. I wave, and they dart upward on a diagonal.

Beside the road are egg-white rocks and from beneath a nearby log a rabbit scurries toward the deeper brambles, where he intends to inform his fellows of my presence. Drawn toward him, I trail along for several steps, and then I see the forest ahead. Even this distant visual contact sends me shying away from those dangers, never looking back, my breath slapping in my chest, my body coated with an icy sweat.

When I slow to a halt at the edge of a summit, the vista below is familiar. I'm looking down at my little house, to which I must now descend. Home is where I've been going, though I didn't know it. Home is where I will reach the climax of my struggles, where I will test the development of my abilities. Home is where I will put into practice those confrontational skills in whose preparation I've been devoted.

Now I see what I must do. I must save Tobias. After moving at a crouch for several steps, I start crawling on my belly, like a savage advancing on the refuge of civilized men. If I've learned anything it's that in the matter of confrontation, it's best to be wild. It's best to be insane. To confront the monster one must be a monster. My plan is to create the impression of an intruder, a burglar on a mercenary raid. I'll steal things I don't need, things I already own. I'll leave behind a scene of random destruction from whose midst I will have plucked Tobias. The newspaper headlines will speculate on robbery, a kidnapping, murder. Having confiscated every photograph she's ever taken of me, I will obliterate them all, every adulteration of my face at which she stares and thinks whatever she pleases, a kind of slime of thought to contaminate my hapless countenance bursting with my innocent feelings, my guile-less eyes. Never again will she violate these stolen figures of my inner-most life, some unconcealed thought, some pitiful sentiment exposed and glossily exhibited before her scorn. I will tear the house to shreds if I need to, but I will find them. I will break the walls and smash the stairs. Nor will her journals escape me. No, no, I'll rip apart the pages of her scribbling. Not a dot or letter of her slander will remain. Of all that she thought to perpetuate in words, I'll create tatters, a rubble like primitive tablets destroyed by a righteous power.

Now I'm darting across the last few yards that separate me from the house. For so long it seemed that preliminary things must consume me.

But now I'm galloping out from my time of preparation into the dawn of action, like a figure from a nightmare into the daylight world. If blood must be the means by which I ransom Tobias, I will be bloody. If horror must be the outcome, I am prepared. I have my knife. I have my ropes. I can barter in gore. I've been trained at her hands by viciousness, by scorn and treachery. With cruel lessons she has taught me, and I am ready to pass her test. Let her screams be my gauntlet. I will leave our house victorious, my little boy delivered like a princely prisoner in a royal war. I will enshrine him in the sanctuary of our cave. I will dress him in leaves and flowers, tree bark for a hat, crystal woven in his hair, and the petals stuck to his cheeks with honey. "We hover upon the earth," I will tell him. "Like flies on the apple's skin, Tobias. We buzz about, tasting, sipping, hungry for the sweetness." This is what I will say, hoping to make him understand. "Blooming in the sun, we disappear. And yet, unlike the flies, who vanish upward into the sky, it is into the very apple on which we have fed that we eventually depart, lying down to be embraced by life. We are not, and then we are. And then we are not. We begin in the bellies of our mothers, and end in the bowels of the earth pushing up daisies." And upon the craggy, dripping heights of our cavern walls I will inscribe crude gouges to express my thought in lines and dots.

Gazing up, I half expect to find a replica of that which rules my imagination rendered in the natural elements, a newborn constellation generated across the gleam of morning.

I'm pressed against the siding of the house, trying to slow my breath. The venture before me demands calm and premeditation. Its best enactment will find me gliding from room to room with the ease of a phantom. I begin to climb the drainpipe to the roof of the back room. From there I can slide easily into the master bedroom to begin my rampage. The joints in the pipe and the clamps that attach it to the house supply a series of paper-thin footholds. Groaning in my grasp, the tube starts to shudder, and I tighten my hold until my hands and fingers ache. The shingled roof is built at a moderate pitch, and when I heave myself over the edge onto my belly, the rough surface clings to the fabric of my clothing. With my left hand, I grab the support of a wrought-iron rod topped by a black rooster-shaped weather vane. Inching along the gritty shingles, I reach the wall and rise until my gaze is level with the window.

Peering into the bedroom, I see Tobias lying in his mother's arms, his little eyes twin pools of adoring bliss. Pressed against the glass, my ear extracts a miniaturized version of their tones and interplay. Words occur, but mainly this exchange is sighs and coos and purrs. She calls him "Little Bubble," and "Monkey-man." He giggles, sightless as a seer in the oblivion of a trance. They sound like elves or doves. Against my ribs, my heart thrashes. Wheeling away, I press my back against the wall while the awesome image of their tender involvement is brought to bear upon everything I see around me in the world. My brain projects a panoramic figure of their intimacy to soak every aspect of day with a ghostly impression of their limbs and eyes, and they are etched into the grass and clouds. They are a gigantic filigree of rapt and phantom fondness, a fantastic cuddling from which I am excluded.

Has he betrayed me for her, my sweet, my dear, my little Tobias? Am I utterly left out? What else can I conclude except that he has abandoned me, turning from me to her, unless I discover some hint of fraud in their embrace, a sign that his behavior has fear or delusion at its base, that he's feigning happiness because of intimidation, or because of fiendish hypnotic powers inflicted upon him. She could find no better tactic to defeat me than to deceive me into believing that I have been jilted by my little boy.

Looking back, I find the room is empty. If they were there as I recollect them, they have fled. The tangled quilt and sheets are proof of someone's occupancy, yet the evidence cannot establish the time of this disturbance. This could be the aftermath of sleepers days ago. Even weeks could have passed.

A nudge against the sill lifts the window in the frame. Though I am careful, the warped wood groans, and as I enter, the floorboards sigh in reaction to my weight. Then I'm standing there, as still as a thief. From the nearby bathroom, I hear sounds of splashing. Tobias yelps, and my wife emits a tuneful sigh while relating a tale about a donkey who meets a clown. In the next few minutes, she sings about a happy puppy and tells a joke about a mouse. Her voice is warm, affectionate, tolerant.

Rising to my tiptoes, I steal across the rug into the hallway and slide, inches at a time, along the polished floor until I'm positioned to peer in the crack between the door and the frame. Like a sniper through his telescope, I squint into their idyll. Crowned in soap and hair, he rules a multitude of bobbing toys as colorful as a discarded deck of cards.

Plastic men in big hats rock amid ducks and paddling dogs in sailor suits, the foamy surface a pleasant sea whose only turbulence is his robust happiness. With a golden sponge, his mother strokes his back in swirls, and he rocks in bliss like a prince in a royal cradle. Trembling probes my knees. My heart grinds, my lungs shrinking to the size of thimbles. The photos, I think. The journal. In them I can substantiate my theories, I can verify my discovery of her planned infanticide. I can find the proof I need. I might even uncover evidence of unnatural powers, because black magic, hexes, sorcery are the only way I can think of to explain the confounding scenes I have just witnessed.

In the bedroom, the third drawer of the second dresser discloses the journal beneath a pile of underwear and T-shirts. When I persist a little further, probing the socks, I'm rewarded with the photo album. The fact that these items, charged with such significance, were so lackadaisically hidden testifies either to her innocence or to the sophistication of her cunning, and I think I know which. Sitting on the edge of the bed, I gather my resources because I must conduct a thorough and focused study of these documents. I start with the journal, reading and analyz-ing every word, looking for clues to obscure meanings, tracing possible patterns, searching for symbolic phrases, or repeated words whose use might betray the existence of a code.

Yet after half an hour or more, all my diligence uncovers is the way she tracked the mundane with a stupefying devotion, as if she believed that the most ordinary of activities, once written down, must reveal unusual virtues. Trips to town are recorded; shopping lists are en-shrined along with errands long ago fulfilled. The weather, as if it's an heirloom whose details must never be forgotten, is enshrined. The dates of luncheons and school events are provided; whom she saw and whom she spoke to. Every page is essentially the same, the narrow spaces stuffed with her rather large, unpretty handwriting, preserving a barrage of trivia through which my presence floats like a neighborly bear, occasionally encountering her to comment on the weather, the light, the temperature.

Nor is there anything sinister in the photos, other than her gruesome inability to properly frame a picture. People are crushed together in a corner, one missing a head, the other lopped off along a vertical seam from skull to crotch. Arms jut into the foreground, displaced and disem-bodied. Anonymous fingers curl in odd, constricted gestures. Some legs are amputated at the ankles, others at the thighs. Occasionally figures survive intact, but at such a remote point in the landscape that, while recognizable as human, they are never identifiable as any particular person. I appear about as frequently as I did in the journal, and for all the distortion and dismemberment I suffer, I can't claim that I am shown in any disfavor. I seem to be always smiling and relaxed, whether I am whole or in parts. Uniformly, I appear as a jocular, affable oaf. If her purpose is to accumulate evidence against me, my crimes are apparently ease and mirth.

Falling from my fingers, the photos whisper to the rug. Nothing intervened, I think. I can hear the tender shuffling of Tobias and his mother as they patter down the stairs toward the kitchen. Judged by the continuing endearments and sighs, the giggles and silly noises, this transit is giving them reasons to escalate the enjoyment already bubbling between them. Through the carpeted floor under my feet, I hear their tittering amid the amiable clinking of pots and cups and spoons as she prepares a meal for them to share.

Envy assails me, a humbling surge. From my toes to the roots of my hair, I constrict, as if I'm in the clutches of some monstrous wrestler who lusts to break my back and pulverize my bones. Falling upon the bed, I close my eyes and beg to be released. Tears writhe in my depths like beasts threatening to rend the misty tissues of my insides if they are not released.

Staggering, I manage to conduct myself from one support to the next. I recoil off the hallway wall and hit the balustrade at the top of the stairs. Like an acrobat making a daring leap, I risk the calamity of a terrible tumble down the stairs. It's a race between my enfeebled legs and raw momentum that doesn't care if it hurts me. I crash into the kitchen. From the expressions with which they face me, I infer the wanton thing I must appear to be. They clutch one another. Only a brute could provoke such an embrace. They hide their eyes, and then peek out, only to duck back, as if the composite of their little bones and skin might preserve them from my wrath were I to let it loose. For they have hurt me, and I think they know it. But I can't hurt them back, for they are good and I am bad. They are right and I am wrong. They have one another.

Looking past their trembling shapes, I am startled by the sight of the window containing the moon in retreat. Immense at first, it is shrinking down as it flies off into an infinitely deepening dark. Night, I am startled to perceive, has taken back the hour. The line of my life is moving through this room. Like a dagger piercing the sheerest tissue paper, I am rushing on from here to where I am charged to go. I am wanted in the night.

In Tobias's glassy eyes, I cannot help but read his fear that my next act will bring him harm. "No, no," I purr. "No, no." From out of the grim uncertainties of my past I hurtled here, my tangent undiminished. I have passed through this day of hopeless desires and deeds as if through a set of shapes drawn on air, nothing to deter my pell-mell course into this house, which I am now about to exit. "Forgive me, I beg you," I say, "I'm sorry, I'm sorry. I'm going. I have no choice." Though they stir, I am not to be delayed. "There are laws," I say, "and I have met them." I have my knife, my ropes, my hats. I have my stocking caps, my gloves and coat. "What awaits me is my fate."

Atop an elevation afforded by the terrain, heaving toward the road, I pause, feeling a tremor beneath my feet, a disturbance of some magnitude moving through the planes and layered plates of the earth, as if a signal is being sent from one point to another regarding something significant that I am certain pertains to me.

Glancing back toward our house, I discover my wife and son padding out onto the back porch. Side by side they peer up at me, their arms upraised to wave. My gesture, returning theirs, stimulates them to huddle together in an urgent little conference out of which they reappear with an increased need to communicate with me. While it is my wife's many rings that catch the moonlight's luster to leap off her hand, it is Tobias's wide blue eyes that blaze. They shout my name, calling to me loudly, beckoning that I come back, begging me to return. But I cannot.

"I have to go," I shout. "I am wanted in the night."

BOOK FOUR

Angels

Chapter Twenty-four

Hastening along the path toward the old two-lane that cuts through the countryside some forty yards in front of our house, I'm startled by a shape on the far shoulder of the road. The silhouette of a man is sculpted against the smoky horizon by the distant yet emphatic moon. Beyond him, the inky tones of the field distinguish themselves by degrees from the black of his suit and the glistening black of his shoes. Elderly and melon-faced, he has a thickish salt-and-pepper beard, and his tufted brows italicize the gleam of his glasses across his brow. A white shirt shows in splinters beneath the open jacket and vest he wears, a scarf flung around his neck.

I've reached the edge of the road now. If he notes my arrival, his response is small. The wind stirs his hair, but his posture remains hunched over, his interests intensely subjective. I'm trying to remember where I left my car. I have to get going, even though I don't know exactly where I'm headed. I'm looking up and down the road, wondering if I should hitchhike. The road is totally without a sign of traffic. Across the way, the man is standing there, inert and etched in light, his head bowed, his total lack of interest in me generating a growing fascination in me about him. Though I'm thinking of other things, I'm staring at him.

When he suddenly breaks from his immobility, striding off along the shoulder, I fear he's leaving. I find myself darting toward him. His manner appears leisurely, but I have to struggle to maintain his pace. In fact, I'm losing ground. On the verge of breaking into a sprint, I'm startled when he pivots and comes racing back in my direction. I assume an idle pose as he goes shooting past. He's pacing, I realize. In order to facilitate his thoughts, his prowling mind has enlisted his body into sympathetic locomotion. Now he goes right by me, his eyes searching behind me, their cast full of alarm and question. By simply turning I can see things from his perspective, and when I duplicate his vantage, hoping to discover the source of his concerns, I see my own house across the road, its ground-floor windows warmly glowing. Why is he so worried? What's he looking at?

As if to answer my questions through a close examination of his manner, I whirl to find him. Having strode off a dozen or so yards, he's hastening back toward me. Behind his glasses, his eyes are panicky, his brow a knot of thought. As he speeds past, I reach out to grab him, but my hand stops short. "What are you doing?" I cry, surprising even myself.

With the effects of my outburst, he hesitates. His eyes seek me out and settle on me gradually, as if we occupy different realms and he must make a series of complex perceptual adjustments before he can see me clearly. For a moment, I fear that I'm like some staticky radio signal that he lacks the patience to tune in. But then he cuts my mounting distress with a voice that is gravelly and paradoxically gentle. "Horrible things have been happening," he says. "I've been trying to find out about them." He's looking off at my house shot through with light, an ember whose excess rises in a canopy against the dark above the rooftop.

"I thought something horrible was going to happen in that house," he says.

"That house over there? The one you were looking at?"

"Yes."

"I thought so, too."

"Did you?"

"Yes."

"Perhaps something horrible did happen. Perhaps it has already happened," he says.

"No."

"But it could have."

"No."

"How can you be so sure? Perhaps it's happening right now."

"I was there."

"You were there?"

"They're very happy."

"Happy?"

"Yes. I checked. I was there."

"Well," he says nervously, his lips puckering. "My evidence was clear. It brought me here. I was very worried. I was certain. Are you sure that everything is all right?"

"Yes."

"Perhaps I've made a mistake. Perhaps I've come to the wrong place." He's beseeching me, his eyes a kind of threat. "My evidence goes no further. Don't you see? It brought me to this place and then it stopped."

"Is that why you came here?" I say. "I mean, *here!*" I retrieve and prepare to reissue the word, as if it's an instrument I've misused. I feel I need to inflict it on the moment, as one might pound his fist against a door. "*Here!*" I say. "*Here!*" He's looking at me as if he finds me increasingly interesting. "What evidence? What evidence?" I say.

"What brought you here?" he says. "Was it the evidence—the evidence you gathered that brought you here? You came here, too, didn't you?" His eyes are fixed on me. His presence crowds me, though he has not advanced an inch. He's drawing from his pocket the mahogany squiggle of a large-bowled pipe, which he packs, tamping down the shredded tobacco with his thumb. "Hmmmm," he says, scanning our surroundings. When he strikes a match, the glass of his spectacles fills with pools of dancing crimson. I see a replica of my own stricken countenance, apparently floating in a realm of fire. "Maybe you're why I'm here," he says.

"Why would you want me?"

"Perhaps we're struggling with the same issue, the same question, but approaching it from different perspectives."

"I know very little," I say. "I just—"

"Often we know more than we think."

"What I do know, I don't understand."

"But there are certain things that you do know."

I don't like the way he's looking at me, but I answer honestly. "I guess," I say.

"We could talk over what you've learned, what I've learned. We could go somewhere and talk over what we've figured out."

"Go where?"

"Just walk."

"Walk where?" I say. "Where?"

"Through the night. Should we end up talking late, my daughter can prepare a dinner for us."

I cannot breathe or speak. The seconds go rushing past me and I stand there frozen. At the edge of my perception, a kind of recognition whirls just beyond my grasp, a thick tugging like a magnetic blur of memory whose specifics refuse to come into focus.

"What's wrong?" His eyes are narrowing on me.

"I don't know."

"What first prompted your attention?"

"What?"

He smiles at me tolerantly. "At the very least, we might have a pleasant stroll. I'm worried about my daughter. I've lost her."

"But you said—you said, 'dinner' . . ."

"If we find her."

"Oh."

"My first clue was the behavior of the moon."

"The moon?"

"Yes," he says. He turns and steps away.

"The moon?" I say, following along after him.

"There were many clues. I pursued them; they led me here, but now there's only you."

"Horrible things were happening. That's what started me."

"I see, I see," he says.

"Horrible things—that's what I saw."

We're moving along easily, gliding through shadows and columns of moonlight, the weeds brushing our trouser legs.

"It wasn't like tonight," he says, "when it started for me."

"Oh?"

He gestures upward at the moon fixed far above us. "It came swooping down into a forest, the moon did. I wasn't there; I wasn't in the forest. I was quite a ways off. I tried to get closer. As I ran, the trees looked like they were on fire. Only silver. Next I heard howling. Who or what was the source of this outcry? I wondered. But by the time I reached that part of the woods where I expected to find this disturbance, everything was quiet. The moon was no longer there. I felt certain that I had made the correct calculations and run to the right spot, but now the moon was back in the sky. I saw it. I saw the stars. I wondered if such an event as this, which I had never seen before—the fall and ascension of the moon—I wondered if such events were more common than I had previously imagined. Was it possible that such things happened with some regularity and I had simply failed to notice? It occurred to me to examine the heavens in order to measure the merit of this new idea against the phenomena I might observe. I decided to mark the stars, and keep a record. Perhaps some previously unnoted pattern would reveal something pertinent to the questions I had to answer. I was worried that I alone had seen this strange event. I was worried that I would be compelled to decipher it utterly alone—unassisted by any other human."

His perplexity accuses me. I cannot deny that I have the power to diminish his concerns. When he looks at me, I say, "I howled. I was there."

"That was you."

"Yes."

"And then you disappeared."

"I ran away."

"I've been looking for you. I wanted to talk to you. Where did you go?"

"I ran away."

"When I couldn't find you, I looked to the sky for guidance, for understanding. After all, it was in the heavens that this strange event had had its beginning. I tried to map the behavior that I found above me, transits and countertransits, ellipses, drifts, and epicycles. I stood as might a sentry abandoned and forgotten by his civilization, wondering at the lonely vastness of what I saw. Comets flung themselves across the dark. I started to wonder if the heavens ended with the last thing I saw, the farthest speck, the final shadow. The end of what I could see appeared absolute and thick as a wall. I tried to designate the point at which my eyesight stopped. This was the frontier of what I knew, but was it the end of what existed? I doubted it. It was the deficiencies of my eyes, I knew, and not this juncture of pure air that blinded me to what lay beyond, which could be nothing at all, or uncountable multitudes of phenomena. How could I ever label as sound or faulty my theories and speculations when I had no idea what lay beyond this point? Worlds could reside out there with occupants who might declare my ideas absolute or make them untenable, or impel me toward the invention of some new set of alternatives. I found my fancy rushing in to populate the void. Angels! Sprites! A world of souls! Facing the sudden possibility of such thriving mystery, I was startled when I began to weep. If the invisible had souls, so did the dead, so did the living. Confused, I longed to reduce, if not abolish, my troublesome emotions. I needed a more rational means by which to go on, by which to live. Looking up, or down, or straight ahead, it seemed necessary to ask, 'What am I looking at?' Fantastic shapes awaited me, colors, darting shots and flashes about which I lacked the power to think. The world, reduced to sensation, was indiscernible, a protean rush.

"Growing dizzy, growing queasy, I understood nothing. How could I continue to assert that I even saw the phenomena around me without some categorization and measurement, some idea serving as a prism through which my mind could flow to refashion the data at which I stared into something known, into knowledge, into understanding? Was it possible to merely observe? And even if possible, wasn't it fruitless without the guidance of some kind of hypothesis by which to interpret and organize what I looked at? I felt myself borne upward by nothing I could perceive to an ungrounded point, where I teetered, sustained only by the momentum of my own mind."

A silence settles between us, and as it lengthens, his hand falls through the air to land on my shoulder. I glance at him and nod. I have been unable to keep myself fully concentrated on him. As if drifting at the margins of sleep, I've listened with a portion of my mind while another part of me sank away through a shimmering reverie at whose center burned the idea of his daughter. When he first mentioned her, I felt my concentration cut in half. Many of my faculties hung upon every twist of his experience and his accompanying philosophical exploits, but at the same time I was lost in anticipation of the ecstasy that I felt his mention of his daughter seemed to promise. And now that we have paused in the yard beside an old farmhouse and started sneaking toward a window bordered in lacy curtains, I am convinced that, when he points inside, he will present her to me.

But I'm wrong. I see an array of moody people seated in sullen interest before a television. A fat middle-aged man is slumped in a recliner, his feet up. A stick of a woman in a housedress sits slackly on a couch covered in plaid slipcovers, her legs tucked under her. Two young boys are sprawled on the floor in their underwear. A little girl in a purple print dress snores in an armchair beside the couch, her head flung back, her mouth open.

"Could something terrible be about to happen here?" he whispers to me.

I stare for a long time through a mist of dizzying possibilities.

"I think it is," he says. "I feel my daughter is in danger. Is she there?"

I'm silent, the possibilities multiplying. "I don't see her," I say.

"No?"

"I don't think so."

"Is something horrible going to happen here? I think it is."

"No."

"I'm worried about her. I'm so worried."

"Where is she?"

"I don't know."

"Well, she's not here," I say.

"You're sure? We don't have to go in."

"No," I say. "We don't."

Looking around, I realize how far we've traveled. Divided as I was, I must have walked for miles, listening to him. The horizon holds nothing familiar. The trees are recognizable as trees, but not as particular trees that I've seen before. The same is true of the rocks, the shrubs through which we're passing.

"We have to find her," he says. "We have to."

"I know."

The next house into which we look is empty and still, the linoleum gleaming with moonlight, the hallways and chairs unoccupied. Dirty aluminum pots and a black iron frying pan clutter the stove. Unwashed dishes fill the sink.

Soon we're crossing a wide dark meadow like a bay surrounded by cliffs and clouds. We've advanced quite a ways in silence before he starts to speak again, his voice quavering with unexpressed emotion upon the fluctuations of the wind.

"There were more clues," he says. "More clues than the moon. And though I was desperate to understand, I couldn't do it. There was no problem accumulating clues, no problem accumulating mysteries. The difficulty lay in interpreting and understanding what I collected. What could be believed? What was true? When was something known to be true? Were the powers of reason and testing and objective documentation the only trustworthy methods? It seemed that it must be so. And yet there were contradictory moments—moments when an interior stirring, a sudden sensation of forceful conviction deep within seemed undeniable, a compelling fount of truth even though it was completely without objective validation."

Now we are peeping through a vertical slit along the side of a window with drawn shades. The dingy room holds two elderly people slumped on a couch. Their eyes gaze vacantly into the air before them. The man wears coveralls. The woman is dressed in a tattered flannel robe.

"Horrible, horrible," he says.

"What?"

"Don't you see it? It's happening to them right in front of us. Look at them." The grief in his voice condemns my inattention, my lack of sensitivity to the plight of these people. But they're old, they're strangers, I don't know them. I feel oppressed by them, though I don't understand how they can be affecting me. "Look," he says.

I don't want to participate in his project anymore. His daughter is all I want. In my imagination, she adorns the glass through which we stare, her lithe legs, the inky lengths of her hair, her hips and pale little ankles, her tits, her moist thick lips. I feel so strange, my heart speeding.

"Look at them," he says. "I think something horrible is happening right now."

The man is wobbling across the floor. The woman is mesmerized by an interior dismay, her wrinkled skin hauling at the stems of her arms.

When I turn to my companion, I see that the misery of this room has infected him. He's pacing back and forth, his shoulders twisted, his manner anxious.

"It was on such a night as this," he says, "that I began my first period of hopeless thinking. Inside me was a thing of fierce yet utterly inarticulate character, a kind of hybrid of warning and accusation. I had to understand it, but I couldn't. It would not let me go, nor would it fully disclose itself. I realized suddenly that there were large fields and sanctuaries of my soul sealed off from my own impassioned inquiry. There was no denying the need I felt, the summons, the significance, the unavailability. I began to wonder about my hidden parts. What was in them? They existed and they were unknown. But were they unknowable? Such was the force and magnitude of this idea that it forced me on until I came face to face with a startling and basic inadequacy in the functioning of my mind, my vaunted consciousness. It seemed these exalted powers operated within a narrow, limited realm. I saw myself as a man who had shone a flashlight into the night and then declared that he saw the world—he comprehended everything—or at the least he saw and understood everything that was worthwhile. I no longer understood my mind. I no longer understood my beliefs. I no longer had confidence that I knew what I was talking about, that I could distinguish between those objects that existed outside my being—such as shoes and socks and trees and cars—and those objects that were known to occupy my interior, such as plans and images and speculations. Pondering this dilemma, I felt myself threatened, overwhelmed. The world was a dynamic flow too protean and mutable for me to abstract it and think about it accurately. I was doomed to a whirl of pointless subjectivity while tumbling through my life like a man caught in a storming sea. Around me was an ocean, and I was falling into it. The waves were reaching up to enfold me, the moonlight flung about in foam. And I had to formulate an explanation for their struggle and need, and as I set out to do this, I saw that I must first explain my own struggle, my own need. What was I looking at? The ocean wanted me, yet I wanted something else. Emptiness, filling my heart, had brought me to this moment. I wanted something I did not have, something I could not even name. Was I to think myself alone in this? Was I to think the stars wandered on and on for some other reason? Or were they seekers, just as I was? If we disowned the order inherent in our minds, there was no other we could claim. There was only this lack to be explained, this lack in everything, as if something essential had been lost, some unity destroyed."

He's so distressed and consumed now that he doesn't even come with me up to the next house, an abandoned, ramshackle wreck, the walls soft with rot, the window cracked. He stands in a nearby field talking.

"I began to envision a separation at the very heart of things, a division at the core of the world, as in the estrangement of two lovers—but lovers who were extraordinary, their sensibilities unparalleled except by the virtues they found in one another, their synthesis as mysterious as the force in living tissue.

"That's when I realized that I was alone. I had lost my daughter. Or rather, I was losing her as I stood there struggling, as I stood there thinking, foundering. I could feel it happening. My bones began to ache. I wanted to stroke her cheeks and kiss her arms and feel her fingers twisting in my hair. But I could not find her. I went from place to place, down roads to mountains and deserts and cities. But I could not find her. I came to a house, your house, but she wasn't there. You came to me and we started to talk. 'My daughter,' I said, 'my daughter. The ocean, the waves, my loss.' It seemed to be the truth. My words seemed to hold the truth, and though I could not back my discourse with absolute claims, my heart rallied in support of the tenets of this small but aching philosophy. My need to convince you of its merit took on sudden, huge dimensions. I had to convince you. And then I realized why. It was because I did not in fact exist. There was only you. I was a memory, a flickering fiction, nothing more. It had all happened long ago and I was just remembering it and I was fading. I had lost her. She was long ago lost. She was gone from me. I was gone from her.

"The stars call out their radiance, each light a signal of pure longing. The rain is yearning. The rain, the wind are mourning. Each blade of grass and arching tree, each flower and ripening fruit rises from an endless yearning. From yearning all is generated; in yearning it flourishes, with yearning it fades. The world, in each and every one of its facets, is the product of my calamity, my separation. What has come from the loss of my great and wondrous love is everything."

Staring in a window at a table set for two, I see her enter the room. I turn to express my gratitude to my companion, but he's gone, leaving an emptiness through which the night is visible. A faint mix of shivering colors convinces me for a second that I've spied him in the distance, and then the colors transform into a cow trundling along a hill. The gap between is a windblown field of weeds that curves like a bowel to hold the dark. The distant shaggy trees that seem an aspect of the sky, and nothing hints at him.

My heart draws drops of ardor as I peer through the window into the room disclosed in warm light. He's vanished, just as he feared he would, having lost his daughter. But I've found her. She's a sylph with dark glossy hair walking across the polished hardwood floor, the furniture carefully arranged throughout the shimmering room. On a long, rectangular table she's setting down a pitcher of water. When she retreats a stride to evaluate the preparations she's making for us, I'm touched by the conscientiousness of her effort.

Two table settings lie on lily-shaped mats on opposite sides of a candelabra with three purple candles flowering up from the brassy base. For the moment that she's stationary, I'm free to examine her as she stands with her weight distributed so that her hip juts out ecstatically, and I find my eagerness for our encounter rising. She leans to pick at some flaw in the tabletop. Beneath her white T-shirt, her breasts are small and perfect. When she glides across the room, they shiver against the rippling cotton. For a moment, she pauses in the doorway, her bare feet set one on top of the other, then she slips from sight.

It's time to go inside. It's time to light the candles. Expecting company, why should she have locked her windows? The hazy, comforting light that I enter bubbles from an overhead lamp ringed with tiny bulbs. In order to make a good impression, I start practicing an earnest, thoughtful speech whose sentiments threaten to press tears from my eyes. I hope I will not be harshly judged for any inappropriate emotion. A clumsy compliment or error in protocol will not, I hope, arouse her disdain, since I have her father's approval.

Tiptoeing to the table, I pass the kitchen doorway and smell the tangy mix of aromas wafting out, some laced with cloves in a background of other complex fragrances I can't identify. The fact that she is working so inventively for us stirs a sense of tender gratitude. Striking a match, I move the tear of light to catch the candlewick. The flame of the second candle flares in duplication of its neighbor as I touch them together, then it trembles and bows to the right. I feel a draft running along my fingers and know that something behind me has shoved the air. I turn and find her standing in the doorway, a bowl of flowers in her hands. Dark and wide, her startled eyes suggest I have arrived earlier than expected.

"Hello," I say. "Am I early?"

"What?" she answers. Through trembling lips she manages to ask, "Who are you?"

Her bafflement startles me. "No, no," I tell her.

And then she shrieks: "What do you want?!"

It hurts to scream the word that comes out of my mouth like flesh ripped from my tongue and spit out: "Love!" I spasm with a humiliated desire to retract what I've said, and then I erupt again: "Love! Love!"

She faints. It happens quickly, and yet in stages. First delirium overcomes her eyes. Her fingers, limp as string, let go of the bowl. The porcelain disintegrates against the floor amid splashing stems and leaves, rolling bulbs, spraying petals. Midfall, she reaches with a kind of flicker of her hand, as if to suggest a different course than the one we've begun. The T-shirt rises to her navel. She hits with a sigh. Before I can move, she's lying there. My heart is trembling. I reach to pick her up. Though dreamy and easy to lift, her form is substantial. Something sweet and carnal rises in her breath. For all her fabulous qualities, her body consists of a dense and amazing softness. I press her to my chest, my arms entirely around her, my fingers fitting into the creases between her ribs, which are like strands of glass. I stroke these delicate indentations. I'm sick of fate, I think. Clutching her, I begin to move. One leg follows the other, our bodies swaying around the room. I manage several turns and then I take a big, graceless leap, and I have to tighten my embrace so that momentum cannot rip her from my arms. Through the cotton of her shirt, I feel her breasts. From her parted lips nuzzled open with my nose, I take a breath.

Intending to lift her hands to my lips, I lay her down on a pile of pillows. But her hands are bound. Ropes are coiled around her wrists, locking them behind her back. The knife, I think. I'll cut her loose. Rummaging through my bags, I find it, but then it's in my hands, the broad blade curving out, the weight compelling, the tip hypnotic. She lies bound in the corner, and fate has put this weapon into my hand. I'm staggering toward the silky bundle she has become, a stew of pillows and ropes and tattered clothing. Am I to destroy her? Am I to kill her and deprive the world of his daughter?

Ardor goes stinging through my veins. The clatter at the window is the moon pawing the glass, working to break the glass with an assault of light more savage than I have ever seen, and I jump as if electrocuted.

Ahead of me, the ropes that wrap around the girl are myriad and tangled. It's as if a spider rather than a man has fallen victim to an overwhelming desire to possess her, though I'm the thing crawling toward her, struggling to cross an intervening distance that defies my efforts. The gap between us consists not of air and space but of a harsher, sterner element, like a stricture against which I have failed to mount a sufficient argument. What? I want to shout. What?

It's a shock when her foot brushes my outstretched hand. I've reached her when I thought I couldn't. Now proximity reveals that the ropes I saw as restraints are in fact a swaddling, winding her in celebratory loops and folds. The smell of her hair is startling. Her skin has a pungency whose effects I can feel in my veins. Tension and confusion make the simple act of breathing difficult, as if I have been transported to an altitude where the air is thin. My fingers strain, and though no one twists my arm, my fingers cramp, my muscles trembling against a hidden longing that could break my arm. There's a clattering when the knife hits the floor. I kick it so it goes rasping off into the corner. Like the rain and clouds and trees, I am filled with yearning.

Strange, I think, to try to elude fate's commands, like a slave attempting rebellion. Won't the vindictive powers who have governed me to this moment simply hunt me down and crush me? Yet I feel defiant, my heart laden with the queasy thrill of abandon and rage in the face of a despot whose vengeful nature is known. And then I glimpse a flaw in fate's ubiquitous control, a flaw through which I can slip to seek a form of freedom. If I must end up enacting fate's decrees in every circumstance, then it doesn't matter what I do. Having stripped myself, I will do the same for her. I will touch her where and how I want to. Infantile is how I feel. I feel ferocious in my desire to plunge into the forbidden. Luminous is how I feel, as if I draw an electric current from whatever part of her I touch or lick or suck. She's not a thing I could give up easily, her clothing strewn among my own, as if we were once a single creature who has now impetuously disrobed. Clutching her, I groan. I am no more master of the muscles of my heart or the pumping of my lungs than of this ruddy hardness risen up between my legs. Witch or dream, sorceress or angel, she is mine and I am hers as I move to enter where she has been made to fit me. For reasons of her own, she mews. Surrendering to an ancient wish, I erupt with yips and yelps. I open my eyes and look into her eyes and see a frightened human being. Why is she so frightened? And then I see that it isn't she. It isn't his daughter. Who are you? I ask. It's just some frightened girl. It's just some frightened human being. Where is his daughter?

And with this realization she disappears, and rushing up to replace her is someone else, or something else, something huge and authoritative, a storming imperious creature in whose hands I am small. I can't escape. I'm lying with my arms outstretched on what seems a plate of air, while she, with her own anatomy composed to be my perfect match, fits herself upon me, pressing in such a way that I cry out with appetites aroused to accept and swell this fearful symmetry. I cry again, louder, warning myself to resist, for she is overwhelming me, merging into me. I writhe and shout in protest. Mutability is a vast and comprehensive dimension, and in it she is entering into me, vanishing into me. The most steadfast of objects is revealed as a composition of quaking specks. My discrete and multiple molecules are acquiescing; they're struggling to adapt and find an exact accord to her, and in the blast and fusion of the sudden resolution of our differences, she is a radiant explosion filling me.

"Let's go," she says.

I don't know where we are.

"Don't worry," she says.

For quite a time we sail through a brooding penumbra before the gloom begins to resonate with roars and howls. Terrible, heartrending voices give evidence of grotesque ceremonies proceeding in the surrounding murk. Who suffers in this unnatural dark? Am I being brought to join them? Am I being delivered in accordance with the laws of fate and men? I have sinned against both. Is this hell? As if my questions are a clutter against which my foot has struck, I stumble. I clutch the only thing I can find, the fingers of my guide, to keep from falling.

Now a hand lunges up from the dark alongside me. The fingers snatch at the extremities of my coat, snarling in the tattered hem. The force of my recoil hauls my assailant partway into view. His eyes petition me, while his stricken face acknowledges that he's lost. He falls away. As he submerges, his features depart in lingering phases. The loss I feel is so excruciating that I leap into the forest's depths. Pawing at an object that appears to be an arm, I find him flailing under me. Once I have him, it's not hard to bring him up, gurgling and hiccuping, his gratitude like a baby's. To reassure him, I look directly into his eyes. Something familiar in his features is growing stronger, as if he's gaining detail under the effects of my contemplation, like a photographic print responding to the perfect chemical solution, until I realize that this figure is not entirely unknown to me. This phantom is no stranger, but the one I abandoned beneath the tree that day the Old Man tied me up, the day he shot the bird and taught me lessons. Now the figure reaches toward me, and in the ease of my acceptance of him he is dissolving, as if he's air and I can breathe him in.

Next thing I know I am running off to investigate a frightful growling. I see a tawny beast lash out a paw that rips the eye from a tinnier, catlike opponent. Impulsively, I pick up the eye. Dipping the tattered pieces into the shallows of a nearby creek, I hope to heal them. My guide wants to know what I've found, what I have in my hand, so I uncurl my fingers and see the animal's eye looking up from my palm.

"We're here," she says. Turning toward her, I face a deep and layered darkness that ends the visible world. Her voice emerges from out of these impenetrable shadows. Inching near, I feel a moist updraft icing my skin. On my tiptoes, I lean forward. What awaits me is a pit.

"Where are you?" I say.

"Here," she replies.

"Come back and get me." I am inching forward to test whether or not the terrain will sustain me.

"There's nothing between us. Just come across."

"Across what?"

"Don't you hear me? I'm waiting."

"There's something there."

"You have to jump."

"Come and get me."

Now I'm listening and talking to the dark. I lean into the emptiness, hoping to glimpse her.

"You have to jump," she calls.

I see a distant flicker, but nothing more. Still, I'm alarmed. I'm certain I've just detected the first signs of something horrible approaching. My stomach does a whirl. I see a surging shape, like a creature rising through the sea, a thousand waving, scheming coils. Several icy loops are ringing my ankle, while another moistly strokes my throat. Peering up from within the monster's nearing mouth is my half-digested face, lacerated and dripping gore. My skin feels rubbery, a sheath of scales, my nostrils flared. My eyes, frozen in the monster's gullet, are lunar and despotic, a dead and pitiless gleam. Loudly, I start to curse. Rising on an increasing furor, this appalling egoism, this murderous appetite, is me. In my desperation, I writhe, and we are a single viper squirming on a mirror. I teem with preparations to be devoured, for he is licking me and beginning to draw me in. He does a nauseating permutation, and while he swirls in a most abhorrent manner, I pray that, though he will gnaw my limbs and suck my bones, my heart is hers, and then I try to jump. Thunderously, I pass through him.

In a blaze of gratification she awaits me, and what the flame of her figure illuminates is a valley stretching out behind her, its slopes and crevices filled like a bowl crammed with flowers. Only this landscape is not packed with flowers, but with dogs, a field of moist black noses and shiny eyes. Dogs of every kind in a sea of fur, and they are singing, their tails wagging happily, or raised like banners, or curled to fondle their neighbor. Wandering their ranks, I see puppies at various stages and adults of every age and breed. Big dogs rest their heads on little ones, and long-haired dogs mix with fuzzy ones, and all of them are singing. Soprano spaniels and baritone collies elevate their cries. Some, apparently, have flutes and cellos in their throats. Hidden in the guts of others are harps and violins stroked by the ebb and flow of their breath. They're flawless, their effort glorious, verging on the transcendent. Though I'm drawn to join them, and clearly encouraged by their manner, my tongue lies dead in my mouth. They're holy, I feel; they're sacred. Certain that I would only sully their powers with my intrusion, I cannot make a sound.

As I move deeper into their number, the melodies they've introduced are starting to return in variations, and with an advancing complexity that feels nearly sublime. Lulled by the extent of their accomplishment, I'm drifting in a kind of dreamy serenity when I'm jolted by the introduction of a series of sour notes. I look around in dismay as this dissonance continues, and then I find a behemoth Saint Bernard. Head back, mouth open, he relishes his shameful bleats. I don't understand how he can sing so loudly when he has no talent. Like me, he should be quiet. His ineptitude is appalling. His lack of sensitivity is inexcusable. Indifferent to the harm he's causing, he continues bellowing, growing even louder. I'm on my way to tell him to shut up. His offense seems so heinous that I'm preparing to slap him in the face to enforce my demand, when three notes of such sincerity emerge from him that my heart shrinks with shame at my arrogance. To the deep and secret orchestration on which this music is based, he is necessary and faultless.

As if rich and passionate brass and woodwinds have been added, the voices of the beasts escalate. Advancing out of their prelude, they celebrate some new and valued development, and I can only think that the understanding I've just reached has brought them a kind of fulfill-ment. Under the influence of their seductive voices, I'm slipping into their midst, their melodic creaturehood sweeping aside my individual existence. I am singing and bumping about amid them. A shepherd puts his paw on my foot, a cocker spaniel nudges my knee. I'm licked by Afghans, sniffed by collies. A poodle winks at me. A playful wolfhound wags his tail. What had seemed a mere bestial eruption is revealed by my participation to be a musical apotheosis both primordial and sophis-ticated in its nature and development. It comes again, a tidal repetition tumbling over me and bearing me into their throbbing heart, from which our voices are lifted together, my throat tingling, for the subject of the singing of these dogs is my life. I surrender, bellowing without the slightest reservation now, my arms thrown back, my commitment so extreme that I am light-headed, dropping to my knees.

And then the noises that I am making are no longer melodic. They're strangled, suffering. My breath is harsh, my tones desperate, and the savagery against which I am flailing is almost over before I realize it has commenced. The dogs are devouring me. They've fallen on me, their tongues, their jaws and teeth sprung on me in a frenzy of snarls and spittle. They're licking, tearing, slavering, gnawing. My thighs and calves, my ankles peel away. Gouts of blood spray past my eyes, blotting away my sight. Awash in a deepening inky splash that keeps reoccurring without letup, I'm swallowed in geysers of horrifying blood. I feel my powers ebbing. By the time I even think that I should run, they've swarmed me and I'm on my back and it's too late. I know what's happening. They are eviscerating me. In seconds, it's over. It's a swoon, the pain evaporating in a weird corollary generated in concert with my recognition of my plight. Like a penitent in his pew, I'm submissive, desolate, servile, defeated, empty. Having eaten me and transmuted me into some gaseous distillation of themselves, they are breathing me out into the air like steam from a kettle. I'm rising off the swampy ooze of their insides in the very fabric of their song now, for they are still singing. I can see nothing but I can feel the valley reverberating around me and with me, a subtle cathedral in which every sound and crevice is informed with resonance, every melody and its reprise, every chord and contrapuntal murmur a mesmerizing instruction.

When I open my eyes, I see the girl lying on the floor in the corner. Her breath sounds like that of a baby without its mother. She's weeping beyond all hope of her own regulation. The room is a shambles, but she is alive.

And still I hear the song of the dogs, each and every member of their meaty, shaggy, nuzzling, snorting, fart-ridden horde continuing to bay his heart out to the immense and majestic unknown. And what they're singing is that I have to go to the Old Man. I have to go to the Old Man and tell him the truth. I have to tell him what happened, and take the consequences.

When I slip out the door, I look into a morning sky. The song is fading and the light along the horizon is like the skin of a partly eaten apple, something fleshy lurking beneath a tattered red. I set off quickly, marching back the way I came, headed for the Old Man's farm.

Chapter Twenty-five

As a painter, I know that violet contains the colors red and blue. But it is not my habit to remind myself while viewing violet that I am looking at red and blue. I think only of violet and not the secret that violet contains. Perhaps it's this way with everything. Wind is not wind but high and low fronts of air and heat, gases on the move, clumps of molecules like enlarged pans of popcorn. The addition of a bullet to a dashing dog with dotted ears, a plume of a tail, and a rascal's eyes creates a slightly heavier dog and what else? Does the dead dog contain the secret of the dashing dog and flying bullet? What is one dead dog with all foolishness blown from his head and maggots devouring his belly? Can it be said then that a digestion other than his own is proceeding in his gut? And what about the maggots? Do they then contain a distillation of the dead dog, the running dog, the bullet? What about the trees that peer down through the umbrella of their own shade over him? What do they see and what do they obscure? The rocks surrounding him are a clue to some incomplete revelation. Purple is purple and green is green and wind is wind, but what is concealed in green, what is the secret of purple, the riddle of wind?

Ahead, I see the Old Man's house, a bulge of frame and shingles around a web of glinting windows. In a way, I didn't even want to shoot the dog. It was the cows that made me do it. Their moist eyes, glowing with ignorance, disturbed me. They seemed unable to understand that the dog was the source of their terror, even as he bounded after them, nipping at their heels. They fled in a state of blankness, rumbling like spellbound boulders around that pasture on their scrawny legs. In a pastoral setting, I had believed my work would flourish, no more crass, honking interference breaking through my windows. Nothing but the subtle urges of my own interior world. Instead, I had this beast beating the air with his exclamations, his bragging howls of self-aggrandizement. Down he would swoop, a marauder from the hills, his exuberance trampling our tranquillity. The cows were a game to him. As they charged around the prison of their pasture, he foamed at their heels, my powers flying with them.

One morning, black coffee in my mug, I went out the door clad in my pajamas and robe to rescue them. Their bleats had been ringing through the walls. He saw me coming. Midstride, he seemed to hover in the air. Then his four paws dug into the dirt, and he veered to meet me. Our eyes collided. He responded with an exhibition of arrogant brawny dexterity and barking, admonishing me to beware of him, as if I were one of the cows.

From that hour on, I felt ashamed. When they rampaged in their dumb terror from tree to fence and back again, I was thundering helplessly with them, no hope in our stinking ranks to appeal to this animal drunk on domination. Never would he renounce his relish of the hysteria to which he could reduce us with a single yip. So overweening was his relish that he would sometimes, in a froth of zeal, outrun himself so that he skidded and toppled over, baying even louder to keep us in his fearful thrall, though he himself was on his back and crashing into a tree.

The anxiety that evolved in me had all the cows' meaty dread behind it. This was the dog of every innocent's dread and he came each day with an increasing appetite, the joke of our cumbersome humiliation intoxicating him. I could not work. Any attempt at aesthetic concentration was overrun by the obscene sport this creature found in his tormenting his fellow beings, the cows and me. Across my thoughts he galloped, then down the steep backsides of my dreams. His face, forever beastly, came and went like an image projected on a screen, a series of superficially varied depictions of a monster, intrinsically the same.

I watched the cows lose weight with fear and indigestion. Dog or no dog, they ran now sometimes in the night. The moon, as if it might reveal a feral nature, made them queasy. They panicked at the rustle of the grass, or the unexpected shadow exaggerating the fall of a leaf. They began to sleep in ungainly piles, peering out of their beefy conglomeration. More and more, they sniffed the air. They had come to think of themselves as permanently in peril, a condition that quickly left them paranoid and superstitious. No longer did they cavort in awkward play as they once had in the sun's lingering at evening's onset. When I moved among them, they appealed for protection, as if I were somehow immune to their distress. I was one of them, I shouted. Startled by the explosion of my voice, they mistook me for a sibling to the dog. They fled and I ran after them. My wife screamed that I was scaring them worse than the dog. The shock of her accusation was enough to bring me to a halt. In the middle of the field I paced about, while in the corner the cows collected, their slobbering nostrils pumping fear.

Hoping to disassociate myself from their misery, I tried again to work. It was humiliating that this beast reveled in the free exercise of his brawn while I was like an impoverished seed, shriveling up around some nub of inadequacy. I saw the dog descending to herd the cows in disruptive jolts across the canvas on which I longed to paint, around and around the helpless consternation of my mind. Had I uprooted myself to travel here for nothing better than the humiliations of this cur? Would I let him degrade me and my fellow creatures forever?

Rushing out, I screamed at him. When this tactic failed, I tried to lure him close with food. I imagined that I might tame him. He kept his distance, as if he knew the enmity racing through me. He scorned my offerings. I took up affable poses in the driveway along the pasture's fringes, trying to look like someone who would be a dog's best friend. Nothing succeeded, and my frustrations festered in me. My sensibility sank through wells of self-loathing, like the scum of a foul pond in which vipers began to appear. Passively, I looked into their prehistoric stare. And all the while the cows in waning optimism fled from sunrise into the dusk, and the days were the dog's to rule. Then the ripples of the pond swirled inside me and parted, and up to the surface swam a serpent with a thought, and in it was a blast of anger that, when it subsided, left a gun and a gun's inclination. It would eliminate the dog, and bring peace to the cows. It would return the quiet and release my stymied abilities to work and paint. Of guilt and remorse I could make my themes, of bloody aftermath my inspiration. From these effects, I could reap my gory and aesthetic harvest. Or so it promised and then swam away.

Looking up, I saw the cows in a cloud of beefy consternation against the glittering sunset, and drove to town that evening to buy the gun.

As I cruised along the winding country road, I made my vow somberly. I could not allow these events to continue. I could not stand idly by any longer while this dog played as if life were a game and not a manly duty; as if it were a festival for his prowess and zeal and my diminishment and degradation. Staring at the sun, I made my vow in my own name and with priestly dedication. I invoked honor and duty and order and civilization. I made my pledge to art and God himself, as I felt his overwhelming presence in that moment, a wave of aggrieved and punishing wrath. I could no longer tolerate the misery I knew the cows endured when I looked into the harried vista of their eyes.

I purchased a Marlin lever-action .30/30 rifle at the hardware store and talked to the clerk about the habits of rodents and raccoons. In order to use the bathroom before I left, I had to descend to the basement, where I peed for a long time. I had nothing worth cherishing. My wife and I were like strangers, seeking out ways to avoid one another day after day, our purposes bitter, the bitterness veiled. My mother, my father, where were they? My son wandered from room to room, the wide glaze of his eyes informing me that he knew well the plight of the cows. My wife was having endless affairs, and though she had avoided telling me about them, I knew. Just as I knew of her infatuation with the dog and his exploits, even though she said nothing to reveal herself until after he was dead. Still, I knew, and I felt repudiated, inherent traits that I valued mocked, delicate intrinsic elements ridiculed, my very essence condemned. In the mirror, I saw a figure with eyes hooded in shame. I looked like a man to whom a specter lurking in the shadows had made an obscene proposal whose acceptance I was contemplating.

When I got home, I found a note declaring that my wife and son had taken the train to the city for a few days to visit a friend. I stayed awake throughout that night. I felt large impersonal powers reordering my circumstances. In the alchemy of my anger I compressed every wound, every disappointment and injustice from which I'd suffered, every insult and failure, into a tiny metallic projectile of gray lead. With this missile I would ram my injuries into the dog's head and out of my own. Fatigue could be a hallowed state, I learned, as I sat drinking black coffee and waiting for the dawn, my grievances glowing in an eerie tier of flickering candles, my skull a kind of church. In exhaustion I found my thoughts scattered and broken, like a set of runes whose disclosures I could not clearly read, my resolve disappearing under their uncertain instruction. And then I turned, and oozing toward me through the flickering aisles of my skull was a wall of bankless sleep. It was the cows the dog pursued, but it was me he wanted. I saw myself about to vanish and swore that upon his next appearance the dog would die. I shouted that I would kill the dog and liberate the cows. Like a condemned man at the gallows, I toppled out of consciousness as if this cry had sprung the trap beneath my feet.

I crashed awake to yowling. In their extremity, the cows had burst through the fence around the pasture, so that now they were a ruckus in every corner of my yard, the dog flying in persecution from the heels of one to the rump of another. They trampled flowers and stuck their heads through kitchen windows, knocking over pots and breaking vases. To my amazement, I saw a spotted, high-strung Guernsey scampering off down the road, her panic blinding her to the fact that she was going to end up lost and far from the herd.

The call for butchery mooed and stampeded around me. Yet my violent aims fell back in confusion, and the gunsight lifted off the cur bolting through a bed of flowers. Meanwhile the cows were every-where. In desperation, I fired into the air. The cows went crazy. The dog, engrossed in his gaming, scarcely noticed. His hurtling was slowed no more than a step as he sped on toward a heifer tangled in a bush, his yammering bark infused with a kind of cruel taunting.

What could I do, with all the cows in disarray and a warning shot fired but utterly unheeded? I had my motive, I had the means, and what's more, I had my vow. Duty fell upon me, as I knew the hammer must in seconds drive the firing pin into the bullet. How, if I broke my vow to myself, would I ever be trustworthy again? A schism would open within me, leaving me glaring forever in mistrust across the turmoil and treachery of my suspicious thoughts.

As if this promise were an autonomous entity, usurping all control and understanding of my present actions, the vow took over and elevated the gun until the dog was sitting on the sights. Somewhere in the forest, a cow was bawling. Everywhere they bleated, sobbed, entreated the skies for vengeance and relief. Scaring one dumb beast into such a frenzy that it tried to jump a fence and failed with a crash that sent the creature bouncing on its belly along the dirt, the dog skidded, leaped into the air with satisfaction, and I fired.

To bring together the myriad knotty threads of my life, and through some witchcraft of my psyche to put them on the pinpoint of a bullet and then shove that bullet through the body of this animal as if to change his mind about something; as if to change his mind about what he thought was significant. As if to impress upon him the fact of my existence. As if to impress some point upon the life he brimmed with. As if to alter the course of that life in some small, irreversible way. As if to let life know that I am around and that death is around and that death is with me—for countless reasons I could name, which in their aggregate were a reason I could not know—I fired.

Chapter Twenty-six

"I see," the Old Man says, "he's dead."

"I'm sorry."

"He's dead."

"I didn't know how to tell you."

"You killed him."

We're sitting at the table in his kitchen, drinking coffee. I've just finished my story. My coffee is black; his is pale with cream. He's dumping in and stirring a second heaping spoonful of sugar. "He's dead," he says.

"Yes."

"Well, that explains why he never come back." His voice is hoarsened by the depths from which he is managing to speak. His preoccupation seems a trance that has removed him from the kitchen, leaving me behind. "He'd have come back if he was alive."

"I bet he would have."

"He would have," says the Old Man. "I'm sure of it. I'm absolutely sure. This is terrible."

"I know. I feel awful." The coffee heats my lips as I drink. It irradiates my tongue, curls down my throat.

"What are we going to do about it?" he says.

"I don't know. See, I promised myself. I made a promise. I just wanted to tell you and get on with things—take the consequences and get on with things."

"Get on with what things, though? That's what I don't know. What is it we're gonna get on with—each one of us—that's what I want to know."

"Well . . . ," I say, and falter. Begun on an introductory impulse, the word opens into a blankness.

"I don't know what to do," he says. He rises and begins to prowl the room, as if random movement might take him to the thing he needs, or at least ease the aggravation he feels. "We gotta figure something out." He pauses at the sink to cool his coffee with a spurt of water from the faucet. "You promised yourself, huh? You promised yourself, so when he came, you had no choice." Methodically, his voice has placed these words in a careful sequence, as if they are objects that must be balanced on a narrow ledge. "Is that it?"

"Yes," I say.

"You know all the little reasons, but you don't know the big reason."

"Yes."

"I wonder what it is." It's obvious that he feels there's peril and volatility haunting this moment, along with a degree of excitement.

"I don't know."

"It was like the promise you made to yourself took over."

"Can you understand that?"

"I think that's what I'm talking about here," he says. "Because I promised myself something, too. I made a promise, too. That's what I'm gettin' at."

"Oh."

"You see what I mean. I'm not a fool. It occurred to me he might be dead, or that he might not come back. That occurred to me. Or that he might die before he got back. What I mean is, it occurred to me that, one way or another, he might die without me ever seein' him again, you know, and never gettin' to twist his ears the way I liked to. That occurred to me."

It feels as if the wood of the chair beneath me flutters, threatening to turn to dust, and I shift and clutch the edges in my hands. I feel pervaded from within by an aching light. "I didn't know that," I say.

"Well, you coulda figured it out if you'da taken a second to think about anybody but yourself."

I just sit there staring at him, waiting.

"See, what I promised myself," he says, "is that if he died and there was somebody who was responsible in some way, either that they kept him prisoner until he died or they didn't give him food or something when he was tryin' to get back after he escaped, or if—you know, worst of all—if they was actually part of it—actually involved in what happened to him. I mean, responsible somehow for his dying. Well, I promised myself they would have to pay. That's what I promised."

Because he's turned slightly away from me, I can't use his expression to define his meaning. I'm moving, hoping to steal a peek and get away without being noticed, when his eyes come sweeping toward me and suddenly we lock with a violent jolt, a surge of frightening connection from which I duck.

"That's what I'm getting at," he says. "They would have to pay."

"Right."

"I mean, you promised yourself. I promised myself. I mean, you of all people understand the way a promise made to yourself can work. What are we going to do?"

"See, I just wanted to get on with my life—to tell you and—"

"But what about me? You selfish hunk of shit. I made a promise, too!" His vehemence startles me, though it shouldn't. He bolts a step toward me, his flushed face bulging, the veins squirming, his swelling eyes like sacks of puss.

"Things were getting too complicated for me almost everywhere. I had to tell you. That's all I wanted," I say.

"But I mean, you said about the consequences. You said something about the consequences before, didn't you?"

"Yes."

"What'd you say? What about the consequences? I'm just trying to get things straight. Something about takin' the consequences, right? What'd you say? Let's have a drink."

From a cabinet beside the window he grabs a quart of Heaven Hill bourbon along with a tumbler and a coffee cup. The muttering amber liquid slops from the bottle into the tumbler and cup. Shoving the cup in my direction, he flings his head back, gulping the liquor the way a field hand might drink water after hours of sweating labor.

"Shit," he says. "Goddamn. Piss. Fuck. Cunt. Cow dung. What are the goddamn consequences? What are they? I don't think there are any. You look to me like you got away completely unscathed. Not a scratch."

"No," I say.

"Looks that way to me," he snorts, refilling his glass. "You ingrate. You butcher. You love anything?"

He's lurking by the window, his back toward me, so that I'm forced to imagine his darkly twisted expression. I remain seated at the table, sipping my drink and fiddling with a splinter on the leg of my chair.

"You love anything?"

"I didn't know about your promise," I say.

"You got any pets? Whatta you got? I'm sick of being the one who gets hurt." He starts to cry. It's an ugly, miserable series of snorts and growls and tears, a stunted grief, disfigured at its roots.

"I don't love anything," I say.

"What about your pets?"

"I had some cows, but I don't have them anymore."

"You got a kid, though, I know you do. What about him?"

"I don't love him."

"He's your kid, whatta you talking about?"

"That's right, but—"

"People love their kids."

"No."

"Does he know that? Does he know how you feel?"

"I think he does."

"Let's see if he does. I wanna talk to him. Let's see what he thinks about all this."

"He's at school."

"Smart, huh?"

"He's just at school."

"So we don't wanna bother him, I guess, if that's the kinda kid he is. But we can see him after. That's all the better and worth waiting for— that's what I think. I mean, if he's so smart maybe he can help us figure this thing out. What's his name again?"

"He always has a play date after school. He goes to a friend's house. He won't be home."

"What's his name again?"

"I think we can figure this problem out without involving him."

"No, no. You know how kids are. He'll be real interested in this. What was his name again?"

I turn from him, putting my back against him like a wall, as I cross to the sink. I turn on the faucet and cup my hands beneath the running water, my silence hard and defiant.

"Tobias," he says.

"What?" I turn and look at him.

"I remember," he says, his grimace gleaming through his tears and stretching the skin over his skull.

Hours later, he pulls his car from the garage. The big stately vehicle oozes into the wavering hours of an afternoon. It's an old two-tone Chrysler, a more emphatic gray on the chassis than on the bulge of the roof. Filigrees of rust and rubber erupt around the doors, and the car, filling up with unease around us, cruises to the road through a kind of vacuum characterized by a sense of slow, distorted motion. Time has visited me with a disorientation like this before, I remind myself. I'm fluctuating in and out of a set of deep, isolating meditations, like a row of lightless rooms.

We find Tobias in an empty lot a short distance down the street from his friend's home. Galloping about in T-shirts and shorts, the two boys clutch big balls of string unwinding at a slant up into the cloudless blue. Their kites, one dragon shaped, the other gaudily aquatic, are bobbing in the winds. Both boys are giggling as we arrive, their overlapping shouts a series of escalating dares about the damage each kite would inflict on the other in a collision.

When I call Tobias and tell him to join us, he stops and looks at me. After handing the ball of string to his friend, he approaches the car, his little face more exasperated than wary.

"Can you hurry up, Dad, because I really want to get back and play with James, okay?"

He has a smudge of dirt on his nose, and I climb from the car and moisten my finger and clean him off.

"Can I go now?" he asks. He seems to have forgotten completely our last encounter. "I want to go play," he says.

"No," says the Old Man.

"No," I say, and pluck him up into the car, settling him down on the backseat. I slam the door and climb back into the front.

As we explain the situation, shadows curl down to loop around

Tobias's pale features like arms reaching in from the oak tree beneath which we have parked. Tobias moves his eyes back and forth between us, their beaming interest like fading sunlight in a darkening day. When we finish, he turns and looks out the window. After several seconds spent in a thoughtful silence, he shakes his head and scans us quizzically, then fades away as if to revisit the more elusive points of what we've told him. At last, with an expression of tender regret, he offers me a shrug and a shake of his little head. "That's terrible," he says. "The poor doggy dying and everything. I hate dying."

"That's an idea," says the Old Man.

"Hmmmmmmmm?" Tobias glances at the Old Man.

I catch a disastrous scent and retreat from the present like a beast sinking into the anonymity and camouflage of his inhuman surroundings.

"That he die," says the Old Man. "That we kill him. Or at least bury him. That's an idea."

As the Old Man speaks, his gaze is leveled at me with the menace of the shotgun he once aimed. He's looking directly into my eyes. I am the object of his words. Tobias is the subject. The moment is hypnotic.

"You don't want me to break my promise to myself, do you, Tobias?" says the Old Man.

My boy and I are linked by a breathless suspense. Tobias's unblinking eyes are fixed on me, as if he intends, by force of will, to oblige me to speak and give him guidance. But it's as if I'm drugged, some numbness stupefying my powers.

The Old Man puts his arm around my shoulders in a parody of the reassurance I cannot give my son. The effect of his closing fingers ices my groin. "I know your dad doesn't want me to break my promise," he says. I can feel his breath on the nape of my neck, his stinking mouth inches from my ear. "Do you?" he says to me.

When I look at him, I see he's turned to stare at Tobias. His brittle fingers flex on my neck. Tobias watches me from a place of perplexity and concern. But with everything up to me, I'm disappearing. It's the promise that I made to tell the truth and take the consequences that has me in its grasp. In a sense, the consequences have come. As if to flee them, I clamber over the seat, my arms reaching for Tobias. I hear a lot of grunting behind me and look around to see the Old Man following. He falls heavily into the back, wedging himself between us.

"You know about promises, don't you, son?" the Old Man says, his voice a dogmatic hiss. "I'm sure you do."

"Yes," Tobias admits in his little voice, a glassy sheen falling over his eyes.

"Nothing's more important. Nothing. I don't *think* anything is, anyway. I don't know, though, but it's what I feel. Your father killed my dog, after all."

"Did you?" Tobias says, scrutinizing me.

"He was chasing the cows."

Outside our windows misting with our breath, the bright world seems exempt from our swampy secrets, our crippled ardors.

"Where was I? Was I here?" says Tobias.

"What do you mean?"

"Where was I?"

"You weren't home. You were away. You were away with your mother."

Tobias exhales in a way that's irresolute and searching, and the Old Man transforms this confusion into an opportunity to advance his own interests. Ruffling the boy's hair so it sticks up at angles like a cropped bush, he says, "Okay. It's settled then. We'll kill him."

"No," I say.

"What?" the Old Man says, glaring at me.

I'm surprised by the remove at which my voice is originating, the distance it has to travel to reach us. "You said we'd bury him."

His impassive eyes move slowly over me. "Sure," he says. "That okay with you, Tobias? It's good enough for me."

"It's fine with him," I say.

"It's really the same thing anyway," says the Old Man.

"Are you going to bury me?" Tobias says, his mouth tensing as he prepares some further statement to which his question was clearly introductory.

"You just shut up and do as you're told, you hear me!" My voice is like a gunshot, like a gavel on a table, imperious, judicial, and final.

Tobias punches his little fist against the back of the seat, but before his rebellion can grow, I stop him. "You do as I say," I shout, my manner tyrannical. He pouts, sucking on his finger. He gnaws a hangnail, causing a trickle of blood as he rips off a shred of skin.

I notice the countryside sailing by and realize we are on the move.

The Old Man has climbed to the front seat and started up the car. He's driving so fast the fence posts blur, the telephone wires flash. Low grayish clouds leap in and out of view at intervals regulated by stationary clumps of roadside trees, as we shoot by.

"I really think I ought to get my choice," Tobias cries. "I don't want to be buried when I'm alive. If I'm going to be buried, I want to be dead!"

I spin and grab his shoulders in both hands. I shake him and fling him down. When I slap him, my fingers tingle and the air explodes. "Just shut up!" I yell. I can no longer tolerate the righteousness of his immense blue eyes; his whiny voice has gotten on my nerves. "Just shut up, goddamnit!" I scream.

Behind the shock of his expression, he starts to drown. I see him make a dreadful realization, and I don't want to watch it happen. He's remembering the stolen night of tenderness we shared when I swept him to the safety of the cave. Because it's now his benefactor who is his persecutor, his plight is not simply cold and brutal but a flowering of overwhelming treachery. My betrayal corrupts his treasured trust from virtue into a curse, a source of humiliation. Not only must he contemplate a helpless future, but every kindness in his past must be reenvisioned as a mockery, a deception. "Dad," he says.

"Just shut up! Shut up!"

He puts his hands over his eyes. Despair crushes the breath from him and leaves him loathing himself for ever having loved me. I want to bury him and get the whole thing over with. I just want to forget everything. I want to get rid of him and be done with it all. I close my eyes.

The Old Man drives us deep into the woods, turning unpredictably but progressing steadily. I peek every now and then and find us moving through endless trees. At one moment they're deployed in parallel lines, and at the next they're chaotic. Veering one way and then another at subtle angles, he conveys us along a pathway that he seems to know well, as we sink deeper into an unearthly, uncharted sector of the wilds. Only once does he make a mistake and have to back up. He eases off in the correct direction, crooning with pleasure, the wheels turning soundlessly on the mattresses of sod and grass, until after a lengthy sail into this solitude he pulls to a halt.

It's there that we set to work, panting under the towering visages of the trees, while the wind moves past us, ghostly in the leaves. We fling the dirt up in large bleak clots. The spades cut into the soil with thud after thud, and nothing is spoken between us until the deed is done. The boy is stuffed into the suitcase, the suitcase wedged into the ground, and then the dirt is returned in large desolate hunks, the spades spanking the black sod smooth and hard.

When we're back in the car, driving down the road, the Old Man says, "I saw what you were doing." His voice is a menacing, a chilling promise of dire consequence if he's crossed. "I saw you trying to make a map of the route we took, the spot where we put him. That's no good, you know."

"I know," I say.

"You have to promise you'll never go back and get him. Never. Do you promise?"

"I promise."

"I don't think I can trust you. I think I'm going to have to lock you up to make sure."

"I promise," I say. The words are like feces in my mouth, and they prompt a stab of queasiness that knots my guts. I bow my head between my knees, but I can't reduce or escape this spiraling nausea. I reel back against the seat like a drunk fighting not to puke—I hate how I feel— and as I rock forward my eyes pass over the hood of the car, and that's when I see an angel sitting there, this figure with wings, his big eyes and radiant sensibility afire with horror and shame. At first I think he's the most enormous hood ornament I've ever seen. Shocked out of my preoccupation with my sickness, I'm flopping sideways in my seat and puzzling over the figure of this angel who looks about eight feet tall and vaguely triangular, like an evergreen tree. His wings rise out of him in white, curving arcs like a pair of rolled-up mattresses, his robes encir- cling him in a cushioning, cottony oval.

Alarmed and amazed, I turn to the Old Man, wondering about his response, and from the dull grimace with which he holds our course, I see that the angel's presence has gone unnoticed, or has had no effect on him. Or perhaps the angel has lifted off and flown away.

Looking back, I find him riding where I first saw him, and as the disorientation of my initial shock fades, I begin to see him clearly. His uncommon countenance seems to rush at me, growing in detail and focus, and he's an anguished seraph. He's an angel in mourning, and the intimations of his mood and emotion resound in my head, stirring the slop of my lobes with a charge of sparks leaping from the pole of my brain and the pole of my heart: Heaven has sent him because heaven is in need of help. Against this idea, my mind rebounds. The thought of an importunate heaven confounds me. Yet before me stands this angel whose eyes are pools of aching petition. Again and again he is shaken with the pain of his yearning and privation, which he clearly believes I can address, his gaze imploringly fixed on me.

"I want to get out here. Right now," I shout.

The Old Man's eyes narrow. "No!" His voice is a razor slashing at me. "No, no, no."

I'm speaking without thinking, the words rushing from me. "Right here. Right now!" I shout. "Right now!"

"No."

I wish the angel had never come. Yet there he hovers. I have to get out of the car. The nausea has returned in a violent surge and I'm going to puke. "Really. I just want to go for a walk. I'm not feeling well. I'm going to throw up. I'm sick. I'm going to throw up."

"Stick your head out the window."

I have a picture in my mind, and in it I'm walking in a field. There's a nimbus around the picture, a beneficent halo. "I have to walk in that field," I shout. "That one right there—just to the left—" I'm pointing out the window, my hand jiggling in the direction of a pasture above which half a dozen blackbirds are elevating. "Right under the black-birds."

"Shut up," he says.

"I want to walk in those little bushes." I am telling the absolute truth, as nearly as I can manage it, and in the picture to which I'm referring, pathways are formed by little pines and hemlocks in neat, cordial rows, and the angel and I are strolling along, chatting and sharing a consoling exchange as he tells me exactly what he needs.

"You want to go back and dig him up," the Old Man says.

"What?"

"I know what you're thinking about."

"No!"

"Your kid. Your goddamn sonofabitch of a kid. You want to ruin my life!"

"No," I say.

"Bullshit!"

"That's not what I'm thinking about at all."

"I know you," he says. "Promises to yourself you keep, and dogs you want to shoot you shoot. But a promise to me you wanna flush down the crapper with the rest of your shit."

"I just want to walk around."

"Well, it ain't going to happen! We're going back to the house. I'm keeping my eye on you. I'm locking you up in a fucking room! In the goddamn closet, so I know where you are!"

Turning to the door, I'm groping for the handle. I'm willing to jump to escape, I don't care how fast we're going. But I can't find the handle. It's gone, or in some weird place on the door. Then the Old Man lunges at me from behind, a mountainous impression of suffocating heft and gnarly limbs, his fingers seizing me by the hair.

"No you don't," he snarls, accelerating the car and pulling me back by my hair.

"All I want is to go for a walk with the angel," I scream. I feel as if I'm crumbling, splitting apart under the pressure of a chill light blasting through me. "That's all I want. Just to go for a walk with the goddamned angel!"

"What angel?"

"He wants to talk to me."

"What angel? You crazy sonofabitch!"

"I'm exploding," I shout.

"Good."

But it isn't good; it's rage and hate and fear in some irreversible transformation about to swallow me. "Please," I say. "He wants to talk to me!"

"I've lived all my life without ever talking to any goddamn angels, you little shit! Who the fuck you think you are?" He's laughing a loud, gagging laugh, as if someone's kicking him in the stomach and it's making him happy.

"He wants to talk to me!"

"Tell him to talk to *me!*"

"He doesn't want to talk to you!"

"Get him to whisper in my ear, you asshole!"

"I can't."

"He'll talk to me if you ask him."

"He doesn't want to. He's an angel! He does what he wants."

"He likes you; he'll do it." He's mocking me now. Each word is a little needle he's sticking into my arm. "Just ask him for me, you sonofabitch! If he likes you, he'll—"

I lunge, grabbing the steering wheel. "Stop the car! I have to get out!" I can't stand what's happening. But my attempt to usurp his control of the car infuriates him and starts him roaring. He smashes his fist into my face. An insulted, murderous part of his brain is gaping at me out of his eyes.

"Let go! Let go!" he's screaming, but I hang on. He pounds me in the face. From side to side we rock, veering wildly across the road.

"The angel wants me, you sonofabitch!"

"There is no angel—there is no goddamn angel, you crazy piece of shit! You wanna kill us!"

Though he knocks me loose, I pounce back, attacking the wheel as if to rip it from the steering column. With a shout, he clamps both hands down on the opposite half of the wheel, jerking savagely. Left and right the wheel spins between us, and the car cavorts across the divider line and back again, our speed mounting, then receding, our tires knifing to the left and then the right. Because he's bigger, he thinks he's going to dominate, but I'm seething with a manic energy, which translates into a kind of brawn. The car skids and squeals with the fluctuations of our struggle, and all the while the angel clings to the hood, his feathers a turbulent whirl. When I meet his innocent gaze, I see that he's imploring me. I howl, driving my shoulder into the Old Man's chest, crushing him back against the door. My elbow slams into his throat and pins him there as I pry his fingers loose. I'm straining to keep him immobilized. I'm heading for the shoulder to bring us to a stop, when he retaliates at a magnitude of force I could not have anticipated. Spasming like an epileptic in a convulsion, he butts his head into mine and his foot stomps the gas. Tires burning, rear end swiveling, we catapult down the road. Oblivion appears to strike him as an irresistible opportunity—if he can't beat me, he's going to kill me.

As the car bursts through a fence with a screaming sound of suffering metal, I hear him calling, "Help, help!" and we go flying off the road. Midair, we begin to tilt. He looks at me. A pause slips into our struggle. We're airborne. There's a stillness, except for the whistling of the wind. The angel takes a breath but does not lift himself into the safety of the air, as he could with his wings. The ground is rushing toward us, its onslaught booming. The Old Man screams, and the car digs its nose in the dirt while the rear end elevates. Then everything twists, and our acrobatic angle becomes a spiral that launches us down the hill. We're a jumble, flailing and crashing off the walls, and yet we persist, as much as possible, in our murderous desires. Snarling, grunting, our savagery fills the car. The elemental forces of the crash press us upon one another in a mockery of an embrace, then pry us apart so we claw the air. Sliding along with the engine upended, the car teeters for a moment before it wheels in a total revolution that sends it end over end into a boulder. And throughout this dizzying uproar, the Old Man and I are eye to eye in our lethal toil, like demons in service to a depraved and everlasting master. On the hood of the car the angel rides, an amazing hope and optimism still surviving in his vast transcendental eyes. The car is a clanking round of dust. But this huge seraph keeps himself upright, his majestic wings like gigantic loaves of bread wavering for balance as he clings to the hood of the car. He's going all the way, I see, even though he doesn't understand this carnage or how it can be part of heaven's aims. Which I don't understand either. But it's all occurring in beats and flashes, each second a dense and infinite resource, far richer and more complex than I ever imagined. I see suddenly that the deeds I am about to initiate are already an influence upon the events that are in progress. As the car embarks on another roll, a grinding convolution accompanied by screeching clangs, I see Tobias in his grave, and the Old Man and I intensify our grim battle while the angel spreads his wings, improvising a means to stay rooted to the car so that he can witness, as is his duty, our ordeal. What asserts itself now is clamor and inarticulate bawling, and in this blur and chaos there is a moment in which the dirt is rising off Tobias; he's being lifted from the ground. It is as if the lid bursts off his grave, the suitcase splitting open like a ruptured strip of flesh, and the dirt gives him up with a splash of exuberance like the earth bubbling open at the advent of a flower. And he has one in his mouth, a rose, blooming and gleaming, its silky layers parting like petals of lace. It rises from his guts, where it's rooted and where secretly it was fed until it grew to this shocking bounty shooting up through his mouth. It feels as if my own mouth is engorged with such beauty also, and only then do I realize that my teeth are sunk into the Old Man's throat, and the car has come to a rest at the base of a gully, and all that now remains of our havoc is the Old Man's feet thrashing against the air and rattling against the dashboard in a futile struggle to escape me. But

I am snarling, ruthless, invincible. My mouth blooms with his blood. The angel is pale, his once-pink cheeks chalky as he wavers over me, positioned in the air a few feet above the tip of a crumpled fender, fumes of dust and smoke rising past him. Though it was his commission to oversee this fleshy and brutal vendetta, he was not ready. Now he attends me with a bleak wonder, his wings shifting to hold him steady, his eyes full of awe. In the rigors of this gauntlet there was a lesson for him as well as for me, and he's beginning to see it. Lifting himself suddenly a hundred yards vertically into sudden song-filled flight, he is aglow against the sun, having come through his own travail to his own exaltation, his figure translucent with epiphany as he has grasped at last the gift it is to be an angel and free of the earth. Never before had it occurred to me to think that angels knew discontent and envy, imagining some other, less vexing life for themselves. Without the horror of me, he would not have grasped the miracle of his own nature, and without his flighty though enduring and demanding presence, I would never have known that an angel could need me, that an angel could come, that an angel could intervene.

When I climb from the car, it's snowing. The Old Man's death is everywhere. It's his vengeance, his envy and outrage, his vindictive soul tumbling in huge flakes from the gloom that has subjugated the sky with a spooky suddenness. I should have known this was coming. I've been forewarned. It's his unrelenting meanness, his spite—his covetousness to destroy all the world if necessary, so that nothing remains after him. Great soggy clumps fall. Tiny particles whirl in spirals beside turning columns and spheres that drill large shifting clouds, which his disembodied howl shreds. Snow filigrees the tree limbs and starts to blanket the hillside down which we have tumbled. Dirt and boulders, concrete and grass are all vanishing under him. Gazing into the escalating melee above me, I see that the depth of this storm is limitless. I look into a world disappearing in the swirls of his vengeful purpose. I see what he wants to do. He's going to hide the way back to Tobias's grave by transforming every turn, every tree and bit of shrubbery into a blur of snow. Direction will be impossible to determine, the way to rescue untraceable beneath his desolate downpour.

As I clamber up the slippery hillside, the Old Man's snow is gathering on me like plaster. He mixes it with the gouts of blood that cover my hands, my mouth and shirtfront, until I'm coated in a stiffening scarlet membrane of ice. By the time I reach the road, the pandemonium at this higher elevation almost knocks me over. With the temperature dropping, his damnation is weighing me down, encasing me in a gleaming immobility. I'm on the highway, trying to run, my clothing crinkling, my big old coat a frosted mosaic. Tobias is dying, expiring in an airless box. It's a blizzard, walls of arctic wind hurling spite and venality and petty rancor in a melee of snowing particles so plentiful they seem a crumbling mountain. I have to hurry. I have no choice. Yet I'm barely able to move, when I see a car negotiating a careful approach and I try to wave it down. The driver slows as if to stop, and then, aghast, speeds off.

With the arrival of the next auto, a station wagon emerging through the onslaught, I place myself before it and make a hideous face. Threatening to run me over, the car veers at the last second and I run after it as it fishtails to a halt. The wheels struggle in a high-pitched frenzy to back up. When I rip the door open, the frightened driver tries to resist me. I bite his hand and fling him whimpering onto the road. There isn't time to explain.

Leaping into the car, I race off. The storm is colossal, the winds accelerating to hurl the whiteness already deposited into a dizzying veil as the Old Man struggles to detain me, to divert me, to confuse me, to freeze me.

But now that I have the car, I have hope. I find the woods, I find the trees, I find the path we took into their midst. In spite of the Old Man's wintry vengeance, I manage to retrace our steps and find the hole in whose depths we left Tobias. I claw him from the ground. His poignant look is worth all my effort, and holding him, I see that, though despair has gnawed him, he has not surrendered every shred of hope, as the snow begins to lighten and then to stop.

Sitting there, I rock him in my arms; I caress his little head so exquisitely alive I can hear the blood flowing in its infinity of veins. To comfort him, I hug him and stroke him, but he is inconsolable.

"The dog is dead," I say. "I know, I know. The poor dog is dead." My chest crumples down around him to enfold him in the hollow that I seem to be, my shoulder blades bulging out behind me like stubby wings, and then a quavering consumes me as might result from flight, but what I am borne into is an opening of grief. Something resolute in my chest is collapsing to unleash a turbulence beyond my management, a rush of damned and hapless tears. Then I sing, and somewhere in my singing a lullaby takes form, and of its haunting rhythms I make a reiteration, and round it goes, a moan rising upward through me, as if the earth on which I kneel has spoken, my mouth its orifice, my flesh its shivering tongue. I sing it over and over, this snatch of sound, this primordial grunt, while Tobias, soothed and sighing, slips off to sleep.

Eventually the police come. First there are sirens in the distance. Then they grow louder and nearer, and with their approach I become silent. There's no way they won't arrive. They follow a trail of blood and bitten hands, battered cars and stolen ones, and wheel marks turning off the road to plow into the woods upon the otherwise flawless snow.

There's about eight of them at first, and they appear with stricken looks, their coats molted in snow, their eyes somehow shy and diffident above their ruddy cheeks and below the frosted feathers of their brows and lids. With their guns drawn, they pace around me, stirred by a mix of wan awe and dread. Then they advance and arrest me. It's for auto theft, they say, and assault and battery, which is their term for what I did to the motorist when I bit his hand. They take Tobias from my arms and bear me off to jail.

Chapter Twenty-seven

Once begun, my imprisonment has no end, for as I expect, they soon learn of all my crimes. My arrest becomes a national event. My trial, though spectacular and complex in many aspects, is tedious as far as I'm concerned.

The judge is a fatherly bumpkin who turns unexpectedly churlish on certain days. After a while, I start to think his moods are dictated as much by the well-being of his bowels as by anything pertaining to the trial. The jury is a democratic mix of age and race and sex. In the beginning they take their involvement in my affairs quite seriously, though as the weeks wear on, their eyes are often glazed. Among the spectators, a surprising number return every day, as if they believe their presence essential. Some view me curiously. A few have a warm, nearly tender attitude. From others I feel a sickened loathing. The reporters amuse me, especially the grizzled elderly fellow who frequently sleeps. More than once, I see him start awake to scribble down a note as if his job is to recount his dreams.

As far as the overview developed in the dialectic between the prosecutor and the defense, the theoretical patterns devised by both could

not be less insightful or applicable. The expert witnesses spew contradictory jargon, while my character witnesses look humiliated by their
task. In the end, the summations of both the defense and the prosecu-
tion leave little room for the real strangeness of the way things actually
transpired. It's all rhetorical questions and heated claims, filling the
courtroom with reassuring sentimentality and convention. I could protest and I think about it more than once; I have the impulse, but not the
motive. There are those in the courtroom who look at me urgently, and I
know they're wishing that I would arise in my own advocacy. I shake my
head, hoping not to appear smug. But I know their encouragement is
really a ploy inspired by a prurient desire to have me bear my soul
publicly so that they can learn my secrets. If I could imagine any benefit
in such a thing, I might take the chance. However, it's obvious to me
that only the most marginal and daring among the spectators will accept
my version of things. The course of the trial will go on unaffected.
Besides, my lawyer has determined not to call me as a witness. Were I to
leap up, shouting, my behavior would only confirm the view of those
who think I'm completely mad. I hold my tongue. The end result is
predictable and satisfactory, really, as far as I'm concerned. It isn't much
of a contest and concludes with the foregone verdict that I'm guilty,
which of course I am, and I'm sentenced as I should be. Regarding the
handling of these matters, I have no quarrel with anyone or anything
central to their outcome. Wholly misinterpreted, I'm accurately judged
and correctly condemned.

    I sink into my prison routine slowly. Time has a strange quality, and
for all my previous experience with its capacity to distort itself, the form
it takes here is one I've never run into before, a thickness and a sense of
layered simulation in which everything feels remote and muffled even
when right in front of me. Sometimes at night I lie in my bunk and listen
to the cavernous ringing of the halls, imagining the tiers of metal and
stone around me. It's like living in a sepulcher, a hollowed rock, or in a
gigantic empty bucket. Of course, I'm still cold. I end up twisting in my
covers, my body knotting up as it struggles against a fit of tremors. This
happens with some regularity, but it goes unnoticed for the most part,
though the other night a guard paused at my door to ask if I was sick, did
I have a fever?

    "No," I told him. "I'm just cold."

    "Then what the hell's the matter?"

Through my rattling teeth, I said, "I'm cold. That's all."

"It's summer," he told me. "Jesus Christ, it's summer. I'm sweating." Grumbling, he paced away.

For a while, I lay there wondering if I might be the single piece of matter in the universe lacking the heat of light but still possessed of the terrible speed, so that I outdistanced all natural warmth and was condemned to subsist that way, singularly bereft. On my way to the infirmary the following morning I passed a window and looked out, expecting to see barren, wintry branches, a desolate landscape, but what awaited me was a rim of green, smudges of light, a fuzz of leaves. I was looking into a web of treetops just beyond the walls.

At lunch, I sit sometimes near a fellow who tells incessant, unrelated stories. He laughs at almost everything he says, and careens from one anecdote to another unguided by either logic or a chain of discernible associations. He appears completely at the mercy of frenzy and impulse, his babble the perfect mirror for the nihilistic rush that was his life. In spite of my dismissive appraisal, I'm drawn to him. I sit as close as I can without drawing attention to myself, relishing his absurdity and ignorance, the perfection of his folly.

And then one day, there's a shard of his history that separates itself from the steady norm of stories squirting through his lips in their perpetual snarl. His mouth is like a wound that keeps ripping open; he will not let it heal. Something leaps at me, the first phrases of an anecdote alerting me to listen, as if that's not what I've been doing. The exact cause of this sensation is elusive and emphatic, yet its presence seems to have had no effect on the man himself. His hard little eyes and intonations reflect only the routine sadness and sadism that always accompany his accounts of mayhem, revelry, and outright savagery.

One night, apparently drunk and bored, he and some of his buddies broke into a zoo. After peeing in the duck pond and trying to light a fire on a swan, they stole an orangutan. As they prepared to flee on their motorcycles, the monkey was put into the charge of the man at my table, because his vehicle had a sidecar. The hapless beast, already drugged with tranquilizers and Jim Beam whiskey, was stuffed into the seat of this metallic oval, and was then covered with a tarpaulin bound down by rope.

Late in the night, roaring down the highway at a delirious speed, our friend was in a dream when he noticed the tarp stir and then burst loose and sail off behind him. Up came the orangutan's head, bleary-eyed and baffled, emerging from its packaging to our friend's dismay. Disoriented, the beast pawed the air and hiccuped. After a horrified perusal of its situation, the trembling brute gave a mournful cry and began to climb onto the back of the motorcycle. The man, clenching the handlebars and screaming to his associates, who could not hear him over the engines, was sure the animal was going to kill him, seeking vengeance on the only living thing in sight. Managing an acrobatic transition, the animal arrived and, straddling the bike, put his furry arms around the man's middle, pressed his head into the meat of his back, and hung on for dear life. They went that way for a hundred miles.

"It was the craziest goddamn thing," he says to us in an edgy, almost annoyed voice. "It was the thrillingest, most heartbreaking goddamn ride, the happiest night of my life." And then, gulping an agitated breath, he rushes on to his next story, a chaotic, Byzantine yarn about hijacking wine, while I sit there thinking about the dog.

For the next few days, I struggle with the fact that something recessive in the tale of that monkey and the man has the power to haunt me, raising slowly but inevitably a sunken desire in me. A week later, I give in. I request and am granted the right to paint. I work on bland, pointless projects like apples, keys, beds, and all the while I'm hoarding small portions of the supplies I'm given each day, until I have enough hidden away to begin what I really want to do. I take as much as I can steal of one whole night and work into its eerie depths, covering my entire cell as if it were a canvas on which to render my definitive portrait. When the guards discover what I've done, they stop me. They curse me and in the morning try to scrub the walls clean. The stains and forms that they fail to wash away, they cover up in a dull and dreary gray slopped on with cloddish brushes. It doesn't really matter, though, because I've seen it. I write a letter to my lawyer ordering him to destroy all the work I've done previously. If they will obliterate the finest I've ever accomplished because of institutional regulations that view it as defacement of the prison walls, then I will certainly eliminate from the world all I know to be inferior to an embarrassing, disheartening degree.

It was a wondrous self-portrait, bold and untrammeled, and in it I had capes and cloaks, a wild dragon's garb. My hair was a mix of all the women's hair I've ever known strung into one abundant stream, a shock in each stark color. My face was Barney's, as was my body, shaggy and firm, precisely his duplicate in every aspect beneath my furled, sculptured garb, and I had flowers for my ears, exploding bits of sun. My eyes were Tobias's eyes exaggerated and turned into orchids; circles were wed to circles, the iris, the eyeball, the pupil, the petals unfolding. Roses sprang from my mouth, sunflowers bursting out the sides of my head like shimmering horns ripe with seeds. And when I beheld this figure, it seemed not a fantasy, not an invention, but a form that I once filled. How dare they have robbed me of my robes and capes? After all, have I not the powers longed for throughout all the aeons of time? Have I not the brain that the dinosaur pined for but could not imagine, fancying that escape was possible by some means other than those he could devise as he stood in the pool of his doom, pondering his imponderable fate upon his ponderous legs stuck into the imponderable mud? I'll paint the dog I want on my prison walls any color I want him to be, and I'll remember him exactly as I portrayed him, even though they've scraped his image from the stones.

If you've never murdered a dog, or done any of the other things I've done until you could no longer bear the mess and toil of them, then you will have to believe that when these things happen, they happen the way I've said. I have, to the best of my ability, accepted and rendered their magnitude and terror, neither exaggerating nor minimizing my graces nor my truly grievous faults, but attending all with honesty and as much accuracy and flourish as has seemed balanced and necessary, a principle whose nature dictates its own articulation as the end approaches.

My fellow inmates often wonder why I am almost constantly humming in the days following the painting of my cell. As the months wear on, they grow increasingly aware of and bothered by the constancy of my habit. Some among them find it so irritating that they threaten me, each in his idiosyncratic way, but of course they never saw the valley of dogs. I tell them that when the moment of their own death comes, they may better understand me. It's an idea, of course, that's on all our minds, the guards included, especially at night. After all, our line of cubicles is called Death Row. I hear my fellow inmates screaming about it, their voices thick with dreams in which they want to escape it, they want to inflict it. I have the highest hopes for mine. The spirits of the women I murdered will, of course, pluck at me in fury, as they should,

until they see that I'm much like them and that the great abyss will make
certain I endure every ounce of calibrated pain I need, and that the
volume of their horrid screeching will do them no good whatsoever, but
will merely incline them to some further confusion, and that all their
ferocious acts of retribution against me only serve as interruptions of my
own excruciating, self-inflicted abominations, far more extensive than
anything they can ever visit upon me. They must come to see that if they
do not forgive me, or at least forget me, they will never move on to their
own accounting. That's the most heinous of my atrocities. To have
instilled in them such a sickness of rage and hatred, such an urge for
vengeance that it blocks their view and blinds them so that they cannot
see beyond it to the airy things they are themselves, quite ethereal and
free.

Fiends will bite at me and suck my soul, as well they must, and
mournfully I will glimpse the life I might have lived along with some
elegant, innovative explanation of the heavens. As if I am a sacrificial
offering to a demon at a ritual at which I am also priest and congrega-
tion, I'll pronounce my own damnation and witness my own soul hurtling through the darkest mass, the opaque hole of my own dissolution.

And yet I have a kind of optimism even now, for however terrible the
end will be, I think I have discerned a concealed and cunning kindness
at work. While some states execute their prisoners with bullets, others
utilize gas or lethal injection, I have ended up in one where the legisla-
tion has decreed the civilized method of execution is electricity.

And so I have that final moment to look forward to, because it's my
hope, and quite a viable proposition to hold, that in the violence of those
charging electrical currents like the mad judgments of God crashing in
my blood to burst my arteries and rupture my heart with light, it will
occur that—if only for an instant and only at the very end—in the
terminal force and raging of all that thunderous voltage, sundering my
components and scorching my brain white, I will be, however briefly,
warm.

Rabe   Rabe, David

Recital of the
dog

#19.95